T0354502

TRIALS
OF A CHRISTIAN TEENAGER

SHERRY DEE

WESTBOW
PRESS®
A DIVISION OF THOMAS NELSON
& ZONDERVAN

Scripture taken from the King James Version of the Bible.

WestBow Press books may be ordered through booksellers or by contacting:

WestBow Press
A Division of Thomas Nelson & Zondervan
1663 Liberty Drive
Bloomington, IN 47403
www.westbowpress.com
1 (866) 928-1240

ISBN: 978-1-5127-5978-5 (sc)
ISBN: 978-1-5127-5979-2 (hc)
ISBN: 978-1-5127-5977-8 (e)

Library of Congress Control Number: 2016916712

Print information available on the last page.

WestBow Press rev. date: 10/14/2016

CHAPTER 1

As the church bus whizzed down the highway, filled with Christian teenagers, everyone present felt excitement. Though weary from their long hours, they had faithfully put in at church camp, lifting, challenging and reviving their minds and spirits were the best reward of all. Though some arrived at camp with their light barely shining for the Lord, they were leaving with radiant glows of peace within, excitement to return to the world, witness to friends and loved ones about their friend and Savior, Jesus Christ.

Strumming her guitar strings, Darla Roberts sang beautifully as she led teenagers in a praise chorus, sincerely wanting to share her spiritual experience with the entire world. Wherever the Lord sent her, she was willing to go. Whatever his request, she was willing to do.

With tired, sore fingers, Darla placed her guitar back in the guitar case. Some teenagers began chattering while others settled back in their seats quietly. Staring out the bus window in deep thought, Darla longed to see her parents.

"What are you thinking about?" Kelley Peterson asked as he returned to his seat next to Darla, gently taking her hand in his.

"I am thinking about a lot of things." She answered with a smile.

"Did any of your thoughts include me?" Kelley asked.

"As a matter of fact, yes." She answered, looking into her boyfriend's eyes.

"Are you going to share your thoughts with me or are you intending to keep me in suspense?" Kelley Inquired.

"I will," Darla said. "I was thinking how surprised my parents will be when I tell them that Kelley Peterson, president of our youth group is my boyfriend."

"I trust your parents will allow us to date." Kelley responded.

"I sure hope so." Darla said, tightening her grip on his hand, looking into his eyes.

"Maybe I should talk to your dad. I would rather ask permission to date you. According to my father's rules, this is my duty. Pastor Roberts is easy to talk to, and it is not like we are strangers; we have known each other's families since we were kids." Kelley said.

"I appreciate your offer, but I must be the one to ask my parents. In fact, I had better be the first one to tell them you and I started liking each other at camp. My parents do not like being the last ones learning anything about me."

"I suggested five weeks ago that you call your parents to ask their permission. You and I both know how fast news travels to the church."

"I know, you warned me. Asking permission to date you is not the only surprise my parents are in for." She said.

"I have also changed in other ways during this summer. I have thought many times how surprised my parents will be with my many changes, but … " She broke into a soft beautiful laugh.

"But what?" Kelley asked.

"When I tell my parents about us, I am not sure if it will be a surprise or a shock." She said, tickled even at her boyfriend's puzzled expression.

"You are a terrific guy, Kelley and you are a dedicated Christian and a gentleman." Taking both of Kelley's hands into hers, Darla grew serious.

"My parents gave me a lecture before I left for camp about my childish and spoiled behavior. My mother told me it was time for me to grow up. My change will be the shock my parents receive. I do not think they expected me to grow up so quickly."

"I am sure if your parents are seeing you maturing, it will please them." Kelley said.

"I hope you are right." She replied.

The bus came to a screeching stop in front of the Christian church in Ragweed. The teenagers hurried to their feet, all wanting to be the first off the bus and into their family's arms.

"Darla, can I call you in the morning?" Kelley asked looking into his girlfriend's eyes as they made their way down the crowded bus aisle.

"I would like that." She said.

2

Kelley escorted Darla from the bus carrying her guitar and suitcase as she searched the crowd of awaiting parents.

"There is your mother." Kelley said, pointing.

Darla hurried toward her mother, forgetting her uncertainties.

"Hi Mother!" She exclaimed, hugging her mother tightly.

"Welcome home, dear." Mrs. Roberts said, hugging her daughter back. "It feels as though you have been gone forever."

"Hello Sister Roberts." Kelley greeted.

"Hello Kelley." Sister Roberts said.

"If you tell me where your car is Ma'am, I would be glad to carry Darla's things for her."

"That would be nice, follow me." Mrs. Roberts said.

Darla watched with silent admiration as Kelley placed her things in the car.

"Thanks Kelley." She said.

"You are welcome. I will see you at church Sunday."

"Where is Dad?" Darla asked as her mother started the car.

"He got a call to go to the hospital just as we were leaving home to come and get you. He was not happy about missing your arrival, but Dad is a twenty-four hour minister.

"I understand." Darla said.

"Tell me about camp." Mother said.

"It was excellent! I could not believe how exciting and rewarding hard work could be. I experienced everything you said I would. All the girls had millions of questions about scriptures, Christianity, even personal subjects. I always thought being a Christian meant reading my Bible, attending church services and being considerate of others, but I never noticed before camp, how many kids my own age find it difficult to utter the name of Jesus. Some were confused and filled with questions about how to be a Christian. When I answered one girl's questions, saw the confusion in her face, replaced with joy and peace, it was the most rewarding experience in my life. I would not change my summer camp for anything, and I cannot wait until next summer." She said.

"I am happy for you sweetheart, I am also proud that you gave your best. I questioned whether I should have insisted you be a counselor this year or just attend camp for a week or two."

"I am glad you insisted." Darla said. "I understand now why you and dad give all your time to the Lord and to others. If you had not, I probably would not have learned anything this summer. I would still be thinking I was just another preacher's kid stuck at camp."

"You would also still be complaining about." Mother laughed.

Darla excitedly shared her summer activities during their twenty-mile drive home to Ragweed. With her mother's help, Darla unpacked her suitcase and took a leisurely bath.

Prepared for the desert climate she had returned to, Darla slipped into a cool pair of shorts, a light cotton blouse and sandals.

"When will Dad be home?" Darla asked, joining her mother in the front room.

"I do not know. Are you getting hungry?"

"A little, yes." Darla said, looking out the picture window.

"No tennis shoes? I thought you could not stand wearing sandals." Mother said.

"Now tennis shoes are dumb, and sandals are in." Darla explained, with a smile.

"I agree on the shoes, the make-up, however, I am not sure. You know how Dad feels about young girls wearing make-up."

"I am only wearing clear lip gloss and mascara." Darla said.

"I will back you on this, but you do not need to wear any other make-up dear. Is this a deal?"

"It is a deal." Darla agreed.

"Barely home and you are already bored." Mother said.

"I am sorry; I did not mean to look bored." Leaving the picture window, Darla sat next to her mother on the sofa.

"I guess I am trying to understand myself. I changed over the summer." Darla said as she looked into her mother's wise, gentle eyes.

"What do you mean?" Her mother asked, putting her arm around Darla's shoulder.

"I do not know how to put it all in words." Darla said.

"I am not sure I understand all of the changes myself. I have always cared about my appearance, but I want to look my best all the time now.

"Are you saying you want to look attractive?" Her mother asked.

"I guess I am, but I do not mean to appear prideful." She assured her quickly.

"Darla, there is nothing to be embarrassed about. You are on your way to becoming an attractive and pleasant young lady." She patted her daughter's leg and then with the doorbell ringing, rose to answer the front door.

"Good morning, Lisa." Mrs. Roberts greeted, as she invited Lisa in.

"Good morning, Sister Roberts." Lisa replied.

"It is good to see you again." Darla said, happy to see her closest friend from church.

"Hi, Dar, I missed you!" Lisa said as the girls exchanged hugs.

"I missed you. Our cabin was not the same without you keeping everyone laughing."

"If I had known my Dad was going to be a grouch all summer, believe me, I would have gone to camp." Lisa chuckled.

"Besides, I was not about to belittle myself having a counselor younger than I am." She added.

"Thanks a lot, pal." Darla replied, laughing.

"I am kidding, Dar. I hear you did a fantastic job. I am proud of you." She patted her girlfriend on her back.

"I am going to take that as a compliment, even though I am not sure you meant it that way." Darla said, leading Lisa to her bedroom, turning on her radio and closing the door.

"Tell me about you and Kelley Peterson." Lisa asked, as she sat on Darla's bed, eager to hear all the details.

"I did not want to say anything in front of your mom. I have been dying to ask you!"

"How did you hear about Kelley and me?"

"My sister Brenda wrote home while she was at camp saying you and Kelley were the main topic in their cabin."

"What did she say?" Darla asked.

"That you and Kelley make a great couple."

"I have not told my parents anything about us." Darla said.

"Why not, you are always open with your parents. I am the one who has to keep secrets. What's wrong?"

"I do not know how to tell my parents, I have never asked them if I could go on a date."

"What about after church on Sundays when our youth group goes out for tacos? Some of the guys have sat by you and bought you a Coke and your parents did not object."

"That is not the same as a date." Darla said.

"Have you forgotten you are a sophomore? Your parents said you could date when you become a sophomore." Lisa reminded.

"I know, I guess I just do not know how to discuss guys with my parents, but I promised Kelley I would ask my parents today." She sighed.

"You should tell Kelley to ask your parents if you guys can date."

"Kelley wanted to ask my dad, but I told him not to. He even said I should call my parents from camp."

"You should have, Darla. Now you have to face them." Lisa laughed.

"You are probably right." Darla said, forcing a smile.

"Darla?" Her dad called, knocking on the bedroom door.

"Hi Daddy!"

"Welcome home, Darla." Pastor Roberts said, giving his daughter a tight hug. "Mom and I missed you; it has been quiet all summer." He teased, winking at Lisa, bringing smiles to the girl's faces.

"I missed you and Mother too."

"You look great, Darla."

"Thank you."

"Mom has lunch ready, so you girls better wash up." Her dad said.

"We will be right in." Darla said.

"You can stay for lunch, can't you?" Darla asked, as she brushed her hair and then started for the bathroom to wash her hands.

"Sure, just so I am home for bed check." Lisa laughed.

"Lisa, you should not cut your parents down." Darla said.

"They cut me down."

"Oh, you, let's go eat."

"By the way, Darla, I think you and Kelley make a terrific couple. Kelley is so good looking."

"I think so."

"How are you, Lisa?" Pastor Roberts asked as the girls took their seats at the table.

6

"Fine, thank you."

"Good. Darla, will you do the honors?" Pastor Roberts said, as he bowed his head for prayer. Darla asked the blessing over their lunch.

"I hear you traded in your tennis shoes for sandals and you wear make-up now." Pastor Roberts said, as he handed his daughter the salad bowl.

"Everyone wears sandals." Darla said politely. "I only wear mascara, Mother said this is acceptable."

"You are taking on a new appearance." Her father looked at her. "You look great."

"Thanks, Daddy."

"What is going on between you and Kelley Peterson?" Pastor Roberts asked, bluntly.

Darla's face suddenly turned red, her heart pounding so hard, she was sure everyone could hear it. Her mother ate slowly and Lisa kept her eyes on her plate, while Pastor's eyes remained on her, patiently awaiting an answer.

"Have you been dating Kelley at camp?"

"Not exactly, we attended services together, but we did not have a real date. I would like to date Kelley. I was planning to ask you and Mother today for your permission."

"Kelley is a dedicated Christian and he is responsible. I think you made a wise choice, so you have our permission." Dad said.

"Thanks Dad."

After a quiet dinner, Darla walked Lisa home. Darla was pleased and happy as she helped her mother with the cleaning of the kitchen. After Darla had a leisurely bath, she went to her bedroom and thanked God that her first day at home from camp had turned out perfect. Darla was very happy as she drifted off to sleep. When she awakened to the sunshine on her face, Darla's heart was still bubbling with happiness.

"Darla, you have a telephone call." Her father said.

"Good morning, Daddy." She greeted, with a tender smile.

"Good morning, Darla. Kelley is on the phone." He said and left her room.

"Good morning, Kelley." Darla said. "How are you?"

"I am fine. I hear you are a sleepyhead this morning."

"Which one of my dear parents is telling you my secrets?" Darla asked, as she slipped out from under her covers and sat at her desk. "I have some good news for you, my parents granted me permission to date."

"I know, your dad has informed me of our dating rules. I assured him I would keep each and every rule." Kelley chuckled.

"I hope he was not too hard on you."

"No harder than my dad is on me about fulfilling my responsibilities."

"I understand your dad is as strict as my dad, therefore, I feel for you. Are you sure you would like to date me?" She asked, with a soft laugh.

"Most definitely, I have waited forever for you to reach dating age." Kelley said, chuckling as he confessed.

"This is nice to hear, thank you. I have some nice comments to share with you. Dad said, and I quote, "Kelley is a dedicated Christian and responsible, I think you made a wise choice.""

"I appreciate your father's comments."

"What are your plans for this beautiful sunny, Saturday?"

"I start working for Brother Hillman at his drug store in a couple of hours. I have to make some money so I can take my girlfriend out. I get off work at six. I want to take you out for dinner this evening if you do not have other plans. I already checked with your dad and he gave me his approval."

"I accept your invitation."

"Great, I will pick you up at seven, if that is okay with you."

"Thank you." Darla replied.

Putting the telephone down, Darla was so happy. Turning her radio on, she began making the bed.

Pastor Roberts appeared in his daughter's doorway.

"You have another call, Macy is on the phone."

"Thanks, Daddy."

"Welcome home!"

"Hi Macy, did you have a nice summer?" Darla asked, bubbling with excitement, taking the extension to her bed, still wearing the baby doll pajamas, as she sat down Indian fashion.

"Yes, I have had a blast the entire summer!"

Darla's entire morning was filled with her many friends from both church and school calling, renewing friendships.

"Dear, you have been on the phone long enough, we need to go shopping." Her mother informed.

"I will be right there." Darla assured.

"Connie, I have to go. I will see if my parents have plans for Monday. I will call you tomorrow, bye."

"What do you want to do Monday, missy?" Her mother asked, as she and Darla left their home for their shopping date.

"I would like to have a few friends over for lunch, if it is okay with you."

"Who would you like to have over for lunch?"

"I would like to have Connie, Macy, Karla, Debbie and Lisa over."

"I trust you intend to be the chef? I have to work Monday." Mother said.

"I do."

"Check with dad first, however, I do not mind."

"Thanks."

Darla was silent as her mother took care of her errands. Her thoughts were on the school year, which would bring new acquaintances, activities and Kelley, her excitement of having her first boyfriend.

"I need to have your prescription filled, and then I will be finished with my errands. We then may shop for school clothes." Entering the drug store, Darla was pleased to see Kelley.

"Hi Sister Roberts, hi Darla." Kelley greeted, as he stocked boxes of cologne on a shelf.

"Hi Kelley." Mrs. Roberts greeted, and then proceeded to the pharmacy where Darla's prescription was ready.

"Congratulations on your job." Spoke Darla, enthusiastically.

"Thank you, it has worked out great so far, I am able to see you today." Kelley shared, pleased.

"Perhaps fate is on our side." Spoke Darla, pleasantly, with sparkles in her eyes.

"Sure it is. We make a great couple." Kelley agreed, confident.

"We may shop for you now, dear." Her mother informed.

Darla tried on several dresses.

"Oh mother, this dress is nice." Darla said, modeling her choice dress.

"No." Spoke her mother firmly, for the fourth time. "It is too short also." She scolded.

"Mother, every dress I like, is too short; they do not come any longer in my size. The style is to wear them short." Darla reminded, pleadingly.

"You can make them longer, you sew well. We will look at patterns and material." Her mother said.

"I do not want them longer; I want to dress like everyone else." Darla said.

"You will not wear your dresses six inches above your knee; a couple of inches are short enough." Her mother finalized, upholding her modest standards.

With patterns chosen and material decided on, they left the shops.

"Shopping with you is becoming a chore." Her mother confessed, with a weary smile as they returned to the car.

"I am sorry; I just want to dress like my friends." Darla explained, still somewhat disappointed.

"Not all your school friends wear their dresses short and only a couple of girls from the church do."

"This, I know." Smiled Darla half-heartedly, but wanting to be nice.

"Oh it is not that bad." Her mother soothed, gently pulling her daughter's long hair. "What do you say we drive to Ragweed and look at shoes?"

"I would like that too." Darla agreed, not wanting to make her mother feel bad or upset her day.

With their shopping completed, Darla glanced at her watch. Excitement arose within her as she silently stared out the car window with the thoughts on the date, while her mother drove towards Dunes, their small hometown.

"A penny for your thoughts." Her mother spoke in her gentle way.

"I am thinking we had a great day together." Darla answered kindly, looking into her mother's eyes, hesitant.

"Is there anything else?"

"I am excited over my date with Kelley, in one hour, forty-five minutes and twenty-six seconds." Darla answered, happily.

"The truth comes out." Mother said with a soft laugh. "You were quite serious when you informed me yesterday you had changed in several ways, weren't you, dear?" She asked, patting her daughter on her back.

"Yes." Darla answered, giving her mother a smile.

"I assure you dear, dad and I both are pleased with our daughter. You make us proud by your gentle, loving ways and your walk with the Lord. Kelley is a terrific young man and he is fortunate to have your interest in him, as you are to have his interest in you. Remember dear, put the Lord first in all things, including dating and you will truly enjoy your teenage years. This should be a fun and exciting time for you."

"Thank you, Mother, Lisa is right; I do have very understanding parents. In fact, I think you and dad are the greatest." Darla shared, touching her mother's heart.

After her leisurely bath, Darla entered her room to prepare for her evening out. Dressed in her newest pant outfit and dress shoes, she stood before her full-length mirror, briefly observing her 5'5", 105-pound figure. Allowing her dark long hair to flow freely down her back, she picked up her matching purse and left her room to await her caller.

"You look nice, Darla." Her father complimented, as Darla joined her parents in the front room watching the news on the television set.

"Thanks, Daddy."

"Won't Bill be shocked with seeing Darla when he returns home on leave from the Army next month?" Her father asked, pleased.

"No more shocked than you were yesterday when Darla returned from camp." Her mother answered, surprising her husband with her bluntness in front of their daughter, bringing smiles to each of them.

"True." Dad agreed with a chuckle, his face reddening as he left the sofa to answer the front door.

"Come in, Kelley." Pastor Roberts greeted.

"Thank you, sir. Hi Sister Roberts." Kelley greeted, politely.

"Hi Kelley."

"What time am I to have Darla home, Pastor Roberts?"

"Have her home by ten at the latest."

"Are you ready, Darla?"

"Yes." Darla answered, getting up from the chair.

Kelley escorted his date to his car, being the perfect gentleman. Closing the car door behind Darla, he hurried to the driver's side, he too anxious to begin their night.

"My parents would like me to bring you by so they can see you. I promise we will not stay long, if you have no objections?"

"I have no objections." Darla agreed, pleasantly.

"Good, dad gave me orders to stop by with you. Personally, I like to stay on his good side." Kelley shared with a grin, bringing a smile to Darla's gentle, pretty face.

Arriving at Kelley's home, Kelley politely opened the car door for Darla, taking her hand into his as he escorted her to the door. Entering his home, Kelley let go of Darla's hand.

"Mom and dad, I brought Darla by." Informed Kelley, as the young couple entered the den.

"Hi, honey. We are glad you are home." Mrs. Peterson greeted.

"Thank you, Sister Peterson, I am glad to be home." Darla replied, in a gentle soft voice.

"Kelley, Darla looks pretty." Aaron grinned, Kelley's younger brother.

"Darla always looks pretty, Aaron." Replied Kelley, looking down into his dates eyes with admiration, causing Darla to blush, yet he brought a smile to her face.

"Aye, this is true, missy." Mr. Peterson agreed, in his Irish way.

"Thank you."

"Kelley, you make sure you have Miss Darla home on time." Spoke his father, sternly.

"Yes, Sir, I will." Kelley agreed his face now red from his father's orders in front of his girlfriend.

"My dad is a real riot." Kelley mumbled, as he escorted Darla from his home, forcing a grin.

"It is nice to learn I am not the only teenager remaining in our generation with strict, rule abiding parents." Darla replied with a tender smile, to ease her dates embarrassing moment.

"Aren't you and I the lucky ones?" Kelley remarked with a laugh.

"Of course we are." Darla assured, pleasantly.

Darla awoke to the ringing of her alarm clock. Dressing quickly, she slipped into a delicate, lime green and white dress and her new white dress shoes. With her long, dark waist length hair brushed, she let her hair hang down her back. She fastened her dainty pearl necklace around her neck and then inserted her post-pierced pearls in her ears. Touching up her eyebrows, ensuring they were perfectly arched, she applied mascara to her eyelashes and clear lip-gloss to her lips. After checking to make sure her long nails were perfect, she removed her white purse from her closet, quickly filling her purse with her necessities from her brown purse. Taking her Bible and Sunday school quarterly from her desk, she was ready for Sunday morning services in the large church, just yards from her backdoor.

Mother had just begun playing the organ softly, as Darla quietly tiptoed down the aisle sitting down by her girlfriends like every Sunday morning. Her father sat on the platform, playing his guitar along with her mother. Darla sat with her shoulders straight, and her eyes looking ahead, wondering if Kelley had arrived yet.

"The Pastor's daughter is not supposed to be late." Kelley whispered, as he slipped in next to her.

"Who says Pastors and their families have to follow stricter rules than other Christians?"

"I am not sure, isn't this the way it is, though?"

"Just about." Darla confessed, with a tender smile.

Kelley gently took Darla's hand in his as the service began. Darla felt happy inside to be sitting with Kelley and to be back home, spending Sunday services in her home church.

"It is good to have you back, Darla."

"We have missed you; you always have a smile for everyone."

"You have really grown over the summer, Darla." Several elders of the church greeted at the close of the services.

"Thank you." Darla replied, though blushing over some of the comments, she politely shook their hands.

Kelley politely walked Darla to her backdoor.

"I have a ball game at two this afternoon, would you like to attend with me?" Kelley asked, hopeful, as Darla unlocked her backdoor.

"I would enjoy going, but my parents will expect me to have dinner with them today. We have been invited to my Grandmothers in Ragweed."

"Perhaps tomorrow evening, then, I have my last game of the season at six." He suggested, understanding.

"I will check with my parents." She assured, pleased with his invitation.

"Great, I will see you at youth service this evening. Enjoy your day."

"Thank you. You enjoy your day too."

Entering her home, Darla changed her dress for a cool short outfit and sandals. Pulling her long hair back, she braided her hair, putting a matching ribbon on the end of her braid.

"Hi, Dar." Lisa and Debbie greeted, entering their friend's bedroom, quickly making themselves at home in her room.

"Hi! What are your plans for the day?" Darla asked excitedly, turning her radio on then sitting down on her bed with her girlfriends.

"Deb is spending the day with me, you are invited also." Lisa offered.

"Thanks, but I have not seen my Grandmother since I have returned from camp and we are having dinner at her home. I will be home later this afternoon if you would like to come over when I return."

"Okay, we will be back." Lisa agreed, as the girls got up from Darla's bed, leaving for Lisa's home.

Darla enjoyed having dinner at her grandmother's country home with her parents, aunt, uncle and cousins.

Parking the family car in front of the parsonage, excitement arose in Darla as she noted the ballgame in the high school field across from her home.

"Is Kelley playing ball today, Darla? I see his car." Pastor Roberts inquired.

"Yes."

"What do you say you and I walk over and see if he is as good of a ball player as my daughter?"

"I would enjoy this."

"Mom, would you like to join us?"

"No, thank you. I believe I will take a nap before this evening's service. You two go ahead and have fun."

"Would you like to borrow my last year's softball cap before you go?" Darla asked happily, looking up into her father's eyes, and bringing a tickled laugh from him.

"If it will make you happier Darla, I will be glad to." Her father answered with a teasing grin.

"I am happy enough dad, I assure you." Darla objected with a soft laugh as they walked toward the baseball field together.

Darla felt proud with Kelley noting she and her father's presence watching him play. She was sure he felt pleased by their attendance.

"Good afternoon, Pastor, Miss Darla." Mr. Peterson greeted.

"Hi, Brother Peterson." Pastor Roberts greeted.

"You have a good player out there." He complimented.

"Aye, not bad." Kelley's tall, strong Irish father agreed, pride clearly on his face.

"Do you know my boy will play college ball next year?" Brother Peterson asked, proudly.

"No, I did not know."

"This is great, is there a chance of Kelley receiving a scholarship for college?" Pastor Roberts complimented, impressed.

"Aye, yes, he will get one. That will help the great expense of college."

"Dad, Kelley would like a coke, please." Aaron informed, running up to his father.

"I get drinks for us, Pastor, come help me."

Darla stood near the backstop admiringly while the men went for soft drinks.

"Hi Lisa. Hi Debbie." Darla exclaimed, motioning to her friends.

"Hi, Darla." The girls greeted.

"Connie and Macy are coming." Debbie informed, pointing, waving at her and Darla's school friends.

"Hi." The girls greeted.

"We heard you are dating Kelley Peterson, Darla, he is so cool." Macy said, happy for her friend.

"He is good looking too." Connie Added.

"And a fantastic ball player." Darla said, excitedly, as her friends and the crowd cheered as Kelley ran the bases, trying for a home run.

"Slide, Kelley!" Mr. Peterson yelled excitedly, as he watched with admiration.

"Aye, that's my boy!" He added.

The crowd roared with excitement, applauding as Kelley slid in home, beating the catcher from tagging him by a split second. Darla and her friends chattered excitedly over Kelley's accomplishment.

"Here is your drink, Miss Darla." Mr. Peterson offered, with pride clearly showing on his face.

"Thank you, Kelley is doing great, Brother Peterson." Darla complimented, excitedly.

"Yes, not bad." The girls politely smiled at the modest ways of Kelley's father.

As the game ended, Darla lingered with her friends secretly hoping for the opportunity to converse with Kelley as the crowd cleared. As Kelley neared their group, her heart seemed to skip a beat.

"I am your boy, huh dad?" Kelley asked, with a pleased grin.

"Aye, it is the Irish blood in you that makes you good." Kelley's father answered, bringing laughter from Kelley's admirers. "Do not tell your mother what I say; she does not understand these things."

"You can bet on it." Kelley agreed, with a grin.

Dressed for the youth group service, Darla silently sat at her desk listening to her favorite songs on her radio, in deep thought of her busy fulfilled day.

"Dear, you have a caller." Her mother informed.

"Thank you, Mother." Replied Darla, her radio turned off, she picked up her purse and Bible from her desk.

"I will warn you, Dad is in one of his moods." Her mother whispered.

"Who is his victim?" Darla inquired, hesitant as though already knowing her answer.

"I am afraid you are." Her mother answered with a smile.

"Great." Darla sighed, slowly leaving her room, somewhat curious of her fathers intended teasing.

Entering the front room, Darla found Kelley quietly sitting in a chair with his hand covering his mouth to control the laughter that wanted to escape him. Her father sat in his recliner wearing his suit for Sunday services and her softball cap, causing Darla's cheeks to redden quickly.

"Hi, Kelley." Darla greeted politely, avoiding eye contact with her father, attempting to ignore her father's ridiculous outfit.

"Hi Darla." Kelley greeted.

"I would like to walk you to youth service if this is acceptable." Kelley explained, working hard to conceal the laughter that wanted to escape him.

"I accept, are you ready to go?" She asked, secretly hoping to escape her father's silliness without further embarrassment.

"You kids do not need to leave yet, it is too early." Pastor Roberts interrupted, winking at Kelley with a grin.

Darla refused to look toward her father, her face its reddest. She silently glanced at Kelley, knowing he wanted to laugh. She quickly took her eyes from his and silently sat down on the sofa looking down at her long nails, as she sat with her hands in her lap.

"Darla, is something wrong?" Her father questioned.

"I am not sure." Darla answered slowly, glancing at Kelley, she now noting the half-grin his hand was attempting to conceal.

"Do you like my outfit?" Pastor Roberts inquired, enjoying his teasing.

"I would rather not answer." She replied, still avoiding eye contact.

"But sweetheart, I really want your opinion." Her father informed, getting up from his recliner, sitting down next to his daughter, putting his arm around her shoulder and bringing a smile to her face. "What do you think, Darla? Hey, look at me." He insisted.

Darla slowly raised her head, looking at her father.

"How about this?" He asked, slanting the ball cap on his head, raising and lowering his eyebrows.

"You like this?" He continued, forcing both Darla and Kelley to laugh, with embarrassment clearly on her face, she offered no reply.

"Have you told Kelley how I made you laugh during your moody, complaining stage?" Pastor Roberts asked, with a grin.

"Dad, you're embarrassing me." Darla informed, with a nervous laugh. "Where's mother?" Darla asked looking for protection, causing her father to laugh, becoming tickled.

"I quit, babe." Her father assured, removing the ball cap from his head. "Don't get mom on me." He added, causing the teenagers to laugh again with his remark. "Come on kids, I'll unlock the fellowship hall for you." He offered, calling an end to his teasing.

With Pastor Roberts next door in his study, Darla sat on the front pew. She and Kelley were the first to arrive, like most Sunday evening services. Kelley sat down next to Darla, taking her hand in his.

"I thought your brother was overseas in the military?" Kelley asked, with a gentle smile.

"Now you know where Bill gets his teasing, it's a real blast when the two of them get together." She shared with a laugh.

"I'm sure it is for them." Kelley agreed, with a sensitive smile. "They're lucky you are such a good sport." He added, pleased with Darla's gentle ways.

"Do you honestly think I have a choice?" She asked with a soft laugh.

"Probably not, they both are a bit bigger than you." Kelley laughed.

Now sitting with her girlfriends, with the fellowship hall filled with teenagers, Darla listened attentively to Kelley's message he brought forth. Everyone's heart could not help but be stirred by his sincerity to live for the Lord. Darla thought back over her childhood, Kelley had always been sincere in the ways of the Lord, as were his parents, she and her parents. Perhaps it is Gods planning for Kelley and me to date and work for the Lord as a couple.

Dressed for bed, tired from her busy weekend, Darla entered the front room where her parents sat conversing.

"Excuse me."

"What Darla?" Pastor Roberts questioned.

"Kelley invited me to attend his last game of the season tomorrow evening, may I go?" She asked, politely.

"What do you think, Mom?" Her dad asked, leaving the decision to his wife.

"When does Kelley need an answer, dear?" Mother questioned, rubbing her eyes, wearily.

"Not until morning."

"I'll sleep on it; I'll give you my answer in the morning."

"Okay." Darla agreed, considerately. With goodnights said, Darla called it a night.

Awaking earlier than most mornings, filled with excitement over her plans for the day, Darla dressed for another warm, sunny day, made her bed, then started for the kitchen.

"Good morning Mother and Daddy." Darla greeted in her pleasant, gentle, respectful way, giving both her parents a kiss. "I feel great today, don't you?" She asked, with excitement in her voice, causing her mother to laugh.

"Ask me after I have had my fill of coffee, dear."

"It does seem that some mornings our carefree, happy-go-lucky daughter makes us feel old, right Mom?" Her father asked, refilling his wife's coffee cup for her.

"Yes." She confessed with a soft laugh.

"You look tired, Mother, do you feel okay?"

"Do I tell our all grown-up daughter what my problem is, Dad?" Her mother asked, her face turning red as though daring to betray a hidden secret.

"Mother," Scolded her husband, "Darla isn't that grown up."

"But I want to complain to someone, Dad." Her mother teased lightly, blushing over her honesty.

"Times like these are when we take our complaints to the Lord, Mom." Her father reminded compassion on his face for his wives upset.

"I know, dear, I'm being silly." Her mother replied, taking hold of her husband's hand, as though secretly, desperately, attempting to gain strength from her spouse.

"You're not being silly Mom, you are being human." Her father comforted.

"Daddy, would you like for me to leave you and Mother alone?" Darla asked, feeling for her parent's heartache.

"No, this is not necessary, dear." She answered before her husband could respond.

"I'll get my act together, in fact, I already feel better due to you and Dad being here. Your zealousness and happiness have a way of rubbing off." Her mother assured, with a tender smile.

"Thank you, Mother." Darla said, giving her mother a comforting smile.

Pastor Roberts picked up the receiver from the wall telephone, quieting its ringing.

"Roberts' residence." He greeted.

"Hang on a second if you would please. I'm in the house; give me a minute to get to my study." He replied.

"Babe, hang the phone up when I pick up my phone in my study, please." Pastor Roberts instructed.

"Okay, Dad." Darla agreed, now concern on her face for her parent's hidden worries, noting the strain on her father's face with the telephone call. With the telephone receiver returned to its resting place, Darla slowly searched her mother's eyes with hers.

"Mother, is Bill okay?" Darla questioned, slowly, fearing her mother's answer.

"Hey, quit worrying sweetheart. Your brother is fine, Dad and my upsets have nothing to do with you or your brother, so quit worrying, and that is an order."

"Yes Ma'am." Darla agreed, forcing a smile.

Getting up from the table, Darla made some toast for her and her mother to share, cheering up her mother, placing her favorite jam on the table before her.

"You may attend Kelley's game with him this evening, since this is his last game of the season. After this evening, one date per week, unless your involved in a group function." Her mother instructed.

"Yes Ma'am." Darla agreed, giving her mother a loving smile.

"I'm going to get ready for work. I want you to enjoy your luncheon date and have a wonderful day." She said, giving her daughter a hug.

"I will, I promise."

"Good." Her mother approved.

The kitchen tidy once again, Darla began working at the sewing machine to make her dresses for her new school year to begin in one week.

After a while of sewing, Darla got ready for her four guests to arrive. They all decided to go across the street to the high school's grassy field to talk and practice.

"Darla, have you asked your parents about cheerleading tryouts?" Connie asked.

"No, and every one of you remembers mums the word. If my teachers and fellow students vote me in, then I'll ask my parents just before tryouts." Darla answered.

"Darla's parents think cheerleading is of the world." Debbie explained, Darla's only Christian friend present.

"Pray before you ask, Darla." Macy advised.

"Your prayers always get answered." She added.

"Thanks for the advice." Darla said, giving her friend an appreciative smile.

The girls practiced their flips, cartwheels and splits repeatedly as they each hoped to make the varsity cheerleading team in three short weeks. With the sound of a car horn, the girls stopped to observe.

"It's Kelley, excuse me."

As Darla hurried toward Kelley's car, Kelley got out of his car, meeting her halfway.

"Hi." Darla greeted happily excited with his visit.

"Hi, you looked great out there, what are you trying to prove?"

"Would you believe you're looking at one of the future varsity cheerleaders?"

"Of course I believe you, you will get my vote." He assured her.

"Perhaps I should have you campaign for me."

"That would not be a problem for me at all, I assure you." Kelley informed, with a big grin.

"On second thought, I think I would rather let nature take its course." Darla refused quickly, with an excited laugh.

"Darla Roberts, don't you trust me?" He scolded.

"Of course I don't, Kelley Peterson."

"Actually, I am in a bit of a hurry, or I might be tempted to stay and watch you and your friends. I am on my lunch break from work. Will you be attending my game with me this evening?"

"Yes."

"Great, I am looking forward to this evening, Miss Roberts." Kelley assured, with a pleased look.

"Thank you. Bye Kelley." Darla replied, smiling with his choice of words. She felt warmth toward Kelley by his mere presence and her heart filled with even more happiness knowing she was his girlfriend.

Darla and her friends talked excitedly over their hamburgers Darla had prepared for them. They could not wait until next week to begin their new school term. By three o'clock, Darla had the kitchen in order and said good-bye to her last guest. Anxiously, she returned to her sewing machine and the unfinished dress she had begun earlier.

By the end of the week, she had completed her wardrobe. She excitedly waited for Monday to arrive for the first day of school. Her parents had approved of Kelley taking her to and from school and she just knew this school term would be her greatest year yet!

Arriving at school in Kelley's car, even more excitement arose in Darla. All of Darla and Kelley's classmates would soon learn Darla and Kelley were now a couple, this seemed to please her most.

"Are you always this excited to attend school?" Kelley asked, taking his girlfriend's notebook from her politely, holding her hand as they left the school parking lot, for the high school campus.

"Yes." Darla answered with a smile, blushing. "I have always enjoyed school, Bill says I am strange."

"Between you and I, what does Bill know?" Kelley asked with a grin for her defense.

"I like your way of thinking."

Their lockers located, Darla caught sight of some of her friends. Excited, she now led Kelley toward the group.

"Hi Darla!" Karla greeted.

"Hi! It is so good to see all of you." Darla said, excitedly, in her bubbly way.

"Cheerleading tryouts are next week, Darla. Can you tryout?" Janis asked, excitedly.

"I have not asked yet, if I am voted for tryouts I will ask then."

"I thought we were only going to say hi." Kelley reminded, appearing bored.

"I am sorry." Darla apologized, blushing, forgetting Kelley's presence, with her excitement of seeing her friends. She was not intending to be rude.

"Kelley, my friends are, Peggy, Janis and Karla." She introduced.

"Girls, meet my patient boyfriend, Kelley."

"Everyone knows Kelley." Peggy informed.

"Oh really?" Kelley asked, surprised, his expression clearly showing all he hoped for an explanation.

"Sure, you are on the baseball team. Everyone knows the athletes." Peggy explained, admiringly.

"I had not realized how popular you are." Darla said, smiling proudly, as she looked into her boyfriend's eyes.

"This makes two of us." Kelley confessed, with a chuckle.

School had been terrific! Darla had renewed her friendship with each of her girlfriends. She found her classes exciting and challenging. Her boyfriend had even walked her to several classes. Being a sophomore was going to be fantastic! She was experiencing the time of her life.

"May I give you a ride home?" Kelley asked, as he arrived at Darla's locker.

"You may." Darla answered, pleased, as she closed her locker. Kelley politely took her books, relieving her heavy load.

"What are your plans for the evening?" Kelley asked, as they approached his car.

"My plans are my studies and practicing my cheerleading routine, lots of both." She answered, with a gentle smile.

"May I ask your plans?"

"Yes, two hours of work at the drugstore, after work, I too have a date with my textbooks."

"We live interesting lives." Darla remarked, with a soft laugh, bringing a smile to Kelley's gentle face.

"We are a peculiar people, this is the best kind."

"You are right." Agreed Darla, most pleased with both their relationships with the Lord.

Darla's first week of school had passed so quickly. She secretly wished it were Monday all over again.

"Darla, Deb, Macy!" Connie exclaimed, running toward the group of girls, with a paper in her hand.

"I have the cheerleading list."

Excitement seemed to consume Darla, as she silently waited to see the list.

"Your name is on the list, Dar." Kelley whispered, as he joined her near her friends.

"Really?" She asked, surprised, wishing her friends would finish with the list so she could see for herself.

"Really, you received the most votes." He shared.

"Oh Kelley, this is too much." Darla said, in a half-whisper.

"This has always been my secret dream." She shared with happy moist eyes.

"You prayed, didn't you?" Macy asked.

"Darla does not have to pray, she is a natural cheerleader." Peggy remarked.

No, Peggy, Macy is right. I prayed and I prayed and I prayed." She confessed, with an excited laugh.

"Now you have to pray your parents will give their permission." Macy reminded.

"I have already begun."

"It is as good as done, then." Macy assured, confident.

"Why isn't Macy attending our youth group?" Kelley whispered, shocked at the non-Christian teenager's faith in Darla's prayers.

"Our church does not believe in dancing. She loves to dance." Darla answered smiling at Kelley's shocked expression.

"She attends Peggy's church because they have dancing parties."

"I was not aware Peggy attends church."

"This is because she has never become a Christian; she attends for the parties also."

"Like I said, you and I are peculiar people." Kelley remarked.

"Very true." Darla agreed, leaving her friends with Kelley.

"You do realize today is Friday, right?" Kelley asked, with a boyish grin.

"Of course, this is the evening my kind boyfriend is taking me out."

"Your kind boyfriend will pick you up at six sharp." Kelley informed, as he walked her to her front door.

"I will be prompt, I assure you." Kelley looked into Darla's eyes, with tenderness on his face.

She silently hoped he would kiss her. With a light goodbye kiss, Darla was on cloud nine. Entering her home, Darla unloaded her books on the coffee table. Going to the kitchen, she removed a note from the breakfast table.

Darla,
Mom and I will meet you at the church
booth at nine p.m., as planned.
Be on time.
Love,
Dad

With the completion of her bath, Darla dressed for her date. Dressed in her light blue cords, fuzzy pullover sweater and white deck shoes, she impatiently awaited the hands on the clock to move. The doorbell finally rang, so she hurried to the door filled with excitement.

Kelley escorted Darla inside their favorite Mexican restaurant. He politely assisted her with her chair. He gently held her hand as he asked the blessing over their dinner.

"You know, Miss Darla, as my dad would say ... " Kelley began, bringing a smile to Darla's young pretty face, her thoughts quickly on Brother Peterson's special unique ways.

"I will always appreciate this summer and this week of school. I feel as you today, it seems I have admired you forever from a distance. I thought you were tops from a distance. You allowing me to be on the inside of your circle, being a part of your life, I know you are tops."

"Thank you for the kind words." Darla said, deeply moved.

"I have learned to listen to people, really hearing them by observing you and your many terrific ways." Kelley confessed, with red cheeks, as though scolding himself.

"I do not know what to say." Darla replied, slowly searching his eyes with hers.

"Then be still and listen, I have this speech well prepared." Kelley assured, with a boyish grin.

"You are devoted to each individual friend whether Christian or non-Christian. You offer encouragement, you compliment everyone on something and you listen to what each person has to say as though it is important, whether it is or not. You are truly devoted to your parents, you do not harbor rebellion and you live Christianity every second. I admire you in many ways."

"Thank you." Darla's heart seemed to swell with tenderness toward Kelley. With a tender smile, she silently allowed him to take her hand in his.

"Are you sure you are two years younger than I am?" Kelley asked, with a chuckle.

"Positive." Darla answered, her face glowing, her eyes sparkling.

"I would like for you to accept this small gift." Kelley informed, placing a tiny, gift-wrapped box on the table before her.

"Oh, Kelley, you should not have gotten me anything." Spoke Darla, both surprised and touched.

"I wanted to, open it please."

Taking the gift into her hands, Darla began opening it with great care. She removed from the box, a dainty gold bracelet with Kelley's class ring attached.

"This is beautiful, Kelley." Darla assured, thrilled.

"Will you be my steady girlfriend, Miss Darla Roberts?"

"It would most definitely please me. Yes!" She exclaimed, surprising Kelley with her excitement, bringing a happy smile to both their faces.

Kelley fastened the dainty bracelet around her thin, tan wrist, proudly.

"Thank you, Kelley."

"You are most welcome."

"I realize it is our custom to exchange class rings." Darla stated slowly, as she removed her ring from her finger. "But … " She hesitated, glancing at her class ring in her hand.

"But what?" Kelley questioned, puzzled.

"But … if you lose this ring, I will be in serious trouble." She warned, handing her ring to Kelley.

"Darla, I promise, I will not lose your ring." Kelley assured, putting her ring on his smallest finger.

"Are you ready to go to the fair?"

"Yes!" Darla and Kelley rode ride after ride at the fair and the faster the ride, the better. They laughed and yelled on the scariest rides until their voices seemed hoarse.

"Oh Kelley, stop, I have to see the livestock." She insisted, quickly going to the fatten calf, gently stroking him.

"Isn't he beautiful?" She asked excitedly.

"He looks like all the other calves to me." Kelley answered, bluntly. Darla smiled with Kelley's lack of interest in the livestock.

"I have seen the calves; we may go to the church booth now." Darla suggested, as she returned to her date's side.

"Apparently you like animals." Spoke Kelley, taking her hand in his.

"I love animals, especially horses. Dad has promised to get me a horse when we move to the country, by the time dad decides to move, I will probably be too old to ride." She shared with a gentle smile.

26

After donating their hour at the church outreach booth, along with Darla's parents, the young couple said their goodbyes.

Darla's head was spinning by the end of her night. She felt she was the luckiest, happiest girl in the entire world.

"God is truly good to me." She silently thought.

CHAPTER 2

It was another beautiful Saturday. The early morning air was chilly, yet the sky was clear and the sun bright. Within a few hours, the temperature would raise producing a nice warm day. With her devotions completed, Darla slipped into a pair of jeans, a blouse of white with bright tiny violets and sandals.

"Good morning." Darla greeted politely, as she joined her parents at the breakfast table.

"Good morning." Her parents greeted pleasantly.

"Did you sleep well?" Her father asked.

"Yes, thank you."

"How many pancakes would you like, dear?" Her mother questioned, as she prepared breakfast.

"Two please." Darla answered, as she took her medicine like every morning.

"Mother, Dad, may I try out for cheerleading?" Darla asked, hopeful, secretly crossing her fingers under the table.

"Cheerleading?" Her father questioned, appearing doubtful.

"Yes please. This past week every girl wishing to tryout submitted a form to each teacher she has, the teacher either approved or disapproved according to classroom participation and behavior and grades. Wednesday, the entire student body voted on each applicant. The list approving who made it, try out on Friday. I made the list. In fact, I received the most votes." She shared pleased.

"Whew, congratulations." Her mother spoke, also pleased.

"Thanks, Mother." Darla replied, with a gentle smile.

"If I have your permission, Monday through Friday I will have practice learning the cheer for tryouts a week from Monday." Darla explained.

"Daddy, please, I have always dreamed of becoming a cheerleader someday, this is my chance." She added.

"I don't know." Pastor Roberts answered. "I have not seen much good come of worldly fame."

Darla was silent now, respecting her father's uncertainties. She silently prayed for her wish to come true, as she ate her breakfast.

"What do you think, Mom?" Pastor Roberts asked after several long moments of silence.

"It would be nice to have a Christian in the spotlight for a change. It would be a great witnessing tool for Darla. Our daughter is strong willed and I do not believe this activity would come between her and the Lord. I think it would be fine." His wife answered, confident with her opinion.

Darla's heart secretly leaped with joy.

"Oh Dad, please." She silently repeated repeatedly.

"You may try out. You will keep up your grades and no wearing yourself out, or I will make you quit if you do make the cheerleading team." Pastor Roberts instructed.

"Thanks Daddy." Darla replied, thrilled. Getting up from the table, she gave her concerned father a kiss.

With all the happiness and excitement Darla felt inside with being allowed to try out for cheerleading along with her friends, made her Saturday morning chores go quickly. She felt relieved knowing she would not have to pass up what she and her friends felt a great honor and privilege in representing their school.

Putting her dust cloth aside with the ringing of the doorbell, Darla hurried to the front door.

"Hi Sis." Greeted her brother, standing tall and proud in his military uniform.

"Hi, welcome home!" Exclaimed Darla, as she hugged her brother. "Mother and Dad were expecting you next weekend. They will be disappointed they missed your arrival."

"I know, but I received my leave earlier than I expected, so I am home." Bill explained, getting comfortable on the sofa.

"This is great!" Darla exclaimed.

"I see Mom finally gave in, allowing you to wear jeans." Bill noticed, pleased for his sister.

"Not entirely, I may wear jeans at home and to Grandmas. My going any place else in jeans is forbidden. It does not matter to Mother that most of my friends I have wears jeans. She keeps quoting me the scripture from the Bible that speaks against wearing men's apparel." Darla shared, with a soft laugh.

"That sounds like Mom." Bill confessed, with a chuckle.

"Whose ring do you have?" Surprise was clearly on his face and noted in his voice.

"Kelley Peterson's, he gave me his ring last night. He is my first steady boyfriend." Darla informed, proudly.

"Kelley is okay." Darla's older, protecting brother Bill approved.

"I think he is more than okay." Darla defended, with a soft laugh, her eyes sparkling.

"Kelley is very good looking, he is a lot of fun, he is popular, and he is a gentleman and a wonderful Christian. In fact, I cannot think of anything Kelley is not." She shared, blushing over her bluntness with an excited laugh.

"It sounds like my kid sister has grown up while I have been away." Bill noted with approval.

"What else is new, besides Kelley?" He added quickly with a grin.

"Daddy is allowing me to try out for cheerleading next week." Darla answered excitedly, with a radiant smile.

"This is great, Sis, I am happy for you."

"Thank you, I thought you would be."

"I would like to know how you talked Dad into allowing you to become a cheerleader. In my high school days, the church considered such involvement of the world. Sounds like you still have Dad wrapped around your finger. Maybe it is the way you say Daddy." Bill mocked, enjoying teasing his sister.

"Perhaps it is." Darla smiled, never allowing her brothers teasing to upset her.

"I just wish I could do the same with Mother." She shared with a soft laugh.

"All I heard last year while you were away in the military was how 'Bill never got by with acting spoiled.' You know, having you for an older brother can be a pain sometimes."

"Thanks a lot, I love you too, Sis." He laughed, quickly remembering his parent's ways.

Everything was going perfect for Darla, in her eyes. Her brother Bill was home on leave from the military, she was going steady with the president of her youth group, most popular guy at church, and well known and liked at school. Last, but not least, she soon would be trying out for cheerleading.

"How has your Monday morning been?" Kelley inquired as he set his lunch tray down next to Darla's tray.

"It could not have been better, thank you." Darla answered, in her soft, pleasant manner, with a sweet smile.

"Darla, how can you be so nice after that horrible Algebra test we just took?" Peggy questioned, with disappointment on her face.

"Because it is a beautiful day, I have Jesus in my heart, and I spent most of my weekend studying for the test." Darla answered.

"You went to the show and a party over the weekend." Doug, Peggy's boyfriend reminded her.

"I do not believe Darla knows how to be unhappy." Macy remarked.

"I would not go that far, I have my down days also."

"Yeah, every time she does not get her way." Kelley teased, bringing a smile to his girlfriend's face.

Kelley was waiting at Darla's locker as the last period bell rang.

"May I give you a ride home?" Kelley asked.

"I would appreciate a ride, but I have cheerleading practice now." Darla reminded him, excitement in her voice.

"May we study together this evening then?" He asked, hopeful.

"Yes." Darla answered, with a gentle smile.

"I will see you at seven." Kelley informed, letting go of his girlfriend's hand now, as they neared the girl's locker room.

"I will be waiting."

Darla practiced and practiced the arm and leg movements repeatedly with the many interested and hopeful contestants. She gave her all, concentrating on each move. It seemed so important to her that she become a cheerleader. With goodbyes said, Darla slowly began her two block walk for home with tired, aching muscles.

"Dar," yelled Peggy, through Macy's open car window, as Macy pulled close to the curb. "Macy and I are going for a hamburger then to my house to practice more. Would you like to come with us?"

"I would love to, but my parents are expecting me for dinner and I am expecting Kelley this evening, also." Darla answered.

"See if you can come tomorrow evening." Peggy suggested.

"I will invite Debbie and Connie also." She added.

"I would like this." Agreed Darla, thrilled over her girlfriends idea.

With dinner completed, Darla quickly bathed, dressing in a fresh outfit for Kelley's arrival.

"I am glad you offered to study with me, this evening." Darla said pleasantly, as she sat down next to Kelley at the kitchen table, placing a glass of iced tea in front of him.

"I could use your help with my Algebra assignment."

"You want help with Algebra? My offering to assist you with your homework was simply an excuse to see you tonight. I was hoping we could go for a coke." Kelley confessed, with a boyish grin.

"Your idea sounds tempting. Would you like to ask my dad?" Darla asked with a gentle smile.

"No, thank you. Your parents said one night a week; I have no intentions of crossing either one of them." Kelley refused, quickly.

"Looks like I am stuck with Algebra." He complained lightly, as he opened his girlfriend's textbook.

It was ten o'clock when Darla completed her studies. With goodnights said to her family, she went to her room closing her bedroom door behind her. Though tired from her busy day with school and practice, she practiced her cheerleading routine several times before going to bed.

The alarm seemed to ring much too early as it awoke Darla to a new day. It took her twice as long to prepare for school as usual. Finally dressed, she hurried to the kitchen to join her parents like most mornings. To her surprise, she found no one present, but a note instead.

"Great, I do not have time for breakfast this morning, anyway." She thought sighing a breath of relief, as she now hurried to the front door where Kelley waited, forgetting to take her medicine.

"Good morning."

"Good morning, Miss Darla." Kelley replied cheerfully, kindly taking her schoolbooks from her, and then escorting her to his car.

"Where is Bill off to at this early hour?" Kelley asked as he started his car.

"I do not know. I woke up to an empty house. In fact, he and my parents have been gone a lot. I am usually the last to hear of my family's doings, especially if there are upsets." She explained slowly, she now curious of her family's whereabouts.

"I will gladly trade you places." Kelley informed with a gentle grin, attempting to relieve her concerns.

"I do not understand."

"I would much rather be the youngest member in my family being spared, then the oldest expected to help with solutions. Would you like to trade?"

"No, thank you. I best leave well enough alone, I believe I enjoy being the youngest, according to Bill, I am spoiled." Darla answered with a smile, blushing.

"I disagree; we both know Bill enjoys teasing you."

"Those girls are always loitering near your locker." Kelley remarked, as they neared Darla's locker.

"Those girls are my friends, Kelley." Darla scolded, poking him gently in his side.

"Hi girls." Darla greeted cheerfully, joining her friends as she opened her locker.

"Can you come over after practice, Darla?" Peggy asked.

"Yes, I get to stay until eight o'clock."

"Great! Macy, Debbie, and Connie are coming also. We will have a blast!" Peggy exclaimed.

"We will show all the other girls up when we try out Monday." Macy said, sure of herself.

"I trust you are right, Macy." Spoke Darla pleasantly.

"Darla, I will walk you to your class." Kelley interrupted, taking her hand in his.

"We have fifteen minutes until the bell rings." She informed him, as she left her friends, going with Kelley.

"I am aware of the time. I want to spend this time alone with you. It is too early in the morning for me to be listening to a group of chattering girls." He explained, bluntly.

"Thanks a lot." Darla replied, though giving Kelley an understanding smile, as Kelley leaned against Darla's classroom, putting his arm loosely around her waist.

"You girls are really giving 100% at making cheerleaders." Said Kelley, pleased for his girlfriend's wishes.

"Of course, we intend to be the future cheerleading squad." Darla replied, confident.

"What happens if you do not make the squad?"

"This is unthinkable." She confessed with a beautiful smile, making Kelley laugh.

The girls were having a great time as they chattered excitedly over their hamburgers and cokes after cheerleading practice. The tension grew in each girl as she worried and wondered if she would learn her routine well enough to be picked as a cheerleader. It was difficult to concentrate on studies. Nervous stomachs found it hard to eat properly. Sketchy dreams of becoming a cheerleader were constantly interrupting the girl's nights of sleep, making it difficult to return to sleep.

The girls practiced in Peggy's front yard until eight o'clock. Weary and tired, they each sank to the ground, the moist grass cooling their sweaty bodies.

"After we make the squad, I plan to sleep an entire week." Debbie moaned, rubbing her aching legs.

"I plan to sleep an entire week also." Darla agreed feeling drained.

"Here comes your dad, Darla." Peggy informed.

"Thank you, Lord, for answering my prayer." Spoke Darla aloud, slowly gathering her books in her arm and picking herself up from the ground.

"I will see each of you tomorrow; I had a lot of fun." Darla assured, happily.

Darla walked toward her father's car as he waited patiently.

"Hi Daddy."

"Hi babe." Pastor Roberts greeted.

"How was your practice?"

"Tiring, but I believe it went well."

"Why were you still at Peggy's?"

"I was not convinced my legs could make the walk home." Darla answered, with a smile.

"I told you to be home by eight, not leave Peggy's at eight. Mom and I were worried."

"I am sorry, Dad." Darla apologized compassionately, not intending to bring worry to her parents.

"You will cancel your plans tomorrow. The next time I tell you to be home at a certain time, you be there."

"Yes Sir." Darla agreed obediently, with reddened cheeks.

"Do you have studies to do?"

"Yes."

"You get to your studies, and then get to bed, you look tired." He ordered, allowing his concern to show.

"Yes sir."

Darla ran her bathwater before beginning her homework. The warm water felt relaxing and soothing on her tired, sore muscles and overly tired body. She closed her eyes, relaxing in the warm bath.

"Sis, Darla?" Bill called, knocking on the bathroom door.

"Yes?" Questioned Darla, awakened by her brothers knocking, quickly removing the stopper from the tub.

"You have been in there for an hour." He complained.

"I will be right out." She assured, quickly drying.

"The bathroom is all yours, Bill." She informed, politely.

"It's about time." Bill replied, in his often-complaining way.

"Lucky for me, I only have one sister." He added.

Setting her alarm clock two hours earlier than usual, Darla went to bed, planning to do her homework in the morning before school, she was just too tired to stay awake any longer.

The alarm clock waking Darla, she sleepily turned the ringing off, returning back to sleep.

"Dear, hey, wake up." Mrs. Roberts said, as she shook Darla awake.

"Darla, you have thirty minutes to prepare for school." Her mother informed.

"Great." She remarked, hurrying from her bed to dress.

"I haven't time for breakfast, Mother." Darla said.

"I know dear, do take your medicine on your way out." Her mother reminded, as she dressed for work.

Again, in her haste, Darla forgot to take her medicine as she hurried to arrive at school in time. Darla sat down at her desk when the tardy bell began to ring. She let out a sigh of relief.

Catching up on her homework in second hour study hall, her assignments were completed, ready to turn in.

"Where were you this morning, Darla?" Peggy asked, as Darla and Debbie joined their friends at the lunch table for lunch.

"I overslept." She answered pleasantly, as she opened her biology book, preparing to study for a test.

"Hi girls, Doug, Brian." Kelley greeted politely, placing his tray next to Darla.

"Where is your lunch?"

"I am passing today; I have a test to study for."

"I believe it is important you eat regular. Your parents always seem worried you might miss a meal." Kelley remarked, concerned.

"My parents spend half their time worrying over my brother and me; skipping one meal cannot possibly hurt me." Assured Darla, and then returned to her studying.

Dressed for Wednesday night church service, Darla sat at her desk listening to her radio, thinking about her busy week and how tiring her schedule was for her.

"I just have to hang in and keep up until I make cheerleader, only a few more days." She told herself.

"Sis, Kelley is here." Bill informed.

"Thank you." Slowly standing, she pushed her chair up to her desk.

"Surely I will feel better by morning." She decided silently and then left her room with her Bible and purse in her hand.

"Hi." Darla greeted, pleasantly.

"Hi, are you ready?" Kelley asked, pleased to be escorting his girlfriend to church.

"I am ready."

Kelley took Darla's hand into his as the service began. Bill soon arrived with his date, stopping at his sister's pew. Darla and Kelley politely scooted down the pew, making room for the couple. Kelley did not take Darla's hand back in his with Bill's arrival. Bill politely introduced his date to Kelley and his sister. The two couples were silent now, with the service already in progress.

"Kelley, I do not mind if you hold my sister's hand if she does not mind." Bill whispered, causing each ones cheeks to flush except his own.

"I do not appreciate your observance of your sister and I, but thank you for granting your permission, Sir." Kelley replied with an embarrassed smile, causing Bill to grin with his return feistiness.

"I will get even, Bill." Darla whispered, scolding.

"I am sure you will." He replied he now with reddened cheeks, his sister's remark bringing smiles of approval to Kelley and Bill's date.

The couples remained silent now, giving their attention on the service, with Darla's hand once again in Kelley's hand.

With the conclusion of the service, Darla tarried in the foyer with the teenagers, visiting.

"Darla, some of the teens are going out for a taco. Would you like to go?" Kelley asked, hopeful.

"Yes, but I can't go, I am sorry." Darla answered, disliking missing an opportunity to do something together.

"Sure you can, Terry and I are going and so is my sister." Bill informed.

"Bill." Darla quieted, with flushed cheeks. Though both Bill and Kelley looked puzzled, neither one said another word, as the crowd of teenagers seemed to surround them.

"Babe, Mom and I are going out with the kids. Since you are grounded, you will wait at home." Informed Pastor Roberts casually and then returned to his after service affairs.

Darla briefly closed her eyes with flushed cheeks. She knew she was now free game for teasing with her father's remark. Bill and Kelley now understood her silence moments earlier.

"Oh great." Lisa remarked rolling her eyes up as Rhonda came closer.

"I heard you are grounded, Darla." Rhonda said with a sly grin, as though she was pleased, causing Darla's cheeks to turn their reddest.

"What did you do?"

"It is none of your business, motor mouth." Lisa mumbled, her comment and Rhonda's, bringing silence to the crowd of young people.

"Girls, this is not the time or the place, we are in the Lord's house." Kelley reminded.

"Rhonda, come on, we are leaving." Her mother informed, as she passed by the teenagers.

"Will she ever grow up?" Bill asked shaking his head as the fifteen-year-old teenager left the church.

"It is not likely." Lisa answered, in her complaining way.

Kelley silently took Darla's hand in his, leading her away from the crowd.

"May I walk you home?"

"Yes, you may." Darla answered.

"I am sorry, Kelley." Darla apologized.

"Your apology is accepted, Miss Darla." Kelley assured.

"I do have one question. Is our date still on for Saturday night?" Kelly asked.

"Yes, I am only grounded for tonight. I stayed too long at Peggy's last night." Darla answered, with flushed cheeks.

"I know something Miss Rhonda does not know." Kelley replied, with a boyish grin, uplifting his girlfriend's spirits.

"That you do." Darla agreed, with a soft laugh.

"Thank you for rescuing me and for quieting Lisa."

"You are welcome. I intend to always be your rescuer." He informed, touching Darla's heart with his wishes.

By Friday night, Darla felt as though she was ready to collapse, as she and her friends completed their practice at Peggy's once again. She lay still on the grass with her eyes closed, afraid her legs would give out under her if she stood up again.

"Darla, are you okay?" Macy asked, with worry in her voice.

"I think so, I feel weak, but surely I will be okay in a few minutes." She answered, sounding out of breath.

"Come on, I will give you a ride home." Macy offered, helping Darla to her feet.

Once home, Darla put her every effort into feeling normal and well, as she entered her home as not to alarm her family.

Quickly excusing herself from her family, Darla went to her room, lying down on her bed and within a few minutes, she was sleeping soundly.

Sleeping until noon, Darla felt better. She remembered to take her medicine for the first time all week. After a warm relaxing bath, she spent her day doing her Saturday chores and relaxing until time for her date with Kelley.

Darla sat on her bed strumming her electric guitar, softly singing her favorite songs.

"Babe." Pastor Roberts spoke.

"Yes."

"Mom and I will be leaving now. We will not be home until late, so make sure Kelley has you home on time after your date. Bill will be in and out."

"I will Dad."

"Enjoy your evening, babe."

With the time nearing for Darla's date with Kelley, she turned her amplifier off, leaving her bedroom.

Leaving her home, locking the front door behind her, she sat down on the front porch, hoping the fresh air would make her over-tired body feel peppier as she awaited Kelley's arrival.

"Good evening, Miss Darla." Kelley greeted, as he approached his date.

"Good evening to you." She greeted pleasantly, picking up her purse, as she stood up.

"You look beautiful." Kelley complimented, escorting his date to his car.

"Thank you." Darla replied, blushing at his openness.

"I would give you a kiss, but your dad is probably watching through the window." Kelley informed, opening his car door for her.

"Kiss me anyway." Darla encouraged, with a sparkle in her eyes, blushing at her forwardness, surprising Kelley with her open wishes.

"Not on your life." Kelley refused, he chuckling over her feistiness.

"No one is home, Kelley." She confessed with an excited laugh.

"Aye, in that case, Miss Roberts, your wish is definitely my command." He approved, with a boyish grin, giving his date a gentle kiss.

"I passed Bill a few minutes ago dragging main. He asked if you and I still had plans to go out this evening. He seemed disappointed we have plans." Kelley informed, holding his dates hand in his, as she sat close to him.

"Did he say why?" Questioned Darla, surprised with her brothers actions.

"He did a bit of complaining about your busy schedule. He said he has barely seen you since he returned home." Kelley answered, looking down into Darla's eyes, as she let out a sigh, realizing her brother was right.

"Where would you like to have dinner?" He asked, quickly changing the subject, as they now were dragging main, waving at their friends as they passed one another.

"To be honest, I am not hungry." Darla answered in her gentle way.

"What? We are dressed to have dinner out together and you are not hungry?"

"I have not felt well today. I truly thought I would feel fine by now."

"Would you rather I take you home?"

"No, we set this evening aside so we could be together. I would like for you to have dinner." She insisted, as she rested her head on Kelley's shoulder.

"You look tired Dar, are you?"

"Yes a little."

Kelley drove around the plaza and down Main Street several more times, talking very little.

"I am taking you home. We can go out some other time when you feel better." Kelley said, breaking their silence, with authority in his voice.

Darla remained silent with Kelley's decision, yet lifted her head from his shoulder as not to worry him further.

"I am sorry about tonight." Darla apologized, as Kelley held her hands in his, standing on her front porch.

"Do not worry about it."

"Please do not mention my not feeling well to my family." Darla said, as she unlocked the front door.

"Why should it be a secret?" Kelley questioned, puzzled.

"I don't want my family worried." She answered with a tender smile and then allowed her date to kiss her goodnight.

Relieved her parents and brother were out, Darla went straight to bed feeling tired and drained.

Darla did a terrific job keeping from her parents how terrible she felt over the weekend.

Her alarm ringing at four a.m., Darla felt as though she had butterflies in her stomach when awakening. Today was her big day; she practiced and practiced her routine in front of her dresser mirror, until perfecting each move.

"Good morning, dear. What would you like for breakfast?" Her mother inquired.

"I cannot eat, Mother. I am too excited over tryouts this afternoon. Thank you anyway." Darla answered, as she gathered her schoolbooks together.

"I will grant you your wish this once because this is a special day for you."

"Will you and Dad be at tryouts?"

"We intend to. Kelley called and he is running late, so he will not be picking you up this morning."

Darla left her home through the backdoor. Once outside, she leaned against her home, catching her breath. Her body once again felt weak. She felt light-headed with a sharp pain in the side of her head that seemed to pound harder and faster as she began to walk the two blocks to school.

The morning classes seemed to last forever. Darla did not understand what was happening to her, she felt terrible.

"Once I get to the cafeteria I can rest." She told herself repeatedly as she neared the lunchroom.

"You are not eating again?" Debbie asked, as Darla sat down.

"No, I do not feel well." Darla answered, as she folded her arms on the table, laying her head down.

"Are you going to be okay?"

"Sure, I am just tired." Darla answered, with a weak reassuring smile as she closed her eyes falling fast to sleep.

"What's wrong with Darla?" Kelley questioned, placing his lunch tray on the table, taking the seat next to his girlfriend.

"She said she does not feel well." Debbie answered.

"Maybe she needs to rest." Kelley replied.

"Darla has seemed overly tired today, I think something is wrong. She has always been energetic." Macy remarked.

Kelley silently ate his lunch thinking about Macy's remark, about Darla's parents concern over her appetite and recalling Darla's mother having a prescription filled for her at the drug store where he works.

"Darla." Kelley spoke, shaking her arm. Darla opened her eyes slowly, her eyes looking drowsy.

"How do you feel?" He asked, brushing his girlfriend's long hair from her face, with tenderness in his eyes.

"Tired, but I cannot go home, tryouts are after school." She reminded, barely above a whisper.

"Your face is warm, let me take you home. Nothing is more important than your health, not even being a cheerleader." Kelley scolded his concern for her apparent.

"After tryouts you may take me home." She assured, with a gentle smile, re-closing her eyes, resting.

Darla put all her effort into looking and feeling fine. With standing up, ready to leave the cafeteria, her head pounded even harder. Putting her arm around Kelley's arm, she secretly used him for support as they left the cafeteria.

"I will meet you at your locker after last period." Kelley said, and then gave her a light kiss.

"Okay."

"Hey, Darla, Mrs. Yaro is showing a film, maybe you should rest. You do not look well at all." Peggy suggested, as the girls entered their last class for the day.

"I hope I do not look as bad as I feel." She replied, releasing a weary sigh.

Taking Peggy up on her suggestion, Darla slept through the entire film, feeling better when awakened by her friend.

"I hope I do not mess up when I turn a cartwheel." Peggy worried, as the girls changed their dresses to their gym shorts, in the girl's locker room.

"You will do great." Darla assured, though she too was nervous.

Leaving her friends, Darla hurried to her locker where Kelley waited.

"Are you ready?"

"As ready as I will ever be." Darla answered, pleasantly.

"How do you feel?" Kelley inquired, taking Darla's hand in his, as they started toward the gym.

"Better." She answered, giving her concerned boyfriend a reassuring smile.

"Good, I was worried."

"Sis, Mom and Dad could not make it." Bill informed.

"Good luck." He encouraged.

"Thanks." Darla replied, leaving her brother and boyfriend, joining her girlfriends and other contestants.

Darla waited impatiently and nervously with the other contestants, until her name was called from the judge table. Picking up her pompoms, she hurried to the platform.

"Ready, hit it!" Darla yelled, as she did her cheer. She did well, but felt more nervous now as she waited for further instructions.

"Darla, do the splits, a cartwheel or whatever you can do." One of the judges instructed.

Putting her pompoms aside, Darla turned a cartwheel, followed by a flip, ending in the splits.

"Thank you." The judge replied, impressed.

"That was good!" Her friends congratulated, as she sat down.

"Thank you." She replied kindly.

As the remainder of the girls did their cheers, Darla sat with her head once again aching so bad, she felt like crying. Doing her routine was too much, for her over-tired body.

"Our new cheerleaders are as follows: Peggy Smith, Macy Williams, Darla Roberts, Debbie Johnson and our two substitutes are Connie Waters, and Tracy Bell, congratulations, girls."

The excited girls laughed hysterically, as they congratulated one another.

Darla remained sitting, trying to pull herself together. She felt too weak to move. It was as if all of her strength had drained from her.

"Congratulations Sis, you looked great." Bill complimented as he and Kelley joined Darla.

"Thank you."

"Sis, what is wrong?" Bill asked his excitement for his sister quickly replaced with worry.

"I do not feel well." She answered, rubbing her aching head, with her weak now trembling hand.

"Could I get you two strong guys to take me home?" She asked, forcing a weak smile.

"I do not think I can make it alone." She added, her eyes becoming drowsy.

"Sure Sis." Bill answered, compassionately.

Darla drifted off. She felt as though her body was floating. She tried desperately to keep her eyes open and remain awake. She heard many voices, yet she could not make out whom the voices belonged to or what was said.

"Kelley, get your car." Bill ordered, as he picked up his one and only precious sister.

Darla's many friends and acquaintances now moved back with frightful stares, allowing Bill room to hurry to Kelley's car.

"Are we heading to the hospital?" Kelley asked, carefully helping Bill inside his car, with Darla in his arms.

"Yes and as fast as you can." Bill answered.

Bill and Kelley were silent, as Kelley drove, appearing calm, yet both had looks of deep concentration on his face, trying to conceal the worry and fright they felt.

For two days and nights, Darla lay sleeping with tubes feeding her body the nourishment she needed. Nurses entered her room often, giving shots and taking blood from her motionless arm. Her parents, brother, and Kelley joined hands in prayer several times in her hospital room praying for a quick recovery. Friends and relatives prayed in earnest in their separate homes.

With the binding together of Darla's family and brothers and sisters in Christ, the Lord answered their prayers.

Darla opened her eyes, moving her head slowly, searching her unfamiliar surroundings. Her father sat with his eyes closed, with a look of concentration as though in deep prayer. Her mother sat near her father, her head resting on his broad shoulder. She appeared tired and drained. Bill sat thumbing through a magazine, in his impatient, fidgety way. Kelley stood with his back toward Darla, staring out a window.

"What am I doing here?" Darla questioned, barely above a whisper.

Her parents and Bill quickly sprang to their feet, going to the side of her bed. Kelley went to the foot of her bed, in his calm way.

"You are here to rest and get your strength back, Babe." Pastor Roberts answered.

"How do you feel dear?" Her mother questioned lovingly, soothing her long hair.

"Weak and tired, but I do feel better than I did." Answered Darla, not wanting to worry her family anymore then she already had.

"Sis, why did you quit taking your medicine?" Bill asked, in his impatient blunt manner.

"My medicine … " Repeated Darla, closing her eyes briefly, then reopened her eyes, with flushed cheeks.

"I am sorry. I do recall forgetting several days lately."

"You blow an entire weekend with me, Sis. I had planned to take you horseback riding" Informed Bill in his complaining way, yet gently held his sisters hand in his.

"I am sorry Bill," Darla apologized, tightening her grip on her brother's hand realizing how worried he was for her.

Darla drifted back into a deep sleep, mumbling how sorry she was for worrying everyone. She now truly realized how important her prescribed iron medicine was to her body. She was now able to understand the depth of worry her parents bore with her eating and resting properly.

Awaking the following day, Darla was able to remain awake. She felt much stronger.

"I guess I owe each of you apologies." Darla began, slowly, as her family and Kelley gathered around her bed.

"Perhaps you owe a couple of apologies." Pastor Roberts said with a chuckle, not wanting his daughter burdened at this time, giving her a kiss on her forehead, bringing a smile to her face.

"Is our cheerleader finally awake?" A nurse asked, entering Darla's room with a bouquet of flowers.

"Perhaps not ready for cheering yet, but she is awake," Answered her mother, with a soft laugh of relief.

"Good, I will have a lunch tray sent up," Informed the nurse, giving Darla a kind smile.

"Thank you." Her mother replied.

"Have you noticed all your flowers, Sis?" Bill asked, cheerfully.

"No." She answered, straining to see.

"Here, Babe." Her father said, raising the head of her bed.

Darla's eyes quickly widened at the many arrangements of flowers sitting in her room.

"Perhaps we should start a flower garden Mom." Bill suggested.

"That is an idea." Their mother agreed, with a weary smile.

"Babe, Mother, Bill and I are going to go home now. Eat all of your lunch so we can get you home. Mom will be up this evening." Pastor Roberts informed.

"Okay Daddy, I love you." Replied Darla, as her family exchanged kisses with her.

"Kelley, you have five minutes son."

"Thank you Sir."

Kelley now went to the head of his girlfriend's hospital bed, taking her hand in his.

"Welcome back." Spoke Kelley, with gentleness in his voice and tenderness on his face.

"Thank you." Darla replied, happily.

"Are you too weak for a kiss? I have not given you one for three days, sleeping beauty."

"No, I am not too weak for a kiss." Darla answered, with a soft laugh.

Kelley kissed his girlfriend's lips gently.

"I must go now. I assure you, your father is timing me." He informed with a grin, bringing another laugh from his girlfriend. "I will visit this evening, please eat and rest."

"I will. Bye Kelley."

"Here is your lunch missy. Do try and clear your tray." Spoke the kind nurse with a pleasant smile, then quickly left Darla's room.

Eating her lunch slowly, Darla found her arm tired quickly simply from feeding herself. Though it seemed just a chore to clear her tray, she completed her task. Pushing her tray aside, resting her head back on her bed, she was sleeping within minutes.

Resting peacefully, Darla slept the entire afternoon until awakened by a nurse for dinner. The food looked and smelled delicious. Eating slowly once again, her arm seemed to last longer before tiring, then it had at lunchtime.

"Hi Darla." A young teenage candy stripper greeted, as she neared Darla's bed.

"Hi Queena." Greeted Darla, pleased to see a classmate.

"I am supposed to cheer you up. What may I do to cheer you, besides sneak Kelley Peterson up here?" Queena asked, bringing a laugh from Darla.

"I am sure having your company would help." Answered Darla kindly, pushing her tray away and resting her head back against her bed.

"I would like that too." Queena agreed, with a sweet smile.

"I brought more flowers in while you were resting."

"Thank you. Perhaps you could read me the cards on the flowers; I have not the slightest idea who they are from."

"Sure." Agreed Queena, excited to share each special arrangement.

The kind actions of so many dear ones she knew, deeply touched and moved Darla's heart.

"You are so lucky, Darla."

"Lucky?" Darla questioned, as Queena returned to her bedside.

"Yes, you are so popular. Everyone at school likes and admires you."

"Perhaps I am not as popular as these flowers make me appear," Replied Darla, with flushed cheeks.

"How can you even think such a thought? I know what it feels like to be un-popular. That is me."

"I do not believe I am deserving of my popularity then." Darla corrected, giving her confused classmate a gentle smile.

"Perhaps if you have time to stop in later, I will explain what I mean. I am tiring quickly."

"Yes, of course." Queena agreed, quickly lowering Darla's bed then removing her dinner tray.

Lying in silence, resting her tired heavy eyes, Darla reviewed her activities over the past week, before entering the hospital. She had wanted to become a cheerleader more than anything she had ever wanted. She had allowed one desire to take top priority in her life. She had neglected her daily duties at home to allow extra time for cheerleading practice. She had not left any free time to spend with her only brother while he was on leave from the military. She had betrayed her parent's faith in her by not keeping her agreement in getting her proper rest in order to cheerlead.

"Charity begins in the home." She mumbled, and then drifted off to sleep.

Sleeping through the evening visiting hours and the entire night, Darla felt much stronger, awaking before breakfast.

"Good morning sleepy head." Her mother greeted with a loving smile.

"Good morning." Darla greeted, pleasantly. "Have you been here long?"

"I stayed the night." Kindly raising her daughter's bed, she began brushing her hair.

"You should not have stayed Mother. You must have been miserable sitting in a chair all night."

"We came to visit you last night. When you kept sleeping, I decided to stay and make sure you were okay. I am a bit stubborn when it comes to caring for my family." She confessed, with a pleased smile.

"I know you are Mother." Darla replied, understandingly.

"I spoke with Dr. Paul earlier and he says if you have a good day today, the nurses will be getting you up this evening," Informed Mother pleased, with her daughter's progress.

"Good morning girls." Pastor Roberts greeted, in his cheerful manner, giving his wife a kiss, then his daughter. "How are you Babe?"

"I feel much better." Darla answered, with a gentle smile.

"Good." Her father approved. "Since you are doing better maybe you can help dear Dad convince Mom she needs to rest."

"I will do what I am able." Darla agreed, now realizing how tired her loving mother looked.

Darla enjoyed her parents company having their breakfast with her in her hospital room.

"Bill was throwing a fit when I left home this morning." Pastor Roberts informed with a chuckle.

"Why?" Her mother inquired concern on her tired, drawn, yet gentle face.

"The telephone woke him. It began ringing at 6:30 this morning. It was still ringing when I left."

"Were the calls questions about Darla?"

"Yes, Bill said the next call that came in he was telling the caller Darla had moved." Pastor Roberts answered, bringing smiles to his wife and daughter, they each knowing what a grouch Bill was first thing in the morning.

With their breakfast completed, Mother stayed on to assist her daughter in freshening up for the new day, while Darla's father returned home to study for his Wednesday night sermon.

"Mother, go home and rest." Darla suggested, compassionately, as she grew tired.

"I realize I am already in serious trouble with Dad when I get well, so if you become ill from wearing yourself out, I will be in double trouble," She added, bringing a weary smile to her compassionate mothers face.

"I will heed your suggestion. Rest now dear, so we can get you home." Her mother replied, kissing her daughter's forehead.

With her room now empty of visitors, Darla closed her heavy eyelids, silently praying. "Lord, forgive me for what I have done to my body, the temple of God. Forgive me Lord, for putting a worldly desire before you. I did not intend to allow becoming a cheerleader to become an obsession. I neglected my daily prayer time and Bible studies with you Lord, as well as letting my family down, my friends down, and myself down. Please forgive me Heavenly Father, as I undo the problems I have created."

With another day of bed rest, Darla was slowly able to make her way to and from the bathroom without assistance by evening.

With the head of her bed raised, Darla sat reading her Bible, strengthening her spiritually as well as physically.

"Look who I found." Spoke Queena, as she entered Darla's room, with Kelley close behind her.

"Hi Kelley." Darla greeted, happily, closing her Bible.

"Hi." Kelley greeted, kissing her lips.

"How is my favorite girl?" He asked.

"I am getting better every day," Darla answered pleasantly.

"How did you get out of class early?" She questioned, glancing at her watch.

"Mrs. Thorton has a crush on me. She's putty in my hands." Kelley answered, with a boyish grin, bringing smiles to the girl's faces as they thought of the seventy-year-old English teacher.

"Darla, I have some notes for you." Queena said, handing them to her.

"I will see you two later." She added.

"I have something for you also." Kelley said, showing Darla an elegant vase with one red rose.

"Oh Kelley, this is sweet of you. Thank you." Darla said, her face now glowing and her eyes sparkling.

"You are welcome." Kelley replied, now setting the vase on her nightstand. Removing the card from the vase, Kelley politely handed Darla the card, his face now growing solemn as he silently awaited her response.

To a very special girl, I love with all my heart.
Yours always,
Kelley

Darla read silently. Returning the card to the envelope, Darla felt warmness in her heart towards Kelley. She did not realize he cared so deeply for her.

"Thank you for the card, and the special words." Darla said, taking Kelley's hand in hers lovingly.

"You are welcome. Given a few more dates with you, I plan to have the nerve to verbally say to you, what I wrote." Kelley replied with a gentle smile, his cheeks flushed.

"I will be looking forward to that date." Darla assured, with a smile, blushing over her forwardness, bringing pride and content to Kelley's young strong face.

"I appreciate knowing this." Kelley shared, kissing her lips lightly.

"Excuse me." Bill said, slowly entering his sister's room, with his present girlfriend Terry.

With flushed cheeks, Kelley let go of Darla's hand, moving aside for Bill to see his sister.

"Hi Sis." Bill greeted with a kiss.

"Hi Bill and Terry." Greeted Darla, pleased for their visit.

"Dad says you are becoming a grouch." Darla shared, with a sympathetic smile.

"What, me becoming a grouch?"

"Yes, you are a grouch. He says you intend to tell my friends I have moved when they call in regards to my well-being." She answered, bringing a laugh from her brother.

"Trust me. Dad would not mind if I told that white lie. The telephone is ringing from early morning, until late at night."

"You mean was ringing." Terry reminded, with an amused laugh.

"My dear brother apparently put a stop to my calls." Darla remarked with a sigh, not trusting his methods for solutions.

"I did not offend anyone, Sis." Her brother assured quickly, to relieve her from worries.

"I called the high school suggesting to the secretary she announce over the intercom you are still in the hospital, suggesting the telephoning cease." He added.

"Did Miss Clara make the announcement, Kelley?" Darla asked, not sure if her brother was completely leveling with her.

A grin appeared on Kelley's face as Bill gave him a "be quiet" look.

"I heard the announcement this morning. It was much as Bill said." Kelley answered, his grin gone, Darla knowing he had taken her brothers side.

"When do you get to come home?" Terry asked, changing the subject.

"In another day or two and I cannot wait to get back to school." Darla answered in her soft gentle way.

"Nor can I wait to get even with my brother." She added with a soft laugh, bringing smiles to her visitor's faces.

Her room once again empty of callers, Darla picked up the envelope of notes Queena had delivered to her while she awaited her dinner tray.

Hi Dar!
We all miss you! Your brother suggested
we send notes to you since your doctor will not
allow us to visit since you need your rest. He
said if we do not quit calling your home, writing
you notes instead, he personally will inflict
bodily harm. We all know Bill is a bit on the
crazy side, so we took him at his word. Ha.
We miss you! Hurry back!
Love, Macy

Darla laughed aloud at her brothers forward; unpredictable ways at getting things accomplished what he wished. Although, the notes were a great idea, Darla felt she was a part of her friends with reading about their doings. This made her want to get well even more.

"I am going to miss our talks when you leave the hospital." Shared Queena, as she and Darla slowly walked down the corridor to the patio.

"I had hoped we would remain close friends." Replied Darla, looking at Queena puzzled.

"I thought you would rather we not mingle at school."

"Why would you think this?"

"I have my friends, but I am not in the "in crowd" like you." Queena answered, feeling self-conscious over her confession.

"Queena, please do not think this way of me, I am probably the biggest square of squares." Darla shared, blushing with a soft laugh.

"I am a Christian and I do not belong to any group except the Lords group. Believe me; most of my friends tolerate me because they feel I am too religious." Darla added.

"Mine too." Queena replied with a shy smile.

"You are a Christian?" Darla asked, excited.

"Yes."

"This is terrific!" Darla exclaimed, giving her friend a tight hug, surprising her new friend by her actions. "Excuse me for my excitement. I have not learned to be as reserved as my family when involved in matters of Christianity."

"That is okay, I guess this is what draws people to you. You are not ashamed of being a Christian."

"Of course I am not ashamed of being a Christian. My personal relationship with Jesus is my life." Darla answered, excitedly.

"Would you help me overcome being ashamed at times?"

"I would be honored." Darla answered, giving her friend an understanding smile.

Darla was thrilled inside, as she remained on the patio alone. It felt good to know Jesus was hers. Regardless of her goofs, momentary actions of being side tracked, He loved her, mistakes and all and she loved Him.

"Hi." Kelley greeted, pulling a patio chair up next to her.

"Hi. How are you today?" She inquired happily, allowing Kelley to take her hand in his.

"I feel great."

"Good. It is such a beautiful day today." Darla said, looking up at the sky.

"I never realized how many of God's creations I took for granted until I could not enjoy them this past week. The trees, the flowers, and everything look much prettier than they did a few days ago." Darla shared, with a happy radiant glow to her face.

"I think we all are guilty of taking things for granted." Kelley agreed, honoring her mood.

"The Lord has been dealing with me for several months." He shared, his face growing serious, as he looked into Darla's eyes with gentleness in his eyes.

"I had been ignoring Him, in regards to totally committing myself to Him. Seeing you lying here in the hospital wanting to make you well but could not, really got to me. I knew I could no longer ignore God. I felt so helpless not being able to save you from your illness. With the leading of the Holy Spirit working through me, it is possible for me to lead others to the Lord receiving eternal life. When I begin college next fall, I will be studying to be a minister." Kelley informed, with pride in his voice.

"This is terrific!" Darla exclaimed, giving her boyfriend a hug. "You will make a perfect minister." She encouraged.

"You would make a perfect minister's wife." Kelley said, sincerely surprising Darla.

"You are a Christian, you study the Bible and you have a compassionate heart." He explained, looking into her eyes, with great compassion.

Darla was speechless, as she looked into Kelley's gentle eyes. The most she had thought about her future was going to college, somewhere, at some time, to become a Nurse. She had mixed and confused feelings of Kelley's remark, yet her heart again seemed to grow closer to him.

"We had better get you back to your room so you can rest and I best get to the drug store before Brother Hillman fires me." Kelley suggested, quickly rescuing Darla from her inner questions brought by his news.

Darla was relieved to learn she could finally leave the hospital, to return home. Walking slowly along the sidewalk near her home, Darla tarried. She reviewed her hospital visit. Her devoted family at her side, Kelley sharing his inner feelings and hearts desires with her, Queena's often visits to her hospital room to cheer her had brought her a new close Christian friend.

"Hi beautiful." Kelley said interrupting Darla's thoughts, as she quickly turned toward the approaching handsome high school senior.

"Kelley … " She scolded, blushing, nervously glancing up and down her street for a possible observer overhearing his forwardness.

"May I join you in your stroll? I promise not to embarrass you further, although, you are even more beautiful when you blush."

"You may, but do refrain from making me blush."

"May I hold your hand Miss Darla?" He inquired rising and lowering his eyebrows, with a boyish grin knowing his girlfriend would blush at his play.

"Yes, you may." She answered blushing, becoming tickled.

"I hear you will be returning to school Monday."

"You have heard correctly."

"Bill tells me you resigned from your cheerleading position before your dad had the opportunity to force you to and according to your brother, you no longer feel worthy of holding the position."

"Yes. I am back to the simple, uninteresting life of a Preacher's kid and Christian teenager. I guess I am stuck with the simple life of being a peculiar person." She answered with a gentle smile.

"You had fame for one day. Besides, Miss Darla Roberts, you are not apologizing for being a peculiar person, are you?" He asked, stopping their walk, looking into her eyes.

"I will never apologize for being peculiar." She answered, with a happy smile.

"Good. I love you, Miss Darla Roberts. You are a very special peculiar person." Kelley assured, with a pleased grin, making his girlfriend laugh.

CHAPTER 3

Summer was nearing, bringing long, warm, sunny days. The grass was a pretty green. The many flowers surrounding the Roberts home filled the air with a lovely fragrance. Darla especially loved this time of year, when Gods beauty in His creations, stood out clearly. The faint sound of voices awoke Darla from her sleep.

Dressing in a cool pair of shorts, tank top, and sneakers, with her long hair in a braid, she was ready for her Saturday morning chores. Quietly closing her bedroom door behind her, as not to disturb her two overnight guests, she left her room.

"Good morning." Greeted Darla, pleasantly, joining her parents at the breakfast table.

"Good morning."

"Who was your visitor?" She inquired, removing a cup and saucer from the table, placing it in the sink.

"Brother Smith." Her mother answered, rubbing her head wearily.

"At this hour, is something wrong?" Darla asked, sitting down at the breakfast table with a bowl of cereal.

"He had some things on his mind." Her father answered, looking as tired as her mother looked.

Darla respected her parent's privacy, as she quietly ate her cereal, with no further questions on her parent's caller.

"Are Macy and Queena still sleeping dear?"

"Yes, I plan to do my chores early this morning. I would like to go to town with Macy and Queena if you do not mind, Mother."

"I do not mind." Her mother answered.

"Aunt Martha called late last night. Mom and I have agreed to assist your hard-headed cousin through her next two years of high school." Pastor Roberts informed.

"Why?" Darla asked, surprised.

"Cindy has created problems for herself at home, school, and with the police. She has been involved in shoplifting and drugs. She just completed three months in juvenile center." Her father answered his heart going out for his sister's only child.

"I would like Cindy's past kept quiet, she needs a fresh start."

"Sure Dad." Darla agreed slowly, disbelieving her ears.

"When will Cindy arrive?" Darla asked.

"Cindy will arrive sometime late this morning."

"I will cancel my plans for the day then."

"No canceling plans on Cindy's account, while she is with us, babe. Do not treat her as a guest. I am sure you will not find her company too pleasing. With time, a lot of prayer, and a

Christian environment, perhaps we will have our old Cindy back." Pastor Roberts instructed.

Cindy had changed so much since Darla's visit to her cousin's home a year ago. Darla stood speechless, with her two girlfriends preparing for her shopping date, as Cindy arrived and Darla and her parents welcomed her into their home. The once attractive, out-going teenager now appeared cold and withdrawn. Make-up caked her pretty face. Her teased hair was so high it looked like a beehive. Her skirt was surely the shortest of mini-skirts. Nonetheless, Darla, along with her parents welcomed Cindy warmly.

With Darla, Queena and Macy's departure, Mom and Dad Roberts took Cindy aside, explaining the do's and don'ts of being a member of their family.

"I cannot believe your parents allowed your cousin to enter their home the way she is dressed." Remarked Macy, as the three girls walked the six short blocks to town.

"I am sure Mrs. Roberts will give Cindy a crash course in "proper attire." Queena said, with a laugh, bringing smiles to the girl's faces.

"I am sure by the time we have returned from our shopping Cindy's appearance will be different." Darla agreed, with a gentle smile.

"There's Lisa." Queena informed, as the girls passed the ice cream stand.

"Hi Lisa." The girls greeted.

"Would you like to come shopping with us?" They asked.

"I can't, but thanks anyway. My dad is on my case." Lisa answered disappointment on her face.

"Perhaps you will be able to join us later this afternoon. Kelley is borrowing his father's truck, taking whoever would like to go swimming." Darla suggested.

"The outing has been changed from swimming to bowling. Kelley called inviting us."

"There goes my excuse to buy a new swim suit." Macy sighed.

"You do not need an excuse to buy a new swim suit, Macy." Lisa remarked with a smile, her down mood lifting.

"I know she gets everything she wants." Sided Queena

"That is not true." Defended Macy, though not annoyed by the girls teasing.

"If that were true, I would be driving to town instead of walking." She added, bringing laughter from the girls.

"Lisa, did Kelley say why he changed the plans from swimming?" Darla questioned.

"No, but you may ask him. Here he comes."

"Good morning girls and Miss Darla." Kelley greeted, pulling up next to them, they each greeting their youth leader in return.

"Hello Aaron." Darla greeted, with a tender smile to the ten-year-old sitting in the truck with his brother. Aaron stared at the floor, deliberately ignoring Darla's greeting, causing Darla's cheeks to flush.

"Darla said hi." Kelley said, lightly bopping his brother on top of his head, disapproving of his action.

"Hi." He mumbled, though his eyes remained on the floor of the truck.

"Lisa says swimming is cancelled." Spoke Darla, pleasantly, pretending not to notice Aarons continued mood.

"This is correct. I was not thinking when I suggested swimming. Bowling sounds like fun. It is something we have not done for a while." Kelley replied, enthusiastic.

"I love to bowl." Queena agreed.

"Bowling is okay, I guess." Macy said.

"What happened with the swimming idea? It is a perfect day for swimming."

"Pastor Roberts will not let us go swimming." Aaron blurted out stubbornly, folding his arms across his chest, as though proving his disapproval.

"You should have gone to San Diego with Mom and Dad." Kelley said, quickly hushing his brother with his stern tone.

"My Dad cancelled our plans, Kelley?" Darla asked her cheeks now their reddest, as her friends grew silent with compassion for her embarrassing moment.

"Yes." He answered, hesitant, not wanting to make his girlfriend feel badly.

"The activity falls under the subject of modesty. The church does not approve of mixed bathing." He answered, attempting to humor his girlfriend with his choice of words.

"You know how your dad is, Dar. He probably thought us girls intended to wear bikinis." Lisa comforted quickly, with laughter, setting the group at ease.

"You are probably right." Darla added, with a smile, blushing.

"What about a new outfit for bowling, Macy?"

"That is a great idea!" Macy agreed, excited over her shopping obsession.

"Where do I pick you girls up?" Kelley asked, starting his father's truck.

"You can pick us up at my house please." Darla answered.

"Lisa?" Kelley asked, politely.

"I will be at Dar's by then." Lisa said.

"See you girls at four and invite your friends, the more the merrier." He encouraged.

"Kelley will probably have the back of his truck filled with kids by four o'clock. There will not be room for our friends." Lisa joked, as the girls politely waved goodbye to Kelley.

"You have that right, Lisa." Darla agreed, pleased with Kelley's drive to witness for the Lord and encourage Christian fellowship.

The three girls enjoyed one another's company as they browsed through the shops of their small desert town.

Returning to Darla's home, Macy with her new outfit in her shopping bag, the girls took turns calling their individual friends to attend their bowling outing. Placing the telephone back on the hallstand, Darla turned her radio on and excitedly visited with her guests.

Cindy entered Darla's room, forcing a greeting to her cousin and friends, as she hung her clothes in the closet. Cindy wore very little make-up now. Her hair had a soft, shiny look, with the rats combed out. Her flashy dangly jewelry and mini-skirt replaced with a modest style.

"It will be fun having you here, Cindy." Darla said in her loving way.

"You will not mind sharing your room?" Cindy asked.

"Of course I won't mind sharing my room." Darla answered quickly.

"It will be nice having you here. It is too quiet with Bill away in the military." She assured, pleasantly.

"Do you enjoy bowling?" Queena asked, politely.

"Not really." Cindy answered, as though she obtained no interest in anything as she continued putting her belongings away.

"If you would like to join us, Cindy, several of our friends will be going bowling at four. We would love to have you join us. I cannot wait to introduce my favorite cousin to everyone." Darla shared, enthusiastic.

"Thanks anyway, but Aunt Mary mentioned she and I going shopping this afternoon for longer dresses for school." Cindy was speaking with kind words, but Darla as well as her girlfriends, sensed coldness. Cindy was deliberately putting a wall between them to prevent them from being close like they had been in the past.

"I hope you enjoy sewing."

"I have never sewed." Cindy replied, puzzled.

"It will be a good idea if you learn. The shops do not make dresses long enough for mother, since mini-skirts became the style." Darla warned, with a sympathetic smile.

"Maybe I should go bowling, instead of shopping." Cindy complained.

"Yes, you probably should." Darla agreed, with an encouraging smile.

The entire first week of Cindy and Darla becoming roommates was trying. Darla had gone out of her way to make her cousin feel welcome and comfortable, at home; school and church, yet Cindy seemed to withdraw, more and more from her. Nightly, Darla silently prayed for her troubled cousin, asking the Lord to save Cindy's soul, taking away her bitterness and sadness, replacing her heart with love and peace.

"Cindy, Dad said to hurry or we will be late." Darla informed, as she removed her purse and Bible from her desk.

"That is just too bad." Cindy replied hatefully, in a half-whisper.

Though Cindy had hurt her cousin's feelings terribly, by her rudeness, Darla did not retaliate. With flushed cheeks, she quietly left her room and sat down in the front room, where her parents already sat awaiting the teenagers, to attend the once a month Friday night, youth rally in Ragweed.

"Darla, is something troubling you?" Mrs. Roberts asked as Darla sat, picking at her long nails, her cheeks still flushed.

"It has just been a hectic week, Mother. I will be fine." Darla answered, forcing a smile.

"Babe, has Cindy been giving you a hard time?" Her father asked.

"Daddy, I will be fine. Cindy is the one needing our concerns."

"You will not be treated rudely in your own home." Her mother defended, sternly.

"I did not say Cindy was rude to me, Mother." Darla replied quickly, for her cousin's defense.

Cindy entered the front room, stopping abruptly, sensing she had been the topic of discussion, with looks of annoyance apparent on her Aunt and Uncle's face.

"You snitch." Cindy accused, snapping at Darla, surprising the Roberts by her outburst.

"I did not ... " Darla started.

"Darla has not said one word against you, Miss Smarty pants." Pastor Roberts defended, extremely putout with his niece.

"Mark, Darla and I will go ahead. We will see you at the rally." Spoke Mrs. Roberts, her face showing her concern.

"I think that will be best." Pastor Roberts agreed, remaining in his chair.

Inside her mother's car, Darla remained silent, with her head toward her door window, as she desperately fought to hold back the tears that wanted to escape over her cousin falsely accusing her.

"Are you okay?" Mrs. Roberts asked, gently pulling her daughter's long hair away from the side of her face, in attempts to see her facial expressions as she drove.

"I will be okay." She answered with watery eyes, glancing at her mother giving her a re-assuring smile.

"Are you sorry Cindy is with us, sweetheart?"

"No Mother." Darla answered, quickly. "I do feel frustrated because I do not seem to have the understanding to reach her."

"Oh, I think you do, dear. Do not under estimate yourself. I am sure Cindy has picked you as her sounding board because you understand what she needs most. She will come around, dear. Just keep doing and being yourself, allowing your life to be your witness before her. I assure you, someday, she will thank you." Her mother said, encouragingly.

Darla enjoyed attending youth rallies, as did most of her friends. The rally enabled the teenagers from other towns and churches to come together, uniting in a time of praise and prayer, strengthening their Christian tithes as a dynamite witnessing team. Locating her friends, Darla joined them on their choice pew.

"It looks like Kelley received a promotion from President of our youth group, to President of all youth groups." Debbie informed, pointing to the platform.

"He does look handsome up front." Darla remarked, with an excited laugh, blushing with her bragging.

"He does at that." Agreed Debbie, also laughing knowing her girlfriends modest ways.

"What is Kelley doing up front, Dar?" Lisa asked, as she, Macy, Queena, and Peggy arrived."

"I do not know, Kelley does not tell me everything." She answered, smiling at Lisa's curiosity.

"Excuse me." Cindy spoke, waiting for Peggy to slide down so she could sit next to her cousin."

"I am glad you came to sit with us." Darla said, giving her cousin a loving smile.

"Uncle Mark insisted." Cindy replied, ignoring her cousin's kindness, bringing silence to the talkative teenagers.

Darla silently looked ahead, her cheeks once again flushed by her cousin's rudeness, as she felt her girlfriends' eyes on her.

"Who is your new friend, Darla?" Dan asked, sitting in front of Darla with his friends from his church.

"This is my cousin, Cindy. Cindy, Dan Phillips."

"It is nice to meet you Cindy." Greeted Dan, forcing his handshake, surprising Darla, her friends, and even Cindy.

"Cindy must take after your dad's side Dar. She is a bit spunkier than you." He added, teasingly, and then took his seat.

"Church boys … " Cindy whispered, with a sigh, bringing smiles to Darla and her friends, they knowing all too well Cindy considered all present to be squares.

"What is your boyfriend doing on the stage? Do not tell me they are allowing him to preach?" Cindy asked, with sarcasm.

"I haven't the slightest idea." Darla answered, she now with a sigh, becoming annoyed with Cindy's constant rudeness and sarcasm.

Cindy was quiet now, with flushed cheeks, with Darla expressing her disapproval in her cousin's manner for the first time.

Everyone seemed to be enjoying the rally except, Cindy. However, she had ceased her sarcasm and for this, Darla was thankful.

"For those teenagers sitting patiently wondering why Kelley Peterson, President of Dunes youth group is sitting on the platform, I will tell you, you are not alone in your question. Kelley has been sitting through this entire service wondering the same." Pastor Finks informed, causing Kelley to grin, along with the congregation's laughter.

"We, meaning myself, along with fellow pastors, keep hearing strange comments about this young man." Pastor Finks began, causing Kelley's face to turn red quickly. "I will rephrase my meaning, Kelley." Pastor Finks chuckled.

"I would appreciate that Pastor." Kelley replied, bringing laughter from the crowd.

"In all sincerity, joking aside, we have heard comments regarding Kelley's doings, and activities. Kelley is a remarkable young man. In these times of drugs and hippies, our young people go through trials and tests daily. Yet, Kelley holds an outstanding record of accomplishment. He has a good approach before man in his daily walk with the Lord. I have learned of Kelley's enrollment at Southern California University for the coming fall semester and his goal is to become a minister. I think we as pastors, teachers, parents, and friends should show our support to Kelley, verbally, through our prayers now, and in the future." Spoke Pastor Finks with admiration. "Kelley, come join me." He instructed.

"Did you know Kelley intends to be a preacher, Dar?" Debbie asked, excited and happy.

"Yes." Answered Darla, she too happy and pleased for him.

"Welcome to your first speaking engagement, Kelley." Pastor Finks informed with a laugh, as he raised the microphone for Kelley's tall height, causing Kelley's face to turn its reddest, the Pastor stepping back from the microphone.

"I will remember when I do become a minister to never put anyone on the spot, Pastor Finks." Kelley said, with a nervous laugh, bringing laughter from the pastor as well as the audience.

"I believe standing up here, all alone, with no outlined speech before me, I now have more insight to how Daniel must have felt alone in the lions den." Kelley confessed, with a grin as he attempted to calm his nervousness.

"The pastor said, "You folks do not bite." Kelley relayed.

"Apparently Pastor Finks does not know you teenage guys and gals as well as he thinks he does." Kelley said.

Pausing briefly, Kelley's face grew serious. "Like the pastor said earlier, all joking aside, I truly love the Lord with all my heart." Kelley spoke, now looking out into the audience, his nervousness under control, as he appeared calm and sincere.

"As my Irish father often says, 'Aye, the Lord makes one feel good inside.'" Kelley shared with a grin.

"I like feeling good inside and sharing how I feel with others. I have been blessed from start to present in my eighteen years. I have Christian parents, a Christian girlfriend, and fine Christian friends. Each of these special people at one point and time has encouraged me in my Christian walk. To all of you present who will be praying for me as I obey the leading of the Holy Spirit, I thank you for assisting me in getting this far, and for achieving my goal. Thank you." Kelley said, now calmly stepping back from the microphone.

"I think he did fine without an outlined speech." Pastor Finks approved, leading the audience in applauding.

"Thank you, Kelley. May God continue to use you and richly bless you." Spoke Pastor Finks, shaking Kelley's hand.

"Thank you, sir."

With the rally dismissed, Darla could not wait until the crowd around Kelley thinned out, so she too could congratulate him. Catching sight of his girlfriend, Kelley motioned for her to join him, making a way for her through the crowd.

"May I drive you home?" Kelley asked.

"I will ask my parents."

"I will ask your parents." Kelley corrected, politely.

"Thank you. I accept this."

Darla enjoyed keeping Kelley's company, as they stopped for a coke after the rally along with other teenagers. He made her feel proud she was his girlfriend. In her book, Kelley Peterson was the greatest.

"Hello Cindy." Darla greeted, as she and her girlfriend entered Darla's home.

"Hi." Spoke Cindy, as she sewed on the sewing machine.

"Which dress are you making?" Darla asked, picking up the pattern envelope.

"More like, trying to make." Cindy complained.

"Lisa, did you make this dress?"

"Yes."

"If you need help, Lisa and I will be glad to help."

"I do not need any help." Cindy snapped.

Darla stood with flushed cheeks, at her cousin's shortness, but remained calm, as she silently watched her cousin sew.

"Where are Mother and Dad?" She kindly questioned.

"Someone called a board meeting. They are at the church."

"I wonder why? There have been several meetings already this month." Voiced Darla, hoping there were no serious upsets in the church.

"It gives our parents something to do." Lisa remarked, with a laugh, relieving her concerned friend.

"Perhaps you are right, Lisa." Darla smiled, though doubting her reply.

"Cindy, Lisa and I are going with Kelley and others to the sand dunes in a couple of hours. Would you like to come?" Darla asked, enthusiastic.

"No. I do not need your friends, or you trying to help me in anyway, Darla. I can do it on my own." She snapped.

"Okay. Enjoy your day." Darla Replied, as she left the dining room to Cindy and her sewing.

"How do you put up with her?" Lisa whispered, turning on her girlfriend's radio, as she sat down on Darla's bed.

"Your parents allow her to live here and you share your room with her. What more could she want?" Lisa questioned, in her blunt way.

"Mother says Cindy is under conviction. I believe Cindy wants to receive the Lord into her heart, but wanting and doing are two different subjects. I pray she yields soon, so she can be happy." Darla answered, feeling troubled for her cousin.

"She is not only rude to us, Dar. She snubs everyone at school too."

"I know, do not mention her attitude to my parents. Dad would be furious if he knew her attitude at school."

"Are you girls going to the sand dunes?" Pastor Roberts asked, standing in his daughter's doorway.

"Yes." Darla answered.

"Kelley and the others are here."

"Daddy, do not forget to bring the drinks when you come." Darla reminded as she opened the front door to leave.

"I won't babe."

"Cindy, aren't you going with the kids?" Pastor Roberts asked.

"No." She answered, as she struggled with her sewing.

Kelley drove his father's pick-up truck through the town of Dunes inviting any and every teenager he saw to participate in his outings of straight, clean, fun. He was a terrific youth leader. He always seemed to know how to keep the teenagers interest in Christ-like activities.

"What is on your mind?" Kelley asked, taking his right hand from the steering wheel, taking Darla's hand in his, as he looked into her eyes.

"Mm, wouldn't you like to know?" She asked with a teasing smile.

"Keep your eyes on your driving, Kel." Roger teased from the back of the truck, causing Kelley to laugh.

"Sit down, before you fall and mind your own business." Kelley ordered, enjoying his play.

"I think I am growing tired of this chaperoning job." Kelley whispered with a boyish grin.

"Do not grow tired, you are very much needed in keeping us younger teens entertained and revived." Encouraged Darla pleased.

"Kel, you can park the truck now." Lisa suggested putting her head near the open passenger window, as Kelley deliberately drove around the sand dunes, teasing the teenagers.

"Sure Lisa, as soon as I am finished visiting with my date." Kelley replied, causing Darla to blush.

"Come on, Kelley." Macy and Debbie yelled.

"Kel-ly, stop it." Darla insisted, blushing.

"Sure baby doll." Kelley agreed, making Darla laugh and blush more by his choice of words.

"You are a terrible tease."

"My dad has warned me of this problem a time or two."

"Now I am warning you, do not embarrass me in front of anyone else, or I am staying in this truck."

"I promise to act my age." Kelley assured, his teasing ceased parking the truck. He politely assisted his girlfriend from the cab of the truck.

The teenagers laughed, joked, teased, sang, and shared with one another as they enjoyed their hiking in the desert and on the dunes. Some of the braver, more carefree teenagers rolled down the dunes on their sides, regardless of their ages. For now, they would play, but when their activity ended, they would return to their more mature sides to his and her personality.

"I am dying of thirst. Dar, when is your dad bringing the drinks?" Debbie asked, sitting down on the sand, after their exhausting hike in the desert surroundings.

"Soon, I hope." Darla answered, she too dropping to the ground resting her weary body.

"You girls are weaklings." Teased Jay, as all the teenagers began sitting down.

"Why didn't Cindy come?" Kelley asked, putting his arm around Darla's neck, squeezing it lightly.

"You are supposed to influence her our way."

"Kel-ley, I invited her." Darla defended, quickly removing his arm from her neck, in others presence.

"Here comes Pastor Roberts." Marty said, getting up from the sand, starting toward the approaching car. Each teenager found the strength to stand to their feet to meet the car that carried the drinks their dry lips longed for.

"Would you like to have dinner with me tomorrow after church?" Darla asked, hopeful, as she and Kelley lingered behind the others.

"Of course I would like to." Answered Kelley, pleased for the invitation.

"Hi Darla, what's happening?" Roxanne asked in her slang, talk.

"Quite a bit, I have Jesus in my heart." Darla answered with a smile.

"I knew you would say something like that."

"I am glad you came today. Will you be at Sunday school in the morning?" Darla asked, hopeful.

"We have missed you not attending." Darla added.

"I will probably be there."

Darla and Kelley joined the others helping themselves to a cold pop. Cindy stood off to herself, looking miserable. Hand-in-hand, Darla now led the way to her cousin's side.

"Hi Cindy, you should have come earlier. We had a great time." Shared Darla, hoping her enthusiasm would rub off on her cousin.

"I am here only because Uncle Mark insisted. This is not my idea of a party." Cindy said, sarcastically.

"You struck out again, Dar." Kelley remarked, sympathetic for his kind, considerate girlfriend. Darla remained silent, slowly drinking her coke.

"I am sorry for making you feel bad Darla." Cindy apologized, for the first time since her arrival.

"You and your parents live a completely different lifestyle then I have and as much as I want to be a part of it, I do not fit in yet. To change sixteen years of living is not easy." Cindy shared, beginning to open up.

"I understand." Darla said, with a comforting smile.

Within a few weeks, Cindy had come out from behind her wall. She was often quiet, keeping her activities near home and church functions.

She had a pretty smile. She had accepted Jesus Christ, as Lord and Savior of her life.

"Cindy, you have a telephone call." Darla informed, setting the extension on her desk.

"Is it a male or female?"

"Male and his name is Dan Phillips." Darla answered, with a gentle smile, happy for her cousin.

"Dan Phillips the church boy from Ragweed?" Questioned Cindy, with an excitedly laugh.

"Yes, dear cousin. It is the same Dan Phillips that has called you every evening at this time for the past four weeks."

"Would you mind if I stay in the room while you talk?" Darla asked, getting comfortable.

"Yes, I mind." Answered Cindy quickly, beginning a laugh from both the girls.

Darla politely left her room giving her cousin her privacy. The girls were becoming as sisters, sharing their up times as well as their down times. Even Kelley and Dan had become good friends, allowing the two couples several good times together, double dating.

"Cindy, has Lisa come by?" Darla asked, placing her schoolbooks on the coffee table, as she returned from school.

"No, but she did call. She and her dad had an argument and he will not let her use his car, so she is walking over."

"Great." Darla complained, slipping her shoes off. "Sometimes Lisa's dad … " She started, and then quickly bit her tongue.

"Now, now, you must remember who you are young lady." Cindy said, bringing a laugh from Darla, her cheeks flushed.

"I am thankful I am only the niece and not the preacher's daughter." Cindy confessed, cheerfully.

"Personally Darla, I do not care what you say about Lisa's dad he is nothing but a fake, along with a few other hypocrites in my dear Uncles congregation."

"You know something that I do not?" Darla asked, not sure, she wanted to hear of any wrong from Christians she had faith in.

"I know plenty. Aunt Mary and Uncle Mark are tops and they do not deserve the way they are treated. They, you, the Peterson's, and a few others are true Christians. Trust me, there are not very many truly sold out Christians. I have met lots of fakes though."

"Are you trying to tell me there are serious problems in the church?" Darla asked, hesitant.

"Yes."

"This is why my parents have been involved in numerous board meetings and their sudden interest in leaving for the day on short trips?" Darla asked.

"Yes."

"Do you know if Bill knows of these problems?"

"Bill definitely knows. According to your parents, Bill blames giving up his salvation on the hypocrites that have hurt his parents."

"Why do you know these things, yet I do not?" Darla asked, disbelieving her ears.

"Maybe it is because you and I, you and most everyone are different. I had to have God's existence proven to me; you naturally accept God's existence. A Christian has to prove to me he or she is worthy of the title, you automatically accept. In other words Dar, you always look for the good in people, overlooking their flaws. I, like most people are not as kind, we see ones flaws first."

"This sounds like I am naïve, perhaps even immature." Darla replied, searching herself.

"Please do not think that Dar. Your parents will kill me if they know I have shared this much with you. You are different from everyone I have ever known. Everyone sees this in you. You are not immature or naive by any means. You are just super nice. It is as if you are too nice and too filled with love for this crazy, mixed-up world. You are a one-of-a-kind person. Do not ever allow anyone or anything to change you."

"Thank you for the kind words." Darla replied, forcing a smile, attempting to conceal her concerns for her parent's happiness.

"I suppose you are sworn to secrecy in regards to my parents upsets?"

"I am definitely sworn to secrecy." Cindy answered.

"How would you like it if I drive you and Lisa to Ragweed so your shopping plans are not disrupted? I am going to Ragweed anyway to see Dan."

"Thank you. I would like this." Darla accepted, kindly. "I best change. Lisa should be here any minute."

Cindy and Darla were extremely quiet as Cindy drove the twenty miles from Dunes to Ragweed. Lisa, upset with her dad, complained of his unfair ways.

"Cindy, wait. Stop the car." Lisa ordered, suddenly.

Cindy quickly pulled off the road, shocked by Lisa's order.

"There is my dad and Sarah." Spoke Lisa, barely above a whisper, as she began to sob. Cindy and Darla sat motionless, as though in shock, as they witnessed Lisa's dad, Sunday school superintendent, holding hands with Sarah, their church pianist.

"Please take us home, Cindy." Spoke Darla, as tears made their way down Darla's cheeks also.

"Sure." Agreed Cindy, turning her car around quickly, in hopes the adult couple would not see them.

"Darla, please do not tell your parents about my dad." Lisa pleaded, as her sobbing continued.

"I cannot promise you this, Lisa." Darla replied, tears streaming down her cheeks.

"I am not asking you to protect my dad, my mom does not know and I do not want her hurt."

Darla was silent now, as she felt for her friend. Their loyalty toward one another had grown since grade school. To be loyal to her friend over the breaking of God's law and betraying her parents for teaching to keep God's law, Darla knew was wrong.

With Lisa at her home, Cindy returning to her dinner plans with Dan, Darla made herself a sandwich, turned on the television set and sat down on the sofa, feeling miserable.

It seemed as though she stared at the television forever, rehearsing repeatedly in her mind, how to tell her parents.

It was after midnight when Darla heard her parents unlock the front door.

"Hi." Darla greeted.

"Why aren't you in bed, dear? It is late." Her mother scolded.

"I need to talk with you and dad. It is important." Assured Darla, worry on her young troubled face.

"What is so important, babe?" Pastor Roberts questioned him and his wife sitting down, getting comfortable.

Darla shared her learnings of Lisa's father with her parents, as tears once again streamed down her thin tan cheeks.

"Mark, it is time to tell Darla." Her mother said, her face baring the pain she bore, over her daughter's upsets.

"Babe, Mom and I already knew about Lisa's father. I am sorry you had to find out. I have always tried to protect you and Bill from hearing such nonsense." Pastor Roberts apologized.

After several long silent moments, Pastor Roberts cleared his throat, looking at his daughter with compassion.

"Babe, I will be resigning the church Sunday morning."

"We have to leave because of Lisa's father?" Darla asked, disbelieving her ears.

"Not, entirely. The church needs a new pastor, I have been here long enough, and it is time for us to move on."

"Where will we move to?" Darla asked slowly, not sure if she wanted to hear her father's answer.

"You have always wanted to move to the country. We will be moving into our home in Ragweed."

"You mean our rental?" Darla asked, with tears once again sliding down her cheeks.

"Someone lives there." She reminded, hopeful.

"The renter's moved out yesterday. Monday we will begin preparing the house for our move." "Daddy, I have lived here practically my entire life. I only have two years of high school left. Why can't we get a house here, and stay in Dunes?" She pleaded as her tears came more quickly.

"We have a house in Ragweed where we will live, and you and Cindy will attend school next fall." Her father informed, bringing silence to his daughter.

"It is late, dear. Come give us a kiss goodnight. We will talk more in the morning." Her mother suggested, she too wiping tears from her face.

Quietly entering her room, as not to wake her cousin, Darla slipped under her covers.

"Are you okay?" Cindy asked in a whisper.

"I am sure I will be."

"Who knows, maybe you can talk Kelley into moving in with Dan, that way we both will have our favorite guys living in our new town with us."

"Kelley will be away at college next fall." Darla reminded, finding no humor in her cousin's suggestion.

"Sorry Dar, I tried."

"I know. Thank you for your efforts, Cindy." Darla said, more pleasant.

Awakened early by the sound of dresser drawers, Darla turned her radio on, and then pulled her covers back over her.

"Good morning." Darla greeted, with a gentle smile. "Why are you up so early?"

"I have a job." Cindy answered, excitedly.

"Where is your job?" Darla asked surprised, sitting up in her bed, eager to hear more.

"I got a job at Sam's hamburger stand in Ragweed. Now I can see Dan more than once a week." She added with an excited laugh.

"I am happy for you. Perhaps when I turn sixteen next month, you can offer me a job."

"Of course, those were my thoughts. I know you are dying to purchase a car."

"I definitely want to purchase a car." Darla agreed, excitement beginning to rise in her.

"I cannot believe I get my license next month." Darla added.

"I have to get out of here or I will be late." Cindy informed, placing a stack of folded clothes on the desk.

"What are you doing?"

"Aunt Mary said she refuses to pack any more than necessary when we move. I never wear these clothes, so Aunt Mary is taking them to the mission." Explained Cindy, and then hurried from the bedroom.

Darla's excitement over a job, a car, and her license quickly faded; as she remembered she soon would be moving. She fluffed her pillow, placing it against her bookshelf and leaned back. Pulling her knees up closer, she slowly glanced around her room she had occupied since she was five, as she quickly closed her eyes tight as not to allow any tears to escape.

"Good morning. Cindy said you were awake." Her mother greeted, sitting down near her daughter on her bed.

"Would you like to talk sweetheart?" She asked, with tenderness in her eyes and understanding in her voice, she taking her daughter's hand in hers, soothing her.

"Yes, please." Darla answered, her eyes becoming watery.

"Your first question is?" Her mother asked, in her slow, patient, gentle way.

"Why do we have to move?" Darla asked, unable to hold her tears back any longer.

"You know this house is not ours. It is a parsonage, belonging to the church. The house Dad and I own is in Ragweed."

"Mother, that house is tiny. What will we do with most our things?"

"Dad is a very handy carpenter. I am sure he will make sure his family is comfortable. I assure you, no one will have to leave any of their things behind. Sweetheart, maybe Dad and I are too protective of our children at times, with Dad being so more than I am. I, unlike Dad, feel you should know Dad's position, so you can understand more clearly his decision."

"I would like to understand, Mother."

"Dad will not, or can he, in good conscience remain the pastor of a church where board members allow Lisa's father to keep his leadership position in the church, instead of dealing with the problem, and cleaning it up. He will not be a part of condoning unchristian acts. Therefore, Dad has no other choice, but to resign his position."

"Poor Daddy, he must be crushed by his friends turning on him." Spoke Darla, barely above a whisper, now fully realizing her compassionate father's pain.

"And you also, Mother. I am sorry I have added to your pain by only thinking of my losses by our moving."

"Dear, you are not a selfish person." Her mother assured, hugging her daughter, she now releasing her own tears.

"You were simply sharing your uncertainties and wishes with your parents, as you will always be expected to do." "Look at us, we look terrible." Her mother said with a soft laugh, letting go of her daughter, reaching for the Kleenex box, bringing a smile to her daughter's compassionate face.

"Mary? Are you two okay?" Pastor Roberts asked, standing in his daughter's doorway, worry on his face.

"We are okay, Dad. We were talking girl-talk." Darla answered, quickly rescuing her sensitive, burdened mother, setting her father at ease and relieving her mother from her awkwardness.

"Are you okay enough to talk to Kelley? He is on the telephone."

"Of course I am." Answered Darla, excitedly; bringing laughter from her parents, as she quickly vacated her bed.

Darla put her upsets aside, as she helped her mother with the Saturday house cleaning and sorting of her clothes as her cousin had done.

Leaving her home, Darla walked to the drug store for a fountain coke, hoping to see Kelley at work. Lingering at the counter, sipping her coke slowly, wishing Kelley would appear Darla soon found herself accompanied with friends.

"Whoops, your boyfriend caught us Darla." Doug teased.

"Excuse me please." Spoke Darla, leaving the bar stool, with her coke in her hand, approaching Kelley.

"Hello Dar." Greeted Kelley, pleased to see her. "What brings my favorite girl to town?"

"I was hoping to see you." She answered with a beautiful smile.

"I have a thirty-minute lunch break in a few minutes. You are welcome to join me."

"I would like to." Darla agreed, starting to return to the fountain counter with her friends to await Kelley.

"Dar … " Spoke Kelley, gently taking hold of her arm. "I am a jealous man. I would appreciate you sitting on the other side of Connie, not Doug." Kelley shared with flushed cheeks, as though a small boy, with his confession.

"Yes Sir." Darla replied playfully saluting, bringing a pleased smile from Kelley as he continued his work.

Returning to the counter and her friends, Darla sat next to Connie.

"We are alone at last." Kelley said, as he started his car, politely giving his girlfriend a light kiss, bringing a smile to her young, troubled face.

Driving the few blocks to the hamburger stand, Kelley ordered his and his dates hamburgers.

Sitting down at the picnic table, Darla silently ate her hamburger, secretly questioning whether she should burden Kelley with her disturbing news or not.

"Dar, you may talk to me. What is bothering you?" Kelley asked concern on his young, strong, but calm face.

"Too many things to blurt out in ten minutes, I would not want to shock you with my concerns, then tell you goodbye." She answered considerately.

"Perhaps I should review my thoughts this afternoon and talk with you this evening when you pick me up for our date."

Kelley's face grew white and tense as he searched Darla's eyes with his.

"I do not want my ring back." He informed, not taking his eyes from hers.

"Kelley." Darla scolded, lightly. "You are not getting your ring back. You gave it to me, remember?" She asked, with a gentle smile.

"I remember." He answered, letting out a sigh of relief. "I will see if I can get off early. We will make a night of our date."

"Okay. Call me with the time, please."

"I will. I have to get back to work. Would you like a ride home?" He inquired, glancing at his watch.

"No thank you. I enjoy walking."

Darla remained at the picnic table for some time, picking at her half eaten hamburger.

"Would you like a ride Miss Darla?" Brother Peterson asked, as he stood before her, his tall, masculine height towering over her.

"No thank you sir." Answered Darla, momentary startled by his sudden appearance.

"I frighten you. Excuse me, please." The tenderhearted man apologized, his cheeks reddened. "I sit with you?"

"Yes, please."

"Thank you Miss." Kelley's father said, sitting down across from Darla.

"Aye, you are daydreaming." He smiled. "This is good if the daydream makes your heart laugh. Not so good if the daydream saddens the heart. Perhaps you have worries, and not a daydream." The wise man suggested.

"Yes Sir." Darla confessed, with a smile.

"My boy, Kelley, he called me. He asked me to check on you, in case you would be here. My boy worries, my wife worries, I worry." He explained with a sigh.

"I am sorry. I ... " Darla started, blushing.

"Please, Miss Darla, no apologies. We Peterson's are close family, like you Roberts." Brother Peterson interrupted, with pride in his eyes. "Your heart aches for your family happiness, true?"

"Yes Sir." Darla answered, now taking her eyes from the compassionate man, staring at her uneaten hamburger.

"Look up, Miss Darla." He ordered, pointing toward the sky. "Never look down. Hold your head high, like your father, your mother. Always look up toward the Heavens. Be proud of your parents for their strength to obey God, regardless the price. Your pride in them will put an abundance of happiness in their hearts, and big smiles on their faces, as they, for you. In the Heavens lies all your happiness and answers. Our Heavenly Father's home." Brother Peterson shared, putting a smile on Darla's face.

"You make everything sound easy, almost magical." Darla said, feeling a peace and happiness within.

"Aye, yes I do. You know, Jesus walking on the water, Moses parting the Red Sea making the water dry, Elijah entering the heavens in a chariot, the virgin birth of our Savior, Magical and magnificent. Look up above man's eyes, into the wonders of God's eyes. Do not worry of man's weakness for this saddens ones heart. Dwell on God's strength and mighty love. This puts a song in everyone's heart. Yes?"

"Yes." Darla answered, with a happy smile and sparkles in her heart. "Thank you for making me feel better, Brother Peterson." She added, giving him a hug.

"You are welcome, Miss Darla. I tell Kelley you be okay." He informed, with a pleased smile.

"Yes, please." Darla replied pleasantly, getting up from the picnic table.

Walking home, Darla sang chorus after chorus, praising and thanking the Lord. She just knew God would see her parents through their upsets, as well as her own upsets.

"Hi." Darla greeted excitedly, as she left her home with her date.

"Hi, I confess, I agree with your mood change since lunch time." Kelley said, assisting his date inside his car.

"Aye, yes, everything looks much brighter." Replied Darla, happily, causing Kelley to laugh.

"Did my dad help with that?"

"Aye, yes, your dad did." Darla answered, with a soft laugh.

"Dad said his visit with you went well. I am glad. You look radiant."

"Is it possible he sprinkled some magic dust on me?" She asked with a pleasant smile, sending Kelley into a tickled laugh.

"You are definitely one of a kind Miss Roberts."

"So is your dad."

"Most definitely, my dad is one of a kind."

Though Darla had butterflies in her stomach as she dressed for Sunday morning service, the peace she had obtained the day before was steadfast within her. She did not know what the town of Ragweed held for her and her family. She did know the Lord was with them in Dunes and He would be with them in Ragweed.

Kelley seemed to hold Darla's hand with an extra firm grip as they sat through Sunday services, as though he sensed she could use his support. Her heart went out to her father, as she listened to the beautiful words from his Bible, that he patterned his life after. She knew her father's heart must be broken, yet he stood before the congregation harboring no resentments toward those committing their acts of sin, or toward those upholding the sin. *He truly is a man of God.* Darla thought proudly, her tears slowly making their way down her cheeks.

Pastor Roberts closed his Bible as he completed his sermon. Clearing his throat, he looked over the congregation, slowly, silently, for a few seconds. It was so quiet, Darla felt uncomfortable. Kelley tightened his grip on Darla's hand once, politely handing her his handkerchief.

"I have been the pastor of this church for ten years. My son and daughter have grown up in this church, along with many of your children. Both Bill and Darla have enjoyed and appreciated being a part of the family of God with you many wonderful people, as have my wife and I. We have been through some tough times and we have shared many good times."

Pausing for a few seconds, once again, Pastor Roberts' eyes now became moist, as he looked into the faces of his family in Christ.

"It is now time for me to follow God's leading and move on. I will be preaching this evenings service, making it my last. Starting with the mid-week service on Wednesday, a pastor will be here with you to try out for the pastoral position." Pastor Roberts informed.

"Before I close, I once again, want to thank each of you for myself and my family, for supporting and backing us over the years."

Darla stood, as did everyone else, as her father dismissed the service in prayer, with tears streaming down her cheeks.

"You have to be strong for your parents." Kelley whispered.

"I will be." Darla assured, forcing a smile, quickly wiping her tears away.

"Babe, come join mom and I in saying our goodbyes." Spoke Pastor Roberts politely, escorting his daughter to the foyer.

"What do I say?" Darla asked, looking up into her father's eyes.

"Just a sweet Christian smile as you shake their hands will work."

It was a touching morning as Darla stood with her parents, just inside the church doors, shaking each person's hand as they left the church building. Several were shedding tears as they approached the Roberts family. Others hugged their necks, telling them how much they would miss them, causing both Darla and her mother to fight to control their tears.

"Miss Darla … " Brother Peterson greeted, shaking her hand politely. "Look up, always look up." He encouraged, with a pleased smile.

"Yes Sir." Darla agreed, returning a warm compassionate smile.

"We love you honey. You will always be a part of our family." Sister Peterson said, giving Darla a hug.

"Thank you Sister Peterson." Darla replied with a happy smile, wiping more tears away.

With most everyone gone, Kelley now, though silent, brought comfort to Darla by standing at her side.

"Do you have plans for lunch?" Kelley asked.

"I do not know." Darla answered and then looked to her mother for the answer.

"We are going to Ragweed. Grandma is expecting us. Kelley is welcome to come." Sister Roberts responded, as she wiped her eyes with her Kleenex.

"Thank you for the invitation, I accept." Replied Kelley, politely.

"I would like to change before we leave for Grandma's." Darla informed.

"Go on ahead, Dad and I will be home shortly." Her mother instructed. "You and Cindy make sure you are ready."

"Okay." Darla agreed, politely.

Kelley walked Darla home then patiently waited in the front room for his girlfriend to join him, visiting with Cindy and Dan.

Darla's dress and dress shoes changed for a cool pant outfit and sandals, the two young couples went outside. Leaning against Dan's car, with his car radio playing, the couples enjoyed one another's company.

"I do not suppose I could talk you kids into riding with us old timers?" Pastor Roberts asked, with a teasing grin.

"Mark, I thought it would be nice if it was just the two of us." Spoke his wife, slipping her arm through his.

"Mother, please not in front of the kids." He teased, making his wife blush as the teenagers laughed.

"We will see you later kids. We have a date." Pastor Roberts said, escorting his wife to his car.

Having dinner at grandmas was nice. The Roberts were able to relax and unwind with no interruptions by the telephone or doorbell.

With the dishes washed and put away, the young couples slipped out the backdoor. Darla loved her visits to Grandma's especially when she was troubled. The country surroundings and wide-open land seemed to calm her with an inner peace. The two couples now parted, walking in silence, as they walked away from Grandma's house. The hot sun beat down on Darla and Kelley as they neared the small irrigation ditch that carried water to Grandma's land.

"I wish I knew what to say to make you feel better and ease your pain." Spoke Kelley, as Darla silently stood looking down into the water.

"My dad has never shared his magical talents with me." He added, bringing a gentle smile to Darla.

"Just knowing you understand and are with me today is enough." Darla assured, looking up into his eyes with tenderness on her young pretty face, as she loosely put her arms around his waist.

"You always have something nice to say even when the chips are down. You are a special person, Miss Darla Roberts." He complimented, giving Darla a long, gentle kiss.

"I love you." Kelley said, looking into Darla's eyes. "When I leave for college in the fall, returning home on the weekends to visit, I would like to spend much of my time with you. When I complete college, I want to marry you." Shared Kelley, sure of himself.

Darla was both surprised and flattered. Though speechless, she felt pleased he cared so deeply for her.

"I would like to know how you feel." Kelley informed, patiently.

Darla looked into Kelley's eyes, with sparkles in her eyes and happiness in her heart.

"I love you too. I would be proud to become your wife after we complete college." She shared with a beautiful smile.

CHAPTER 4

The Robert's family spent two weeks cleaning, painting and building on the once rental, preparing it for their future home. The small, plain, four-room house now had six rooms, wall-to-wall carpeting and the smell of fresh paint.

"Cindy, it is time to get up." Darla said, gently.

"It is too early." Cindy complained, slowly getting out of bed.

"Your parents are slave drivers. Surely there is a law against parents over-working their teenagers."

"I never thought I would say this, but I will be glad when we are completely moved to Ragweed. I had forgotten what it is like to have a normal evening after school." Darla said, as she wearily opened her closet door.

"I had forgotten what it is like to have a normal evening after school and a normal weekend." Cindy agreed, as she slowly made the bed.

"I feel like Cinderella, scrub this, sweep this, pack this, hurry up, it is getting late." Cindy Mocked.

"My parents can be a bit trying at times." Darla agreed with a weak smile, as she dressed for school

"They can be a bit trying?" Cindy questioned, as though in shock.

"It is too early and I am too tired for your attempts at humoring me." She complained, as she now went to the closet.

"Would you like a ride to school with Kelley and me?"

"Yes, I do not think my legs can make the two-block walk." Cindy answered, forcing a smile as the girls left their bedroom.

"Good morning." The girls greeted as they entered the kitchen.

"You girls look tired." Pastor Roberts said, as he sipped his coffee.

"I would not know why, Uncle Mark." Replied Cindy, half-heartedly.

"I am convinced you and Aunt Mary have Dar and I confused with Cinderella." She added, causing her aunt and uncle to laugh.

"Do you feel as your cousin does, babe?"

"Yes. Daddy let us move and be done with it. I have no social life, I am developing bags under my eyes, and I have lost my sense of humor." Darla answered, siding with her cousin.

"Mark, tell the girls." Mother ordered, hushing her husband's teasing as she left the table to answer the doorbell.

"The last of our belongings will be moved over this morning. Tonight will be our first night in Ragweed. Mom and I do appreciate all you help, girls."

"Thanks."

"Good morning." Kelley greeted politely, as he helped himself to a chair.

"Good morning, Kelley. Meet Cinderella number two and three." Pastor Roberts said with a chuckle.

"My dear parents have been working us to death on our new home, Kelley." Darla explained, with a pleasant smile.

"Cindy is seventeen, I will be sixteen in two days, yet we both feel at least ninety."

"Your hours of serving hard time have paid off. Your home looks beautiful." Kelley said, as Darla gave her parents a kiss goodbye.

"Darla, I will pick you up after school, be out front dear." Her mother instructed.

"Cindy, do you still have a ride after school?"

"Yes, Dan is picking me up." Cindy answered, excitement in her voice bringing smiles to each present.

Darla was glad it was Friday. She waited in front of her high school, as she watched for her mother's car. Her thoughts were on her new home she would be spending her first night in and her new town.

"Hi Mother." Darla greeted pleasantly, as she got inside the family car.

"Hi dear, how was your day?"

"I had a good day." Darla answered, with a kind smile.

"Good. Off we go, our new home awaits us." Her mother said, with a gentle smile.

"Great." Darla replied halfheartedly.

"Cheer up dear; you will make friends in Ragweed quicker than you think."

"I am sure you are right."

"Aunt Martha and Uncle Don are visiting for the evening."

"This is nice. I am sure Cindy has missed her parents."

"I am sure she has. Uncle Don brought Cindy's horse."

"Terrific!" Darla exclaimed.

"I cannot wait to ride her." She added her face aglow and her eyes dancing.

"You come inside and visit your aunt and uncle before you get involved with Cindy's horse."

"I will Mother." Darla assured, respectfully.

Entering her and Cindy's large new bedroom, Darla changed her school dress for a pair of jeans, soft, cool cotton blouse and tennis shoes. Leaving her room, she started for the front room to greet her aunt and uncle as instructed. Deeply moved, Darla stopped in her tracks, finding the room decorated for her sixteenth birthday and filled with her many friends from Dunes.

"Happy birthday!" The crowd yelled.

"Thank you."

"We get to have a slumber party." Cindy said excitedly.

"This is great. Thanks Mother. Thanks Dad."

"You are welcome." Her parents replied, pleased with her happiness.

"Open your gifts." Cindy suggested, excitedly placing the gifts before her cousin.

Opening her gifts, taking great care as though each gift was priceless her friend's thoughtfulness deeply touched her.

With the gifts opened and thank you said, Kelley handed Darla his gift. Taking the tiny gift into her hands, Darla opened it with great care.

"Your parents gave their approval of this gift, I assure you."

"Oh Kelley, this is beautiful." Spoke Darla barely above a whisper, her eyes growing moist.

"Sorry I could not get you a bigger diamond, I am a poor man." Kelley replied, though touched by her look of admiration.

"This is perfect." She exclaimed, regaining her composer and giving Kelley a tight hug.

"Cindy, let's saddle your horse, so you kids can ride." Uncle Don said, getting up from his chair.

Kelley held Darla's hand as they, along with Darla's friends and cousin followed Uncle Don and Pastor Roberts outside. Darla was surprised to find a mini barn and corral area behind the garage at the end of her parent's property.

"Now you know how I earned my calluses." Kelley said.

"You helped Dad build this?"

"Yes, my dad and I."

"Then I owe you two special kisses when we can arrange the time alone." Darla said, excitedly.

"I will be pleased to accept them." Confessed Kelley, with a grin, making Darla blush, bringing a laugh from her.

"Happy birthday, babe." Spoke Pastor Roberts, handing his daughter the reins to a second horse in the corral.

"This is for me?" She questioned, shocked.

"This is for you." Her father answered, pleased to be fulfilling his daughter's heart's desire.

"Her name is Princess."

"Thank you, Daddy." Excitedly, Darla hugged and kissed her father. "Thanks for the best birthday ever."

Completing her turn on her horse, Darla watched with admiration as her friends took turns riding her and Cindy's horses.

"I would not say our moving was so terrible." Her mother said joining Darla, giving her a tight hug, happy for her happiness.

"You have a beautiful new room, your dream horse and a special ring."

"I am the happiest I could be, Mother." Darla assured, returning her mother's hug.

The teenagers made themselves comfortable on the lawn as they ate their hamburgers and visited.

Slipping her arm through Kelley's, the young couple walked away from the other teenagers.

"How late can you stay?" Darla asked.

"We guys may stay until ten."

"I guess this ring means we are stuck with each other."

"I am trusting for good." Kelley replied, taking Darla into his arms, kissing her tenderly.

"You kids keep in mind that ring is a pre-engagement ring." Pastor Roberts ordered, startling Darla and Kelley, their faces turning their reddest.

"You have other company visiting, Darla. I suggest you be a good hostess."

"Yes Sir." Darla agreed, blushing.

"Your dad has a way of getting to the point." Kelley remarked, embarrassed.

"I know." Darla agreed in a half-whisper, as she and Kelley returned to her guests.

Sleeping late from their long night of activities and talk, Darla's girlfriends assisted her in tidying her room. After several turns riding Darla and Cindy's horses, the girls walked to town having lunch at the hamburger stand where Cindy was busy at work.

"I think it would be neat to live here, Darla. At least Ragweed is bigger than Dunes." Macy said.

"Ragweed is barely, bigger, Macy." Darla replied, with a pleasant smile.

"There is a really cool church here." Queena reminded.

"I know. Cindy's boyfriend attends here. Truly, I am thankful for everything because I know I am fortunate. If each of you could move here, attending Ragweed High with me, everything would be perfect." Darla said.

"Next year will not be the same without you at Dunes high, Darla."

"Connie, we are supposed to encourage Darla to fall in love with this town. Besides, I want the dollar Pastor Roberts promised us if we are successful." Lisa scolded.

"You are teasing, Lisa?" Darla asked.

"She is teasing, Dar." Debbie answered.

"Are you girls about ready for me to take you home?" Sister Roberts asked, as she parked her car near the picnic table.

"We decided we like Ragweed better than Dunes, so we are moving in with Darla." Debbie answered.

"Okay. I will tell my husband to add a couple more bedrooms." Mrs. Roberts agreed with a soft laugh.

"I will meet you girls at home in one hour." She added.

"Okay Mother."

As the girl's returned to Darla's new home, they placed their overnight bags in the trunk of the car.

"Darla, I think you should rest, dear while I drive the girl's home."

"Bye Darla. See you at school Monday. We had a great time."

"Thank you. Bye."

Darla watched until her mother's car was out of her sight. Entering her home, she went to her room and picked up her electric guitar as she played her favorite praise choruses to prevent the lonely feeling that was trying to creep in with the departure of her friends.

After playing and singing for some time, she felt revived. She had so much to be thankful for, so she knew she must not give in. Putting her guitar down, she went to the ringing telephone.

"Hello, Roberts' residence."

"Good morning Miss Roberts." Kelley greeted in his cheerful manner.

"Good morning Kelley." She greeted the sound of his voice bringing a warm smiling to her face.

"Do you still have guests?"

"No, Mother has taken them home."

"Is our date still on for this evening?"

"Of course it is." Darla answered, excitedly.

"I was worried your dad might have cancelled our plans after last night." Kelley shared, with a nervous laugh.

"He has not said anymore."

"Good." Kelley replied, as though releasing a long sigh.

"I will make sure I do not put either of us in the position I did last night, again. It was a foolish move on my part."

"I am just as guilty, Kelley. I should have contained my excitement until our date this evening."

"Perhaps we have both learned a lesson. I will see you at six-thirty."

"I will be waiting, bye."

Leaving her home, Darla went to the corral. Her heart filled with happiness, as she mounted her beautiful horse. Trotting down the road, in front of her home, she passed her neighbors home, wondering what their names were. Seeing two teenage girls in the distance, standing, conversing, she slowed Princess to a walk. Nearing the girls, they observing her approach, Darla stopped her horse.

"Hi." Darla greeted, in her friendly, cheerful, way.

"Hi. We love your horse." They informed, impressed, gently patting Princess.

"Her name is Princess and my name is Darla Roberts. My family and I just moved here."

"I am Candy, I live here. This is Susie." Candy introduced, kindly.

"Will you be attending Ragweed High?" Candy asked.

"Yes, next fall. I will be a junior."

"Great, I will be junior." Candy said.

"Susie will be a senior next year."

"Do you have a sister?"

"You mean does she have a brother." Susie interrupted, with an excited laugh.

"Yes and yes." Darla answered, with a gentle smile.

"My brother, Bill is away in the military. Cindy, she is actually my cousin, but we are like sisters. She lives with my family. She will be a senior next year."

"Does Cindy work at the hamburger stand, on Palm Avenue?" Candy asked.

"Yes."

"I love her car." Candy shared, excitedly.

"So do I, her dad gave her the car for her sixteenth birthday."

"Would you like a ride on Princess?" She asked, kindly.

"Sure!" Both girls exclaimed.

Darla felt better knowing she had at least one neighbor her age. Candy and Susie went to Darla's home with her. They sat on the corral fence, visiting, while Darla brushed and cared for her horse.

"Darla, we are going to a party tonight. Would you like to come with us?" Susie asked.

"I have a date in a couple of hours, but thanks for inviting me."

With good-byes said to her two first friends in her new town, Darla entered her home to prepare for her date.

"Deary, you and I need to talk." Her mother informed, as Darla passed by the kitchen.

"Come in, and sit down, please."

Entering the kitchen, Darla sat down at the table, giving her mother her full attention.

"Dad seems concerned you and Kelley are becoming too serious, too quickly and I am too. Kelley assured Dad and I the ring he gave you was a pre-engagement ring, with the understanding you would date as in the past. You would date as boyfriend and girlfriend with no plans for engagement, until you are at least college age, if you and Kelley still like one another at that time. Yet, Dad walks upon you and Kelley kissing. He was shocked to say the least, with the way you were kissing."

"Mother, Kelley and I have never done anything wrong nor would we ever dare. Surely this is what you and Dad thinks." Darla said with reddened cheeks, surprised at her parent's thoughts of her.

"Wait a minute." Mrs. Roberts said quickly.

"I am not suggesting any such thing, do not get excited. If we thought there was wrong going on, believe me, you both would know it." Her mother assured.

"Do you remember our talk we had before you went on your first date?" Her mother asked.

"I remember it well. I have abided by your every word Mother, I assure you." Darla answered, defensively.

"Explain to me what Dad saw." Her mother suggested, patiently.

"Mother ... " Sighed Darla, embarrassed with her mother's suggestion and openness.

"Dear, I want to know from you." She insisted, with her firm tone.

"Kelley kissed me. It was a special kiss, but that is all. I was not intending for anyone to see, especially Dad." Darla explained, with flushed cheeks.

"I should not have been with Kelley and ignored my other guests. We only slipped away for a few seconds to discuss him giving me the ring. He kissed me and then we would have returned to the others, only dad arrived while we were kissing." She added, with a frustrated sigh.

"Dear, stay with your group. Do not allow yourself to be in such a situation. Lucky for you, dad walked upon you, than another."

"Lucky? Mother, I would rather anyone had seen us than Dad. You did not see or hear him. He looked at Kelley and me as though we had created the unpardonable sin."

"Oh, come on, Darla." Her mother replied, breaking into a laugh over her daughter's words, and humiliated expression.

"Mother, it is not at all funny."

"I know. Excuse me for laughing." Her mother apologized, regaining control of herself.

"Mothers are extremely cautious of their daughter's well-being, but dads are both cautious and possessive. I give you fair warning, dear; do not allow this to happen again."

"I won't, Mother." She assured, blushing.

"Good, I am taking you at your word."

Darla dressed for her date with Kelley with her radio playing, as Cindy prepared for her date with Dan.

"Darla, I spoke with my boss today. He said he could put you to work as soon as school is out for summer, if you are interested." Cindy informed.

"I am interested." Darla replied, excitedly.

"This is great. Oh Cindy, maybe I will be able to get a car by the end of summer."

"You will get your car because you are a miser." Cindy said, with a laugh.

"Honestly, I believe you are becoming more like Aunt Mary every day."

"Perhaps you are right." Darla replied, with a gentle smile.

"Cindy, Dan is here for you, Dear." Her aunt informed.

"Thank you, Aunt Mary. Has Kelley arrived? We are double dating this evening." She explained, hopeful.

"He has arrived, but Uncle Mark has him detained for a few minutes. I am sure they will not be much longer." She answered, glancing at her daughter, as though she hurt for her, bringing silence to both girls, as her daughter's face reddened.

"Are you ready, Darla?" Cindy asked, breaking their silence.

Cindy visited with Dan in the family room while Darla silently sat feeling terrible for Kelley. She knew her father was giving him a lecture in regards to their conduct last evening.

"Dan, go get Kelley. It is getting late." Cindy suggested, anxious to leave on her date.

"I feel much safer right where I am." Dan replied, with a grin, bringing smiles to the girl's faces.

Kelley finally entered the family room, with reddened cheeks and reserved, with Pastor Roberts behind him.

"Are you ready Kelley?" Cindy asked, pleasantly, as though Kelley was his usual cheery self.

"Sure." He answered, as he politely held the door for the girls and Dan to exit first.

Kelley was quiet, as he sat next to Darla in the back seat of Dan's car, while Cindy casually visited with Dan, turning his radio on to their favorite pop station.

"I am sorry Kelley." Darla spoke, looking up into his eyes, breaking their silence.

"You have nothing to apologize for." He replied, letting out a sigh, now gently taking Darla's hand into his.

"I had it coming to me." He added, forcing a smile to comfort Darla's uneasy feelings.

Though Darla enjoyed her time with Kelley, she could not help but notice he was upset with himself for concerning her father. She knew Kelley had an abundance of respect for her father, and he felt he had failed Pastor Roberts.

"Kelley, would you please quit punishing yourself?" Darla asked, as Dan now drove toward the girl's home, their date nearing an end.

"I am working on it, so be patient with me." He said, with a tender smile, his cheeks flushing once again.

"Of course I will be patient." Darla answered, with an understanding smile.

With the first weekend ending in their new home, the girls were excited to return to Dunes High and their friends.

"I cannot believe we only have two weeks of school left." Cindy said, as she pulled out of their drive.

"Next fall, we will be attending school with Dunes rivalry." She added.

"I am considering skipping all sports activities next year." Darla confessed, with a soft laugh.

"That makes two of us." Cindy sided.

"I do not care to acquire the nickname, 'Trader'."

"Cindy, honk your horn." Darla ordered, waving at Susie and Candy, as they passed Candy's house.

"You know them?"

"I kind of know them, I met them Saturday."

"Be careful, Darla. They both are nice and they hang out at the hamburger stand, but I am sure they are not your type because they party a lot."

"What do you mean they party?" Darla asked slowly, puzzled.

"I mean they drink and they do drugs. I cannot say to what extent, but I am sure they smoke pot."

"Thank you for telling me." Darla said, now concerned for the girls lifestyle.

"Let me guess." Cindy started, with a laugh. "You are presently planning your strategy to win Cindy and Susie to the Lord."

"Why of course." Darla answered, with a pleased smile.

"You, my dearest cousin, are definitely one of a kind." Cindy said, proudly.

The school week had come and gone too quickly for Darla. She lingered at her locker visiting with her girlfriends, knowing she would not be seeing them over the weekend.

"Excuse me." Spoke Kelley, joining Darla. "May I walk you to Cindy's car?"

"Yes, of course." Darla answered, with a sweet smile.

Good-byes said to her friends, Darla silently walked with Kelley toward the school parking lot.

"The weekend will be over before you know it, Dar." Kelley said, tightening his grip on his girlfriend's hand.

"I see I am easily read."

"Too easily read, Miss Darla. People see you coming from a mile away." He agreed, with a comforting smile.

"Darla, I am going to be late for work." Cindy reminded, impatiently waiting at her car.

"She cannot wait to get Ragweed so she can see Dan." Darla whispered, as though she was jealous, making Kelley laugh.

"I will see you tomorrow evening." He reminded, with a quick good-bye kiss.

Cindy drove fast to Ragweed, letting Darla out at home, and then heading off toward work.

Unlocking the backdoor, Darla found her home empty of her parents. Changing her school clothes, she left a note on the kitchen table.

Mother, Dad
I went riding.
Love, Darla

Guiding her horse to the nearest country road, Darla kicked her, running her fast. She loved the thrill of her horses speed. She loved the feel of the air hitting her face and she felt as free as a bird, flying through the air.

Taking the long way home, Darla slowed Princess, as she neared traffic at the edge of town. She rode to Cindy's work, purchased a coke, lingering, visiting with her cousin.

"Here come your new friends." Cindy informed, with disapproval on her face.

Darla turned toward the approaching girls. Cindy was right; Candy and Susie were definitely taking some sort of drug.

"Hi." Darla greeted, with a smile, as the girls approached the order window.

"Hi." The girls greeted with glossy eyes and smiles that appeared permanent.

"Cindy, this is Candy, our neighbor, and her friend Susie." Darla introduced, as Cindy gave each girl a coke.

"Would you guys like to come to a party with us tonight? We could introduce you around." Susie suggested.

"What kind of a party?" Darla inquired.

"It is a dance party. Candy's boyfriend plays lead guitar in the band. … it is a really cool band." Susie answered.

"Thanks for the invitation, but I do not attend dances, I am a Christian. Maybe we can do something else sometime."

"Sure." Susie agreed.

Returning home, Darla brushed Princess until her coat was shiny.

"Babe … " Spoke her dad, approaching the corral, dressed in a suit.

"Hello Dad." Darla greeted, with a loving smile.

"Hi Babe, how was your day?"

"It was okay." Darla answered, leaving the corral.

"You look nice, Daddy."

"Thank you. Mom and I are going out for dinner with Pastor Finks and his wife. You are welcome to join us."

"No thank you. I have semester exams I need to study for which is the highlight of my evening." Darla shared, as she and her father walked toward the house.

"I know you feel restless, with not having any activities here in Ragweed, Babe. Have you given any thought to signing up for summer school here? It would give you the opportunity to meet some kids, plus you would earn extra credits."

"This is a thought." Darla replied, looking at her father in deep thought, with his suggestion.

"We need to find something for you to fill your restlessness." Her father confessed concern on his face.

"Dad, please do not worry about me. I will find my way here, in the Lords timing." Darla assured, considerately.

"I do not doubt you in the least, Babe." Pastor Roberts replied, pride now in his eyes, as he gave his daughter a hug.

With her books on the family room floor, Darla became absorbed in her studies.

"Darla, we are leaving now." Her mother said. "Cindy will not be home until late, so keep the doors locked and Dad will call later to check on you."

"Okay, have a good time."

Returning to her books, Darla was soon deeply engrossed in her studies. After an hour of studying, the ringing of the telephone caught her attention.

"Hello, Roberts' residence."

"Good evening, Miss Darla." Kelley greeted.

"Hi." She greeted, happy with his call.

"Why don't you come visit me?" Darla asked.

"Because your dad would have me shot. We get one date a week, remember?"

"I know, but my invitation is a nice thought." Darla said, with a loving smile.

"Yes it is. So, what is my girlfriend doing this evening?"

"I am having a blast studying for exams for Monday and Tuesday." She answered, with a soft laugh.

"At least you are doing something constructive."

"Kelley, we both know I do not have a choice. Dad may have resigned the church, but he is still a minister, which means I am a preacher's kid for life, I am doomed." She reminded, blushing over her teasing.

"What is happening with you, Dar? At school, you were jealous with Cindy being able to see Dan more than we are able to see each other and now, I believe I detect self-pity." Kelley teased with a chuckle, bringing a laugh from his girlfriend.

"Guilty as charged." She confessed, with a gentle laugh, her cheeks flushed again.

"Your call has lifted my spirits. It does get lonely here, but for now, I best let you go. I know this call is costing you.

"I will heed your warning. I love you, Darla." Spoke Kelley, sincerely, touching Darla's heart.

"I love you too. Bye."

Darla felt great after hearing Kelley's voice. The lonely feeling she briefly had, was gone. Going to the kitchen, she made herself a sandwich for her dinner. Turning the television set on; she sat down Indian fashion on the floor with her sandwich. Returning to the kitchen with her saucer and empty glass, she slowly, very quietly, placed her dishes in the sink, thinking she heard a noise on the front porch. There it was a faint knock on the front door. Quietly, going to the front door, she looked through the peephole.

"Oh no … " She whispered, as she quickly unlocked the door. "Oh, Candy, come in." She invited, quickly locking the door behind the battered girl, her face, hair, and hands covered with blood.

"Thanks Darla. I am sorry." Candy apologized, holding her hands up to her bloody nose and mouth to catch the streaming blood.

"You said you are a Christian, so I thought you would help me."

"Of course, Candy." Darla assured, as she quickly blotted her friends face with cold towels to stop her bleeding. "Candy, what happened?"

"My dad is drunk. He and my mom were fighting and the next thing I know, my dad started hitting on me." Candy answered, her hands shaking from fear, as she sobbed.

With the bleeding finally stopped from Candy's nose and mouth, Darla led her to the family room, making her comfortable in the recliner. Taking Candy's hand in hers, Darla closed her eyes, in reverence.

> *My Heavenly Father, who art in heaven, I*
> *bring Candy before you, asking in*
> *Jesus' name that you remove all pain from her*
> *Lord, I also ask for your protecting hand upon her,*
> *that her father will never harm her again.*
> *I thank you Lord, for answering my prayer. Amen.*

Opening her eyes, Darla looked at Candy with great compassion. "Would you like to spend the night?" Darla asked, politely.

"No thanks, I do not want to put you out."

"You will not be putting anyone out." Darla assured.

Darla left Candy's side going to the ringing telephone.

"Babe, it is Dad. Are you okay?" Pastor Roberts asked.

"No." Darla answered, hesitant not wanting to alarm her friend. "Will you come now?" She asked, in a low whisper.

"We will be right home." Her father answered, hanging up the telephone quickly without a good-bye.

"You will have to come over and go horseback riding with me some Saturday." Darla invited, as she returned to her neighbors side.

"Thanks. I would love to." Candy accepted.

Darla's parents, along with Pastor Finks and his wife soon arrived, each with worry on their face.

"Dad, Candy has been hurt." Darla informed, relieved for his assistance.

Darla's father quickly went to Candy's side, examining her cuts and bruises.

"Where do you hurt, Candy?" Pastor Roberts asked.

"I do not hurt since Darla prayed for me. I have a little soreness, but no real pain."

"I am glad you had faith in Darla's prayer, or you would be having one terrific headache. You have some terrible bumps and bruises."

"Darla is different than most kids. You can tell what she says is true, I believed every word she prayed."

"This is good." Spoke Pastor Roberts, touched by his daughter's good deed.

"Babe, take Candy in your room, so she can lie down. She will be spending the night. When you have Candy settled Pastor Finks would like to speak with you."

After helping Candy to her room, Darla returned to the family room, where her parents and guests waited her return. Quietly questioning why Pastor Finks felt the need to converse with her, she sat down on the sofa next to her mother.

"Darla, how would you like to help me in getting the serious Christian teenagers from our church involved in street witnessing?" Pastor Finks asked.

"It sounds interesting; I have never done any witnessing of that type." She answered, hesitant.

"I am aware of this. I have been discussing you participating with your parents tonight. After hearing your friend's faith in you, I am even more convinced you are right for this outreach project."

"I did what anyone would have done." Assured Darla, surprised at his comment.

"This is my point, not everyone does help, but you did. Furthermore, you shared Jesus with your caller. She believed in you therefore, believing what you had to say. This sense of trust and believing is needed so badly on the streets with kids your age." Pastor Finks explained.

"I could give it a try." Darla agreed.

"Good. I appreciate your help."

Darla was becoming excited over the street-witnessing project. She met twice weekly, with Pastor Finks, 2 young adults, 3 teenage boys, and 2 teenage girls. Their meetings taught them the slang talk of the people living on the streets, how to present their ministry and safety precautions.

The excitement over her new project was beginning to feel her loneliness and emptiness.

Excitedly, watching through the family room window for Kelley's car to appear in her drive, Darla found she was looking forward to completing the school term. Her new town was filling with exciting new events involving her.

"You are late." Darla scolded lightly, sliding onto the front car seat next to Kelley, giving him a good morning kiss.

"I overslept." Kelley explained, as be backed his car out of Darla's drive.

"Dunes graduation ceremony was beautiful last night and of course you were the main attraction." Darla complimented, in her soft, gentle, way.

"Thank you."

"Oh, Kelley, we begin witnessing next week. I wish you would join us." She encouraged, with sparkles in her eyes and excitement in her voice.

"I have been giving it a lot of thought. I might attend to observe, but I am not sure if that type of ministry is for me."

"I would appreciate you giving the ministry a try." Darla concluded, with a sweet smile.

"By the way, Mr. Kelley Peterson, you look handsome in your suit." She added.

"Thank you. You look very beautiful. I see you got a new dress for my senior breakfast this morning."

"It was a good reason to talk Mother into the new dress I have wanted for weeks." Darla shared, with a soft laugh, her cheeks now flushed, bringing a laugh from her boyfriend.

"We seniors received our yearbooks last night after our ceremony. If you would get it from the back seat and turn to page fifty-seven, I believe you will be impressed."

Doing as instructed, Darla's face was aglow, as she discovered a picture of her and Kelley standing near Darla's locker, under the title "The couple most likely to succeed."

"Oh, this is great Kelley!" She exclaimed, giving her boyfriend an excited kiss.

"I like that. Now turn to page eighty-one."

Darla's eyes now grew moist as her eyes slowly read about herself, along with the varsity cheerleader squad. There her picture was, even though she had resigned, under the title "Most school spirit."

"I like the part where you say if you had not put a worldly want before the Lord, you would have remained on the cheerleading squad." Kelley shared, putting his arm around her shoulders, bringing her closer to him. "One more page, Miss Roberts. Number eighty-nine."

Turning the yearbook pages, Darla felt her findings a bit much. Once again, there was her name, and picture, under the title, "Best dressed."

"I would say Dunes High honored you quite well for your last year attending." Kelley said, giving her a kiss on top of her head.

"Yes they did, very well." She agreed, with an excited laugh, brushing her tears of happiness away.

Darla was silent now, as she thumbed through Kelley's yearbook, as he drove the twenty-mile drive from Ragweed to Dunes. Turning to the index, she found Kelley's name, with several page numbers following. She silently turned to each page, reading about her modest boyfriend.

"I see Dunes high has honored you quite well also." Darla informed, with a loving smile, holding the yearbook up for Kelley to see her findings.

"I did not do too badly."

"Kelley, you did great!" She exclaimed. "Best personality … " Darla began, to prove her point. "Four pictures of you on the baseball team, besides the article of you receiving a sports scholarship. The picture and article of you and me and this picture and article of you receiving a separate scholarship for being an honor roll student. Congratulations."

"Thank you, Miss Roberts. We both have had a terrific year and God has been very good to both of us."

"Yes, He has. We are truly blessed." She agreed, with a happy smile.

"So, Dar, how does it feel to be dating a college man?" Kelley asked, escorting his date into the restaurant to join Kelley's senior class for breakfast.

"I feel like a princess." She confessed, with an excited laugh.

"You are a princess." Kelley replied, with sincerity in his voice, warming her heart.

Darla enjoyed her last day of school. She stopped friends, having him or her sign her yearbook, as she signed theirs in return. Even with the noon dismissal after school, the campus remained crowded with excited teenagers having their books signed by their friends.

"I believe everyone has signed our yearbooks and us theirs. I definitely have writer's cramp." Kelley said, with a pleased grin.

"I know." Darla agreed, with a radiant smile.

"Oh, Kelley, I am going to miss this high school, all our friends and you walking me to class." She shared with watery eyes, though she forced a smile.

Kelley put his arm around her, comforting her. "Next year will be different for both of us, Dar. If you and I continue to allow our light to shine for the Lord, we will have another, fulfilled, exciting year. Personally, I intend to live all week for the weekends when I return home to see my girlfriend." Kelley said, in his wise, mature manner.

"I like this." Darla replied, with an excited laugh, brushing her tears away, quickly. "You always know what I need to hear before I know myself."

"Another reason why I believe you and I are meant for one another." Kelley replied, looking into Darla's eyes with tenderness, quickly comforting her. "We have a worldly party to attend. Are you game?"

"I am most definitely game to attend a worldly party to San Diego and the beach." Darla answered, excitedly.

Darla and Kelley enjoyed their afternoon at the beach, one hundred miles away from their hot, barren, desert land. As the sun went down Kelley's senior class made a huge campfire, cooking hamburgers and hotdogs along with radios blaring, laughter and loud talking. Darla observed that some teenagers had brought beer and wine in their ice chests. She also observed a group sitting in a circle passing a joint around. This was her first experience witnessing first hand, what she knew many teenagers, even her own age were doing.

"What do you say we leave before this party becomes too wild for us?" Kelley asked picking their blanket and beach towels up from the sand.

"I say, you know best."

Ragweed had become an exciting town to Darla. After her week break at the start of summer vacation, her days were busy and exciting. From eight in the morning until noon she attended Ragweed high for summer school, meeting and making friends quickly. From one in the afternoon until six in the evening, her weekdays were spent working at the hamburger drive-in with her cousin, saving her pay checks to add to her savings her parents had started for her when only a toddler, hoping for her choice car. She became active in the young group at Ragweed Christian church, besides her two nights weekly working with the street-witnessing ministry. Kelley had become active also in the street-witnessing ministry. Candy was now a dear friend of Darla's, visiting often.

It was August already and the days were long and extremely hot. In only three short weeks, Kelley would leave for college, Cindy would begin her senior year of high school, and Darla her junior year. The Christian teenagers seemed to grow and mature so quickly. Their interests and goals leading them in different directions at times, yet the bond they had developed over the years were never broken.

Darla was awake and dressed early. Though it was a hot, humid Friday, to Darla it was a beautiful morning as she entered the kitchen to join her parents having their coffee.

"Daddy, could you spare a couple of hours this morning? I have my down payment saved for a car and I know which car I want." Darla informed her dad.

"Sure, Babe, we will go this morning."

"Bill is home, he arrived late last night." Her mother shared, pleased.

"Terrific! I can take him for a ride in my car." Darla replied, her face aglow happy her brother was now home to stay.

"I am sure your brother will expect to receive the first ride, dear." Her mother confessed, with a soft laugh.

Filled with excitement, Darla proudly led her father to her choice car. "This is the car I want Dad, the gray mustang."

"This is a pretty car, Babe."

"This red interior is beautiful." Darla said.

"Yes, this is a beautiful car." Her father agreed. "Are you aware this is four-speed?"

"Yes."

Pastor Roberts accompanied his daughter, as they took her gray mustang for a test drive.

"I think it sounds cool when I shift gears." Darla shared excitedly, as she drove her father through town, bringing a laugh from him.

"I suppose this "cool" sound is the only reason you want a four speed." Pastor Roberts replied, with a chuckle.

"Yes. Isn't it neat?" She asked, with a radiant smile.

"Sure, Babe, it sounds "cool". Her father teased, tickled with her reasoning and excitement.

"Daddy, may I get this car? Please?" Darla asked, excitedly, as they vacated the mustang.

"I realize you have enough saved for the down payment, Babe. There is still the matter of the balance owing. The balance will be your responsibility, your mom and I will not make the payments for you."

"I understand Dad. I have a job."

"Which means with school and a part-time job, I will not allow you to participate in softball or cheerleading. I will not allow you to run yourself down, as you did last fall."

"I understand. I really want this car, Daddy."

"Okay, I see my little girl is growing up. Before I know it, mom and I will be sending you off to college." Pastor Roberts replied, with pride clearly in his eyes and on his face.

"Thanks Daddy!" She exclaimed, giving her father a tight hug.

"You are welcome, Babe."

With the necessary paper work completed, Pastor Roberts walked his daughter to her car.

"You drive careful. I will meet you at home." Pastor Roberts instructed.

"Okay, thanks again." Darla replied, feeling her happiest.

Darla excitedly shared her news of her car with her mother, brother, and cousin. She was pleased to hear their compliments of approval.

"Bill, I am going to Dunes to show Lisa my car. Would you like to come with me?"

"I will come only if I am the one doing the driving." Bill answered, with a grin, winking at his parents.

"Bill, I just got the car." Darla refused, tapping her brother on his stomach for teasing.

"I do not know if I trust your driving, Sis."

"Darla is a good driver, son. Enjoy your sister's company." Their father defended.

Darla drove toward Dunes with her window down, allowing the wind to blow her long hair with her radio playing loud. She could not wait to share her excitement.

"I find it hard to believe Dar that I am sitting in the passenger seat of my little sister's car." Bill spoke, with an approving smile.

"Even kid sisters grow up, dear brother."

"You are telling me." Bill agreed, with a chuckle.

"I am definitely proud of you, Sis."

"Thank you. I am a bit prideful when it comes to my older, over-protective brother, also."

Darla complimented, bringing a smile from her brother.

Darla patiently waited on Lisa's doorstep, with ringing the doorbell.

"Oh, Dar, you are so lucky. I love this car." Lisa said, as Darla drove her car up and down Main Street with her girlfriend and brother.

"Isn't that Kelley?" Bill asked, pointing.

"Yes. I must catch him." Darla answered, excited to see her boyfriend and share her new car with him.

Pulling her car up next to Kelley's, Darla honked the horn as her boyfriend started toward the order window of the hamburger stand.

"Wow, this is sharp." Kelley said, approaching his girlfriend as she, Lisa and Bill got out of Darla's car.

"Thank you." Darla said.

"I do not recall you having a new car during your high school days, Bill." Kelley remarked, with a grin.

"Darla has always been Mom and Dad's favorite." Bill replied, as he ordered lunch for everyone.

"This is not true."

"It is good to see you Bill." Kelley said, shaking Bill's hand.

"It is good to see you, Kelley." Bill assured, politely.

"I cannot get over how fast each of you has grown up while I was off fighting a senseless war. You are not exactly the skinny little kid you use to be, Kelley." He complimented, patting Kelley on his back.

"Kelley is a college man now, Bill." Darla informed proudly, as they ate their lunch at a picnic table.

"This is what I hear. Congratulations, Kelley."

"Thank you."

"Darla, I was going to call you later. I will not be able to make the street witnessing meeting tonight." Kelley informed.

"Why?" Darla asked, disappointed.

"I have to work late, again."

"You will be leaving for college in a few weeks. We have barely seen one another all week." She complained, lightly.

"I need the money for college, Dar." Kelley apologized.

"My Irish father is a tight wad." He added, with a grin, uplifting his girlfriend's mood quickly.

"I am going apartment searching in San Diego tomorrow, come with me. We will make a day of it."

"You are not actually involved in that street ministry stuff with my sister, are you?" Bill asked.

"Yes, I am." Kelley answered. "Though I confess, I have not learned as quickly as Darla has. She is a natural with the street people."

"Kelley is learning quickly, Bill. I have simply been involved longer than he has." Darla assured.

"Personally, I think Darla needs her head examined for mingling with those freaks." Bill said, shocking all present by his cold choice of words.

"Bill." Darla said sharply, to hush him.

"You have no right to pass judgment on others. They are people with souls, just like you and me." She reminded, her sternness, bringing silence to Lisa and Kelley.

"You have become considerably brave since my last leave, Darla." Bill remarked annoyed with his sister jumping back at him, as though he was a child.

Darla's cheeks now flushed, surprising herself with her sudden bravery to go against her brother. She bit her tongue saying no more, remaining in silence, for several long moments, calming herself.

"Will you call after the street ministry Kelley? I will ask my parents if I can go with you tomorrow."

"I will call." Kelley assured.

"Be careful, Darla." He warned.

"I have to return to work. Lisa, Bill, see you later."

"Bye Kelley." The three young people replied.

"Dar, I would like to go with you tonight." Lisa said, whispering, as the girls threw away their hamburger wrapping.

"This is terrific. Come home with me now and spend the night." Darla suggested.

"Okay." Lisa agreed, excitedly.

Darla turned her car radio on to fill the silent tension between her and her brother as she left the town of Dunes, heading toward Ragweed.

"I am sorry Bill, for snapping back at you. I know you are afraid for me and I realize you do not understand the type that hang out in the City Park where we witness. I am so happy that you are home to stay, yet I have already been rude to you."

"I owe the apology sis, as usual. I guess I have been in the military too long and at war so long, I have forgotten my manners." Bill apologized, with gentleness in his voice

"I would be glad to teach you manners." Darla replied, with a tender smile.

"Alright, do not get cute." He warned with a grin, pulling his sister's hair playfully.

"What do you say sis, if I treat you and Lisa to a game of bowling?"

"We thought you would never ask." Lisa said, with a laugh, causing Darla to laugh also.

"You girls always stick together." Bill mumbled in his teasing, complaining way.

Bill treated the girls to several games of bowling. His mood was once again carefree and happy, making the girls laugh, as Bill had always done during Darla's youth.

"Bill, come with us tonight, to the park ministry." Darla encouraged excitedly, as she walked with her arm through his, as they were leaving the bowling alley. "Come see first-hand how the people really are."

"No way, sis, I am not going to the park ministry"

"It would be like old times, when you were President of the youth group in Dunes. I will even let you drive Lisa and I to the meeting in my new car." She pleaded, in her excited, bubbly way.

"Besides, Kelley will not be attending. You could go as my protector. It comes so natural for you."

"No. Now take me home. I have my own plans for this evening." Bill replied, as he got inside his sister's car.

"Bill … " She started once more.

"Darla, you know I am not into religious doings. Do not ruin our day, by pushing religion at me."

"Okay, I give up."

Returning home, Lisa went horseback riding with Bill. Darla studied her Bible scriptures at her desk for her evening meeting of witnessing. She spent much time in prayer, building her spiritual strength.

"Lisa, you will need to change before we go. Take your pick." Darla offered.

"We can wear jeans?" Lisa asked, surprised.

"Yes." Darla answered, with a soft laugh.

"It is okay, Lisa. It took Pastor Finks forever to convince mother the street people relate better to simple, hippie dress. We will be allowed to leave the house wearing jeans."

"I am in shock, Dar." Lisa teased.

"My mother is still old fashioned with her ideas of dress, but your mom has my mom beat."

"Mother simply wants me to be a lady, Lisa." Darla reminded, with a gentle smile.

Dressed in jeans, short sleeve sweatshirt, and deck tennis shoes, Darla carried only her Bible and guitar into her large city park. Along with Lisa, Mark, and Brother Jones, Darla's group went in one direction, while the second group went in the opposite direction.

The street people stopped the group of Christians often by one reaching out for love, safety, and a way of escape from their life of drug dependency. Each person felt desperate to have his or her need met.

"Hey Angel." A familiar voice yelled as Darla neared several teenagers sitting on the ground.

"They look creepy." Lisa whispered.

"They are harmless." Darla assured, comforting her nervous friend.

"How are you doing, Angel?" A skinny, longhaired teenage boy asked.

"I am doing great, Slim." Darla answered, with a beautiful smile as she joined the group sitting down on the ground Indian fashion.

"Who is she?" A tough looking, stocky girl, with stringy hair asked.

"It is okay, Marge." A tiny frail girl assured, putting her arm around her friend's shoulders to calm her.

"She is with Angel. She is cool, or Angel would not have brought her here."

"Angel. Is that you Angel?" Marge asked, crawling close to Darla.

"It is me." Darla answered.

"Feel my long hair?" Darla asked.

"It is Angel." Marge agreed, with touching Darla's hair, now calming her.

"I am really stoned on Jesus, Angel." Slim informed, in his hippie talk. "Me and my old lady got back together. I even started to work." He shared excitedly.

"Slim is a Jesus freak now, Angel." Marge informed with a boisterous laugh.

"Check this out." Slim said pulling his long shirtsleeves up, exposing his needle scarred arms. "I have not shot up since you shared Jesus with me."

"This is terrific, Slim. You are set free from a dependency on drugs, through faith in Jesus. Now you are enjoying a spiritual high, which is free and everlasting, just for the asking. We must remember to depend entirely, and only, on Jesus." Spoke Darla, thrilled for the miracle of salvation at work again.

"In the Bible, there is a scripture that reads, "Make a joyful noise unto the Lord!" Let's tell the world we love Jesus." Darla encouraged, excitement in her voice as she picked up her guitar.

"Dar, that guy by the tree is shooting up." Lisa whispered.

"Shhh, pray." Darla hushed quickly, as she began strumming her guitar strings.

"You may sing with me, clap your hands, or meditate on Jesus. Just allow the Holy Spirit to lead your heart and mind, not me or any person." Darla said, with sparkles in her eyes and a happy, radiant glow on her face.

The many teenagers within hearing distance came closer. All the members in the witnessing group were making their way through the crowd to be of assistance to one seeking prayer, guidance, and seeking the way to salvation. Some teenagers began clapping their hands. As Darla sang, many joined in singing the simple song she had chosen to fit the needs of these people, while the Holy Spirit dealt with hearts.

Jesus is a soul man,
Jesus is a soul man,
Jesus is a soul man,
And I'm sure sold on Him.

As the hour grew late, many of the teenagers began slipping away into the darkness. With the witnessing team together again, they left the park for their vehicles. With each member safely in his or her cars, Pastor Finks got inside his car.

"That was scary, Darla. I am still shaking, yet you are and were so calm." Lisa shared, as Darla pulled away from the curb.

"Lisa, this type of ministry is not for everyone. Perhaps it is not your calling." Darla comforted, kindly.

"I know it is not my calling." Lisa replied with a nervous laugh, bringing an understanding smile from Darla.

"Did you get my Bible?" Darla asked, suddenly remembering it.

"No."

"Oh, I left it on the grass. I have to go back." Darla said, quickly turning her car around.

"Darla, I heard Pastor Finks stress, "sticking together" for safety precautions. Go back tomorrow when it is light out." Lisa suggested, worried.

"I know what Pastor Finks said. My mother just bought me that Bible and if I go home without it, I am dead." Darla explained, as she parked her car.

"I will only be a minute." She assured.

"Okay, but hurry Darla." Lisa coached, fear on her face.

Barely able to see due to the dimness of the park lights and many grassy, rolling hills, Darla finally located her Bible. As she picked up her Bible, someone grabbed her from behind, bending her arm behind her back. She screamed for help, as loud as she could.

"Shut up." A huge, ugly man ordered, bending her arm even harder. Darla felt as though her arm had snapped and then fear, panic, and hate filled her tender, compassionate heart, as she kicked at her attacker.

"Stop it!" Darla screamed, as tears flowed down her young, tender face.

The brutal man grabbed Darla's long hair. Jerking her by her hair, he pulled her to him until they were face to face.

"I told you to shut up. I will fix you." Pulling his arm back, the wild man hit Darla in her face with his fist. She felt stunned, with blood now streaming down her face. He then threw her to the ground and she felt as though her head had hit a boulder. Her vision became blurred and she felt as though she was going into a deep sleep.

"I cannot sleep." She thought.

"I have to fight, I cannot sleep." She said this repeatedly in her mind fighting desperately to stay awake.

"God please help me." She begged, as the man ripped her blouse from her body.

Taking every ounce of strength she could find within her half-conscience mind, she screamed. "Somebody help me!"

The crazy man jerked Darla up from the ground, throwing her to the bottom of the grassy hill, as Darla was in and out of consciousness.

"Do I hear sirens?" She questioned, silently.

"Please God; I cannot take any more pain. Am I finally safe? Is help coming? Where is that horrible man?" She questioned, as she lost consciousness again.

"Darla, I am so sorry Darla." Lisa sobbed, as the ambulance attendant brought Darla from the park on a stretcher.

"Oh, what has been done to my little girl?" Sister Roberts questioned, kissing her daughter's bloody face, causing the attendant to stop.

"Sir, we need to get your daughter to the hospital." One attendant informed.

"Honey, come on, move back, so the men can get Darla to the hospital." Pastor Roberts comforted, putting his arm around his wife's shoulders, allowing her to cry in his arms.

"Mark, I must go with Darla." Sister Roberts informed, pulling from her husband's embrace.

"Okay Babe, I will meet you at the hospital." He agreed, than assisted his wife inside the ambulance.

"Come on, Babe." Pastor Roberts said, putting his arm around Lisa's shoulder.

"Let's get you out of here." He soothed, calming the seventeen-year-old.

Pastor Roberts entered the hospital with Lisa at his side. Stopping at a payphone, he telephoned his home.

"Roberts, Bill speaking."

"Son, I can use your help." Pastor Roberts said, his own eyes growing moist and his voice shaky.

"Dad, what is wrong?"

"It's Darla, she has been brutally beaten. Mom and I are at the hospital." Pastor Roberts said, pausing, clearing his voice and wiping his eyes.

"I will be right there, Dad." Replied Bill quickly.

"I would appreciate you coming, but first we need to get Darla's car off the street and home. It is still at the park. In addition, Lisa is here with me. We need to get her out of here and get her home. She is a nervous wreck."

"I will take care of Dar's car, and then I will be by for Lisa."

"Thank you, Son and we will see you soon."

Pastor Roberts returned to Lisa. "Hey, calm down Lisa. Darla will be okay, babe. She always bounces back. She is a bit stubborn like my wife in that manner." He assured, comforting, and soothing the broken-hearted teenager.

Bill soon arrived with Cindy at his side.

"Dad, how is Darla?"

"I do not know yet, Son."

"What happened, Uncle Mark?" Cindy asked, impatiently.

"All we know now babe is Darla has been beaten." Pastor Roberts answered, his voice cracking, he slowly walking away to regain his composer.

"Cindy, would you mind taking Lisa home? I would like to stay with Dad."

"Yes, of course." Cindy agreed.

"Come on Lisa." Cindy said, assisting her still sobbing friend to her feet.

Bill now went to his strong, compassionate father, putting his arm around his broad shoulders.

"Dad?" Bill questioned, with the departure of the girls.

"She looks bad, Son." He answered, his face bearing the strain of him holding his own eager tears back.

Bill let out a long sigh. It was as though his impatience suddenly kicked in, taking charge, going quickly to the information desk.

"I would like to see my sister, Darla Roberts."

"Your mother is with her."

"We know this." Pastor Roberts said, placing his hand on his son's shoulder to calm him.

"It would make us both feel better. We just need a couple of minutes." He assured, politely, yet firmly.

"I understand." The nurse said, with a compassionate smile.

Pastor Roberts and Bill entered the room where Darla lay unconscious. Sister Roberts stood at her daughter's side holding her hand, with tears streaming down her cheeks. Pastor Roberts went to his wife's side, putting his arm around her, comforting her. She released her tears, more quickly with her husband's comforting touch.

"Why did you ever allow Darla to step foot in that park filled with crazies?" Bill asked, as his eyes remained on his sister's battered face.

"Oh, Mark. Why did we?" Mrs. Roberts asked, looking up into her husband's strong face, her tears coming uncontrollably.

Putting his arms around his wife's shoulder, pulling her close to him, Pastor Roberts soothed and calmed her.

"Mom, we have to keep our heads thinking straight. We must be strong for Darla's sake as well as our own sake."

"Bill, be strong for your mother and your sister, they need our strength. Do we understand one another?" Pastor Roberts asked patiently, yet firm, with disapproval of his son's question at such a time.

Bill stared at his father for a split second, amazed with his great strength. He glanced at his weeping, broken mother, whom had never broken to his knowledge in his twenty-four years as her son. His anger calmed, replaced with love and dedication to his family.

"I am sorry Dad." Bill apologized.

"Mom, Dad is right, we have to be strong for Darla and get her through this." He added, looking into his mother's eyes, giving her a kiss.

"I will wait outside. I need to get a grip on my sudden rage." He confessed, bringing understanding smiles to his parent's faces with his open honesty.

"I am trying so hard to be strong, Mark, although I do not seem to be making any progress, I know I must for Darla."

"Mom, you may cry on my shoulder anytime you would like. You will have the strength as you need it."

"Excuse me." Spoke a nurse.

"The doctor has ordered some tests for Darla. Mrs. Roberts, if you would like to come with us, this might be best, in case your daughter wakes, your presence may calm her."

"Yes, I want to come." Sister Roberts assured, leaving her husband's side.

Pastor Roberts returned to the waiting room, finding both Bill and Cindy patiently waiting.

"Uncle Mark, apparently Lisa called Kelley, informing him of Darla's misfortune. He just called saying he is on his way. I could not talk him out of coming." Cindy informed, hesitant.

"It is okay, babe." Her uncle assured her, kindly.

It seemed with each minute that passed, it was an hour long, as Pastor Roberts, Bill, and Cindy silently awaited news in regards to Darla.

Kelley quickly came through the door into the waiting room with fear on his face, followed by his parents.

"Brother Roberts?" Kelley questioned.

"We do not know anything, son. We are still waiting."

"We are praying, Brother." Brother Peterson assured, shaking the pastor's hand.

"We appreciate your prayers."

"My wife and I would like to stay. Share your burden with you, if you want this." Offered

Brother Peterson.

"I believe we each could use some support."

"Aye, we like this. We go out in hall, me, and you?" Kelley's father questioned compassion on the strong Irish man's face.

"Sure." The pastor agreed, as though relieved to leave the waiting room.

Sister Peterson silently went to Cindy's side, putting her arm around her shoulders as she sat next to her.

"Have you seen Darla, Bill?" Kelley asked, anxious for some word in regards to his girlfriend.

"I saw her briefly." Bill got up from his chair, going to the window, staring out into the darkness for a few silent moments.

"Lisa said Darla was beaten." Kelley informed slowly, as not to intrude on Bill's thoughts and upsets.

"She was beaten badly, Kelley." Bill said.

"I promise you, whoever did this will pay." He threatened, his anger once again appearing on his face, bringing silence to Kelley, and more tears to Cindy's eyes.

"Is there a Mr. Roberts present?" A police officer asked.

"I will get your dad, Bill." Kelley offered, quickly leaving the room. Kelley returned with the pastor and his father.

"Mr. Roberts, my partner and I would like to talk to you alone." The officer informed.

"We are all family. What may I help you with?"

"Sir, we want to let you know, my partner and I will be here. We have the man in custody that attacked your daughter, due to your daughter's girlfriend calling for help so quickly we were able to catch him before he could get away. He is an escaped convict and his previous conviction was rape and murder. We do need the doctor's report on your daughter. Your daughter will also have to identify her attacker. From you Sir, after you have talked with your daughter, you will need to file charges."

"If I may add, sir … " Spoke the second officer. "Your daughter is lucky that she is alive."

"I will do whatever is necessary in regards to filling charges. I appreciate what you both have already accomplished.

"Mark?" Mrs. Roberts questioned, as she entered the waiting room, seeing the police officers.

"The police officers have the man in custody that attacked Darla." Pastor Roberts explained.

"Oh, thank the Lord." She replied, somewhat relieved.

"I do want this kept out of the newspaper." She ordered, firmly.

"Yes Ma'am, your daughter is a juvenile." The officer replied.

"Oh Patricia, I am so glad you are here." Sister Roberts said with a weary smile.

"Our friendship is steadfast, Mary." Mrs. Peterson assured.

"Thank you." Mrs. Roberts replied, taking a seat next to Cindy, giving her a gentle smile.

Avoiding everyone's eyes on her, she knowing their silent wishes to learn of Darla's condition, she regained her composer, attempting to make herself strong.

"Darla will be coming home." Started Mrs. Roberts, glancing around the room forcing a weak smile, as sights of relief came from more than one present.

"This will not be easy for her, but she will be safe with us." She added, as tears once again started down the broken-hearted mother's cheeks, bringing looks of deep concern from the others.

"Mary, you do not have to say anything." Sister Peterson assured, hurrying to her side, comforting her.

"Oh, but I do. Then, then ... " She sobbed,

"I do not ever intend to repeat this again." Taking a deep breath, and then letting out a long sigh, she managed to stop her sobbing.

"Her face looks terrible, but the doctor says it will heal. She will not have scars, not physically anyway. Her lip split, but they stitched it inside. She has a broken leg and arm. They are putting the cast on her now. She has a terrible bump on the back of her head and a concussion." She informed, now hesitating, her face becoming tense.

"The doctor advised we leave her here for the night." Mrs. Roberts began again, in her slow way.

"She is in and out of consciousness. She is somewhat out of control due to her nightmares while sleeping. I insisted we take Darla home, Mark." She informed, looking into her husband's eyes now, for his approval.

"Then she will come home." Pastor Roberts agreed.

"Her attacker also sexually assaulted her, so this scar may take some healing." Sister Roberts shared, now putting her face in her hands, sobbing.

Pastor Roberts went to his wife's side, with Sister Peterson leaving her friend's side. Cindy was now sobbing for her tender cousin's pain, with Sister Peterson holding and soothing her. Bill hit the table in front of him with his fist, then hurried from the waiting room. Kelley stood as though in shock, as his strong father came to his aid, putting his arm around his son.

"Why did this happen to Darla, Dad?" Kelley asked, tears now escaping his eyes.

"Your father not this wise, Son, I have no answers. I am sorry. You do right by Miss Darla. You be strong for her. No matter how long you wait, you always love her. She is as you say Son, 'a princess'. "His father said with pride in his eyes, giving his son a hug, as though strengthening him.

"Are you sure you are up to dealing with Darla this evening, Mary?" Pastor Roberts asked.

"I have to be, when she would be conscience, she begged the nurses to take her home. I will get control of myself." She assured, wiping her face with a Kleenex, and blowing her nose.

"Cindy, Patricia, perhaps we should find the ladies room." She suggested, standing up.

"I will find Bill." Pastor Roberts said, leaving the waiting room.

It seemed to take the hospital staff forever to prepare Darla for home. Her family had shed their tears now, though saddened shed no more tears. They were each silently building his and her strength to aid Darla to a quick recovery. The Peterson family, now silent, waited silently saying their prayers to aid their friends, brothers and sisters in Christ and Kelley, his girlfriend.

CHAPTER 5

Darla's first night home from the hospital was a nightmare for everyone. No sooner would Darla fall asleep, she awoke herself with screams of terror as she relived the scene with her brutal attacker in the park repeatedly. Her times of waking were brief due to her concussion. When she spoke, it was not always clear what she was saying. Nonetheless, her family was at her side the entire night, ready to love, comfort, and assist in healing her deep wounds if need be.

Mrs. Peterson kept the coffee brewing and coffee cups filled. She answered the late telephone calls inquiring of Darla, relieving the family of any dealings except their precious daughter's needs. Kelley and Bill, both extremely quiet, were in and out of the house, sitting in the family room for a period, in silence, and then leaving the house going for long walks alone, as Cindy finally fell asleep on the sofa.

Dawn seemed to bring a peaceful sleep for Darla. Pastor Roberts took the telephone off the hook, as he and Bill went to bed for a few hours. Sister Roberts lie sleeping in Cindy's bed next to her daughter's bed, in case Darla needed her at her side.

Brother Peterson had drifted off to sleep in the recliner, while his wife, busy in the kitchen, prepared some meals ahead to prevent her dear friend the bother of meal preparations.

Opening her eyes to the faint sound of voices and the smell of coffee, Darla turned her head slowly toward the clock on her nightstand. "It is almost noon." She thought.

"Good morning." Cindy greeted pleasantly, as she returned from the shower, looking at Darla as though it was another normal morning.

"Hi." Spoke Darla slowly, noting her lips swollen and sore.

"Kelley is here." Cindy informed, as she dressed for work.

"Kelley? Why?"

"He says you and he had planned to go to San Diego today. Honestly, I think he is here because he is madly in love with you." Cindy answered, cheerfully.

Darla did not return her cousin's smile. She remained quiet, trying desperately to keep her eyes open and listen. She did not want to appear rude by falling asleep, but she was still drowsy.

"Would you like me to send Kelley in for a few minutes?"

"My parents will not allow this." Darla answered slowly as though stuttering.

"Do not upset Mom or Dad." She added, barely above a whisper.

"I won't Darla." Cindy assured, feeling for her tender, loving cousin.

Cindy opened the drapes, allowing the warm sunshine to brighten the bedroom. She was determined to do all she could to help her dear cousin, as Darla had done for her when she had become a member of the Roberts' family.

There was a knock on Darla's door shortly after Cindy's departure. Darla lay staring at the door, knowing her voice was too soft for anyone to hear, waiting her caller to enter her room.

"May I come in?" Kelley asked, as he opened the door.

"Sure." Darla answered drowsily, forcing a weak smile, as she remained lying, as not to aggravate her paining body.

"I cannot speak too well this morning, I am sorry." She apologized, slowly.

"My lips are so sore." She added, closing her eyes briefly from the pain her stitched swollen lips brought.

Kelley's arms longed to hold and comfort Darla. He felt tears wanting to come to his eyes. His throat tightened as though he were going to become speechless. He had made a promise to Darla's parents to remain natural, treating Darla as though nothing had happened to her. He had promised.

As Kelley stood seeing Darla's battered swollen face and her motionless position, he was not sure he could keep his promise.

"We have to be strong for Darla. She will need our strength." Kelley heard, repeatedly in his mind, the words Sister Roberts had spoken. "If you cannot handle this, you should leave now, so Darla is not disappointed in you at this time."

"Oh, God, give me the strength to do right by Darla. She is so precious, Lord. Give me the strength." Kelley prayed, silently.

Darla opened her eyes again. She looked at Kelley, giving him a sweet smile.

"Hi." She greeted, as though Kelley had just arrived at her side.

"Hi, Dar how is my favorite girl?" Kelley asked, appearing his old self.

"Not too good today. I do not feel well." She answered with another sweet smile.

"You will feel better soon." Kelley assured, taking her hand into his, kissing it gently.

"I am surprised my parents allowed you in my room." Darla said, with a smile.

"I have been granted special permission, I am a great guy." Kelley replied, forcing a weak smile.

"No, you are the greatest." Darla said kindly, closing her eyes.

"No, Dar, you are the greatest and strongest." Kelley thought silently, with great admiration for his girlfriend.

Darla drifted back to sleep. The weak grip she held on Kelley's hand released as her hand relaxed.

Returning to Darla's family and his parents with Darla's door quietly closed behind him, Kelley appeared as though he had seen a ghost.

"I do not understand Darla is like an angel, sweet, kind, gentle, still concerned for the other guy." He shared, overwhelmed.

"It is like she is too innocent to acknowledge what has happened." He added.

"Darla does not know yet, Kelley." Mrs. Roberts informed.

"The concussion has not worn off. She will remember soon enough because her dreams will not allow her to forget. Until she is fully conscience, we will not know how she is going to react."

"Of all the people, I will never understand why it had to be Darla." Bill mumbled, taking his cup of coffee to the window with him, staring through the glass.

"Me either." Kelley sided, his hands in his pockets, staring at the floor, repeating Bill's question repeatedly in his mind.

"Being beaten and abused all over a group of low life losers." Bill mumbled, surprising everyone with his name-calling.

"Maybe I am speaking out of turn Bill, but you have the street people wrong." Kelley said.

"Every prostitute and drug addict in that park love, admires, and respect Darla. Ten of those street people have turned to Christ in the two months Darla has been witnessing. They would never harm Darla, Bill. Darla is referred to as an angel to the street people."

"You think so?" Bill replied with anger in his voice.

"Where were those precious "street people" as you call them, last night? Where were they when Darla needed help?"

"That will be enough, son."

"I am not a kid anymore, Dad." Bill informed.

"Then start acting like the man you really are." He ordered sternly, disapproving of his son's anger, rudeness, and back talk.

"This is my problem. I am a man, I do not believe in fairy tales, anymore." Bill replied leaving the house, slamming the door behind him and shocking his parents, Sister Peterson, Brother Peterson, and Kelley with his actions.

"I apologize." Started Pastor Roberts humiliated by his son's actions, as was his wife.

"Brother, say no more. I understand. My family, they understand. Upsets and temper do not go well together.

"My poor wife, she is patient with me more than once." Brother Peterson said, with flushed cheeks.

"It is good Bill get this out. He will feel better inside then he will feel foolish." He explained with a chuckle, bringing smiles to each one's face with his open honesty.

"No! Leave me alone! Please do not hurt me!"

Darla's parents and the Peterson couple sprung to their feet rushing to Darla. Kelley followed, with Bill hurrying through the door behind him.

The Roberts' soothed and comforted their daughter, putting aside their own pain. Kelley stared on with helpless actions for the one he cared so deeply for. Bill seemed to fill with more anger over the pain his loving sister was barring and enduring.

"Darla, wake up dear." Spoke her mother.

"Angels do not go through these things, Kelley." Bill whispered.

"I apologize for not understanding you earlier. I had no right to voice an opinion in matters I apparently know little about." Kelley replied, his eyes on Darla and her pain.

"I did not have any right jumping at you. I definitely do not have the Roberts' patience." Bill confessed, holding his hand out to Kelley as a truce. Shaking Bill's hand with a hard firm grip, the two young men looked into one another's eyes, seeing one another's pain for the first time.

"I do understand now. She is your kid sister and the girl I love." Spoke Kelley, holding back the tears he so desperately wanted to release.

"That is the way it is." Bill replied, patting Kelley on his back and giving him support, as Kelley had given him with his wise words.

"We have to be strong, Kelley. We have to get Darla through this." He added, he also with watery eyes.

Darla opened her eyes, looking at first her parents, Brother and Sister Peterson, then her brother and boyfriend. The drowsy look she had had in her eyes was gone. She was now seeing with a clear head.

"How long have I been out of it?" She questioned, looking at her parents with saddened eyes.

"About fourteen to sixteen hours." Pastor Roberts answered.

"Do you think you could eat some soup, dear?" Her mother questioned, with tenderness in her voice.

"I am not sure. It feels like that wild man busted my lip." Darla answered slowly, feeling her swollen lips. "I must look terrible."

"It is the beauty within one's heart, Miss Darla that counts." Spoke Mr. Peterson, bringing a weak smile to her face.

"Perhaps I should start looking up toward the heavens?" Darla asked, with a happy smile.

"Aye, you must always look up, Missy, always."

"What happened last night, Mother?" Darla asked, her pain becoming visible on her face.

"I can feel the cast on my leg, I see the cast on my arm, I barely remember the hospital, and I do not remember leaving the park or coming home."

"I want you to try and eat something first. A visiting nurse will be stopping in soon to examine you and then if you are not too tired and you feel like talking, we will." Her mother replied.

"Honey, my husband and I will leave now. We love you and you will be in our prayers." Spoke Mrs. Peterson, giving Darla a kiss, as did her husband.

"Thank you." Darla replied, with a weak smile.

With Darla's parents walking their guests to the door, then off to prepare her lunch, Bill and Kelley went to Darla's side.

"You both look so sad. You two do understand that I am to blame for this misfortune, right?" She questioned, attempting to comfort the two of the most important people in her life.

"Why would you say this?" Bill asked, disbelieving his ears.

"I broke the most important rule set in our street witnessing ministry. I left the park safe, I returned to the park alone and that was foolish of me. One always pays the price for breaking rules, Bill. Lisa reminded me of the rule and I entered the park alone regardless of the rule and Lisa's warning."

"You are one special girl, Sis." Bill replied, shaking his head at his sister's calmness and gentleness. Giving her a kiss on her forehead, Bill left his sister's room.

"We are alone at last." Kelley said, kissing Darla's sore, tender, lips gently and taking her hand in his.

"I love you, Darla."

"I love you too, Kelley Peterson." She replied with a tender smile.

"I am glad you are here. I have missed not seeing you as often since I moved here. In just three weeks you are going away to college to become Preacher Kel." Darla said proudly.

"I think it is neat when the street kids call you Preacher Kel."

"I think it is special the way they call you, Angel." Kelley complimented.

"I think you are right, Kelley. We do belong together. I hope that as we grow and later marry, we will always make time for the street ministry. They are special people with special needs. Not many people understand the park ministry, especially my family. You, Kelley, and I are fortunate we have the understanding for these special people's needs."

"I believe you are the kindest and wisest girl I have known." Kelley replied, touched by her sincerity, giving her another kiss on her lips.

"I know you will manage this soup now." Mrs. Roberts said, as she and her husband interrupted, returning with a lunch tray.

"I best leave, while still able." Kelley said, blushing. "May I visit Darla tomorrow?"

"As long as you behave yourself, you may visit." Pastor Roberts answered with a chuckle at Kelley's red face.

"Yes sir, this is a promise I will always keep."

Darla ate her soup by sipping it through a straw, along with the rest of her liquid diet.

With the nurse completing her visit, Darla was glad for some alone time, sleeping the remainder of the afternoon.

Awaking to the quiet talk at dinner table, Darla began thinking over her last trip to the park, and what little she could remember about the emergency room visit.

"There is more." She thought, as tears came to her eyes, as she put the pieces together.

"Please do not let my thoughts be true." She sobbed.

"Darla, what is wrong?" Her mother asked, as she entered her room.

"Tell me Mother all that happened to me in the park." Darla said, still sobbing.

"Okay." Sister Roberts started slowly, searching for the right words.

"What do you remember?" She questioned, patiently, looking into her daughter's eyes.

"I remember my arm breaking then being yanked around by my hair. He hit me in the face with his fist." Darla sobbed harder, pausing.

"Mother, please close my door. I do not want everyone hearing."

"Shush, calm down, dear." Mrs. Roberts soothed, gently hugging her daughter until she was able to calm herself.

Mrs. Roberts closed Darla's door. As she returned to her side, Darla knew that by the sad, hurt look on her mother's face, her thoughts were true.

"Go on, Dear. What else do you remember?" Her mother questioned, gently.

"I fell to the ground. He jerked me up from the ground, throwing me to the bottom of the hill and that was when my leg broke. I hit my head terribly hard, so I started having trouble seeing. I felt like sleeping and I was in and out from that point." Spoke Darla, sobbing once again.

"Darla, please calm down." Her mother soothed, handing her some Kleenex, as she wiped her own tears from her face.

"Mother, I-I remember him tearing my sweatshirt off me." She sobbed, humiliated.

"Mother, what else did he do?" She questioned, though fearing her mother's answer.

"He sexually assaulted you." Mrs. Roberts answered with tears streaming down her strong, yet gentle face.

Darla turned her face from her mother's eyes, feeling great shame, defiled, unclean, hurt and angry. She lay sobbing for hours. Her mother's words of comfort, her hugs, nor her kisses did not ease her pain nor was she able to make Darla feel the way she once had about herself. The world now looked dark and ugly, brutal and cruel. The same world that used to look so bright and beautiful filled with excitement and laughter. Nighttime only brought more cruel dreams. She received no peace even when sleeping; even her dreams were dark and ugly.

Morning came all too soon for Darla. She did not want to see the pain she had brought to her family or Kelley, on their faces. She did not want their eyes on her, now knowing, they each knew what had happened to her because it was too painful.

"Good morning." Cindy greeted, preparing for another summer workday.

Darla turned her head away from her cousin silently as her tears were released, streaming down her face.

"Darla, are you okay?" Cindy asked, going to her cousin's side.

"Do not look at me." Darla ordered, putting her arm up, blocking her view from her cousin.

"I am getting Aunt Mary." Cindy said, frightened over her sudden mood.

"Leave Mother alone, she has been through enough. Get Bill please." She requested, trying to calm the anger that kept striking at her.

"Okay." Cindy agreed, nervously.

"What do you need, Sis?" Bill asked, as he entered Darla's room. "Why are you crying?"

"Give me my mirror please, it is on my dresser."

"Why?" Bill asked, hesitant.

"Please, just give me my mirror." She pleaded, trying to conceal the anger within her.

Bill handed his sister her mirror, silently waiting for his sister's response. Cindy stood back, not sure of her cousin's next reaction.

Staring in her mirror, Darla was horrified at her face. The swelling made her face look twice its natural size. Her once tan skin was now red, blue, purple, and green from bruises. Her lips were so swollen they looked as though they belonged on another's face. Suddenly, Darla threw the mirror at the wall, causing it to shatter.

"Darla." Scolded Bill shocked.

"I am getting Aunt Mary." Cindy informed.

"What on earth happened?" Mrs. Roberts asked, as she and her husband entered the bedroom, with hearing the breaking of glass.

"Darla looked in the mirror." Bill said.

"Apparently she does not like what she saw." He added, as he picked up the broken glass.

"I am sorry." Darla apologized, ashamed her parents had heard her childish action, as she sobbed uncontrollably.

"Darla, you have to shake this. You are no different; you are the same girl today as you were a few days ago. In another few days, you will look the same." Her mother assured.

"Will I feel the same again, Mother?" She asked hopeful, yet feeling defeated.

"Only you dear, will determine this, but I hope so, for your sake." Her mother answered, sitting on the edge of her bed, supportive for her.

Darla worked hard at making herself appear more pleasant, as she lay in silence. Hearing the doorbell, Darla listened wondering who had come to visit. She heard Kelley's voice, then Bill, and followed by strange voices.

"Darla." Spoke her father, as he entered her room.

"Police officers are here to visit you."

"Why do they want to see me?" Darla questioned, frightened.

"Babe, it is okay." Her father calmed, patting her hand.

"You have to tell the officers what happened to you."

"I cannot tell them what happened, Dad." Darla objected, tears quickly making their way down her cheeks.

"Darla, do you want the man punished that harmed you?" Pastor Roberts asked sternly, he secretly trying to make his daughter be strong.

"Of course, but …"

"No buts. You will put this guy away for good by speaking with the officers, so another innocent girl is not harmed."

"Dear, this is officers Stephens and Meyers." Mrs. Roberts introduced, bringing the officers near her bed.

"Daddy, please." Darla pleaded, as she began to sob.

"Darla, only a few questions dear, then we will be able to put this nightmare behind us, okay sweetheart?" Her mother asked, gently taking her daughter's hand in hers.

Finally, Darla nodded her head in agreement, yet she turned her head away from the officers, not wanting them seeing her face as they heard of her shame.

"Darla, we will try to make this as painless and quick as possible." Officer Stephens said.

Darla told the story of her horrible night in the City Park again. Her mother once again had tears streaming down her cheeks. Her father's eyes were moist and he kept clearing his choked up throat. Bill and Kelley sat motionless in the next room as they overheard the horrible details of Darla's abuser. Kelley sat with tears streaming down his face, with his face in his hands. Bill shortly left the family room going outside shedding his tears in private.

"Do you know what the man looks like?" Officers Meyers Asked.

"Was he one of the teenagers that hang out in the park?"

"No." Darla answered, quickly, looking at the officers for the first time.

"The street people would never hurt me." She defended.

"If we show you some pictures do you feel you could identify the man responsible?"

"Yes, I see his face all the time."

Thumbing through several pictures in silence, Darla discovered the ugly haunting face in her dreams. His eyes seemed to be staring at her, daring her to scream once more. Her hands began trembling though refusing to scream, her tears escaped again, streaming down her face. She silently pushed the picture toward the officers.

"He is as good as gone, honey." Officer Meyers assured.

"No more nightmares for you." He added.

The visiting nurse arrived immediately following the police officers departure. Detaching the catheter from Darla, she was now able to get out of bed.

"What do you say we have lunch on the patio?" Her mother asked, as she assisted her daughter freshening up for her first trip out of her room since her trauma began.

"It will be nice having you join the family at meal time again."

"It would be better than staying inside." Darla agreed, politely.

Mother left Darla's room to begin preparations for lunch. With the assistance of her crutches, Darla slowly made her way to the vanity in her bathroom. Sitting down she stared into her mirror.

"Pull yourself together, Miss Darla Roberts. There has been enough pain. I have to put the past behind me. I must think about today and tomorrow." Darla silently told herself as she attempted to disguise her battered face with make-up.

"Perhaps with time, I will think and feel as I did before."

Being included with her family for lunch had been refreshing, even though she felt her family's eyes on her often, as though expecting her to react in an abnormal manner. She pretended not to notice.

Cindy and Bill helped mother clear the picnic table, then returned to their jobs.

"Babe, I had better get back to work. Somebody has to make your car payment for the next six weeks."

"Thanks Dad. I appreciate all your help." Darla replied, with a sweet smile.

"Just think of it as a loan until you get your casts off at fifty percent interest." Her father teased, bringing a smile from his daughter.

"By the way Babe, it is good to see you smile again." He informed, appearing relieved and pleased, looking into his daughter's eyes with compassion.

"Thank you Daddy." Darla replied, her heart going out to her devoted father, her eyes growing moist. With a kiss given to his daughter, he left her side.

Blinking hard as to not allow her tears to escape, Darla glanced at Kelley. The young couple's eyes met as Kelley supportively took Darla's hand in his.

"I intend to get past this stage." Darla forced a tender smile, as her tears escaped.

"I do not doubt this. You are, as I have stated in the past, very wise for your age. You are a determined, unique and peculiar person. One that is as an angel to the street people and to me, you are an angel and a beautiful princess."

Darla's tears came uncontrollably, as she continued looking into Kelley's eyes of compassion. Kelley gently brushed her tears away with his hand.

"I have something for you." Kelley cleared his throat, his eyes moist with seeing his girlfriend's broken heart.

Putting his hand in his shirt pocket, Kelley removed the dainty gold bracelet with his class ring attached. He fastened it around Darla's thin wrist. Removing the tiny diamond pre-engagement ring from his pocket, he slipped it onto her finger.

"I love you more today Darla, then I did yesterday." He assured, as his tears escaped.

"Please hold me, Kelley." Darla pleaded, beginning to sob.

"I will hold you as long as you like, as often as you like because we are a team." He soothed, with his arm around Darla, he allowed her to cry her heart out, with her head on his shoulder.

Mom Roberts approached the patio, desiring to check on her daughter. Her heart went out to Darla. She looked into Kelley's eyes, silently questioning her tender daughter's state. Kelley silently pointed to the rings he had given Darla. Mom Roberts now had tears streaming down her cheeks. She was most appreciative of Kelley reassuring her daughter that his feelings for her were steadfast. She silently patted Kelley on his back and then slipped away. Returning inside her home, she shed her tears in private.

Hearing a car enter the drive, Darla removed her head from Kelley's shoulder.

"Great, I look terrible." Darla complained, quickly wiping her tears away.

Kelley quickly stood up removing a handkerchief from his back pocket. Returning to Darla's side, he handed her his handkerchief.

"I am not up to entertaining guests."

"Lisa and Debbie are life-long friends, Dar. You do not need to entertain them." Comforted Kelley, as Darla blew her nose, attempting to pull herself together. He put his arm around her shoulders, bringing her comfort.

"Oh, Darla, I am so sorry for you." Debbie spoke, with tear-filled eyes as she gave her dear friend a hug.

"I will be okay; the Lord is busy mending me." She hugged her friend in return, forcing a weak smile.

"Why did God allow this to happen to you? You did not deserve this and you were witnessing for the Lord. God is supposed to be a God of love." Debbie said, her tears streaming.

"I do not have all the answers, Debbie." Darla soothed, hoping to bring her dear friend comfort.

"I was disobedient and entered the park alone breaking an important rule. My parents have forever told Bill and me there is a price to pay for disobedience.

Trust me when I say, I believe them with a whole heart now." With sincerity on her gentle tender face, Darla wiped her tears away once again.

"How can you blame yourself for what happened to you, Dar? You returned to the park for your Bible. You did this to spare your mother an upset, not to set out to be disobedient." Lisa reminded Darla, she too questioning God's love and mercy.

"I confess I am struggling with God's mercy in my behalf. I cannot afford to dwell on this at this time. When I am older and wiser I trust I will obtain more insight." Darla shared, releasing a deep sigh.

"I do know I am responsible for breaking a most important rule. God is not to blame, both of you truly believe this."

The teen girls looked at one another speechless. They did not understand their dear friend speaking with kindness with a peaceful spirit as she sat, her pretty face severely battered. Her stitched lip causing her pain with each word she spoke and her leg and arm in a cast.

"My parents also have often said ones actions affect others. I have brought great sadness to my family. I have created doubt in you both and now you question God's love and mercy. This is my deepest pain and I apologize." With all sincerity, each felt Darla's deep compassion for her friends. In her humble devoted way, she touched their hearts. She once again wiped away her streaming tears, with Kelley's handkerchief.

"Lisa, if you will exercise your forward ways … " Darla started, with a tender smile. Her statement bringing a smile to each ones saddened face.

"Enter my home and inform my mother I have thirsty guests, please."

"I will help you with the drinks, Lisa." Debbie offered.

With the teenager's departure, Darla looked up into Kelley's eyes.

"I do not wish to dwell on my accident any longer, Kelley." Darla confided, seeking his strength for the visiting girl's questions.

"I will intercede for you when the girls return if this is your desire, Dar."

"Yes, please. I feel exhausted from their questions."

"Then you will answer no more questions." Kelley assured, with authority in his voice.

He tightened his arm around his precious girlfriend's shoulder, silently bringing her comfort as she rested her head on his shoulder from her aching body growing weary.

The teenage girls returned carrying glasses of ice tea and making themselves comfortable at the picnic table. Darla briefly raised her head from Kelley's shoulder, as she looked at her drink, her dry aching lips desiring moisture, yet she silently hesitated.

"Did you not want tea, Darla?" Debbie asked.

"Tea is fine, thank you. I am thinking on how to drink it." She answered, blushing.

"I will get you a straw." Kelley said, getting up from the table.

"You are getting good at reading Darla's thoughts, Kel." Lisa commented.

Kelley smiled at Lisa's comment.

Darla took hold of Kelley's arm, preventing him from leaving.

"And my comforter, my rescuer, my protector, and my dearest friend." Darla added, with a tender smile, looking into Kelley's gentle eyes.

"Thank you, Baby doll." Kelley replied with a grin, surprising the girls with his forward choice of words, causing Darla to blush.

"Good-bye, Kelley." Darla scolded lightly, her response bringing laughter from her girlfriends.

"Yes Ma'am, Baby doll." Kelley kissed his girlfriend's lips lightly for the first time in other's presence, he surprising all presence.

"Kelley." Started Darla and then broke into a tickled laugh, as did Lisa and Debbie.

"Darla." Kelley mocked, leaving the laughing girls for Darla's home.

Darla quickly hushed her laughing, putting her hand over her stitched lips as the pain from her laughter brought tears to her eyes.

"Are you okay, Dar?" Lisa asked, alarmed.

"Yes, I must remember to restrain from laughing a bit longer." She spoke slowly.

Mrs. Roberts soon arrived insisting Darla cease her visiting and rest. Good-byes said to her girlfriends, Kelley assisted Darla inside her home. Darla started toward the sofa at her slow pace with Kelley's assistance.

"Darla, I want you in your room lying down."

"Mother, I … " Darla started, intending to protest.

"Your room Dear, you have already exceeded your time up." Mrs. Roberts interrupted, with concern on her face.

"My mother has always been over protective." Darla whispered, as her mother departed from the young couple's presence. Kelley smiled as he assisted Darla to her room. Slowly sitting down on her bed, she released a weary sigh.

"That was a long walk."

"Yet you did not want to rest?" Kelley asked, taking Darla's crutches from her.

"I cannot bear to close my eyes for fear of reliving the nightmare in the park." Kelley's face quickly saddened, as Darla lied back against her pillows.

"I use to adore this new bedroom Dad built for Cindy and me." Darla briefly closed her eyes, as she lay still catching her breath.

"This room is beautiful. You do not still adore your room?" Kelley asked, desperately wanting to understand her needs completely.

"I feel detached from everyone when alone in here. Then I feel different, not like myself and I despise this feeling."

"You are never alone Dar, the Lord is always with you." Kelley said, taking her hand in his.

"In my heart I know this, but my mind seems to be working overtime, playing tricks on me, clouding my thinking. When I am awake or with others I manage to fight, but when alone or sleeping, I feel another is controlling my mind and emotions. This scares me, when I fear I feel anger tugging at me. I just cannot give in to these feelings, Kelley. Self-pity and anger are sin. I just want to be myself again." With drowsy eyes, tears slid down Darla's bruised cheeks.

"You will feel the same in time, I promise you this. Your family, friends, the Lord, and I are at your side. We each will assist you through this misfortune, always at your side, as you have faithfully been for others."

"I am counting on this to get me past this." Darla confessed, her eyes remaining closed.

Darla was sleeping soundly within minutes. Mrs. Roberts entered her daughter's room and going to her daughter's side, she silently soothed her long hair away from her face. Politely standing with Mrs. Roberts's arrival, Kelley let go of Darla's hand.

"Sister Roberts, I would like to stay as late as you will permit. I realize this would not be allowed under normal circumstances, but Darla truly means the world to me, Ma'am."

"I know your feelings toward my daughter are genuine, dear. I believe your presence is good medicine for Darla. My husband and I are most concerned with the lasting effect of this trauma, Darla will have to contend with, so I grant you permission to stay as long as you would like. I will deal with my husband's passiveness with Darla." With a soft laugh, Mrs. Roberts gave Kelley a quick hug.

"I most sincerely appreciate this, Ma'am." Kelley replied, quickly.

"I have no intentions of crossing your husband." He assured, with reddened cheeks.

"I know this, dear. If you will be kind enough to sit with Darla while I run a couple of errands, I would be grateful. I do not wish for Darla to be alone at this time."

"I will gladly stay with Darla." Kelley assured, respectfully.

With the Robert's home empty except for Darla and Kelley, Kelley silently prayed. He prayed for peace within his girlfriend and her family.

He prayed a prayer of healing for Darla's injuries. Opening his eyes, raising his head, Kelley walked to the patio doors. His hands in the front pockets of his casual slacks, he stared through the glass in deep thought for some time.

"Kelley." Mr. Roberts spoke, standing in his daughter's doorway.

Kelley quickly turned, facing Mr. Roberts, he finding his former Pastor's face most putout.

"Yes sir?" He inquired respectfully.

"Where is my wife?" Mr. Roberts asked, wiping the perspiration from his forehead with his handkerchief, his clothes speckled with sawdust from his long hours of carpentry work in the desert heat.

"She had some errands to run." Though Kelley knew Mr. Roberts was not pleased with his presence in his daughter's room un-chaperoned, Kelley remained calm.

"She left you in charge of Darla?"

"Yes sir."

"I do not believe this." Mr. Roberts remarked, shaking his head. Though holding Kelley's stare thoroughly aggravated, he said no more.

Hearing the backdoor open, Mr. Roberts glanced toward the door.

"I do not believe this." He repeated then entered the family room.

"Hello Dear, how was your day?" Mrs. Roberts asked in her gentle way.

"My day was fine until returning home." Mr. Roberts snapped.

"How could you leave Kelley in charge of Darla?"

"Mark, do not give me a hard time. Furthermore, do not question my judgment because I do not need this at this time."

"Mary, your actions go against our principles. We do not allow a young man to stay in our daughter's bedroom in our absence. I cannot believe you allowed this." Mr. Roberts continued.

"Dear, do you not trust our daughter or Kelley?" Mrs. Roberts asked, as though challenging her husband.

"You know better. This issue is not about trust; it is about proper and improper standards. Don't allow this again."

"Mark, I do not wish to hear anymore, this subject is closed." She said sitting on the sofa wearily.

Most aggravated, Mr. Roberts left the family room to shower.

Kelley remained standing near the patio door, taking in the words exchanged between the Roberts.

"Hi Aunt Mary, how was your day?" Cindy asked, pleasantly.

"I have had better. How was your day, Deary?"

"I had a good day." Cindy answered

"You look tired and drained. Did Darla have another rough day?" Cindy asked.

"No, she had a good day. Kelley seems to uplift her spirits. Your Uncle is presently annoyed with me and if he wants dinner this evening, he better change his tune." Mrs. Roberts said, with a weary smile, Cindy giggling with her aunt's threat.

"I'll never understand how you and Darla remain even-tempered, yet stand your ground, this drives me crazy." Voiced Cindy, still laughing

"This drives your Uncle Mark crazy also, dear." Mrs. Roberts confessed, blushing as she broke into a soft laugh.

Kelley smiled with hearing the women's talk. He looked now at Darla as she lay sleeping. He had never known one as young as she that possessed such self-control. It now dawned on him that she was much like her mother. She was taught well the characteristics of a young lady, of a Christian young lady and this pleased him immensely.

Darla began to stir, as though restless. Her eyes remained closed. Kelley quietly neared her bedside.

"No! No!" Darla screamed, filled with terror.

"Darla, wake up. Darla." Kelley said, shaking Darla awake.

"Get away from me! Do not touch me!" Screamed Darla, her eyes now open.

Kelley moved back, stunned. Mrs. Roberts hurried to her daughter with Cindy close behind her.

"Darla, you are home, Dear. You are in your room and you are safe." Mrs. Roberts said, soothingly.

Looking at her mother, Cindy, then her father standing in her doorway, she began to tremble and her tears came uncontrollably. Her mother held and comforted her. Kelley had tears streaming down his face, so Mr. Roberts put his hand on Kelley's shoulder.

"She did not mean to lash out at you, Son. She was having a nightmare." He explained in a whisper.

"Thank you for explaining." Kelley wiped his tears slowly from his face.

"Daddy ... " Spoke Darla, removing her arm from around her mother's neck.

"Yes Babe, I am here." Mr. Roberts took his daughter's hand in his, as his wife and niece moved away from the bed.

"Please pray these nightmares stop. I am not strong enough to fight this much longer, surely God does not expect this of me."

"I will pray now, Sweetheart." He assured.

"Mom, Cindy, Kelley, let us pray together for Darla." Each present gathered near Darla. They praying silently, while Mr. Roberts prayed allowed.

Their praying ceased, Kelley and Mr. Roberts entered the family room. Cindy took her shower, preparing for her date with Dan. Mrs. Roberts assisted her daughter in freshening up from her nap and crying.

Sitting at her vanity, Darla's eyes quickly filled with tears as she and her mother sat over-hearing Kelley's heartache with Darla screaming at him. Mrs. Roberts continued silently, brushing her daughter's long hair.

"I screamed at Kelley, Mother?" Darla asked, her tears releasing.

"You were having a nightmare sweetheart. You did not intentionally lash out. We all know this is not in your nature."

"Mother, I cannot bear this, everyone in this family is hurting and now Kelley."

"Families have endured tougher times and remained overcomers. We will also be overcomers. I assure you, this will pass with time. In the meantime, we will be strong for one another and we will be sensitive to one another's needs."

Wiping her tears away, Darla nodded her head in agreement.

"I will be strong, Mother." Darla assured, with added boldness.

"Good for you, Dear." Mrs. Roberts gave her daughter a tight hug.

"Let us join Dad and Kelley." Her mother added.

Mrs. Roberts patiently awaited her daughter to make the walk from her room to the family room at her slow pace, slowly walking behind her, prepared to assist if needed.

Mr. Roberts and Kelley ceased their line of talk with the arrival of Darla and her mother. Kelley politely stood as Darla neared him. As she sat on the sofa, he took her crutches laying them aside. He then returned to his seat next to her.

"Mom, are we not having dinner tonight?" Mr. Roberts asked, as his wife sat down.

"This depends on you and your attitude." Mrs. Roberts answered, leaning back in the recliner, she speaking in her slow, mellow, yet to the point way.

"Babe, it is after six and I am hungry, so please get to the point." Spoke Mr. Roberts in his impatient tone.

"Dear, you have been giving me orders since you returned from work. I have yet to receive an apology from you." Kelley and Darla smiled at one another.

"Babe, do not toy with me, I am tired and hungry. I would just like to have dinner."

"I would just like an apology, Mark. Is this request difficult for you to fulfill?" Mrs. Roberts asked, in her passive way, continuing to relax in the recliner. Darla released a soft laugh. Kelley grinned with the adult's ways.

"I apologize for my manner. Now may we eat?"

"Yes dear, as soon as you pick dinner up. The checkbook is in my purse. Bill requested tacos from San Barro."

Releasing a weary sigh, Mr. Roberts vacated his chair. Leaving the room, he went for the checkbook.

"Mother ... " Darla scolded lightly, though smiling with her ability to handle her father.

"Missy, do not take Dad's side. I owe him, believe me." Mrs. Roberts whispered.

She broke into a tickled laugh with the teenager's surprised expressions.

"Mother has no mercy when one gives her a hard time." Darla shared, looking up into Kelley's eyes.

"You remember this Kelley, for the future if you do marry my daughter." Mrs. Roberts warned, as though threatening him. Kelley released a chuckle.

"Yes, Ma'am, I assure you I will." Kelley humored, as Darla and her mother became tickled.

"Mother, Dad left through the front door. He is avoiding you."

"Do you blame him?" Kelley asked, grinning at his girlfriend.

"No I understand how he feels." Mrs. Roberts laughed with the teen's talk.

"Do not pick up this characteristic from your mother, Dar." Kelley warned.

"Kelley it works for Mother, she is my number one teacher."

"Now you inform me, after I have fallen for you. Thanks a lot, Dar." Kelley rubbed his head as though he was already weary, while Darla and her mother laughed.

Kelley and Darla enjoyed time alone on the patio, following dinner. Darla made her apologies to Kelley for reacting when he attempted to calm her when having a nightmare.

Walking Darla to her backdoor as the hour grew late, Kelley put his arms loosely around her waist. Looking into one another's eyes, Darla briefly saw the brutal man's face flash before her. She blinked hard several times to make the face go away.

"Dar, are you okay?" Kelley asked, puzzled.

"I am sorry, Kelley, I am having flashbacks, I am truly sorry." She apologized, her eyes quickly filling with tears.

"I best allow you to go inside. You look tired." Kelley calmed, removing his arms from around her waist. Politely opening the door, he assisted her inside. His goodnights said he left the Roberts home without a goodnight kiss to or from Darla.

Darla stood in silence as Kelley departed, staring down at the floor leaning on her crutches. She felt her parent's eyes on her as they sat next to one another on the sofa.

"Babe, are you okay?" Mr. Roberts asked.

Slowly raising her head, she looked into her father's gentle eyes, as her tears released. Slowly, as though in a daze she shook her head no. She looked into her mother's eyes full of compassion for her.

"Mother, may we talk?" She requested, her tears coming more quickly.

"Of course we may." Mrs. Roberts said, quickly vacating the sofa.

"We will talk while I assist you in preparing for bed." Putting her arm around her saddened Darla, hoping to bring her comfort, she walked beside her daughter to her bedroom. Sitting down on the edge of her bed, Darla began to cry hard.

"Sweetheart, what is troubling you?" Mrs. Roberts sat down next to her daughter, putting her arm around her shoulder.

"I have hurt Kelley terribly, Mother. He could not even kiss me goodnight. When I knew he intended this, I saw that man's face." Darla shared.

"Oh, Sweetheart ... " Mrs. Roberts started, releasing a weary sigh. "I know you must be growing weary, I know your world appears to be turned upside down at present. Do believe me, all will pass and you will feel and react naturally. For now, hang on to this when the trials seem unbearable."

"I am trying with all my might to beat this, Mother."

"I know this. You are a true trooper, Sweetheart." Mrs. Roberts assisted her daughter dressing for bed.

With goodnights said, Mrs. Roberts returned to her husband in the front room, as Darla lay in her bed fighting sleep, fearing she would relive the brutal attack on her in the City Park.

Darla heard Cindy enter her home from her date with Dan. Mr. Roberts turned the television off, as he and his wife gave their full attention to their niece, as she shared her evening out.

Bill entered the home from his evening activity. He inquired of his kid sister's day and emotional state. Darla listened as her mother shared her concerns. Her fears of her daughter folding under all she had to contend with, knowing her mother was crying.

"Mary, we must remain strong. We must see Darla through this. She must only see our strength, so she is able to draw strength from us." Mr. Roberts comforted.

"I know this, Mark. I know better, but I feel as though we are fighting a losing battle. I myself cannot bear to see Darla enduring pain much longer. She does not deserve this."

Tears streamed down Darla's face, as she heard firsthand how heartbroken her family was. They were all hurting because she broke an important rule, with returning to the park alone.

"I must cease their pain." Darla decided. "Somehow I must do this for them."

Darla felt a void when awaking, learning Kelley would not be spending the day with her. He would be apartment searching in San Diego, as he prepared for his first year away at college.

Darla desperately worked on the lonely feeling that tugged at her while her family each went about their separate busy schedules. She wished she could play her guitar, she always felt uplifted when singing and playing praise choruses. With her arm in a cast, this too, was presently impossible to fulfill.

Leaving her patio door where she had sat looking outdoors, she slowly left her room. Entering the front room where her mother was busy dusting, she sat down at the patio. She lightly pecked the keys to her favorite chorus she played on her guitar to the street people. She longed to return and to be involved with others, filling her emptiness.

"Dear, I must go to the office for a few hours today. My cousin is growing impatient with me for me neglecting my duties. Will you be okay? I will not be gone long; I intend to bring my work home." Mrs. Roberts asked.

"I will be fine." Assured Darla, trusting she sounded convincing.

"Dad's prayer did the trick; I did not wake everyone last night with having a nightmare."

"I realize this and this alone is a relief. You are going to be okay, dear." Mrs. Roberts gave her daughter a tight hug. Darla smiled a reassuring smile.

Several days had passed since Kelley's last visit. Sister Roberts was spending more time at the office then she had intended. The lonely feeling within Darla grew. She silently withdrew more and more from her family. She felt empty inside, she had ceased her daily devotions and she felt as though a stranger to herself, her family, others, and God.

"Dear, why are you sitting in your room alone?" Mrs. Roberts asked, entering her daughter's room.

"I adore watching the sunset, Mother." Darla answered, pleasantly.

"Yes, it is beautiful." Mrs. Roberts agreed. With her arm across her daughter's shoulders, she too admired the beauty of the sunset through the patio glass door.

"I am glad Dad put patio doors in my and Cindy's new room. I often wake early and admire the sunrise. I feel most at peace during this time. God's creations bringing us beauty, joy and peace, He is the artist of all artists."

"Do come join you family. Dad is concerned you spend too much time alone these days and I agree with him."

"I am sorry, Mother. I did not intend to concern you and Dad. My intentions are to relieve you of concerns."

"There is no need to apologize, Sweetheart. We are aware of you intentions, but come join your family. We desire your company."

"Yes, Ma'am, I will." Darla agreed with a tender smile.

Slowly standing, Darla balanced herself on her crutches. Entering the family room, her father, her brother, and cousin sat enjoying a comedy program. Their laughter ceased with Darla's arrival, each silently showing their heartache for her misfortune had not ceased. This saddened her because in the past she brought joy to her family and others. Now she brought sadness and uncomfortable feelings between others and herself. With a loving smile, Darla neared her father, he sitting on the sofa.

"Daddy, may I sit by you? I would enjoy your company."

"Of course, Babe, you may sit by me anytime. Kelley does not have you yet, nor will he for a long time." Mr. Roberts teased with a grin.

"Darla will always be a daddy's girl whether she is married or not. This I guarantee, poor Kelley." Bill teased.

"Of course I will." Darla agreed pleasantly, sitting down.

"This is the spirit, Babe." Mr. Roberts chuckled.

"At least you bear with me, Dad, regardless of my many moods."

"Yes, and I always will, Babe." Mr. Roberts voiced though his manner now serious, he looking into his daughter's eyes, silently questioning her comment along with her family members.

"Dar, Kelley sticks by you, as we each do." Cindy replied.

"I have not heard from Kelley for several days, Cindy. Perhaps this ordeal has become more than he can deal with." Darla stated, barely above a whisper, she was feeling sorry for herself, with missing him.

Her family quickly looked at her. She felt their eyes on her, she avoiding eye contact. She stared at Kelley's class ring on her bracelet, she silently questioning the distance she felt between her and him.

"Mom, is Kelley not in San Diego preparing for fall semester?" Bill asked, surprised with his sister's negative remark.

"Yes he is and Darla is aware of this."

"Even little sisters are allowed an occasional pity-party, Bill." Darla shared, forcing a smile, regretting creating more concern within her devoted family.

"Babe, one pity-party per person per year is allowed." He lightly humored.

"Do not entertain this state of mine." Mr. Roberts cautioned.

"I know better, Dad." Darla raised her head, looking into her father's gentle eyes.

"I am a Roberts." She added with a defeated smile.

"I must obey the rules." Mr. Roberts laughed and each family member seemed to relax with Darla's added comment.

Darla relaxed on a lounge chair on the patio with her eyes closed. She longed to be active. She missed riding her horse. She missed friends visiting on a daily basis as they had in her former town and she longed to drive her new car.

"How is my favorite girl?" Kelley asked, approaching.

Quickly opening her eyes, Darla smiled. "Quite bored these days, how have you been?"

"Okay. My first week at college went well, I am pleased with this." Kelley said, sitting down in a chair near Darla, taking her hand in his.

"Would you like to go for a walk to the corral?" Darla asked, finding an excuse to take her hand from Kelley's, as she slowly got up from her chair.

"Dar, are you sure you are up to a walk?" Kelley asked, concerned as he assisted her with her crutches.

"I intend to find out." She answered with a tender smile.

"It would be nice if these crutches came with instructions for us whom have a broken arm." She added with a gentle smile, as she attempted to manage her crutches regardless.

"I will try to hurry before Mother grounds me for attempting this walk."

"I see, you want me to be your escape goat." Kelley said with a boyish grin, at the wrong he knew his girlfriend was committing.

"Why not? Our walk will put a smile on my face and this alone will please Mother.

It took some time for Darla to make the walk, but she made it. She now was silent, as she and Kelley stood watching and petting the horses. She felt as a stranger in Kelley's presence.

"Dar ... " Started Kelley, slowly, his face flushed.

"Yes?" She asked, looking up into his gentle face.

"Is there a reason why you are not wearing the rings I gave you?"

"No, I guess I forgot to put them on this morning when dressing for the day." She answered, silently searching her reasons for not thinking to wear the rings.

"I am sorry for you that you have been forced to experience so much pain." Spoke Kelley, compassionately.

"I think I should go so you may have the time you need to get over what has happened." He added, as though reading his girlfriend's inner thoughts.

"Kelley ..."

"Please do not say anything now, I feel the same about you and I always will. You need time to understand and sort out your feelings, so take your time, please."

"Okay." Darla agreed, respecting her boyfriend's wishes, though she felt bad for hurting his feelings by making him feel uncomfortable, yet she secretly did wish to be alone. She did need time to recapture the old Darla she had been before her accident.

"Would you allow me to assist you back before I leave?" Kelley kindly asked.

"Please, I found the walk difficult." She answered, smiling that she had insisted she could handle the walk earlier.

"I tried to warn you." Kelley replied, with a comforting smile.

"I know, it must be the stubborn side of me, I believe I take after my mother's side." Darla said, glancing toward her home, with flushed cheeks.

"Your mother does not look happy." Kelley agreed, he now noticing her observing their return walk with her hands on her hips.

"Please try to walk more steady, Dar; I want this to look as good as possible. I do not care to be a part of the lecture she is plotting to deliver you." He added with a boyish grin, bringing a soft laugh from Darla.

Reaching the patio, Kelley assisted Darla unto a chaise lounge.

"Darla Roberts." Her mother spoke, as Kelley laid Darla's crutches aside for her.

"I give in, Mother, I promise not to attempt that far again." Darla assured, weary from her outing.

"The walk to the coral did put a smile on my face to see Princess." She added quickly, bringing a smile from both Kelley and her mother. They both knew she was humoring her mother to stay out of trouble.

"You make sure you keep your word, Deary." Her mother instructed, though with a smile of approval with her happiness.

Darla lay back, enjoying the warm sun, resting and relaxing, until falling asleep napping most of the afternoon. Awaking finding her body sweaty from the hot August sun, she decided to bathe and change into fresh clothing. It seemed a slow process to bathe herself with one hand, as she sat at her vanity taking a sponge bath for her first time alone. As she looked in her mirror, she found she had bruises she had not been aware of, bruises on her back, her arms, her legs and even her neck.

"I hate you." She whispered dropping her washcloth in the water, as she thought of the horrible man responsible for all her inner pain, as well as her physical pain.

"Darla." Spoke Mrs. Roberts, knocking on the bathroom door.

"Yes?"

"Are you doing okay by yourself?"

"I could use your help now, Mother."

Darla was silent as her mother assisted her with her dress. "I am a bit old for you to have to help me dress." Darla said breaking their silence, giving her mother a loving smile.

"True." Her mother agreed, with a soft laugh.

"I feel more confident, missy, if the tables were turned, you would be at my side."

"You may always count on me."

"I am counting on you to hurry and get well. Besides my counting on you, you are wearing me out." She added truthfully, with a beautiful laugh, though giving her daughter a tight reassuring hug.

"I will hurry, Mother." Darla replied, with a gentle smile.

"Good, now come entertain your guests."

"Entertain my guests?" Darla asked, her smile quickly disappearing.

"Yes, Candy and Susie are waiting in the family room."

"But, Mother, they will ask questions." Darla reminded, her face now bearing her worries.

"This is true and it is your decision which questions you answer and how. You do not have to share anymore then you choose. I will not allow you to hide for six weeks. You need to be with people, especially your friends so you will truly heal your heart and your mind. When you have successfully completed your visit with your present guests, I have a very long list of calls you need to begin returning." Her mother instructed, in her patient gentle way.

"Perhaps Cindy is right; I do have a drill sergeant for a mother." Darla replied, forcing a weak smile and bringing a laugh from her mother.

"Darla I would be careful if I were you."

"Yes Ma'am." She answered, saluting her mother, tickling her mother with her sudden bravery with her light teasing.

"Darla, go to your guests."

"Hi." Darla greeted pleasantly, concealing her uncertainties with her guests possible questions.

"Darla, what happened to you?" Candy asked shocked, as Darla entered the family room on crutches.

Darla nervously glanced at her mother as she continued her walk to the sofa on her crutches.

"Cindy told us you are not working because you do not feel well, but we had no idea you were in an accident." Candy informed.

"An accident … " Darla repeated, giving her mother a smile.

"It was a painful accident." Darla said, returning her eyes to her friends, as she lifted her cast, placing her leg on the coffee table.

"Mother allows me to put my foot on the coffee table now." She added, bringing smiles to her friends, their concerns fading somewhat.

"What happened, Dar? Were you in a wreck?"

"No. Would you believe I fell down a hill at the City Park?"

"You are kidding, Darla."

"No, I am quite serious." Darla assured, bringing a pleased smile from her mother.

"Did you see Darla's new car girls?" Mrs. Roberts asked; glad to assist her daughter through her ordeal, as Darla propped her broken arm up on the cushions near her.

"Oh, Dar, that is your car?" Susie asked, excitedly.

"Yes. I was able to drive it for one whole day. I would offer to take you for a ride, but my mother is a bit overprotective."

"What kind of pills is Darla on, Mrs. Roberts?" Susie asked surprised with Darla's humor in her present condition.

"My pills are my mother's orders." Darla answered pleasantly before her mother could respond.

"I have been ordered to stop keeping myself from my friends while I am recuperating. Your and Candy's visit is my medicine." She explained, making her friends feel special.

Darla leaned her head back against the sofa now, as the girls excitedly filled her in on events to come with their new school term nearing. The girls ending their visit, Darla's mother walked them to the door.

"You did great, Sweetheart. I am proud of your efforts and pleased with your results."

"Thank you and you made it easier by your presence. You being here kept me from feeling like an outsider."

"Good."

Darla returned her friends calls, with her mother insisting opening the door to her friends to visit, as they liked. Her days with visitors were uplifting, but her days when not having a visitor were long, making her feel lonesome. With the lonesome feeling came indifference, forcing Darla to remember her misfortune. With remembering came hate, often filling Darla with anger.

Lounging on the patio after dinner, Cindy kept Darla company as she waited Dan's arrival for her Saturday evening date.

"Darla, come with Dan and I tonight." Cindy suggested.

"I am sure Dan would disapprove if he was aware of you inviting me." Darla answered, with a kind smile.

"So what?" Cindy asked, with a selfish laugh.

"So my answer is no. I refuse to spoil your one night a week out with the guy of your dreams."

"Then call Kelley and invite him over."

"No, Mother would never allow me to call a guy. Besides, I would rather Kelley not come. Not this evening anyway."

"Oh." Sighed Cindy, as though giving up attempting to fill her cousin's empty time.

"Cindy!" Darla exclaimed. "Dan has Slim with him."

"Who is Slim?"

"Slim is one of the street people."

"Uh … He looks awful."

"No he does not, he looks great. He used to look awful, but now he is straight and he is a Christian." Darla shared excitedly, her face aglow and her eyes dancing.

"I will never understand you." Cindy whispered.

"I know, you feel as Bill and my parents, but Slim understands." Darla replied, as though his understanding made all the difference in the world, puzzling her cousin.

"Hi Slim." Darla greeted excitedly as he and Dan got out of the car.

"What's happening Angel?" Slim asked, in his carefree, happy way.

"I had a slight accident other than that, life is going on. Slow and terribly boring at present, but then life is not without flaws." Darla answered, in her bubbly way, for the first time since her accident.

"Angel, it is cool, we all heard what happened to you in the park. We are sorry we were not there for you. You have always been there for us and had any of us been there, the dude would have gotten wasted." Slim assured her.

"I realize this, but I am thankful no one was there. I could not bear to know one of you were in jail on my account."

"This is our Angel." Slim remarked, looking at Dan and Cindy with a big pleased smile, shaking his head.

"I got to get out of here, most parents do not approve of my kind. I brought you this." Slim explained, handing Darla her Bible, it bringing tears to her eyes.

"Thank you Slim."

"Marge found it. I had a hard time getting it away from her. She said she wanted to keep it, she said it makes her feel closer to Angel and her Jesus." Slim shared with a happy smile, now causing Darla's tears to escape over their love.

"I got to go, when you are working for the man, he expects you to be on time."

"Slim, give this to Marge. Tell everyone I miss them and they each are in my prayers."

"I will." Slim agreed, taking the Bible from Darla.

"Thanks for the ride Dan. Later."

"Bye." Replied the three teenagers as they watched the longhaired hippie leave the drive, walking back toward town proudly carrying Darla's new Bible as though it was priceless.

"Darla." Spoke her mother with a sharp tone, as Darla wiped her tears away.

"Yes?" Questioned Darla surprised with her mothers' tone.

"Who was that?"

"Slim."

"One of those hippie's from the park?" She questioned, thoroughly upset.

"He is not a hippie, Mother, he is a Christian."

"My patience is entirely gone with you. He is a hippie." She insisted.

"He will never show his face here again, or any of his kind." She ordered in her sternest tone, making Darla, Cindy, and Dan uncomfortable with her actions.

Darla silently kept her eyes on her mother's face for fear she would think her disrespectful, even though she disagreed with her mother's actions, and opinions.

"Why was he here?"

"He came to return my Bible, Mother." Darla answered, gently, hoping to calm her.

"Where is it? Where is your Bible?" Her mother asked, as though disbelieving Darla, making her daughter feel confused and more uncomfortable.

"I gave it back." Darla answered slowly, realizing her mother had given her the Bible as a gift.

"You did what?" She questioned, as though shocked with her daughters ungratefulness toward her gift.

"Mother, I am sorry, I should have given Slim my old Bible." Darla apologized quickly. Her act of charity that had made her feel so happy, now seemed to go sour, filling her with shame and humiliation.

Her mother stood a few minutes as though in shock over her daughter's actions. "Make sure this Slim does not return."

Darla felt Cindy and Dan's eyes on her, as her mother returned to the house.

"You did what you knew was right, Dar." Dan said, breaking their silence.

"She irritates me." Spoke Darla; anger now in her voice, as she kicked the empty lawn chair next to her, surprising Dan and Cindy, this action unnatural coming from her.

"Let it go, Dar, do not allow it to eat at you." Dan calmed.

"Your mother is scared for you; she is trying to protect you."

"I truly wish Dan, that you, Mother, Bill, and Kelley would quit trying to protect me. I feel like I am suffocating. I do not even have a life that is mine anymore. Everyone is trying to make me be what I am not and I feel like I am going crazy." Getting up from her chair, Darla went for a short walk on her crutches, to be by herself.

Darla began withdrawing even more from her family she so dearly loved. She understood her mother's fears for her safety. She did not understand why her family felt her desire to work with the street people was unnatural, when it was an activity of her past. The misunderstanding seemed to eat away at her daily, making her feel frustrated, empty and angry.

"A penny for your thoughts?" Bill asked, pulling a chair out from under the patio table where Darla sat, completing her homework.

"Geometry ... " Darla said, putting her pencil down, politely giving her brother her attention.

"It is a pain."

"It is a pain? Since when did you develop a negative attitude toward school work?"

"I am not for sure." Darla answered, with a gentle smile.

"I will be graduating a year early though, so perhaps my past love and drive for school work has paid off."

"Mom said you could graduate this year with Cindy. This is if you attend summer school next summer."

"Correct. I am going for it because high school is becoming a bore as is life." Darla replied, taking her eyes from her brother, staring at her incomplete math assignment.

"Just one more week, Sis, and you will be able to attend school. I am sure your life will be just as full as your past school years have been."

"I hope so Bill, sometimes I am so frustrated with being stuck at home."

"I know." Bill agreed with a chuckle.

"Does it show?" Darla asked, blushing.

"Of course it shows. You are becoming as impatient as your brother is. This is expected of me, Sis, you, on the other hand, never bore my bad hang-ups until your convalescent."

"Then Mother and Dad must be concerned. Am I right?" Darla asked, feeling for her loving parents.

"We each are concerned. Your changing is scary; you are not you most of the time. You know we are each here for you." Bill assured his concern showing on his face.

"I know, I am sorry, I have not intended to make anyone worry. I honestly have been trying to do just the opposite. I will get my act together."

"I will let you get to your studies. I hear your tutor expects nothing less than perfection."

"She is a miserable grouch." Darla informed, smiling at her brother's shocked expression, with her choice of word.

"Will you please quit saying whatever pops into your head before the wrong person hears you?"

"Yes sir." Darla replied pleasantly, saluting her brother, and bringing a laugh from him.

Since Bill's talk with Darla, she worked harder at controlling her moods of frustration.

"Do not make any plans this afternoon, Darla." Mrs. Roberts advised as she and Bill had lunch with Darla.

"I have already made plans, Mother." Darla informed, hesitantly.

"You will have to undo them, after your casts come off; we need to do your shopping for school."

"I would rather shop next weekend."

"Next weekend you will be busy with school events and your job. Besides, I have taken the afternoon off for you, Deary."

"You should be thrilled to be going out with mom; you have been stuck at home for six weeks." Bill sided.

"Perhaps I am not a swinger like you, Bill." Darla replied, forcing a smile.

"Mother … " Started Darla hesitant, crossing her fingers under the table.

"I did make special plans for this afternoon and this evening."

"What plans, Darla?" Her mother asked, annoyed with her daughter's persistence.

"Gail is planning to pick me up on her way from school. She and I were to meet Pastor Finks and the others from the street-witnessing group for dinner then after dinner it would be time for the park ministry."

Darla watched her mother's face change from annoyed to angry within seconds. She put her fork down, pushing her plate of barely eaten lunch away, clearly proving her upset by her loss of appetite.

"You are not going back to that park." Sister Roberts ordered, firmly.

"Mother, please."

"I mean never." She repeated, with fury on her face, surprising her children with her tone.

"I am shocked to say the least, you would consider going to that type of environment after what happened to you."

"Mother, the teenagers are not to blame for what happened."

"Darla Roberts, what more must I say for you to hear my decision and be still?"

"You do not need to say anything more." Darla answered, taking her eyes from her mother's, staring down at her plate with flushed cheeks.

Mrs. Roberts took two aspirins then left the kitchen to change for her shopping date. Bill assisted Darla in tidying the kitchen.

"Cheer up, mom is right."

"Bill, you do not understand, nor does Mother." Darla replied, with a sigh.

Going to her room until time for her shopping date, Darla turned her stereo on then lay across her bed closing her eyes. She felt terrible for upsetting her mother, yet aggravated her need to help others was being pushed aside.

Returning home from her shopping date, Darla was relieved to have her casts removed. Monday she would attend her first day at Ragweed High and return to her part-time job. She could now drive her car and ride her horse.

Dinner dishes completed, Darla slipped out alone to ride. Entering the corral, slightly limping on her once broken leg, she learned both her leg and arm was weaker than she had thought.

"I thought I might find you back here." Kelley said, climbing over the fence.

"Hi Kelley … " Darla greeted, pleasantly.

"I have not seen you for several weeks. How do you like college?" She questioned joining Kelley, sitting on the fence.

"I like college. How about you, have you started at Ragweed High?"

"I start Monday. I have had a tutor the past three weeks, so I am becoming excited." Darla shared, happily.

"I see you still are not wearing the diamond I got you, or my class ring."

Darla was silent now; she did not feel comfortable with Kelley like she once had.

"You and I dating like old times, is still a problem for you?" Kelley asked, politely.

"Yes." Darla answered, honestly, yet she disliked hurting Kelley.

"I am not sure we can ever have between us what we had, I am so different, Kelley." She explained slowly.

"I love you Darla. I feel no matter how far apart we may be now, or in the future, I will wait. It is my choice to make and I have made it. I still have the faith you will become my wife someday." Kelley said, gently.

Darla was silent again. Her heart still loved Kelley; yet she did not feel like the Darla Kelley really cared for. Hurting him more was something she could not and would not do. She knew she would be deceiving him if she did not tell him now.

"The main reason I came by was to see if you are truly coming back to the Park Ministry." He informed, jumping down from the fence.

"Gail called saying you are coming tonight. If you can attend, I would like to take you."

"I want to go and I intended to attend tonight." Darla started, as she placed the bridle on Princess.

"Mother will not allow me to return and she said 'never'. It seems the odds have turned against you and I being together." She added with tear-filled eyes, bringing her saddle near her horse.

"Darla." Bill called, as he entered the corral. "Mom said not to ride yet."

"Why not, Bill?" Darla asked, irritated.

"Do not bite my head off, I am just the messenger."

Darla stood biting her tongue, still holding the saddle in her hands.

"I am riding anyway." She informed, throwing her saddle on her horse.

"Why? Mom only wants to ensure your arm and leg is stronger before your ride."

Darla slowly began to mount her horse. She felt Bill and Kelley's eyes on her, watching and waiting to see if she would deliberately disobey. She did not carry out her wishes and intentions; she was not one to disobey. Angrily, she jerked the saddle from her horse throwing it on the ground, and then kicked the saddle. Bill took hold of his sister's arm firmly, turning her face to face with him.

"What is wrong with you? You pushed Mom past her limit during lunch and now this. Dar, you are heading for serious trouble if you do not a hold of yourself."

"I feel like I am in a cage and I cannot get out." Darla shared, with tears streaming down her face.

"Everything is going so wrong." Walking away from her brother, keeping her back toward him and Kelley, wiping her eyes, she tried to make her tears stop and calm herself. After several long minutes, Darla was able to regain control of her emotions.

"Guys, I am sorry." Apologized Darla, forcing a weak smile, walking back to Bill and Kelley with tears still coming, she brushing them away.

"I do not know what is wrong with me; I guess I have simply had a disappointing day. I believe I had better call it a day." She confessed, still wiping away her continuous tears.

"Go ahead and I will take care of Princess." Bill offered, compassionately.

"Thank you Bill, Bye Kelley." Darla said, forcing a smile.

"Bye Dar. Take care."

Darla kept herself busy with her school attendance and job. She withdrew from her family, locking her emptiness and loneliness inside, not wanting to cause her family any additional pain over her unhappiness.

"Darla, I saw Cindy's engagement ring. It is beautiful!" Exclaimed Candy, as she and Susie joined Darla at her locker.

"I know. Dan gave Cindy her diamond on Valentine's day."

"I wish Mike would get me a diamond." Candy shared.

"Not me. I plan to stay single forever, doing what I want, when I want." Susie remarked.

"Cindy is lucky; she and Dan are definitely a perfect couple." Candy said.

"I agree." Darla sided.

"What about you, Dar?" Susie asked.

"I do not understand your question."

"Do you want a diamond ring to tie you down, or do you intend to always play the field?"

"I am not sure if either appeals to me, ask me again in a couple of years." Darla answered, with a gentle smile.

"Are you going out with Don Jacobs tonight, Dar?" Candy asked.

"No, I have another date." Darla answered, with a mysterious smile.

"Great. Set me up with Don Jacobs and we can double date." Susie suggested, hopeful.

"I assure you, you do not want to double date with me."

"Why?" Susie asked, puzzled.

"My date is with Chemistry and Latin." Darla answered with a soft laugh.

"I do not believe you, it is Friday night." Susie reminded.

"You do not have to work tonight, you never have any fun. All you do is work and study."

"Spend the night with me tonight, Dar." Candy suggested.

"My parents are out of town for the weekend, so we will have the entire house. Susie and a few other friends are staying over."

"Come on Darla, have some fun for a change." Susie sided.

"Okay." Darla agreed, secretly wishing to be doing something fun, also.

"Tell your parents you are spending the night with me." Susie said.

"Why do I need to lie?" Darla asked, hesitant.

"You need to lie for two reasons." Candy answered.

"Number one, your parents would never allow you to stay at my home because of my dad's drinking problem. Number two, we are having a small party with booze present, but you do not have to drink. My parents think I am staying at Susie's house and Susie's parents think she is staying at Tina's house. We do it all the time and we never get caught." Candy explained.

"I do not know if my parents would find out I would be in serious trouble." Darla replied, hesitant.

"They will not find out. Come on, we will have a blast and you deserve to have fun too." Susie encouraged, excitedly.

"Okay, I am game." Darla agreed, letting out a deep sigh.

"Great! I will get Tina and we will meet you at your car, Darla." Susie instructed.

Darla and Candy patiently sat in Darla's car in the school lot for Susie and Tina to join them. Though she felt scared for the wrong she was about to do, she also felt excitement.

She nervously drove to a liquor store as instructed by Susie. Tina went inside, returning with a twelve pack of beer, wine, and cigarettes. Darla felt ashamed now that she had agreed to go with the girls because her parents believed she was spending the night with Susie and they had trusted her judgment in picking her friends. They believed she would act in the ways of a Christian while with friends.

"I cannot change my mind now. Mother and Dad will wonder why I changed my plans, so I have to make the best of it, just this once." She decided silently, as she drove out of town pretending to be enjoying herself.

With the car radio playing, the girls sat down on the ground talking and laughing, as Tina, Susie and Candy drank both beer and wine, having a blast.

"Should I join them? I have not really been happy or had a good time for so long. If not happy with following rules, perhaps I should bend the rules a little and have fun also." Darla thought repeatedly in her mind.

"Have some wine, Darla." Tina offered.

Darla slowly took the wine bottle her friend offered, taking a sip. To her surprise, she found she liked the taste. With several more drinks from the bottle of wine, Darla felt as good as her friends. For the first time in six months, she was laughing even if it did take a little wine to help her relax. She was accepted for who she presently was and pretending to think and feel like the old Darla was not necessary with her new friends, the Darla her parents thought she still was and Kelley hoped for.

As darkness fell, Darla drove her friends to Candy's home. Driving her car into the garage, the girls closed the garage door, hiding her car from any curious neighbors. Candy turned her stereo on as the girls made themselves comfortable in the front room, continuing their drinking.

"Look what I have." Candy said, returning to the front room holding out a baggie filled with pot.

"Alright, it is party time!" Susie exclaimed, setting her beer car down, eager to get started on the pot.

Darla smoked joint after joint with her friends. As soon as they began coming down from their high, they lit another joint. Darla enjoyed her new experiences with her new friends.

Awakened early by Candy, the girls pulled themselves together as they prepared for their separate homes.

Darla's eyes were blood shot from her excessive drinking, pot smoking and lack of sleep. Driving into her drive, Darla hoped her family was still sleeping. Holding her breath, she tiptoed into the house, quickly to her room releasing a sigh, as she closed her door behind her.

"Why are you home so early?" Cindy asked, returning from her shower, causing Darla to jump.

"Oh, you scared me." Spoke Darla, her hand on her chest from fright. "I am sorry."

Darla turned her stereo on, and then lay down across her bed.

"Dar, you will wake your parents." Cindy reminded, quickly turning the stereo off.

"What is wrong? Didn't you get any sleep?"

"Not much." Darla answered closing her eyes, quickly falling to sleep.

It was afternoon when Darla awoke. She showered, slipped into a pair of bell-bottom jeans, a smock, and sandals. Finding no one home, she left a note for her parents and then walked to Candy's home.

"Hi! Come in." Candy greeted, her face appearing strange.

"Thank you." Replied Darla, politely.

"Would you like to go horseback riding?" She asked pleasantly, as she followed Candy to her bedroom.

"I would love to." Candy answered, picking up a lit joint from an ashtray, taking a hit.

Darla sat down on the floor, Indian fashion, next to Candy.

"Would you like a hit?" Asked Candy, holding the joint out toward Darla.

"Why not, my parents are not at home anyway."

The girls sat quietly getting high together and listening to the stereo. Darla enjoyed sitting back relaxing and experiencing her calm, peaceful high. For the present anyway, her thoughts were only on pleasing herself, not others. The telephone rang several times before the girls realized what was ringing.

"Darla, your mom is on the telephone." Candy informed.

Panic struck Darla, as she clumsily took the telephone. She knew her mother would be able to tell she was high, simply by hearing her voice.

"Yes, Mother?" Darla asked, nervously.

"Are you planning on coming home soon, Dear?"

"I will be home in a few hours." Answered Darla slowly, finding it difficult to concentrate on her mother's conversation.

"A few hours, what are you doing that takes hours to do?"

"I am helping Candy with her homework." Darla answered with flushed cheeks for telling a lie.

"I need your help grocery shopping. I will pick you up in one hour, so be ready."

"Wow. You look down."

"My mother is picking me up in an hour." Darla explained, paranoid, as she looked in her friend's mirror.

"Do I look stoned?"

"You look fine, just concentrate on looking and acting together and your mother will never know." Answered Candy, sure of her advice.

Darla was beginning to come down from her high when her mother arrived.

"Hi Mother." Darla greeted nervously, as she got inside her mother's car.

"Darla Roberts." Her mother scolded.

"What?" Questioned Darla, fear stricken her mother knew of her wrongdoing.

"What? You know you are not to wear jeans except at home or when horseback riding." Her mother said, disappointed in her daughter's disobedience.

"Mother, no one wears slacks except little girls and grandmothers." Darla complained, as she stared out the car window.

"Oh this is not true." Defended Mrs. Roberts, irritated with her daughter's sarcasm.

Darla was silent as she pushed the shopping cart for her mother. She felt so much hostility toward her mother for disapproving of her dress. For the first time in her young years, she wanted to dress, act, and speak the way she felt. She had had her fill of people telling her how to dress or to act respectfully and proper. It was time she started thinking of pleasing Darla.

Returning home, Darla assisted her mother putting the groceries away, with few words exchanged.

"Mom, are you girls about ready to leave? Your son and I are hungry men." Pastor Roberts said, as he and Bill entered the kitchen, dressed nicely for their family evening out.

"Just about," Answered Mrs. Roberts, pleasantly.

"Dear, go change so we can go.

"I am already dressed." Informed Darla slowly, standing up for her rights.

"Darla, you will change now, I am not in the mood for this." Her mother ordered, firmly.

"Why can't I choose my own way of dressing, Mother? I am not a child." Darla reminded, bravely.

"Do you have a problem hearing young lady?" Pastor Roberts asked, sternly.

"No." Darla answered releasing a sigh, as she continued leaning against the counter, silently standing her ground.

Pastor Roberts took hold of Darla's arm firmly. "Do I have to paddle you at your age?" He questioned, extremely put out with her actions.

"No Sir." Answered Darla, her sudden bravery quickly dissolved with the sternness in her father's voice and firm grip he held on her arm.

"Go change and hurry up. You have wasted enough time with your nonsense."

"Yes Sir."

Changing quickly, Darla felt both ashamed and aggravated. She felt shame for being disrespectful, yet aggravated for having to dress differently.

Darla's family was extremely quiet, as her father drove his car toward his choice restaurant.

Their meals ordered Darla felt it her duty to break their uncomfortable silence.

"I am sorry for spoiling everyone's dinner." Darla apologized, now truly feeling like a heel.

"You should be." Agreed Mr. Roberts disappointed in her behavior.

"I am sorry, Dad." Darla assured, with gentleness in her voice.

"Mother, I am sorry for the way I spoke to you." She assured, as she gently put her hand on her mother's shoulder to comfort her.

"I do not believe I am ready to forgive you, Darla."

Darla looked at her mother with disbelief, as did her brother and father. Darla had never known her mother not to forgive anyone, yet she was hesitating now with her own daughter.

"I do not know what to say, Mother." Darla confessed in her soft way, with flushed cheeks.

"Perhaps I like it better this way."

Darla now glanced from her mother to her father for support or understanding of what was happening. She had always been so close to her parents, but now it seemed as though her mother was considering breaking her closeness with her.

Picking at her food, she felt even more alone. Mother had always been at her side, through everything and now she had pushed her past her limit.

"Am I going to lose Mother, also?" She silently questioned.

"How is your dinner, Darla?" Mr. Roberts asked, interrupting her silence, attempting to lift his family's spirits during the dinner hour.

"It is fine, Dad."

"Then eat and quit picking at your meal." Her mother ordered.

"Yes ma'am."

Entering the house from their dinner date, Darla was glad to be home even though she knew her evening was far from being over. With reddened cheeks and a nervous stomach, she sat down quickly waiting for her mother's next move. She hoped to get her punishment over with and retrieve to her room behind closed doors.

"It is time for a family discussion, Darla and the topic is you." Her mother informed.

"We will ask the questions and you will give the answers. Is this understood?" She questioned, sternly.

"Yes Ma'am." Darla answered, nervously picking at the hem of her blouse with her long nails.

"What is bothering you? What are you hiding?" Mrs. Roberts asked.

"Are you having problems at school?" Mr. Roberts asked, sounding as desperate to understand his daughter as his wife.

"Everything is going well at school."

"Is everything going well at church?"

"Church is fine."

"If church and school are going so well, why is it you seldom bring friends home, Darla? Why aren't you filled with your usual excitement and involvement like previous years?" Her mother asked, doubting her daughter's answers.

"I honestly do not know, Mother."

"Why do you ignore Kelley?"

Darla's face flushed even more as she hesitated, searching herself for the answers.

"Mother, Kelley is kind of a personal subject." She answered, hesitant, not wanting to appear rude again.

"Yes, Kelley is a personal subject and I want personal explanatory answers." Her mother demanded, her patience wearing thin once again.

"Yes Ma'am." Darla answered quickly.

"I do not feel comfortable with Kelley right now. Kelley is a great guy and I am not interested in anyone else, we just do not have too much in common anymore."

"As far as school and church, I keep busy with my studies and my job. I spend a lot of time caring for Princess and riding her. I receive a lot of pleasure riding. Mother, I am okay. This year is just new and different. I am still trying to find my place in a new school and town."

"How do you explain your sudden outburst of rebellion?" Her mother asked.

"I cannot explain."

"You told Bill you feel like you are in a cage, explain this." Her mother ordered.

"Oh, Bill, I could kill you." Darla thought silently.

"Come on, Darla, your mother is waiting." Her father ordered, impatiently.

"What about you deliberately disobeying today and your rudeness toward me, did you have another bad day, choosing me as your punching bag?"

"I did not intend to upset you, nor actually be rude." She answered slowly, hesitating.

"I have not any excuses for today. I simply …"

"You simply acted like a disrespectful spoiled child." Her mother interrupted.

"Yes, I did." Darla agreed with reddened cheeks, truly ashamed of her actions.

"I had hoped, Darla, we could start tearing down some of those walls that you have built around yourself, perhaps even help you walk freely out of your cage, yet, you still refuse to let us in." Replied Mother, with a sigh, as though weary from her daughter trying her patience.

Now picking at her nails, with flushed cheeks and shame, Darla hated the deep lonely feeling within her, yet she would endure before she would tell her parents how terrible she truly felt about herself since her misfortune in the park six months earlier. She had to spare her dear wonderful parents from that nightmare. She would work harder at appearing pleasant for her parent's sake because she had caused them enough pain and upsets.

Spending the next few Friday nights with different friends, Darla intended to prove her involvement with others to her parents. While away from home for the night, she drank and smoked pot, allowing herself one night to be relaxed, carefree and excited with being included and escaping her present confused feelings.

Staring out the drive up window, between customers, Darla wished she were with her friends partying like most Friday nights.

"Hello in there." Spoke Kelley, startling Darla from her daydream as he stood outside the order window.

"Hi." Darla replied, blushing.

"I am sorry; my mind is not on working tonight."

"May I get you something?" She asked pleasantly, picking up her order pad.

"Can I get a coke please?"

"One coke sir and it is on the house." Darla said, placing his coke on the counter, as he reached for his wallet.

"Thank you."

"You are welcome." Darla replied, kindly.

"How are things at college?"

"My grades could use improving, but I am doing okay."

"What time do you get off work?" Kelley asked, as though impatient.

"In a few minutes, as soon as Cindy returns from her break."

"I would like to talk with you after work, if you do not have other plans."

"I would like this also."

"Hi Kelley." Cindy greeted, joining her cousin at the counter.

"Hi Cindy, I hear you wear diamonds now." Kelley said with a pleased grin.

"Yes, and I love it." Replied Cindy, happily, showing her ring to Kelley.

"I am leaving Cindy." Darla said, now appearing down as she left the counter.

"Okay." Cindy agreed her and Kelley silently exchanging glances at Darla's sudden mood change.

"Dar, Aunt Mary called, she wants you home by ten."

Nearing the backdoor of the restaurant, Darla stopped walking with her cousin's information. Turning toward her cousin, it was apparent she disliked her orders.

"Why?" She questioned, irritated.

"I have not any idea." Cindy answered, irritated by Darla's irritation.

Darla silently looked at her cousin, knowing she was irritated with her tone, desperately attempting to calm herself.

"Thanks Cindy." She replied calmer.

"Is she always this moody?" Kelley asked concern in his eyes and voice.

"She is becoming unbearable, Kel, she reminds me of me a year ago. It is scary and we each are worried. She definitely is not herself."

"Paybacks are a bummer, aren't they?" Kelley asked, with a boyish grin, as Darla neared him.

"Yes, they are." Cindy agreed, now laughing, remembering her past stage of rebellion and giving Darla a hard time.

"Be patient." He whispered and then turned his attention on Darla as she joined him where he waited.

"Would you like a coke or a hamburger?" Kelley asked, considerately.

"No thank you." Darla answered, forcing a weak smile.

"May I offer you the picnic table then?" Kelley asked with a gentle smile, Darla noting he was as handsome as ever.

"That will be fine." She agreed, feeling comforted by his gentle smile and politeness.

Kelley politely stood until Darla was seated then he sat down across from her.

"As your heard my orders, I am down to forty-five minutes before bed check or Mother will send the troops out for me." Darla said with a pleasant smile, bringing a grin to Kelley's handsome face.

"I understand the Roberts' way, so I will get right to the point." Kelley said, his face growing serious.

"I want you and I to begin dating, Darla, I have missed seeing you terribly." Kelley said, bluntly.

"I wish we could Kelley, but it is not this simple." Darla started sadly, not wanting to think of the pain she felt each time she thought of how much she wished she and Kelley could share what they once had together.

"Why?" Kelley asked, impatiently.

Darla sat in silence with her head lowered, as her eyes filled with tears. She tried to stop the tears, yet her efforts were in vain. She did not know why she was crying. She had not shed any tears for any reason for so long.

"Dar, are you okay?" Kelley asked, with compassion and gentleness on his face.

"I did not mean to upset you." He assured quickly, hurting for her pain.

"You have not done anything, Kelley, it is me. I am too different for our relationship to work. I am not even living as a Christian anymore. You are attending college to be a minister and we are two different people with different interests. I am not the way I use to be, or the way you want me to be." She explained between sobs.

"Darla, I will wait until you feel as you use to because I love you." Kelley insisted, his face clearly showing his own pain with her rejecting him.

"You do not have love for me anymore, is this it?" He questioned, frustrated, trying hard to be patient and understanding.

"I have love for you, but I have learned to push it aside." Darla answered, wiping her eyes.

"Push it aside? You have lost me." Kelley replied, becoming aggravated.

Darla looked into Kelley's eyes sadly, as tears continued to stream down her tan, thin cheeks.

"Kelley, I have drifted so far, I am just not the Darla you wish for. I smoke pot and I drink when I spend a night away from home. This is how different I am. The only time I am happy anymore is when I am high. I do not like feeling miserable and I have been pretending I am happy when I am around my family. I hate lying to my parents in regards to my whereabouts and activities. I feel awful caring for you and knowing you care for me. You and I as a couple cannot be.

I am different, Kelley, I did not want to change, but I have." Darla explained, brushing her tears from her face.

"Darla, the Lord can change things in your life. He can take away the pain and give you peace within again and you know this. Turn to God and your family. Do not turn away from the ones who love and care for you, turning to the world for comfort. You have found the world's ways comfort for only a few hours, but it does not last." Kelley pleaded, looking into her saddened eyes.

Darla quickly took her eyes from Kelley's eyes. She could not bear seeing him hurting for her over her wrong.

"Dar, you are developing a lousy relationship at home by lying and hiding what you are doing. You have always had so much love and respect for your family. How can you hurt them be deceiving them?" Questioned Kelley, annoyed with her actions.

"I am sparing them from pain. If my parents knew how mixed up I am over what happened to me at the park, they would be crushed. It is better if they think I am fine." Darla defended.

"If you think you can continue to partake of sin like you are presently doing and your parents never find out, you are wrong. You cannot continue the way you are and not get caught." Kelley scolded.

"I will not allow my parents to learn of my doings and hurting them." Darla insisted, becoming short with Kelley.

Kelley put his hands over his face for a second, and then looked at Darla with calmness on his face and gentleness in his eyes.

"Let me pray with you." He offered, putting his hand over her hand.

"No thank you, I have to get home." Darla refused quickly, as she got up from the table.

"It will be easier on both of us if we do not see one another anymore." She suggested, taking her car keys from her purse.

"I am sorry for you and myself, Darla. I will not give up, so you remember this." Spoke Kelley with authority in his voice, as he remained at the table.

Darla slowly walked toward her car. She wanted so badly to turn back around to Kelley, allowing him to pray, so everything could be as it once had been, yet she did not.

Getting in her car, she locked her doors, turning her radio on loud. She watched as Kelley got in his car driving away. Her tears slid down her cheeks once again, as she longed to be with him.

"I have to pull myself together and quit thinking about what could have been and have a good time, the way I see a good time." Taking a joint out from under her car seat, Darla lit it, as she drove around town getting high looking for Susie's car. After several trips through town, she spotted her friend's car, honking the horn as she approached.

"Hi Dar, what's happening?" Tina asked.

"Not much." Darla answered, as they waited for the green light.

"I thought you had to work." Susie said.

"I just got off."

"Meet us at the hamburger drive-in and party with us." Susie suggested, in her excited way.

"Okay." Agreed Darla, though already stoned.

Parking her car in the parking lot, Darla was no longer crying, she was happy. Everyone and everything she saw made her laugh and she loved feeling carefree and happy.

"I will be back; I have to tell Cindy what is happening." Darla informed.

"I will go with you." Tina offered, getting out of Susie's car.

"Tina, I do not think you or Darla should talk to anyone, you are both pretty messed up." Said Susie, worried.

"Cindy is cool, Susie, do not worry." Darla assured.

Darla and Tina were laughing hysterically as they approached the order window.

"Hi Cuz." Darla greeted happily.

"Hi." Replied Cindy annoyed with the girl's actions.

"Cindy, would you please call Mother, telling her I have to work until midnight?" Darla asked cheerfully.

"You know I do not lie to your parents." Informed Cindy, aggravated by Darla even thinking she might.

"Come on, Cindy. Please? Dad will ground me. I am already late and I would cover for you." She pleaded in her soft voice.

"Darla, listen, you are probably in deep trouble. Your mom has already called asking for you. Bill is out driving trying to find you, so you better get yourself together." Cindy warned.

"Terrific, my own brother is out to bust me." Darla said, with a smile, as though she did not have a care in the world.

"I will wait around for big brother."

Darla walked Tina to Susie's car, with no more laughter from either girl. Stopping at her own car, removing a baggie filled with marijuana from her glove compartment, she returned to Susie's open car window.

"Susie, here is some grass. I have to stay here because my brother is looking for me."

"Darla, you are not straight enough to see anyone in your family."

"I will handle myself." Darla assured.

"Good luck. We would have had a blast."

"Thank you for inviting me."

Bye Tina."

Darla returned to the order window where her cousin stood observing her every move. She desperately tried to appear straight; secretly convincing herself, she would be successful.

"I did not think you would ever ruin your life." Spoke Cindy, concerned for her dearest cousin.

"I thought not too." Darla confessed, now feeling down.

"I am going home."

"Wait for Bill, Darla. If you go home now, your parents will know you are high." Cindy suggested, nervously.

"I am kind of tired, so I will go home and crash and Mother and Dad will never know." Replied Darla, confidently.

Darla clumsily unlocked the front door, entering her home finding her parents awaiting her, with displeased worried faces.

"Hi Mother, hi Daddy." Darla greeted, with a pleasant smile.

"Good night, I am going to crash." She informed, as she started to her room.

"You may sleep later. You are an hour and a half late." Scolded Mr. Roberts surprised with his daughter's casual actions.

"Where have you been?"

"I was visiting with Kelley, he came by the hamburger drive in and we had a lot to discuss." Darla answered, beginning to feel drowsy.

"You are home." Spoke Bill, as he entered his home with worry on his face.

"Are you okay, Sis?"

"Besides being tired, I am fine."

"Daddy, I am really tired, may I please be excused?" Darla asked, attempting to escape her family before they became wise to her drowsiness, dilated pupils, and glossy eyes.

"No you may not. I have questions I want answered now."

Darla sat down on the sofa, trying to appear straight. It took all her concentration to speak at the right time. She felt her brother's eyes on her. She felt some fear if she was able to fool her parents, she might not be as convincing with her brother.

"I want to know where you were and what you have been doing since ten o'clock." Pastor Roberts ordered.

"I was talking with Kelley most of the time and I was upset over our talk, so I went for a drive."

"Darla, you know you are to call when delays come up. Mom and I have been worried sick." Scolded her father, though Darla was sure he suspected nothing wrong.

"I am sorry, Dad. I did not intend to upset you or Mother." She apologized, feeling lousy with her irresponsible actions.

"Go on to bed, you look done in. We will discuss this further in the morning." Her father agreed, softening toward his daughter.

It was a beautiful Saturday morning. After listening to her father's lecture on being home on time, she left her home for a morning of horseback riding.

"Wait up, Sis, I will ride with you." Bill said, as Darla mounted Princess. Darla patiently waited, as her brother saddled Cindy's horse.

"How do you feel this morning?" Bill asked.

"You looked out of it last night."

"Last night I was terribly tired, but this morning I am rested and I feel terrific." Darla assured with a gentle smile.

Bill and Darla rode the horse into the country, enjoying the quietness.

"Mom says you will get to graduate with Cindy's class."

"Yes, I have really crammed this semester; I cannot wait until next fall to begin college." Darla shared, excitedly.

"You are too young to be attending college next fall. You will only be seventeen, Sis." Bill reminded, disapproving.

"I will not be too young; age has nothing to do with maturity." Defended Darla, irritated with her brother's disapproval.

"Are you and Kelley planning to date again?" Asked Bill considerately, changing the subject.

"No, it is over between me and Kelley." She answered, wishing her brother would quit asking questions.

"I spoke with Kelley last week and he was too interested in your activities for his caring for you to have ended."

"Kelley feels the same, Bill, I have changed. I wish you; Mother and Dad could understand this. I like different types of people and I have different ideas and interests." Darla snapped.

"There is no need for you to become angry. I certainly have noticed your change." Bill said, taking hold of Princess's bridle, making his sisters horse stop.

"I would like to understand why you get so irritated at simple statements that never irritated you before. I want to understand why you pretend not to care for Kelley, when it is obvious that you do. I want to understand

165

why you are so unhappy, when you use to be the happiest person I have ever known. I care about you, Sis." Spoke Bill, with tenderness on his strong face.

"Thank you for your concern, Bill. Really, I am okay." Darla replied, calming her hostility.

"Why are you drinking?"

"Who said I drink?" Darla asked nervously, feeling threatened by his accusation.

"I could tell by the way you looked last night. Mom and Dad bought your being tired story, but I did not.

"I am going home; I was not drinking last night." Darla snapped.

"Let go of my bridle." She ordered, trying to pull it from her brother. Bill held the bridle firmly, as his face changed from concern to shock.

"If you were not drinking, then you were on drugs." He accused all tenderness for his sister gone.

"I did not say that." Shouted Darla feeling threatened by Bill invading her secrets, filling with anger toward him.

"This is why Mom and Dad did not suspect you because they could not smell alcohol, you were high on dope." Bill accused, shaking his head with disgust, and disbelief.

"If I ever catch you with any dope, I will break your neck and the person that gives it to you." Bill promised, glaring at his sister.

"You party, Bill, why are the rules different for you?" Darla argued.

"I drink occasionally, I am twenty-four and liquor is legal, dope is illegal." Spoke Bill, trying to remain rational.

"You party your way, and I will party my way. I do not pry into your activities and you have no right prying into mine. Now, let go of my horse." She insisted angrily, glaring at her brother.

Bill let go of Princess's bridle. Darla kicked her horse running her as fast as she could toward home. Reaching home, she jerked her saddle from her horse, allowing the saddle to fall to the ground, taking her anger out on the saddle.

Over the next several weeks, Darla was extremely careful. She eliminated party activities and she spent every free moment studying or riding her horse. She worried her brother would deliberately attempt to end her party nights, so when at home she went out of her way to avoid him.

Summer was nearing once again. Swimming and sunbathing at nearby lakes, with most present either drinking or smoking pot is how Darla and her friends would spend their Saturdays. Darla's new friends lived for Saturdays and although she had declined all party invitations since Bill became wise to her, she longed for activity.

Lying in the hot sun, with several of her friends surrounded by empty beer cans, Darla was smashed, this being her first party in sometime.

"Darla." Spoke Susie, fearful.

"Your dad and brother are here. You have to get out of here."

Darla raised her head up from the ground, looking in the direction Susie pointed.

"Do not worry Susie; they will go fishing on the other side of the lake." Darla said, laying her head back down, without a care in the world.

"We are out of here." Jeff, Don and Jacob said hurrying before they were caught involved in minor drinking.

"You guys are real tough guys." Scolded Susie disappointed in her friends.

"Get real, Susie. Darla's brother alone could take us three on." Jeff defended, gathering his things together.

"I am with them, Susie. If I get busted, my dad will kill me." Tina informed.

"Are you coming, Candy?"

"No, I am not a trader. Some friends you guys are, chickens." Candy added, furious with them.

"We are dead, Candy." Whispered Susie, as Pastor Roberts and Bill approached the girls.

"Darla would stick by us." Candy defended.

"I know she would. Otherwise, I would have been out of here with the others." Snapped Susie.

"Hello girls." Pastor Roberts greeted, with disapproval on his face.

"Hello Mr. Roberts." The girls greeted, nervously.

"Would one of you please tell me why my daughter is lying on the beach sleeping at one in the afternoon?" The girls looked at one another too frightened to speak.

"She is drunk, Dad." Bill said, disbelieving his eyes.

Pastor Roberts' face turned its reddest. He bumped his daughter's bare foot with his shoe to get her attention.

"Are you having fun?" Pastor Roberts asked, anger on his face, yet his voice remained controlled.

"I am having a blast." Darla answered with a smile, the booze in charge of her mind.

"Get your things, your party is over." Pastor Roberts ordered.

"You are spoiling our fun." Darla complained, staggering to her feet.

"I haven't just begun to spoil your so called fun." Her father informed, taking hold of her arm to steady her.

"I can walk by myself." Darla said stubbornly, as though a small child.

"I do not believe you can." Her father replied, steadying her.

"I have Darla's things, Dad." Bill informed.

"You girl's best not allow this to happen again or I may forget I am a Christian. I will be notifying both your parents." Pastor Roberts said, heartbroken over finding his daughter in such a state.

Candy and Susie were speechless as they watched Darla's father and brother assist her to the car.

Putting Darla in the back seat, she slept during her ride home.

Arriving at home, Bill assisted his father with his sister, taking her to her room to sleep off the booze.

"Mark, what is wrong with Darla?" Mrs. Roberts asked, hurrying to her daughter's side.

"She is drunk." He answered, putting his arm around his wife's shoulder to comfort her.

"Oh no, Mark." She spoke barely above a whisper, putting her hand over her mouth, appearing as though she was in shock.

Finally awaking from her morning and early afternoon of partying, Darla glanced around her room.

"Oh no ... " She spoke allowed, realizing she was in her own home. "How did I get here?" She silently wondered.

"Darla." Spoke her father sternly, looking his angriest.

"Yes Sir?" She questioned, as she neared her father, barely able to walk a straight line.

Her father took hold of her arm with an extra firm grip. He assisted her to a chair sitting her in it firmly, as though she was a small child being punished.

"Look around this room, Darla. You take a good look at each person and you think about all the times you have lied, deceived and caused pain to each one of us over the past several months." Mr. Roberts ordered.

"I cannot do this, Daddy." Darla refused, lowering her head as tears filled her eyes. Her father put his hand on her chin, raising her head.

"You will do as I say." He ordered, in his sternest tone.

Darla obeyed her father, fearful of the consequences if she did not. First, she looked at her cousin.

"Cindy, have you ever seen Darla partake of alcohol or drugs?" Mr. Roberts asked.

"No Sir." Cindy answered with tears in her eyes, feeling for her cousin.

"Have you ever seen Darla while she was under the influence of either?"

"Uncle Mark, I would rather not be involved in this. Please, may I be excused?" Cindy asked, with tears sliding down her cheeks.

"No babe, you may not, as cruel as this may seem, this is the only way I know to bring Darla back to her senses. Please answer my question."

"Yes." Cindy answered, barely above a whisper.

"When and where?"

"At the hamburger stand, the night you sent Bill looking for Darla." Cindy answered, she now unable to stop her tears, for snitching on her cousin.

"Dad, ask me, I will tell you. Please do not upset Cindy or anyone else." Darla pleaded, as she began to sob.

"But Darla, I have asked you in the past what was troubling you. Mom has asked you repeatedly, but you have not leveled with us once. We cannot believe what you say anymore. Therefore, what pain is caused or upsets is due to you and not anyone else."

"I will level with you now." She pleaded, desperately wanting to spare her family members of any further pain.

"Be quiet." Her father ordered.

"Cindy, had Darla been drinking or was her high from drugs?"

"I did not see what Darla took." Cindy replied, hesitating.

"What is your opinion, Cindy?"

"I smoked pot, Daddy. I talked with Kelley like I told you I did and I felt terrible, so I drove around in my car getting stoned, because I could not stand the pain I felt for hurting Kelley. After I was high, I felt good. I did not hurt and I could laugh again. I returned to the hamburger drive in and that was when Cindy saw me while I was high." Darla informed, telling on herself because she could not bear to look at her cousin wanting to defend her.

"Is that all you know, babe?" Pastor Roberts asked.

"Yes Sir." Cindy answered, wiping her tears away.

"You may be excused."

"Here, Dar." Cindy offered, kindly setting a box of Kleenex near her cousin, as she prepared to leave the room.

"Thanks. Cindy, I am sorry." Darla apologized, as she continued in her tears.

"I know." Replied Cindy then gladly left the room.

"Dad, why is Kelley here?" Darla asked, burying her face in her hands.

"Your dad asked me to be here Darla." Kelley said, answering his former girlfriend's question.

"I gladly came because I care deeply for you and I cannot bear to see you destroy yourself." He said.

"Brother Roberts, all I know is what Darla told me at her work a couple of months ago. She said she has learned to put her feeling for me aside, because she parties occasionally, drinking and smoking pot. She said when she is partying is the only time she is happy. Her reasoning she gave for her unhappiness is because of what happened to her at the park. She said she could not be the Darla we expect."

"Kelley, you have said enough." Darla said her face still buried in her hands, as she cried her hardest.

"Darla said she could not tell you or Sister Roberts how she really feels because she cannot bear to hurt you more than you have already been hurt."

"Oh, Darla ... " Mrs. Roberts started, going to her daughter's side, hugging her tightly, calming and soothing her.

"How could you think this way, Sweetheart?" Her mother asked.

"Because of the pain in your and Daddy's eyes since that terrible night. I thought if I could act okay, you could quit hurting." Darla explained, sobbing in her mother's arms.

"Sweetheart, we will always hurt when you hurt. This is just the way it is with parents. The worst pain of all pains for a parent is not to know why your child is hurting. If you do not know why, you cannot help them, or comfort them." Her mother assured, lovingly.

"I am so sorry, Mother." Darla said sobbing, hugging her mother's neck tightly.

"Me too, dear, I should have realized your hidden pain. Mothers are supposed to know these things."

"Kelley, thank you. We are forever indebted to you for stepping forward as you have." Spoke Mr. Roberts, shaking his hand and then giving him a hug as he walked Kelley to the door for his departure.

Darla had received the lecture of her life when awaking the next morning, sleeping off her consumption of alcohol and pot. For the remainder of the school year, she spent four weeks of every weekend home, having to participate in every family and church activity, leaving her little time to herself. The constant fellowship was healing Darla's deep wound, allowing her to share her feelings and closeness toward her family was once again developing.

"Darla, I have been accepted!" Susie shouted, hurrying toward her friend with a letter in her hand.

"I get to attend college in Springfield, Missouri!"

"This is fantastic!" Darla exclaimed.

"Maybe you will hear from the University today."

"I hope so." Darla replied, just as excited as her friend.

"If I receive my letter, we have to celebrate this weekend."

"How are we going to celebrate? You are grounded for two more weeks and your parents will not allow you out of their sight."

"My parents are taking Cindy to her parents for the weekend. I have to work tomorrow evening, so I am staying home and there just might be a way I can get away from my brother." Darla explained, hopeful

"I hope so."

"I had almost forgotten what it is like to have a party." Darla shared happily, with sparkles in her eyes.

Hurrying home from school, filled with excitement, Darla entered her bedroom and there it was a long white envelope from the university on her dresser top. Carefully opening the envelope, she read her letter of acceptance. Her heart seemed to skip a beat, as she felt so much joy and excitement. Turning her stereo on, Darla answered the ringing telephone.

"Sis, I will not be home until late because I am in San Diego on business. I plan to be on my way home by midnight. Remember to lock the doors when it gets dark."

"I will. Drive careful and I will see you in the morning." Darla replied.

Darla quickly called Susie. "I have been accepted at the university also!" Darla exclaimed.

"Way to go!"

"We have to celebrate. The party is on at my house and we will have the house until midnight." Darla informed, cheerfully.

Within the next couple of hours, Darla's stereo was filling her home with music, as her closest friends sat on the floor, passing around joint after joint and drinking wine.

"Darla, there is a good looking guy at the front door." Whispered Faye, worried the visitor might hear her.

"Do not leave him outside, invite him in." Susie suggested, in her forward, crazy acting way.

Darla went to the door, quietly checking through the peep whole.

"He is cool." She informed, unlocking the door.

"Hi." Darla greeted, politely. "Come in."

"Apparently I chose the wrong evening to visit." Kelley said.

"Excuse the mess, we are having a party. Would you like to join us?" Darla invited, with slurred speech and glossy eyes.

"This is not my idea of a party." Kelley answered in his calm, to the point manner.

"Dar, you did not tell us you invited guys." Susie joked.

"He was not invited."

"He is good looking." Faye remarked.

"Come on, don't bug him. He is straight, but he is cool." Darla defended, feeling for Kelley's uncomfortable position.

"He must be the reason Darla turns down every invitation to date." Karen said.

"She even turned down Jack Snider." Faye added.

"You turned Jack down, Dar?" Susie questioned, surprised.

"This is my mystery man, Kelley Peterson." Darla introduced, proudly.

"Here, have another joint." Darla offered to quiet her friends.

Lighting up a joint, she took a hit, and then handed it to her friends, as she joined Kelley on the sofa.

"May I ask why you are here?" Asked Darla, happily, as she lit a joint for herself.

"I wanted to see you and see how you are." Kelley answered, hesitant.

"I must be a bit of a shock for you tonight." Darla said, with a laugh.

"Dar, you are needed back at the park. The kids need you and you need them." Kelley said, becoming impatient with her foolishness.

"Do not put that on me, they forgot me a long time ago." She snapped.

"This is not true, you forgot them." He reminded.

"Do you enjoy giving me a hard time?" Darla asked, annoyed.

"I love you and I only want to make you happy." Assured Kelley, shocked by her accusation.

"Then stay out of my life. I do not want to remember you. You are even spoiling my fun at my own party, this is a real bummer."

"Have your fun." Kelley replied, getting up from the sofa, leaving her home.

The remainder of the night was no fun for Darla. She was glad when her friends had left for their homes. She lay on the floor, alone, listening to her stereo, with tears streaming down her cheeks, with her thoughts on Kelley until drifting off to sleep.

Bill returning home at one in the morning from his business trip could hear music coming from inside his home, as he neared the patio. Unlocking the backdoor, he stopped in his steps as he entered the family room. Glancing around the room at empty wine bottles, saucers that had served as ashtrays for pot smoking and a baggie with pot, Bill filled with rage.

"Wake up." Bill ordered, shaking his sister's arm forcefully.

"Stop it, Bill." She complained, barely aware of his presence.

Picking up his sister from the floor where she lay, he put her in the tub with her clothes and shoes still on. Turning the cold shower on full blast, he allowed the water to hit her in her face.

"Bill!" Darla yelled, attempting to stand.

Bill held her arms down, forcing her to remain in the cold water.

"Let me out of here." She yelled, trying to free herself.

Bill ignored his sister's wishes and comments, as though he could not hear her.

"I hate you for this!" She yelled, trying to shield her face, finding it impossible with her brother's strong grip on her.

"Bill, stop it!" She screamed repeatedly.

After several moments of yelling and screaming out her anger and hostility, which had replaced the love she once had in her heart, Darla felt empty inside. Her screaming ceased she began to cry. Her crying seemed to last forever. She cried over missing Kelley, failing her parents, being hateful to her brother and making a mess out of her life. She cried until she could cry no longer.

"Bill, I am freezing." Spoke Darla in a calm pleading voice, her hostility and anger gone for the first time in almost a year.

Turning off the shower, Bill placed a towel across his sister's shoulders, helping her to her feet.

"I do love you, Sis." Bill assured, compassionately.

"I know you do and I am sorry for everything I have done." Darla replied, hugging her brother lovingly.

CHAPTER 6

Darla slipped into a pair of bell-bottom jeans, a beige waist length halter-top exposing her tan shoulders and brown sandals. She brushed her dark, long, waist length hair, allowing it to flow freely down her back.

Entering the family room, intending to clean up from the party she had thrown the night before, Darla found the room already in order. Taking the telephone extension to her room, she telephoned Kelley's home.

"Good morning, God loves you." Kelley greeted.

"Good morning, this is Darla." She informed pleasantly.

"I would like to talk with you in regards to my rudeness last night. May I drive over?" She asked, filled with shame for her behavior.

"If you would rather I not come, I certainly understand." She quickly added, with flushed cheeks.

"I have no plans for the day. You may come, I will be waiting." Kelley answered, politely.

Darla discovered Bill in the front yard washing his car.

"I thought you were going to sleep all day." Bill said as his sister approached him, bringing a weak smile from her.

"Thank you for cleaning the family room, I did not intend to fall asleep before cleaning up." Said Darla nervously, knowing her brother was not happy with her partying actions.

Bill looked at his sister as though disgusted with her. With no comment, he continued to wash his car making Darla feel more uncomfortable.

"Bill, I am going to Dunes to visit Kelley, I owe him several apologies. I give you my word I will not party. I am truly sorry for taking advantage last night and throwing a party in Mom and Dad's home. All I can ask is that you trust me once more."

"Do not let me down, Sis." Warned Bill, his patience gone.

"If you do, I personally am going to deck you." He threatened.

"I cannot believe the nerve you have anymore. You are still grounded from Dad finding you drunker then a skunk and higher than a kite at the lake two months ago. The first opportunity you have alone, you throw a party in our parent's home. You have nerve I never dreamed of having, or you have become heartless." He accused sternly.

"Bill, do not say this. I have been a lot of terrible ways this year, but I am not heartless, I have feelings." Darla defended with watery eyes.

"We each know you have selfish feelings for yourself. How about others, are you sure you have feelings for others, Dar?" Bill asked, glaring at his sister as though daring her to produce proof of her statement.

"Yes, Bill, I do." Answered Darla, as her tears came suddenly, streaming down her face.

"I do not believe you. You have called my bluff one too many times, dear sister."

"So, are you going to ground me, Bill?" Darla asked, becoming annoyed with his lecture and mistrust, when she truly intended to set things right with Kelley and her parents on her own, not because she felt forced to.

Bill suddenly dropped the water hose. With anger on his face, he slapped Darla hard across her face, stunning her with his blow. She looked at her brother as though in shock, as her tears came more quickly. Bill had never laid a hand on her before now.

"Do not ever use me again, or Mom and Dad's home for your wrongdoings."

"I won't." Assured Darla, as her tears continued.

"Then start by changing your blouse and jeans. I personally do not see anything wrong with it, but Mom and Dad disapprove; you are even using me in your dress while they are away."

"I will go change." Darla agreed in her soft, calm voice.

Returning inside her home, Darla washed her face from her crying and changed her choice outfit. Removing her purse and car keys from her dresser, she left her home.

"I am going to Kelley's now." Darla informed, politely.

"Do not be late."

"I won't be." Darla agreed, with tenderness in her eyes and gentleness in her voice.

During her twenty-mile drive from Ragweed to Dunes, Darla reviewed her past several months of foolishness. She still was not willing to change her lifestyle completely, yet her thoughts on partying were over. She had played long enough and it was time she got herself completely together. No more hurting Kelley or her family, there had been enough pain and childish play.

"Hi." Kelley greeted, as he opened the front door.

"Hi." Darla greeted, with a gentle smile.

"Have a seat, please." Kelley offered, as he quickly removed his notebooks and schoolbooks from the sofa.

"My family is away for the weekend, also." He explained.

Darla made herself comfortable on the sofa, sitting straight and poised as a young lady, waiting patiently for Kelley to join her.

"You are much prettier when you are straight." Kelley said, sitting down on the sofa near Darla.

"Thank you." Darla replied, blushing with Kelley's never-ending kindness.

"What happened?" Kelley asked, gently pushing her long hair away from her face, noting a red mark on her cheek.

"My loving brother did not approve of my taking advantage of him or my parent's home last night. I pushed him past his patience tolerance this morning." Darla answered, blushing.

"I will not push him again." She added, with a soft laugh.

"I would not think that wise either, Bill almost makes three of you." Kelley agreed with a grin.

"I owe you so many apologies it is difficult to know where to begin. Perhaps I should begin with last night." Spoke Darla, in her slow, soft way, pausing, with tenderness showing on her young pretty face.

"I am sorry for the way I spoke to you. I said what I felt, but I had no right verbally to express those feelings, at least not the way I did and certainly not while I was high. I am sorry Kelley, for my behavior." Darla said, looking into Kelley's gentle eyes, he remaining silent and expressionless.

"I said what I said out of anger. My anger from my pain of wanting to be a part of you each time I would see you would become more intense. I do still love you, but like I told you in the past, I am different, I am ready to face my feelings for you now, but I am not ready to live a Christian life. A steady relationship between you and I would only work if I gave my all to Christianity." Darla shared, sincerely.

"I would not want us going steady unless you were a Christian, either." Kelley agreed.

"Now that you can deal with how you feel, is it possible that we have dinner dates or share occasional outings? This not being able to be friends or speaking rationally bothers me much more than us not going steady."

"What do you say we be friends and join me for lunch?" Kelley asked, politely.

"I would like to." Answered Darla with sparkles in her eyes, relieved for his forgiveness, acceptance and loyalty.

Kelley opened his car door for Darla, taking her hand in his as he led the way inside the restaurant. Darla felt proud to be sharing lunch with such a wonderful person.

"What were the results of your parents trying to get to the bottom of your upsets the evening I squealed on you?" Kelley asked.

"I never learned what prompted your dad to invite me over that evening."

"Oh … " Darla sighed, her face quickly reddening.

"I could not believe my Dad intended to interrogate you and Bill, as he did poor Cindy. If ever there was a time I wanted to hide and never show my face again, it was that evening." Darla confessed ashamed, taking her eyes from Kelley's and fidgeting with the straw in her soft drink.

"So? What happened?" Kelley asked impatiently, his curiosity aroused.

"Everything imaginable happened." Darla answered with a nervous laugh, her cheeks turning their reddest.

"My dad and Bill stumbled across me at Ragweed Lake. I had been partying with my girlfriends. I was completely out of my head when Dad and Bill discovered me. Besides being both drunk and high, I was sunbathing, wearing a bikini, which Dad made me burn." She shared with a nervous laugh.

"You are a crazy girl." Kelley laughed blushing with her, knowing how her parents felt with such dress.

"Dad took me home from the lake. When I opened my eyes, finding myself in my room wearing the bikini, I knew I was dead. Dad had also searched both my car and my room. He found two joints in my dresser drawer, the morning after you squealed on me." Darla said, smiling.

"While I was fully aware of everything, I was given another lecture, a paddling at sixteen years and ten months of age. In addition, I have two more weeks of grounding. I have had to attend every church and family activity, with no exceptions allowed." She shared.

"Good." Kelley replied, approving.

"You needed your family." He added.

"I needed them much more than I thought." Darla confessed.

"These past two months have been good for me. What rebellion I had left in me, I believe Bill slapped out of me this morning." She shared with a soft laugh.

"What anger and hostility I held unto bottled up inside me, Bill took care of also last night."

Kelley put his hand on Darla's chin, turning her face sideways, examining her face.

"I do not see a hand print from last night."

"Bill did not hit me last night. He rudely awoke me by putting me in the tub with the cold shower spraying in my face."

"Alright, Bill is okay." Kelley approved, laughing uncontrollably.

"Thanks a lot. I should have known you would find Bill's methods acceptable." Darla replied, with a tender smile.

"I screamed my lungs out, until all my anger was gone." She added.

"You screamed at Bill, and he didn't slap you last night?" Kelley asked, surprised.

"No he did not, poor guy." Darla confessed with a laugh.

"I am sure he made up for it this morning." Kelley said, with a grin.

"Yes, believe me I thought I was going to see stars for a few seconds." Darla confessed.

"This morning was the first time Bill ever hit me." She shared, with watery eyes.

Kelley took Darla's hand into his, with gentleness on his face.

"You have been through so much, Dar." Spoke Kelley, comforting her.

"As much as I dislike admitting this, most of my upsets were self- inflicted."

"Self is usually our worse enemy." Kelley replied, letting loose of Darla's hand as the waitress arrived with their lunch.

"Guess what?" Darla asked excitedly, as they enjoyed their lunch.

"What?" Kelley asked, giving his luncheon date his full attention.

"I have been accepted at the University in Springfield, Missouri." Darla said, happily.

"Missouri? That is far from home."

"I know, but it is supposed to be pretty there. One of my girlfriends will be attending also. Besides, San Diego is too close to home, I want to really be on my own when I attend college." She shared happily.

"Your parents are allowing you to attend college that far from home?"

"I have not asked yet." Darla confessed, with a smile.

"I did not think so." Laughed Kelley, knowing how protective her parents were of her.

Darla felt great for the first time in many months, as she drove back to Ragweed. It had been a long hard struggle, but she was back in charge of herself. Her sparkle was once again in her eyes. Her pleasant, calm nature had returned and her face glowed with happiness. She had not re-dedicated her life to the Lord, but the Darla her family had missed and she had longed to be was back.

Straightening the house, making sure everything was in its proper place, Darla waited anxiously for her parents return from their weekend get away with Cindy. Within the next few hours, she would be asking her parent's permission to attend college out of state.

Hearing a car in the drive, Darla checked through the window to see who had arrived. Filled with excitement, she hurried outside to greet her parents and cousin.

"Hello Mother and Dad." Darla greeted, hugging their necks.

"How was your visit?" She inquired politely, assisting her father with their luggage.

"It was nice and we had a good time."

"How was your weekend, Dear?" Her mother asked, sitting down on the sofa, leaning her head back, weary from their long drive.

"It was different." Darla answered, her checks flushed.

"I had lunch with Kelley yesterday." She shared with a pleasant smile.

"Good, Kelley is nice young man." Her mother approved, surprised at her daughter agreeing to lunch, yet pleased.

"There are not many guys like Kelley." Darla agreed.

"We have not discussed my attending college next fall, I would like to now, if you are not too tired from your drive."

"Mom and I feel you should wait a year to begin college."

"Why?" Questioned Darla surprised with their wishes.

"We feel you are too young with graduating from high school a year early. You may start next year."

Darla looked at first her father, then her mother, pleadingly.

"I had planned to begin college this fall, Dad. I will have an entire year wasted if I have to wait." She complained lightly.

"Just think of this year as a year of maturing before going off to college." Her father suggested, not budging in his decision.

"We realize San Diego is only a two hour drive away, but with your actions of wild parties and fellowshipping with a wilder group of kids then we ever thought you would, has brought us to realize you are not mature enough to go off to college at this time."

Darla was silent, as her parent's mistrust in her seemed like a knife cutting in her heart. She had failed her family and herself by giving in to a way of rebellion.

"I know your decision is right, Dad. I have not been trust worthy, so I will prove to you and Mother my maturity over this coming year."

"I honestly hope you fulfill what you say, dear. Dad and I are getting too old to deal with these crazy teen years." Her mother informed.

"May I ask one more question in regards to college?" Darla asked, hesitant.

"Sure Babe." Pastor Roberts answered.

"I do not want to attend college in San Diego." Darla began slowly, as she witnessed her parent's expressions change from calm to concern.

"I want to attend in Springfield, Missouri. I have been offered a full scholarship there." She quickly explained.

"This is out of the question. You will attend close to home." Mrs. Roberts ordered.

"Susie will be starting in Springfield this fall and we want to share an apartment together. I would really like to join her next year, Mother." She shared, in her gentle way.

"You would have to prove yourself before I would agree to you going out of state to school. Under no circumstances will I agree to an apartment, even a year from now. You will stay in the dorm." Her father informed.

"Yes Sir." Darla agreed politely, yet disappointed.

"You attending college and being independent, living on your own, has no connection. You will attend college under my and Dad's supervision, to be trained to go out into the world and become self-supportive. When you reach the point when you are trained in your career and become self-supportive, we then and only then will agree to you having an apartment." Mrs. Roberts explained, patiently.

"Now ... " Sister Roberts began, with a weary smile.

"May we please not discuss college for at least a year? I am getting a terrible headache."

"Yes Ma'am." Darla answered, with an understanding smile.

With summer school completed, Darla quit her part-time job at the hamburger drive-in, working full-time at the hospital as a nursing assistant. She loved her job and the satisfaction she received from helping others in need was worth more to her than her paycheck.

Kelley visited Darla often while home from college on summer break. She enjoyed his friendship, but she held herself back from becoming seriously involved. She appreciated Kelley never pressuring her into making their relationship more than a casual, boyfriend/girlfriend, relationship.

"Dar ... " Cindy began, as she passed her cousin the salad bowl.

"Do not forget the girl's will be by after dinner to try their dresses on." Reminded Cindy, excited over her upcoming wedding.

"Oh, I forgot." Darla replied, slowly.

"You did not make other plans for this evening did you?" Cindy asked, her excitement quickly fading.

"Yes, but I can undo them." Darla assured, pleasantly.

"Kelley is supposed to pick you up in an hour." Mr. Roberts reminded.

"I know."

"Dear, I trust you are not making light of Kelley's friendship. You know how he feels toward you." Mother cautioned.

"I assure you Mother, I am appreciative of Kelley's friendship and sensitive to his feelings." Darla replied, relieving her mother of her concerns.

"He is my dearest friend." She added.

"This is Moms point, Kelley is your dear friend in your eyes, but in Kelley's heart, he wants you to become his wife someday, so wise up Sis." Bill informed with a chuckle, bringing smiles to his families face.

"We both are aware of one another's feelings, Bill. We are completely honest with one another. We also respect one another's right to his and her individual feelings, therefore but out, dear Brother." Darla ordered, bringing laughter from her family by her ability to hush her older brother.

"I cannot wait until you leave for college." He snapped, pretending to be annoyed with his sister.

"Son, Mom and I were wondering ourselves, when you are going to get married and get your own place. We are beginning to think you intend to become a permanent fixture." Spoke Mr. Roberts, shocking Bill, bringing laughter from all present, except Bill.

"Thank you, Daddy." Darla said, with a soft laugh.

"Thank you, Daddy." Bill mumbled, as he got up from the table to answer the doorbell.

"You are welcome." Mr. Roberts whispered, winking at his daughter.

"Dar, come see what Kelley brought." Bill instructed.

"Oh Kelley, he is beautiful!" Darla exclaimed, taking a beautiful Irish Setter puppy from Kelley into her arms lovingly.

"What do you intend to do with a dog, babe?" Her father asked, as Darla brought the puppy to the dining room, followed by Bill and Kelley.

"Love him."

"Oh, Dar, he is so cute." Cindy sided, leaving the table to pet the puppy.

"Daddy, please? Kelley got him for me for my birthday. Please Daddy?"

"What do you say, Daddy?" Bill asked, mocking his sister and tormenting his father, bringing a chuckle from their father.

"Babe, when you are away at college next year, who is going to take care of your horse and dog?"

"I doubt Bill will be married for some time, so he will not mind caring for them." Darla teased.

"You have a point, Babe. I guess you are elected, Bill." Their father informed with a grin.

"You always get what you want." Bill accused.

"Most of the time I get what I want." Darla answered, with a soft laugh.

"If you ever manage to corral my sister, Kelley, I warn you, she does not play fair."

"Bill." Darla scolded blushing, hoping to quiet her brother with his forward talk.

"Gotcha!" Bill said with a boyish grin, he now having the last word, bringing silence, yet smiles from his family.

"Mom, I have a date, I will see you later. Thanks for dinner." Spoke Bill politely, giving his mother a kiss goodbye.

With Kelley away at college, Darla filled her empty evenings after work making Cindy's wedding gown, bride's maid, and maiden-of honor gowns. With working so closely with Cindy on her wedding plans, Darla often wondered what her future held for her, with her completion of college, in regards to marriage.

"Cindy, who is Dan having for his best man?" Darla asked, as the girls drove toward the church for the wedding rehearsal.

"Kelley."

"Kelley?" Darla questioned, surprised.

"I am sorry, Dar, I thought you knew." Cindy apologized.

"I hope you being maiden-of-honor and Kelley being best man will not be a problem for you."

"Of course not, I am sure Kelley and I will play our roles quite well." Darla assured, with a pleasant smile.

Darla was surprised to find herself excited, as Kelley escorted her down the aisle during rehearsal.

"I think I enjoy escorting you, Miss Darla." Kelley said, as she walked with her arm through his, making Darla blush.

"This is simply a rehearsal for Cindy and Dan's wedding." Darla reminded with a gentle smile, attempting to conceal the excitement she also felt toward Kelley escorting her.

"Aye, but fate is on our side, you will see." Kelley replied with a boyish grin, causing Darla to laugh, disturbing the rehearsal and causing everyone to look at the young couple.

"I am sorry." Darla apologized, her face flushed.

Returning home after rehearsal, Darla went to the corral. Climbing on the fence, she sat down petting the horses as they came toward her. She thought of how handsome Kelley was and how he seemed to know her every mood and need.

"Would you like some company?" Bill asked, as he approached with his latest girlfriend.

"Sure." Darla answered, pleasantly.

"Hello Karen."

"Hello Darla." Karen greeted.

"It is pretty back here with all the trees." She added.

"I think so too and I love it here." Darla shared, happily.

"I hear you and Kelley are the talk of Cindy's wedding rehearsal." Bill said, with a pleased smile.

"Yes, those gossipy church women could not wait to spread the news. Fill me in, what about me and Kelley?" Darla asked with a gentle smile, bringing laughs from Bill and Karen.

"Some seem to think you and Kelley will be next to stand before the preacher."

"Perhaps these people know something that I am not aware of. I have four years of college to get through before I say, "I do" to anyone."

"Are you sure you want to gamble? Four years is a long time to keep one wondering. A lot can happen in that amount of time." Bill cautioned.

"I was just asking myself this question and I presently do not have an answer." Darla replied, with a sigh.

"May I give my opinion?" Bill asked, considerately.

"Yes."

"I do not believe you should wait much longer without having an understanding between yourself and Kelley, he is bound to be growing impatient."

"Thank you, Bill. I will think on what you have said."

Darla's year of waiting to begin college seemed to fly by. With the dinner table set, Darla joined her parents at the table, their dinner hour seemed terribly quiet since Cindy had married and Bill seldom coming home until late.

"Babe, Mom and I feel you have more than proven your maturity to attend college out of state. You have become quite a responsible young lady over the past year. We are proud of you." Mr. Roberts informed.

"Thank you!" She exclaimed, leaving her chair, giving both her parents a tight hug and a kiss.

"We do have conditions." Darla's father said as she returned to her seat, bubbling with happiness.

"Yes Dad?" Darla asked, her eyes dancing with sparkles and her face aglow with happiness.

"By no means will you drive that far. You will leave your car home and Mom will fly to Springfield with you, and get you settled. You are to return home for Christmas and summer breaks, but no apartment. Do we have a deal?"

"Yes Daddy, we have a deal."

"Dad and I are visiting Aunt Nellie next week. The following weekend you and I will leave for Missouri. I want you to have plenty of time being settled before school begins and dad has you enrolled already." Her mother said, happy for her daughter's happiness.

Darla wished it were Friday. She untied her slightly muddy nursing shoes just inside the front door. It had been a long hard workweek.

Hearing her parent's voices, she thought it best to greet them before starting her shower. Leaving the family room, starting toward the front room, she froze in her tracks at her parent's tones.

"Mary, we owe Darla the facts." Her father stated, irritated.

"Darla is eighteen, Mark. We have made it through all these years without her knowing of her adoption." Her mother disagreed.

"We will tell her when we return from Nellie's."

"I am not sure Darla is ready for this." Cautioned Mother upset.

Darla, stunned by her newly discovered information, quickly and quietly went to her room. "I cannot be adopted." She thought repeatedly in her mind, as she showered and dressed for the evening.

"I did not hear you come in, Dear." Her mother said, as she entered her daughter's room, her eyes red from her crying earlier.

"How was work?" She asked, in her gentle loving way.

"It was tiring." Darla answered, pleasantly.

"Mother, I realize you and dad will be leaving on your trip soon, would you mind terribly if I do not see you off? I am already late."

"No, we do not mind."

"Tell Daddy bye for me, love you." Darla said giving her mother a hug and a kiss good-bye, then hurried from her room.

Backing her car out of her drive, Darla began trembling, as she heard her parent's conversation repeatedly in her mind. She had lied to her mother, she had no plans for the evening, yet she could not bear to look her parents in the eyes, after overhearing their conversation.

With nearly an hour driving around town aimless, Darla stopped at a payphone calling Kelley's apartment in San Diego, shaking from head to toe.

"Hello, have you prayed today?"

"Maybe, have you?" Darla asked in her gentle way.

"Prayer is the way I begin each day. How are you, Miss Roberts?"

"I have been better." Darla answered, hesitating.

"Kelley, if you haven't any plans this evening, I would like to drive up. I could use a good friend and you are my first choice."

"Come on up."

Darla stopped at a liquor store that sold to minors and she purchased a bottle of wine for the first time in nearly a year. She drove toward San Diego, drinking continuously, as she drove, her body beginning to feel numb and her vision blurry. By the grace of God, she made it to Kelley's apartment safely.

Barely able to walk, Darla climbed the stairs to Kelley's apartment with her tears now streaming down her checks. Leaning against the wall to steady her body, she knocked on Kelley's door and then put her face in her hands sobbing.

"Darla, what is wrong?" Kelley asked compassionately, putting his arm around her shoulders, drawing her close to him. Raising her head up and removing her hands from her face, he sighed, irritated

"You have been drinking." He scolded. "Let's get you inside."

Walking Darla to his sofa, he patiently allowed her to cry on his shoulder, as he kept his arm around her, comforting her.

"Darla, what is wrong?" He questioned again.

"I do not have any parents." She answered between sobs.

"You what, what happened to your parents?" Kelley asked he now upset also.

"I do not know."

Kelley rubbed his head wearily, becoming frustrated with her intoxicated state.

"I will make some coffee." He informed, getting up from her side, irritated with her actions.

Darla continued to cry while Kelley remained in the kitchen calming his emotions until the coffee was finished brewing.

"Here, drink some coffee."

"I do not like coffee." Darla refused, with childish behavior.

"I do not care whether you like it, drink this." He ordered, putting the cup to her lips, assisting her in steadying the cup.

"What is the problem with your parents?" He asked, as Darla regained control of her crying.

"I am adopted, I heard my parents talking. They plan to tell me before I leave for college." Her tears continued.

"You are adopted, so what if you are adopted, why the drinking and the crying?"

"I do not know what to do. I love the parents I have; I do not want to know of any others." Darla answered, once again wiping her tears.

"You go on with your life, Brother and Sister Roberts raised you, this is the important issue."

Kelley listened, encouraged, and comforted Darla until the hours grew late then drove her home.

Darla awoke early with her news of her adoption tugging at her. Slipping out from under her covers, she opened her drapes, admiring the beauty of the sun rising.

Enjoying a warm leisurely bath, she lay in the tub searching for a solution, as not to learn any details of her adoption. She was happy and content and it was not necessary for her father to undo her place in the only family she had known. He had no reason, as far as she was concerned, to tell her of her adoption. She decided she would not hear anymore of her adoption.

Getting out of the tub, Darla dressed quickly into a pair of cut-offs, short sleeve sweatshirt, and tennis shoes. She had only one answer to avoid her father's intended conversation with her. She would not be present when he returned from his trip.

Darla called the hospital, informing her employer she must leave right away for college, apologizing for her short notice.

Quickly thumbing through her clothes, she organized her clothing for her year away at college. She quietly filled suitcases, pushing them under her bed when filled.

"Dar … " Spoke Bill, as he tapped on his sister's closed door.

"Come in."

"Kelley is here to see you."

"Would you please send him in?" Darla asked, as she secretly emptied her desk.

"Sure, I will see you this evening, Sis."

"Bye, have a good work day." Darla said, pleasantly.

"Good morning, Kelley." Darla greeted, with a nervous smile.

"Good morning."

"I am sorry about last night; it seems I am constantly apologizing to you."

"I am just glad I was there for you, Dar." Kelley replied, kindly as he glanced around her room.

"Darla, what are you planning?" He questioned, concerned.

Darla did not answer; she quickly and quietly continued preparing her things for her departure.

"Darla, do you plan to leave before your parents return?"

"I am preparing my things for when I leave for college." She answered, avoiding Kelley's direct question.

"I pray that someday you will quit running. You fight your feelings for me and now you plan to run from your parents because of discomfort to you." Kelley scolded.

"I just want to leave, having my parents, my real parents, Kelley and nothing short of that. As for you, the best thing I can do is get out of your life and stay out, so you can find a nice Christian girl."

Kelley put his arms around Darla loosely.

"You keep forgetting I have God on my side and I live by faith." Kelley reminded, looking down in to Darla's eyes, with gentleness.

"Write me and let me know how you are doing. Do be careful." He cautioned.

"I will." Darla replied with a relaxed smile, he setting her quickly at ease.

With Kelley on his way to San Diego and Bill at work, Darla quickly carried out her plan.

Withdrawing her savings from the bank, she rented a small U-Haul trailer. Arriving home, she quickly loaded the U-Haul with her necessities, bathed Sam, her Irish Setter and then entered her parent's bedroom, placing a note on their dresser top.

Dearest Mother and Daddy:
Sorry I had to leave without saying goodbye. I cannot bear to wait for
your return hearing of my adoption. You are the only parents I care to
know. You both are the greatest. I will be fine. I will stay with Susie and
share the living expenses from my savings. I promise to study hard.
Love,
Your daughter, Darla

Closing her parent's bedroom door, she went to the kitchen placing a note on the table.

Bill,
I will be away for the weekend. Sam is with me. Do not worry.
Love,
Darla

Driving as fast as the small trailer and speed limit would allow, Darla's heart seemed to pound harder, as she worried someone would see her leaving, putting a stop to her plans. She knew legally she was safe because she was eighteen. The guilt she felt for taking off on her own and breaking most every rule her father had set in regards to attending college was terrible, yet there was excitement within her as she ventured out on her own.

With two long days and nights of non-stop driving, Darla entered the city of Springfield, Missouri. Her heart leaped with excitement, as she observed the beautiful colored downtown lights, they were beautiful as they stood out against the dark night. Opening her letter from Susie, she carefully studied the map her girlfriend had sent with directions to her home.

Parking her car in front of a cute house, Darla wearily got out of her car. Knocking on the door, she heard music playing and the shuffle of feet, as a shadow neared the door.

"Darla!" Susie exclaimed excitedly, giving her friend a tight hug.

"You came early. This is great! Is your mom with you?" She asked.

"No, I drove. I would like to take you up on your offer instead of me staying in a dorm, if you still have room." Darla informed.

"Yes, of course, this is great!"

"Guys, this is my new roommate, Darla Roberts, from Ragweed, California."

"Hi." The two young men greeted, as they sat sipping their beer.

"Darla, this is Phil, our neighbor. This is Jerry, Phil's roommate and my boyfriend."

"It is nice to meet both of you." Darla greeted, with a pleasant smile.

"You drove from California by yourself? Boy, your parents must be liberal." Phil said sipping his beer.

"Darla's parents liberal?" Susie laughed at Phil's thoughts.

"Darla's parents are extremely un-liberal, her dad is a minister. Darla is simply strong-willed." Susie explained.

"Do you plan to tell all my secrets my first night?" Darla asked politely, yet secretly hushing her intoxicated girlfriend.

"Would you like a beer?" Phil asked, politely.

"No, thank you." Darla answered, with a gentle smile.

"I forgot I have a friend in my car. May I bring him in?" Darla asked, politely.

"You brought a guy with you?" Susie asked as though in shock.

"No, silly, I brought my Irish Setter, Sam." Darla answered with a soft laugh over Susie's confused expression.

"Oh, sure, I forgot you said you wanted to bring him." Susie said.

Returning inside with Sam devotedly at her side, Darla handed Susie a gift-wrapped box.

"This is a little something from the gang back home."

"Thank you." Susie replied, deeply touched by her friend's thoughtfulness, as she opened the gift.

"It is a pound of grass!" Susie exclaimed.

"It is Colombian Gold." Darla informed, pleased with her friend's happiness.

"Thanks Darla. Let's party." Susie suggested, excitedly.

"I am all for that." Phil agreed.

The four young adults did as Susie suggested with the stereo blaring they smoked pot. Darla was laughing, joking and flying high with her girlfriend and new friends and she loved it!

"So, your dad is a minister. This is far out." Phil remarked, now sitting closer to Darla, as he passed her a joint.

"Yes, he is a good minister too." Darla informed, in her relaxed carefree mood.

"Darla, how can you speak so highly of your father?" Susie asked, as though disbelieving her ears.

"Aren't you proud of your father?" Darla asked in her soft, gentle, happy way.

"Of course, but your dad is too strict. He was always on your case and so was your mother."

"They were only on my case because I have good parents, Susie." Darla exclaimed happily, with a radiant glow on her face from her high.

"Remember when we all went to the lake and you got caught?' Susie asked, laughing hysterically.

"That was not funny; I paid dearly for that party that you threw." Darla reminded, blushing.

"If I remember correctly, you were not laughing then." She added, with a secretive smile.

"I would like to hear about it." Phil said, curious about Susie's new, attractive roommate.

"You guys know Darla and I are from a small desert town. Well, in the spring, a group of us went to different lakes most every Saturday, we would party, and occasionally Darla joined us. This particular Saturday,

Darla was really down, so she really partied!" Susie laughed, enjoying telling her story.

"Then my dad found me, he took me home and I got grounded. End of story, guys." Darla said, lighting up another joint.

"No, no, no, Darla." Susie teased, laughing.

"Darla, this is your life!" She laughed, determined to finish her story.

"Great. I can see it is going to be a riot rooming with you." Darla replied, with a soft laugh, blushing.

"So, Darla had partied heavily, you girls were at the lake, and ... " Phil encouraged, siding with Susie.

"So, Darla is lying in the sun, flying high, without a care in the world. Then her dad and big brother arrive. I am talking B-I-G brother like over six foot."

"Then Susie freaked out." Darla interrupted, laughing.

"I would have also." Phil sided.

"Didn't you freak?' He asked.

"No, I knew how to handle them." Darla answered pleasantly with a sweet smile.

"She did not freak, Phil." Susie informed, excitedly.

"I was going into hysterics, telling Darla her dad and brother was there. Darla raised her head very causally, looked toward her dad and said, 'Do not worry Susie, they will go away.' Then she lies back down, sunbathing."

"Did her brother and dad go away?" Jerry asked, doubting his question.

"No, they headed toward us. I was telling Darla, 'Your dad is coming.' like I was a crazy person. Darla said 'Do not worry about it.' as she remained laying in the sun with her eyes closed.

"I bet he was one angry man." Jerry said, laughing.

"Darla's dad was furious! He asked her if she was having fun. Darla remained calm and cool, answering, 'I am having a blast!'" Susie exclaimed.

The group roared with laughter, each picturing a scene of the incident in his and her separate stoned minds.

"Darla's dad said, 'Get your things because your party is over.' Darla began pouting as though she were a small child, telling her father he was spoiling our fun." Susie shared, sending the group into hysterical laughter once again for several long minutes.

"Oh." Susie sighed, holding her aching stomach from excessive laughing.

"Were there any guys in your group?" Phil asked, digging to learn more about Darla.

Darla looked away from Phil, allowing Susie to answer his question. She was not impressed by his curiosity of her.

"Sure, sometimes, we each had our boyfriends." Susie answered, noting Phil's curiosity also, remaining loyal to her girlfriend.

"I believe I will crash, Susie." Darla said standing up and excusing herself.

Darla left her girlfriend, Jerry, and Darla's too curious admirer Phil, to themselves.

Awake bright and early, Darla pulled her dark waist length hair back in a barrette, slipped into a pair of jeans and a violet under shirt style top, exposing her thin, tan arms and then leaving the house, she unlocked the U-Haul trailer.

"Good morning." Phil greeted, approaching her.

"Good morning." Darla greeted, with a pleasant smile.

"I am surprised you are up so early, with having a late night."

"I am use to tending to my horse early each morning. I guess some habits are hard to break." Darla replied in her pleasant way as she began removing her things from the U-Haul.

"Let me give you a hand with that." Phil offered, taking the heavy box from Darla, their eyes meeting and Darla really seeing him for the first time.

Turning away from Phil quickly, returning to the U-Haul, Darla felt attracted to Phil. She had not really noticed him the night before.

"This is a beautiful desk." He complimented, as he closely inspected the carvings.

"Thank you, my dad made it for me, so if anything happens to it, I am dead." Darla shared proudly, as she and Phil carried the desk inside the house.

With the U-Haul emptied, Phil helped himself to a beer from Susie's refrigerator.

"I wonder where Susie is." Darla voiced.

"She is next door. She spent the night with Jerry."

"Oh." Darla said, surprised.

"I was not aware Susie and Jerry are so close." She added quickly, blushing over her friend's liberal lifestyle.

"Susie and Jerry are just good friends." Phil explained.

"I had best turn the trailer in." Darla informed pleasantly, changing the subject.

"Do you mind if I go with you for the ride?"

"No. In fact, I would appreciate your company. I haven't the slightest idea how to find my way around."

Driving carefully, Darla followed Phil's directions to the nearest U-Haul office.

"I like your car." Phil complimented.

"Is this another gift from your dad?" He asked.

"Thank you. This was not a gift, in my family one does not receive cars for gifts; you work and buy your own." She explained pleasantly.

To her surprise, Darla had enjoyed her morning with her new neighbor, Phil. Returning from the shower, Darla slipped into a soft delicate dress and dress shoes. Checking the wanted ads carefully, she circled her choices for employment. She was sure her parents would be furious with her living alone with Susie. She intended to be prepared to prove her independence and she being responsible to make her own way. She knew it was just a matter of days before she would hear from them and she sincerely intended to have a job before speaking with them.

Darla spent the entire afternoon seeking evening employment that would not interfere with her classes or study time. Applying for each suitable position in the classified, she ended her day with no job prospect. By the end of the week, desperate, she took the only job not needing years of experience. She waited tables in a very elegant cocktail lounge, working four hours each weekday evening. Her co-workers and customers were nice and the tips were great. She disliked taking the job, knowing her parents would not approve if they found out, yet it fit her needs. She hoped sincerely, that they never would.

After a long week of working at her new job, and settling in with Susie, Darla was ready for some enjoyment.

Dressed in jeans, a delicate tailor-look blouse and hiking boots, she picked up her lightweight jacket and left her room.

"All ready to leave?" Phil asked, waiting on the sofa with a beer in his hand, as usual.

"Yes, I am. I cannot wait to go hiking in the Ozarks."

Phil put his arm around Darla's shoulders as he drove away from the city toward the beautiful mountains. The many green trees and grassy green hills along the highway were so beautiful. The scenery was a nice refreshing sight compared to the flat, dry desert land in her hometown.

"What does your preacher dad think of you being a cocktail waitress?" Phil asked, drinking a beer and smoking a cigarette as he drove.

"I am hoping my parents never find out." Answered Darla honestly, blushing with a weak smile.

"This is what I thought." Phil confessed with a laugh.

"This far away from your parents, I am sure you will be able to do most anything without them knowing."

"This is my train of thought." Darla said.

Holding Darla's hand, Phil led the way as they climbed to the top of an extremely high hill overlooking a valley.

"It truly is beautiful here." Darla said admiringly, trying to take in all the beauty that surrounded her.

"I would love to be a hermit living up here getting stoned and enjoying nature. This would definitely be a trip." Phil said.

"Yes, it would." Darla agreed, silently taking in all the beauty that surrounded her.

The young couple spent the entire day hiking and smoking pot. Darla had never experienced as beautiful a high or time in her life. As darkness fell, the mountain air grew chilly. Flying high, Darla snuggled close to Phil, as they sat around the campfire she and Phil had built to warm them. In silence, the couple stared into the fire as they each began coming down from their high.

"You are shivering. I have a sleeping bag in my car. I could go down and get it." Phil offered, rubbing her arms to warm them.

"No thank you. It is terribly late already. I think we should get back."

"You do not want to camp overnight? We can if you would like, I think it would be fun."

"You and I staying the night together would not be right." Darla refused standing, ready to leave.

Phil put the campfire out, without another word about staying. Driving back to the city, Phil refilled his pot pipe, renewing his high, appearing disappointed in Darla for calling an end to their evening.

Each day, Phil checked in at Darla's home when not at work at his summer job. He was becoming a big part of her life and it was fun to be with him.

Darla and Susie cooked steaks out on the grill while Jerry and Phil went to the store for beer.

"Darla, Jerry asked me to move in with him this evening and I told him I would. I hope you will not mind. I will continue to pay my part of the rent, so I can come back if Jerry and I go our separate ways." Susie shared.

"Of course I do not mind." Darla answered.

"What about you and Phil?"

"What do you mean?" Darla asked, slowly.

"Now that I will be with Jerry, you may have Phil move in with you." Susie suggested.

"Susie, I do not love Phil." Darla protested, slowly.

"Who says you have to love another to have a good time? Enjoy a good time while you can because we only live once. Have fun, Dar, our parents do not know what we do, so loosen up. Just be and do what you, Darla Roberts wants and forget what people expect from you." Replied Susie, sure of her advice.

"Besides, everyone lives together before marrying now." She added.

"Darla, your dad is on the telephone." Phil informed from the backdoor.

"I will be right there."

"Oh no, good luck." Susie remarked.

"I knew this day would come sooner or later." Darla sighed, her heart pounding faster.

"Would you like a cold beer?" Phil asked, as she stocked the refrigerator with beer.

"A coke please, thank you." Receiving the coke from Phil, Darla went to the telephone.

"Hello."

"This is Dad, Darla." Her father said anger in his voice.

"Hello Dad." Darla replied, nervously.

"What on earth got into you?"

"I explained why I left." She answered, her cheeks reddening.

"You did not explain anything, you left a note."

"Daddy, my intentions were not to hurt you or Mother. I felt the note would be easier on all of us, then my verbally telling you and Mother."

Overhearing Darla's conversation of her abundance of love and concern for her parents, Phil went to her side to comfort her.

Sitting on the breakfast bar facing Darla, Phil took her hand in his pulling her closer to him, as he looked into her eyes, silently giving her support. Returning his look, Darla felt warmth and comfort.

"You at least should have called, telling us you had a safe trip. We have been worried sick over you. We would have called you a week ago, but Susie's telephone number is unlisted and her parents were out of town until today. We even had to get your telephone number from Susie's parents."

"You are right, Dad. I should have called. I was not aware the number is unlisted, I apologize." Darla said, respectfully.

"Did you have a safe trip?" He questioned his anger calming with concern in his voice.

"Yes, I did."

"Dear, do you still intend to stay with Susie?" Mrs. Roberts asked, on the extension.

"Yes, Mother." Darla answered nervously, glancing at Phil's comforting eyes for more support.

"I am doing fine, Mother. I have a part-time job in the evenings, so I make enough to pay my living expenses and I still have most of my savings." She added quickly.

"When will you have time for your studies?"

"I will have plenty of time for studying. I only work four hours in the evening and my weekends are free."

"Darla, you are making a big mistake not staying at the dorm like you were told." Her mother scolded.

"I assure you, I am fine. I will continue to be fine and I will not let you or Dad down." Darla assured, respectfully.

"I certainly hope not, I am becoming too old for let downs from my daughter." Her mother replied, though her voice seemed to soften.

"Who was the young man that answered the telephone when I called?" Mr. Roberts asked.

"He is our neighbor, Phil, we are having a cookout." She answered carefully.

"I trust you and Susie are wiser, keeping your neighbors outside your home here on out." Her father cautioned.

"Yes Daddy, we will." Darla agreed with a gentle smile, glancing at Phil.

"Do you need me to fly up and help you get settled, dear?" Her mother asked, in her loving way.

"No, this is not necessary. I am already settled and I am working full-time for the next two weeks until fall semester begins."

"Is there anything you need, Babe?" Her father asked.

"Dad, I do not need anything, I am fine and I love it here." She assured.

"You and Mother quit worrying, please." She added, with a proud smile over her parent's way.

"Okay." Her father finally agreed, with a sigh.

"If you need us in anyway, please call, Babe. We are always here for you." He added.

"Thank you, Daddy. I promise I will call if needed." Appreciated Darla, deeply touched.

"Dar, the steaks are done." Susie informed, as she entered through the backdoor.

"Mother, Daddy, I had better let you go." Darla suggested, politely.

"You are going to have an expensive telephone bill." She added.

"Okay dear, we love you." Her mother said.

"I love you too, Mother."

"Oh Babe, Kelley stopped by." Her father informed, sounding pleased.

"Kelley? What did he want?" Darla asked curiously, now taking her eyes from Phil's eyes.

"He was concerned about you and he would like for you to write him. He asked me to tell you hello for him."

"Tell Kelley I appreciate his concern and please inform him I am a terrible letter writer, but I will try." Replied Darla touched by his thoughtfulness.

Putting the telephone down, Darla's eyes did not return to Phil's eyes. The mention of Kelley's name now made her feel uncomfortable alone in Phil's presence.

"Would you like another beer, Phil?" Darla asked kindly as she opened the refrigerator.

"Sure." He answered, though silently noting Darla rejecting him.

Darla enjoyed attending college and her studies were going well. She enjoyed being her own boss, making her way in the world. College and her part-time job had brought many new and exciting friends into her life. She kept extremely busy with classes, studies and work during the week. She spent her weekends going on outings and resting from her busy week. In her eyes, being an independent adult was a blast!

"Only one more hour and I will be off for the weekend." Darla thought, as she hurriedly cleared another table.

Returning to her workstation, Darla noted a tall husky man sitting down at one of her tables with his back toward her. After giving him a minute to get settled, she hurried to his table.

"Good evening, sir. Would you like … " Darla started, in her professional manner. "B-B-ill … " She stuttered, disbelieving her eyes.

"Hello Sis." Bill greeted standing, giving his sister a loving, tight hug.

Darla was surprised with Bill giving her a hug, instead of scolding disapproval for her place of employment.

"Excuse me, Sir." Spoke a huge, husky man.

"John, everything is okay, this is my brother, Bill." Darla explained, quickly.

"Bill, meet John, our bouncer."

"I would hate to run into him on a dark night." Bill chuckled, as he returned to his seat.

"John is a very nice person." Darla assured, with a gentle smile.

"I am sure he is, as long as you are the one he is protecting."

"True." Darla confessed, with a soft laugh.

"Are Mother and Dad okay, Bill?" Darla asked, alarmed by her brother's arrival.

"Other than worrying over you, they are both fine. I came to visit, so I could ensure mom and dad that you are truly okay." Bill answered.

"Will you put me up for the weekend or would I be cramping your style?" He inquired, bluntly.

"I would love to have you stay with me." Darla assured, politely.

"We will have a fun weekend; you will love Springfield, Bill." She assured, excitedly.

"I'm game." Bill agreed, pleasantly.

"My shift ends in forty-five minutes, would you like something to drink?

"Please, I will have a martini."

"Really, you do not want coffee?" Darla asked feeling awkward, the mere thought of her serving her brother a drink.

"I am sure you are keeping others waiting. I would like my drink right away, Miss Roberts; I have had a long flight." Bill said as he lit a cigarette for the first time ever in her presence.

"Certainly, Bill." Replied Darla pleasantly, though secretly questioning his actions in her presence.

Completing her shift, Darla returned to her brother's table.

"I am off work, dear brother. Are you ready to leave? I am beat."

"I am ready." Bill answered.

"I have a rent-a-car, so I will follow you, Sis." He added.

"Okay." Darla agreed, as she slipped her coat on over her short uniform for the chilly, late October night air.

Parking her car in front of the cozy two-bedroom house, which presently served as Darla's home, she had several questions racing through her head with her brother's arrival.

"This is home." Darla informed, pleasantly.

"Not bad." Remarked Bill, impressed with the girl's decor.

"Surely, you did not think I lived in a shack, right?" Darla asked with a gentle smile.

"Me, of course not, Dad, maybe, Mom, probably." Bill answered honestly, as he removed his jacket.

"This sounds like my parents and brother." Darla agreed, with a soft laugh.

"If you will excuse me, I will take a quick shower. Make yourself at home." She instructed, as she hung her brother's jacket in the coat closet.

"Ah, ashtrays, you must have known I was coming. Mom is not as kind." Bill said, with a chuckle.

"If you are wondering if I smoke cigarettes Bill, the answer is no, I do not." Darla informed, pleasantly and then left her brother to browse while she showered.

Completing her shower, Darla slipped into a pair of bell-bottomed jeans, a loose baggy smock with matching socks and no shoes. Returning to the front room and her guest, she turned her stereo on, finding her brother enjoying a sandwich and a glass of wine.

"I am sure you have snooped in every room, drawer and cabinet already, Bill." Darla accused, teasingly.

"I will make it official anyway and give you a tour of my home." She suggested, offering her hand to her brother.

"This of course, is where I do my entertaining. This room serves as a dance floor and a bed for many whom crash on the floor sleeping over after parties. It comes equipped with my stereo, my guitar, my amplifier, my plants, my decor and Susie's furniture."

"Now entering the cozy cute kitchen, we pass the breakfast bar which separates the kitchen from the front room. The bar is well stocked, as you already know and for your information and note taking, I prefer wine, but only when attending a party. No, I am not a daily drinker, regardless of my place of employment and well stocked bar. The refrigerator has plenty of food and beer. Phil, a neighbor and Susie keep the refrigerator stocked with beer. The dishes are some mine, some Susie's." Darla informed.

"Sam occupies the fenced backyard until I return home. The yard is equipped with a grill and patio furniture." She described, opening the backdoor for Sam to enter.

"My room is furnished with my waterbed, my desk, sewing machine and necessities. Assure Mother that I have plenty of clothes." Darla said with a gentle smile, opening her closet door to prove her point.

"The bathroom we share and Susie's room, which you will use. Susie is living next door with her boyfriend for now." She informed.

"Sis ... " Bill started, as he and his sister returned to the front room, sitting down on the sofa, his face serious, yet his voice gentle.

"Yes?"

"I did not come here to pass judgment on you, nor did Mom or Dad send me to check on you. I simply came reassure myself that you are okay. In addition, I would be able to ensure Mom and Dad so they do not worry so much over you. Dad wanted to come himself, but Mom told him to let you be. When I told Mom and Dad of my plans to come check on you, they both were relieved. I assure you, I am impressed with what I see." Bill explained.

"Thank you." Darla said, pleased with her brother's approval.

"I assure you, both Mom and Dad would have been here immediately dragging you home, if it was not for the fact you are eighteen and a half, you being of age." Bill said, with a grin.

"This I know." Darla confessed with a laugh, blushing.

"I do sincerely hope you do two things, as Mom and Dad believe you will do. Come home during school breaks and return home after you complete college. Do not remain here indefinitely." Bill advised, compassionately.

"I promise you each that I will return home. For now, I need my time of independence. If I goof, it will be no one's fault, but mine alone, Bill. Assure Mother and Dad I love them dearly, and I am doing terrific. Please do this for me, Bill."

"I will, Sis."

Darla took her brother to the Ozarks early Saturday morning and Saturday evening she showed him the city's exciting nightlife.

"I am glad you came to visit, Bill. I will always remember this special weekend." Darla informed, as she waited at her brother's side for his flight departure.

"Me too, we will always have good time together. We Roberts are never apart for long because we stick together through thick and thin, right?" Bill asked, giving his sister a tight hug.

"You bet. Love you and tell Mother and Dad I love them. Bye." Darla said hurriedly, as her brother left her side to board his plane.

"Study and get top five percent of your class!" Bill encouraged, as he waved goodbye.

"I will do my best." She called out, happily.

Susie had been next door living with Jerry for three months, which gave Darla the run of the house. Phil conveniently continued to be on

Darla's doorstep whenever Darla had free time. They enjoyed many outings together.

Busy preparing for her Saturday night party and coming guests, a knock on the front door interrupted her preparations.

"Hi." Darla greeted, inviting Phil into her home.

"I thought I would give you a hand preparing for your party." Phil offered.

"Since Susie and Jerry took off for the afternoon, leaving you to deal with the party plans alone." He added with disapproval.

"I do not mind." Darla said pleasantly, as she returned to the kitchen, putting the final touches on the hors d'oeuvres she had prepared.

"You should mind." Phil insisted aggravated, lighting up a joint, then passing it to Darla.

"Have you had a bad day?" Darla asked kindly, taking a seat next to Phil at the breakfast bar, offering to lend an ear if Phil needed a friend.

"No, I have not had a bad day. It makes me mad that everyone takes advantage of you, you are a nice person."

"Who is everyone?" Darla asked gently, not believing Phil's statement to be true.

"Everyone does, man." Phil answered, in his hippie talk.

"You always get stuck with having the parties at your place, plus hosting them. Your boss always cons you into working longer hours, Susie moves out on you, and then she has a fight with Jerry and runs back in on you. Your parents, man, your parents are always doing a number on you. You might as well be living under the same roof with them and they are always mentioning some Kelley guy to you, messing up things between you and me." Phil answered.

"If anyone is taking advantage of me it is only because I allow them to." Darla replied, feeling high now from the pot she shared with Phil.

"I appreciate your concern though and you wanting to protect me." She added, with a gentle smile.

"Have I ever taken advantage of you?" Phil asked, looking into Darla's eyes.

"No, you have never taken advantage of me." Darla answered.

"Why is it everyone uses you and gets what they want? I do not use you and I do not get anything from you."

"What exactly do you want from me?" Darla asked, hesitant.

"I want you to be my girl for the remainder of this school term. We have a good time together. Man, I have liked you since you first arrived. I have wanted to move in with you since Susie moved in with Jerry. Every time I think I have a chance to have you as a real girlfriend, your parents mention that Kelley guy to you and then you pull away from me."

Darla's face felt flushed, she knew that most of her present friends believed it acceptable to live together before marriage. Phil had been correct about her feelings. She was attracted to him and enjoyed his company very much. She also had started to give of herself to Phil, several times, yet did not, because of her upbringing, Kelley's loyalty toward her as a friend and her parents trust in her moral behavior.

Leaving Phil's side, Darla poured herself a glass of wine, thinking over Phil's wishes.

"Darla." Phil spoke, going to her side, putting his arms around her and gently pulling her closer to him.

"Why not give it a try for the next few months until summer break? If something becomes of our relationship, then it will be great and if nothing becomes of our relationship, we simply go our separate ways." Phil suggested.

"What do you say? Are you willing to give us a try?" He asked.

"I am not sure, Phil." Darla answered honestly, feeling confused by her thoughts.

"Man ... " Phil sighed, aggravated.

"What is your problem?" He asked, removing his arms from around her.

"I do not feel I have a problem." Darla answered sharply, she now becoming aggravated.

"You cannot remain your parents little girl forever. Man, your parents have your head all messed up."

"Phil, I would like for you to leave please, before we both say things we may regret." Darla ordered, sternly.

"Okay, if that is what you want, later." Phil agreed, slamming the front door behind him.

Darla returned to her party preparations with tears streaming down her face, asking herself her old forgotten question repeatedly in her mind. "Why do I always feel so different from everyone else?"

With the front room furniture arranged, making room for dancing and the many different dishes prepared, Darla began her own party. She drank wine as though she was drinking water, as she showered and dressed for her party, with her stereo already blaring.

"Hi Dar, I came to offer my assistance with the party preparations." Susie greeted, entering her girlfriend's bedroom.

"Thank you, but I have everything ready." Darla said, pleasantly.

"You look nice." Susie said, admiring Darla's taste in clothing.

"Thank you, I doubt Phil will be here to notice."

"He will show, I guarantee it." Susie informed, with a sly grin.

"You know something that I don't?" Darla asked curiosity clearly on her young, pretty face.

"Of course, I am also here to warn you." Susie confessed with a smile, faithful to the girl's friendship.

"Then warn me, I am curious." Darla ordered, impatiently.

"Phil is really upset over you not permitting him to move in with you, that part you know. Tonight at your party, he has a plan that he will not even tell Jerry about to win you over."

"This is nice to know." Darla laughed, picking up her empty wineglass, leaving her bedroom and entering the kitchen.

"Great! You are up to something also." Susie laughed following her friend to the kitchen, excitedly.

"Have you known me to do anything important that I have not wanted to do?" Darla asked, smiling excitedly, feeling lightheaded from the wine she continued to consume.

"No."

"Whether I allow Phil to move in or not, will be my choosing, not his. Just to throw a monkey wrench in his plan, I will make sure everyone knows that I am making the move to accept him. Of course, I will be discreet about it." Darla shared with sparkles in her eyes.

"Is that weirdo friend of Jerry's, James, coming tonight?" Darla asked.

"Of course, he always attends the parties you attend. Whew. Phil cannot stand James, Dar."

"I know." Darla laughed with a twinkle in her eyes.

"You know someone always requests I play my guitar and I always do and then weird James always asks me to sing. Of course, I never do, but tonight, I shall sing and then Phil and you and all Phil's many friends will learn of my choice to accept or to refuse Phil before he even gets started on his plan." Darla said laughing, filled with excitement.

"This is going to be great!" Susie exclaimed.

"I had best go to ensure Jerry is ready on time. I want to see this from the beginning."

"Susie, can you hear my stereo at Phil's and Jerry's home?"

"You can most definitely hear your stereo from Phil and Jerry's apartment."

"Good, make sure Phil is aware that I am not brooding over our disagreement earlier." She suggested with a smile.

"It is as good as done." Susie laughed as she left the house, returning to her boyfriend's and Phil's home next-door.

Darla set the hors d'oeuvres out, in-between welcoming her guests into her home as they began ringing the doorbell. She loved entertaining and she busily filled her guest's empty glasses.

"Where is Phil?" Darla asked as Susie arrived late, like usual.

"I told you, he will be here. He has to give you time to miss him and to think he is not coming." Susie assured.

"I see your secret admirer is here." She added.

"Oh, yes, James was one of the first to arrive." Darla sighed.

"Doesn't the microphone look inviting?" She asked with an excited smile, trying not to laugh.

"I noticed. How could one not notice, the way you have arranged the plans so perfectly around your microphone stand?"

The continuous drinking was beginning to affect Darla greatly by the time Phil arrived. She was overly carefree and she welcomed Phil into her home pleasantly, the same as she had her other guests.

"Do you feel better now?" Darla asked politely, as she handed Phil a beer.

"No, not really, I was not sure I was still invited to your party after this afternoon." Phil answered, his face bearing his hurt feelings.

"You are always invited, Phil." Darla assured, politely.

"The more the merrier." She added quickly, observing Phil's expression change from hopeful, to discouragement.

"Excuse me, I had better mingle. I do not want to be a poor hostess." Darla said pleasantly, as she refilled her wineglass.

"Darla." Phil spoke, taking hold of her arm gently, preventing her from leaving.

"Yes?"

"How long has James been here?"

"James was one of the first to arrive, I understand you do not care for James, Phil, but he is nice and polite."

"Don't you think you have had enough to drink? I have not seen you drink this much." Phil asked, becoming annoyed with her manner.

"Probably, yet I believe I can handle my own. After all, as long as my parents do not know, it is allowed, right?" Darla asked, looking into Phil's eyes.

Phil silently walked away from Darla aggravated, joining a group of his college friends.

Darla secretly felt sorry for Phil, for causing him to feel excluded by her actions.

As the couples tired from their dancing, there were the usual requests for Darla to play her guitar, which she gladly did.

Phil had avoided Darla the entire evening after his arrival. He had danced several dances with different girls, yet had not asked Darla to dance. Darla had pretended not to notice, as Phil presently pretended not to notice her guitar playing, which he adored.

"Hey Darla, sing something." James suggested, as Darla and Susie had predicted.

"Man, maybe she does not feel like singing." Spoke Phil, finally having his fill of James' presence.

"Excuse me." Darla spoke through the microphone, bringing silence throughout the house, everyone giving Darla his or her full attention.

"I would be glad to sing, James." Darla informed.

Taking her microphone from the stand near the stereo, Darla put an eight-track into her tape player.

The party guests looked first at Darla and then Phil, surprised Darla had sided with James over Phil. Phil looked surprised, yet remained patiently waiting along with the many curious and anxious guests to hear

Darla sing, for the first time. The guests remained motionless as the soft, beautiful music began.

"I would like to sing, for all of you, my guests and dear friends, this particular song, I have chosen for a special friend. I trust the words hold the same meaning to my special friend, as they do to me." Darla said in her soft, gentle way.

As Darla prepared to begin her song with her mike in hand, her eyes moved across the room including each guest in on her song, except Phil. Phil could not stand anymore, so he got off the barstool he was sitting on, heading for the front door, without a word to anyone. Just as Phil put his hand on the doorknob, Darla interrupted his intentions.

"Phil." Darla said, gently through the mike.

"I would like you to stay. This song is for you." She informed, with a beautiful smile.

Phil looked puzzled as he looked first at Darla, then at Susie. His face now relaxed, as he realized the two girls had set him up. He returned his eyes on Darla, with a look of pride as she began to sing.

*"We've only just begun
to live,
White lace and Promises ...*

Darla sang beautifully. Laying down her mike, she went to Phil's side, giving him a light gentle kiss. Her guests applauded both the singer and the joining of Phil and Darla.

CHAPTER 7

Phil had moved in with Darla, as Susie remained living next door with Jerry. Darla had enjoyed her first year of college running her life as she wished with no rules and no restrictions.

"Are you going home for the summer?" Phil asked, as he and Darla prepared for a weekend camping trip.

"For a few weeks at the end of summer, I enrolled for summer semester."

"Will you be returning home, or staying in the city?" Darla asked, knowing their relationship was ending.

"I will probably split sometime next week, going home for a while. My Old Man has offered me a job with him, so I figure I might as well check it out. Maybe we can get together sometime. You have been a lot of fun."

"Maybe we can."

Knowing their camping trip would be their last outing together, Darla and Phil spent the entire weekend hiking in the mountains. With the wind blowing Darla's hair through the open car window, she stared out the window in deep thought, as Phil drove the young couple back toward the city. She would be going home soon and her heart pounded with excitement as she thought of seeing her family again. She had missed them terribly.

Returning to her home, Darla assisted Phil with their camping gear. She said her good-byes to him; as he returned to his home next door to begin his packing to leave the city, now that he had graduated from college.

Checking her mailbox, Darla discovered two letters for herself. Sitting down on her front porch, she opened her letters excitedly.

> *Dear Darla,*
> *I have thought of you often. I keep in touch with your*
> *parents, visiting them when I can and I look at your high*
> *school picture when I really begin missing you.*
> *How is Sam? Are you taking good care of him? I am sure you*
> *are. You were born to be gentle, kind, and loving.*
> *By the time you receive this letter, I will be out of school*
> *for the summer. I imagine you will be also.*
> *Your parents said you would be home for the summer. I would like to*
> *see you, when you return home. By the way, I am still waiting on you.*
> *Love,*
> *Kelley*

Darla barely managed to keep her tears back. She had no idea after all these months that Kelley continued to care for her and was waiting for her to return his caring. She was deeply touched, as she opened her second letter.

> *Dearest Darla:*
> *We are so anxious for you to come home. We miss you terribly!*
> *Be sure and call as soon as you know when you will be coming.*
> *Bill was disappointed you could not attend his wedding.*
> *It was nice and he and Paula went to Hawaii on their*
> *honeymoon. The pictures they took are lovely.*
> *Kelley was by last night. We see him often and he always asks*
> *about you. I understand he still cares deeply for you.*
> *We love and miss you, dearly.*
> *Love,*
> *Mother and Dad*

"Susie, what is wrong?" Darla asked with tenderness, putting her letters aside, as her ex-roommate approached her, crying hysterically.

"Jerry kicked me out. May I move back in?" Susie asked, between sobs.

"Of course, you pay your half of the rent and your room is as you left it." Darla assured, compassionately.

"Come inside, so we can talk."

"I cannot believe Jerry. He said he loved me, Darla. For an entire year, he has been telling me how much he loves me." Susie shared, sitting down on the sofa.

"What happened?"

"I have no idea. Jerry returned an hour ago from a party, informing me our relationship is over."

"Guys can be so cruel." Darla soothed, handing her girlfriend some Kleenex.

"I am glad I had an abortion now because it would be devastating to be pregnant with Jerry's baby, and then have him tell me to get out."

"I had no idea you were even pregnant." Darla said, shocked over her girlfriend's secret and solution.

"Jerry did not know, either." Susie informed.

"I should have known he only wanted to use me." She added, going to her room still crying.

With Phil moving back to his hometown, Susie no longer living with Jerry, Darla and Susie were roommates once again.

Picking up the telephone, Darla dialed her parent's telephone number.

"Hello." Mr. Roberts answered.

"Hello Daddy!"

"It is good to hear your voice, Babe. How are you?"

"I am fine. I made it through my first year of college with flying colors."

"I knew you could do it, Babe." Her father said, pleased.

"So, when are you coming home?" He asked.

"This is one reason why I called … " Darla started, slowly.

"I will not be home until the end of July. I am taking some nursing classes this summer, also." She explained quickly.

"I do not recall you attending classes during the summer part of our arrangement."

"I know, Dad. I will only be in summer classes for four weeks, though." She added with tenderness, not wanting to upset her father.

"You must know, Darla, I am disappointed again." Pastor Roberts said, with an irritated sigh.

"Daddy, I know you are right now. I know you will be pleased with the outcome, though. I am only taking these summer classes to better myself in the nursing field."

"Darla, you best be on a plane for home within five weeks, or I will come get you myself." Pastor Roberts ordered, firmly.

"Yes Sir, I will be." Darla assured, politely.

Darla worked hard in her summer classes. She was so pleased with her results and she could not wait to share her progress with her family.

Sitting on the airplane, it taking Darla closer and closer to her home and family, the excitement grew within her. She could barely wait to hug her parent's neck, visit with Cindy and her husband, and Bill and his wife. Growing up had brought many changes and some hard times between Darla and her family, but no matter how different their opinions, they shared a great bond between them, a bond of love, the bond that could never be broken if you were a member of the Robert's family.

As the plane prepared to land, Darla put her nursing books she had been reading away in her backpack. She brushed her long hair and then lightly touched up her baby-blue eye shadow, mascara and clear lip-gloss. Retying her shoestrings on her hiking boots, she was ready to greet her family.

Standing up along with the other passengers, she glanced out the plane window next to her seat, taking in the beauty of the huge San Diego Airport. Now in line, she pulled down the legs of her faded blue jeans and straightened her light blue sleeveless under-shirt style top, then placed her backpack on her back. Entering the crowded airport, breaking out of line, she searched the crowd for her parents, as her heart began to beat faster with excitement.

"Hi!" She exclaimed, racing to her parents, hugging them both excitedly.

"I have missed you." She informed happily.

"You both look great." She added with an excited laugh, hugging them again.

"We have missed you also, Babe." Mr. Roberts assured, with a radiant grin, putting his arm around his daughter's shoulders lovingly, as she walked between her parents toward the baggage claim.

"You have lost weight, Darla." Her mother said, with concern on her happy face.

"Only five pounds, Mother." Darla assured sweetly, as they stood waiting for the luggage to arrive.

"You look like a bag of bones." Her father sided.

"I do not cook as well as Mother." Darla explained with a gentle smile, bringing smiles to her parent's faces.

"I assure you, Mom will work overtime to put some meat back on your bones while you are home."

"Daddy, the thin look is in now." Darla informed happily, though knowing her parents never allowed styles to change their ways.

"You have always been thin, Babe. Thin I can deal with, my daughter being skinny, concerns me."

"I promise to eat you and Mother out of house and home while I am here." Darla said with an excited laugh, relieving her parents of their concerns.

"When does fall semester begin, dear?" Her mother asked, as they walked through the airport with Darla's luggage.

"The first of September."

"We get you for six whole weeks then." Sister Roberts replied, happily.

"I can only stay for two weeks." Darla said, slowly.

"What?" Her father asked, stopping abruptly in the middle of the airport entrance, surprising both Darla and her mother.

"I could only get two weeks off from my job." She explained with flushed cheeks, knowing her news had hurt her parent's feelings.

"You are home until school begins in the fall." Her father said with authority.

"Dad, I cannot stay longer, I will lose my job."

"You will be home until fall semester begins, which is about six weeks." Mr. Roberts ordered, finalizing their discussion as he began to walk again.

The Roberts were silent as they left the airport for the parking lot. With Darla's luggage and backpack in the trunk of her parent's car, she politely sat in the front seat between her parents, at her mother's request. Silently picking at the seam of her jeans with her long nails, her cheeks still flushed from her father's orders. She secretly hoped her boss would hold her job because she had gotten used to the extra spending money her tips had brought.

"Is there anything special you would like to do while you are home?" Mr. Roberts asked, breaking their silence.

"Yes, lots." Darla answered politely, forcing a smile.

"Can you give me an example?" He questioned, his face once again relaxed and his voice calm and pleased his daughter was home, his manner relaxing his daughter's embarrassment over his scolding.

"I have missed Princess and I cannot wait to go horseback riding, besides visiting each of my friends and family, I just have to go to the beach in San Diego and smell and feel the salt water." Darla answered, her excitement quickly growing within her again, this pleasing her parents.

"Lakes are no comparison to the ocean." Her father agreed.

"Tell me something, dear." Mrs. Roberts spoke, as she lovingly put her arm around her daughter's shoulders, looking into her eyes.

"Did you honestly think you could do all you would like to do within two weeks?" She questioned, with a gentle smile.

"No, Ma'am."

"Then perhaps sometime between this moment and your return to school, you will thank Dad for insisting you stay longer than two weeks." Darla's mother suggested, in her gentle way.

"Yes, Ma'am and I am sure you will remind me if I do forget to thank Dad." Darla replied with a soft laugh, bringing laughter from her parents.

"How did your summer classes go, Babe?" Mr. Roberts asked, as he drove out of the mountains, approaching the desert.

"Fantastic! You and Mother will be so pleased. The university has begun a new program in nursing and they are experimenting starting with fall semester, with a two-year program to receive your registered nursing license. One of my professors asked me during summer semester if I would be interested in being one of the chosen to be a part of the program. Of course, I agreed, therefore, I only have one year of college remaining, instead of three."

"Oh, this is great, dear." Her mother approved.

"Congratulations, Babe. You have always been a go-getter once you have set your mind to something, we are proud of you."

"Thank you, Dad."

"Bill and Cindy will be at home to greet you." Mrs. Roberts informed, as they neared their small desert town.

"Cindy insisted on preparing dinner for your homecoming." She added.

"I cannot wait to see them!" Darla exclaimed.

"Dad, would you please drive faster!" She asked with an excited laugh.

"Do you intend to pay the speeding ticket if I do?" He questioned with a boyish grin, as though glad for an opportunity to drive fast.

"Mark, do not be funny." His wife scolded, lightly.

"Yes, Mother." Pastor Roberts agreed, secretly winking at his daughter as he increased his speed somewhat, regardless of his wife's warning.

Darla gave her father a smile over his teasing play. She had forgotten how happy her parents had always made her feel until now. True, they were strict, yet they contained an abundance of love, which they freely gave and shared, an unconditional love. She was both pleased and happy to be home and truly grateful she was a part of the Robert's family, the family the Lord granted her at some point and time in her life.

"I will make you so proud to be my parents, Mother and Dad." Darla thought, as her father turned down their street.

"I cannot believe I am actually home." Darla said happily, as her father turned into the drive.

"You are home and you will never forget where home is either." Her mother said with an excited laugh, giving her daughter a loving hug.

Entering the Robert's home, Darla truly felt she was home. Her brother and cousin greeted her with hugs and kisses. They were as excited as she was, as the family was re-united.

"Hi." Kelley greeted politely, giving Darla a kiss on her cheek.

"Hi." Darla replied with a tender smile, feeling warm toward his touch, as she looked into his strong, yet gentle face, surprised to see him among her family members.

"Sis, this is my wife, Paula." Bill introduced, proudly.

"It is nice to meet you, Paula." Darla said pleasantly, as she shook her sister-in-law's hand.

"Do I get a handshake also?" Dan asked, as he entered the family room from the kitchen.

"Cindy?" Darla asked, with an excited laugh.

"I do not care if you give him a hug, believe me, the honeymoon has been over long ago." Cindy joked, laughing.

"It is good to see you, Dan." Darla informed, giving him an excited hug.

"Same here, you have been dearly missed."

"Thank you." Darla said, her eyes sparkling and her face aglow from happiness.

As Darla's family made themselves comfortable on the sofa and various chairs, Darla sat down on the floor Indian fashion near her brother's chair with her back straight.

"We do have furniture, Babe." Pastor Roberts reminded with a teasing smile, yet surprised with her choosing the floor.

"I am fine, Daddy." Darla assured, happily.

"What is this?" Bill asked, removing Darla's backpack from the floor near his chair.

"Is this your hippie bag?" He asked teasingly, bringing laughter from his family.

"It is called a backpack." Darla answered, blushing with his teasing, as he freely examined the bag's contents.

"Schoolbooks ... " Bill reported, reclosing the bag.

"Don't you do anything besides study?"

"Yes, Bill." Darla answered with a gentle smile, as her brother returned the backpack to the floor.

"Darla will be graduating from college at the end of this school year, Bill." Mr. Roberts informed, proudly.

"You are not serious?" Bill asked, as though in shock.

"I thought you had four years of college?"

"Originally I did, now I will have my degree in two years."

"My hippie sister is a whiz-kid."

"B-ill, quit referring to me as a hippie." She scolded, blushing.

"I cannot believe mom let you in her car wearing faded jeans. Darla is wearing jeans, Mom." Bill teased, causing Darla's face to turn its reddest and his parents to laugh.

"Bill, leave her alone." Paula said.

"Thank you, Paula." Spoke Darla, with a gentle smile.

Cindy had prepared a feast and Darla enjoyed having dinner with her entire family for the first time in over a year.

"Darla, I have to leave, I have the park ministry to attend." Kelley said.

"May I call you tomorrow?" He inquired, hopeful.

"Please do." Darla answered, pleasantly.

"Cindy." Darla spoke, in a whisper, as the girls washed the dinner dishes.

"Kelley is still involved with the street kids?"

"Deeply and seriously, he says it is one of his main callings for the Lord."

"I do not doubt his calling." Darla replied, with a pleased smile.

"Have you discovered your calling, Darla?"

"No, but I believe I feel a tugging at my heart. Perhaps I will use my vacation time more wisely then I had intended and seek out my calling."

"I hope so because you and the Lord make a dynamite team." Cindy encouraged, kindly.

"Thank you." Replied Darla deeply touched, her cousin's remark reminding her of her past years of living her life for the Lord before she became self-centered.

"Sis, I have the horses saddled. Would you like to join me?" Bill asked, as he entered the kitchen.

"Yes!"

"Go with Bill, Darla, I will finish up." Cindy offered.

"Thanks, you are the greatest." Darla replied, giving her cousin a quick, excited hug.

"I will race you to the corner." Darla replied, excitement in her eyes, as she dried her hands on the dishtowel.

"You are on." Bill agreed, as his sister laid the dishtowel down, he patiently waiting for her.

"I will meet you at the corner." She informed and then ran from the kitchen, through the family room and out the backdoor, hoping to mount her horse first. Reaching Princess, Darla discovered her brother was at her heels.

"Cheater!" Bill yelled as she kicked Princess, her horse darting past her brother, as he mounted Cindy's horse.

Riding her fastest, Darla loved the feel of the warm desert wind stinging her face and blowing her hair. She loved the thrill she felt, as her horse seemed to carry her through the air as though she had wings.

"I won." Darla said with a soft laugh, as her brother joined her at the corner.

"You do not play fair."

"Neither do you." Darla replied, poking her brother in his side, as they walked their horses side by side.

"What have I done?"

"Bringing up my wearing jeans in front of everyone, you know perfectly well my wearing jeans are a sore spot with Mother." Darla answered, lightly scolding her brother.

"There was no harm done, Sis."

"Not yet, but Mother has not had her time alone with me." Darla reminded with a soft laugh, blushing.

"I truly do not believe mom cares how you are dressed because she is too happy with you being home, as we all are, Sis. We will even be happier when you are home to stay."

"Thank you. You each have made me happier today then I have been in a long time. I had not realized how much I missed each of you, until today. I am proud I am a Roberts."

"Once you are in, Sis, there is no getting out." Bill assured, with a grin.

"This is the part I like best." Darla shared, with a happy smile.

"What were your thoughts when you saw Kelley waiting to greet you?" Bill asked, as they returned to the corral.

"That he is more handsome then he was a year ago." Darla answered with an excited laugh, blushing over her openness and bringing a chuckle from her brother.

"I know Kelley is still waiting for you to clear the cob webs out of your head and become his girlfriend. Do you intend to gamble another year away at college to see if Kelley is still waiting?"

"No." Darla answered quickly with a gentle smile, knowing her answer pleased him.

"I am glad, Sis. I know Kelley would always do right by you."

"I know this too." Darla agreed with pride in her voice.

"Bill." Dan said, climbing over the fence.

"Yeah?" Bill asked, looking up from brushing Cindy's horse.

"If you would like, I will take over for you. Paula seems concerned about your absence." Dan explained, politely taking the brush from Bill's hand.

"Thanks Dan." Bill said with reddened cheeks, as though embarrassed.

"Sis, good to have you home." Bill assured, giving his sister a kiss.

"Thank you. Bye."

Darla continued to brush Princess in silence. Something told her, her brother was not happy in his marriage, but it was not her place to meddle in his private affairs.

"Dan, do you and Cindy have plans for tonight? Darla asked, putting her brush aside.

"No, is there something you would like to do?" He asked, considerately.

"Yes, but I need your help."

"I will do what I can."

"I suddenly have this strong yearning to visit the park ministry. I really do not understand why because I have not even attended one church service since I left for college. I promised my mother three years ago I would never enter the park. My parents cannot know if I go. Would you go with me? I know you go with Kelley occasionally."

"I will be glad to take you. Perhaps the yearning you are feeling is the Holy Spirit dealing with your heart."

"Perhaps you are right."

With the horses tended to, Darla and Dan returned to the house, where Mr. Roberts, his wife and Cindy sat visiting in the family room.

"Cindy, what do you say we treat your cousin to a night on the town?" Dan asked, secretly making Darla's way of escape.

"I think that will be fun." Cindy answered, getting up from the sofa ready to leave.

"I really should shower and change first." Darla said.

"You are fine." Dan assured.

"Mother, Dad, I will not be late." Darla said respectfully, giving her parents a kiss.

"Have fun, kids." Mr. Roberts said.

Darla silently sat in the backseat of Dan and Cindy's car, as Dan informed Cindy of Darla's wishes.

"Dar, are you sure you should go to the park?" Cindy asked, with worry on her face.

"I need to go, Cindy. Perhaps if I visit, I will have more understanding in putting my life in order." Darla answered, honestly.

"Cindy would you like to join us, or would you rather I take you home?" Dan asked.

"Home, I am not as daring as my dear cousin." Cindy answered, giving Darla a gentle smile.

"I am glad you are with me, Dan because I do not believe I could ever come here alone." Darla shared, as she and Dan arrived at the park.

"And you never should come alone." Dan advised.

Darla was silent now, as the couple entered the darkened City Park, the dim park lights barely aiding one in finding their way. Approaching a group of teenagers sitting in a circle, Darla spotted Kelley with his Bible in his hands, as he shared scriptures with the group. Taking hold of Dan's arm to prevent them getting too close, Darla not wanting to intrude, she sat down on the grass. Tears were soon escaping, making their way down Darla's cheeks as Kelley spoke on one being a drifter, a drifter from the Lord. Secretly and quickly, Darla brushed her tears away, not wanting Dan to know of her crying.

At the close of Kelley's simple sermon for the simple people before him, Kelley offered individual counseling as Darla had once done.

"We best go, it is getting late and I do not want to worry my parents." Darla suggested.

Returning home and goodnights said Darla took a long leisurely bath. Her thoughts reviewed her past few years of living a sinner's life. What had seemed fun and exciting now brought embarrassment to her and now she questioned herself, how and why she had strayed from the Lord.

Slipping into her nightclothes, Darla sat down at her bathroom vanity, looking at herself in the mirror, as she placed curlers at the ends of her long hair. Her eyes searched her reflection, digging deep into her heart.

"What is my future? What does my future hold for me?" She questioned. "What all have I missed out on in fulfilling God's plan for my life?"

Finished curling her hair, Darla now sat closer to her mirror as she touched up her eyebrows, arching them perfectly. Upon her completion, she took one last long look at herself, her face now flushed, as shame tugged at her.

"Oh no, how could I give of myself to Phil and how could I do this to myself, to Kelley and all before you, God?" Tears now streamed down her young tender face. "Oh, Lord, surely this is the unpardonable sin. How could Kelley ever forgive me of this?"

Leaving her bathroom, Darla removed her Bible from her dresser. It had been so long since her heart had longed to read from the sacred book. She read for hours and it was as though she could not consume enough, quickly enough.

The words, "Come just as you are" seemed to stick in Darla's head, regardless of the many different passages she read. It was as though the words became louder and louder in her head. Notwithstanding the echoing words any longer, she began to cry. She poured her heart out to the Lord, inviting Him, begging Him, to be Lord, Master, Father, Brother, Savior, and Comforter.

"Not my will thus forth Lord, but thine will." Darla promised, as she ceased her praying.

Though it was four in the morning, Darla set her alarm for six. She could not wait to begin a new day, with the Lord in charge of her day instead of herself. She had drifted long enough.

Turning her alarm off, Darla slipped into a pair of jeans and cool top for the warm July desert morning. Quietly slipping out the backdoor, as not to disturb her parents, she went to the corral.

Putting the bridle on Princess, she hopped onto her horse's bare back. She ran Princess until she tired and then slowed her to a trot, then a walk. She rode into town, nearing the City Park. She walked Princess around the park several times, as she yearned to be a part of the park ministry again.

"Is that you, Angel?" A little old man asked, staggering from the park.

Darla dismounted her horse, walking toward the little man. Her heart skipped a beat, as she recognized the wino from her past when witnessing in the park.

"Hi." Darla greeted excitedly, giving the dirty, smelly man a hug.

"I did not know you still live in the park." Darla said.

"Well, Missy, if you would come with Preacher Kel, you would know. I hear you are a college gal now, working on some big degree, I suppose."

"I am working on a small degree." Darla answered with a gentle smile.

"I am going to the restaurant for a cup of coffee. You want to join me, or have you gotten too big for your britches to be seen with the likes of me?" Gino asked, causing Darla's cheeks to redden.

"I would consider it an honor to join you." Darla answered politely, as she slipped her arm through the little man's arm, bringing a pleased smile to his face.

"When you going to come back to the park?"

"Soon, I hope."

"You do not have yourself another boyfriend, do you?"

"No, Sir." Darla answered, with a gentle smile.

"I am glad to hear ya say that because Preacher Kelley is the young man for you. You and he belong together. You know that, don't ya?"

"Yes, Sir, I do know this."

"I figured you did." He replied with a pleased grin.

"Gino, I must be going, my parents are probably wondering where I am." Darla said, getting up from the table.

"I plan to see you next Friday with Preacher Kel."

"I will try to be there." Darla assured, with a pleasant smile.

As she mounted Princess, Darla felt such happiness, knowing the park ministry was hers and Kelley's as a team. The Lord had never changed His plans for her, she had.

Joining her parents at the breakfast table, Darla excitedly shared her news of rededicating her life to the Lord. Her parents were as happy and thrilled for her as she was.

"Babe, the telephone is for you." Her father said, as Darla kindly refilled her parents coffee cups.

"It is Kelley."

"What took him so long to call?" Darla asked blushing, giving her parents a sweet smile and bringing laughter from them.

"Good morning. Have you prayed today?" Darla asked, excitement in her voice, as she took the extension to the kitchen table.

"Yes Ma'am. Have you?"

"Yes, I have." Darla answered, happily.

"In fact, I was up until four this morning praying and studying my Bible, I had hours' worth of confessing and apologies." She shared, observing her parent's happy smiles of approval.

"You rededicated your life to the Lord?" Kelley asked, he just as excited as Darla and her parents now.

"Yes, I did and I feel terrific!"

"It is about time." Kelley said, bringing a tickled laugh from Darla, causing her to blush.

"When may I see you, so I may congratulate you properly?"

"I will find out, just a second please."

"Mother, Dad, do you have plans for me today?" Darla asked, considerately.

"No set plans, dear." Her mother answered.

"Kelley, I am free today."

"Would you like to go to San Diego, to the beach?"

"I would love to!"

"I will pick you up at ten." Kelley said.

"Okay, bye."

Darla returned the telephone to its proper place and then returned to the table with her parents.

"Kelley is taking me to the beach." She shared.

"Now, are you not glad you will be home for six weeks instead of two?" Mr. Roberts asked.

"Yes." Darla answered, excitedly.

"Thank you, Dad." She added, with a loving smile.

"You are welcome, Babe."

"What was Kelley's response when you informed him of your rededication?" Her mother asked.

"He said it is about time." Darla answered, blushing, bringing laughter from her parents.

Showering quickly, Darla dressed in a delicate, feminine short outfit and sandals. Her beach bag packed, she set her bag and purse in the family room.

"Whew, you look nice." Her mother complimented, laying down her dust cloth.

"Thank you." Darla replied pleasantly.

"I am proud of you, dear even if you do like wearing faded blue jeans." Mrs. Roberts said, with a gentle laugh, bringing a smile from her daughter.

"Darla, stick with the Lord, dear. He will make your darkest day seem bright, I assure you. He is much kinder than people are and He will never leave you or forsake you."

"I will, Mother. I have played long enough."

"I agree." Her mother replied with a gentle smile, giving her daughter a loving hug.

"There is Kelley." She informed, as the doorbell rang.

"Have fun, sweetheart."

"I will, Mother. Bye." Darla said compassionately, giving her mother a kiss goodbye.

"Are you ready?" Kelley asked, as Darla picked up her beach bag and purse.

"Yes, I am." Darla answered, pleasantly.

"I will have Darla home no later than ten, Sister Roberts."

"Thank you, Kelley."

"Good morning." Kelley greeted with a gentle smile, as he walked Darla to his car.

"I have missed you." He added.

"I have missed you also." Darla said, pleased.

"I was surprised to see you at the park last night." Kelley voiced, as he backed his car out of the drive.

"I was pleased, yet surprised." He added.

"I had this sudden urge to attend."

"What were the results of you attending?" Kelley asked eagerly.

"I am no longer a drifter or can I wait until next Friday night to return again." Darla answered, her eyes sparkling with excitement.

"Do your parents approve of you returning?"

"I prefer my parents do not know. I will only be home for five more Fridays, so I will attend, but I will spare my parents. I owe them at least these next five weeks of happiness with no worrying in regards to me; I have put them through enough."

"I understand." Kelley said.

"It is good to have you home and it will be great having you involved in the park ministry. You belong there." He added.

"I know I do, and thank you. It is great to be home. I have been flying high since I have returned." She shared, kindly.

"At least you are on a straight high." Kelley said with a gentle smile, causing Darla to blush.

"Yes, straight and free."

"It has been sometime since I have had the privilege of asking you this … " Kelley started, his face growing serious, yet his voice gentle and his eyes held tenderness.

"What are my chances with you falling for me, Miss Roberts?"

"How does a ten sound?" She asked, with a soft laugh.

"Aye, Miss Darla is truly back." Kelley remarked, extremely happy.

"Yes, I am back, one-hundred percent." She agreed, as Kelley took her hand into his, briefly taking his eyes from his driving, looking into her eyes.

"I sincerely love you, Darla."

"I love you too, Kelley." Darla replied, scooting closer to him.

"I have also missed you terribly." She added with an excited laugh, blushing over her forwardness.

Darla and Kelley were silent for some time as Kelley drove toward the mountains, each in their separate thoughts of this special time for them.

"I have something I would like to show you." Kelley said breaking their silence, as he turned off the main highway onto a country mountain road.

Driving for a few miles, Kelley turned onto another road until arriving at a beautiful clear lake surrounded by pine trees.

"Oh, Kelley, this is beautiful!" Darla exclaimed, though patiently waiting Kelley to open her car door for her.

"I thought you would like it." Kelley said, pleased with her happiness.

"Shall we go for a walk?" He politely asked.

"Yes."

Opening the car door for Darla, Kelley extended his hand to her, assisting her from his car. With Darla's hand in his, Kelley slowly led the way to the lake. Stopping near the lake, Kelley turned toward Darla, putting his arms loosely around her waist and looking down into her eyes, as she looked up into his eyes.

"I love you, Darla. I want you to become my wife when we complete college and I even wore my college ring today, in hopes that you would accept it." Kelley said with a gentle smile.

"I accept." Darla said, with a beautiful happy smile.

Tightening his arms around Darla's waist, Kelley gently kissed her.

"Kelley, where is the ring?" Darla asked, with a happy smile.

"In a minute … " He answered, kissing her again and she allowing him.

"One more, I have a couple years of catching up." He added with a boyish grin, as he kissed her once more.

Removing his ring from his finger, Kelley slipped it on her finger, discovering his ring was much too big for her finger.

"Maybe you should put the ring in your purse until you get home. I believe you have a bracelet which you can put my ring on." He suggested.

"Yes, I do and I will." Darla assured with sparkles in her eyes.

"Now you will have to tell your other boyfriend to get lost." He teased.

Darla's smile quickly faded, as her face flushed. She slowly walked away from Kelley.

"Dar, what is wrong?" Kelley asked, taking hold of her arm and preventing her from walking.

"What did I do?"

Darla did not look at Kelley as she quickly searched her heart. Must she tell Kelley of Phil and would this be the last straw? How could Kelley possibly forgive her if he knew?

"Darla, what have I done? Talk to me, please." Kelley tried again, feeling terrible as tears escaped Darla's eyes.

"You have not done anything; it is what I have done." Darla answered slowly, avoiding Kelley's eyes.

"I do not believe it would be fair of me to accept your ring." She informed, as she began to cry harder.

"Darla, I do not understand." Kelley repeated feeling frustrated.

"Did you have a boyfriend?" He asked.

"Yes." She answered barely above a whisper, as she stared at the ground, her sobbing continuing.

"So? What is the big deal? You were under no commitment to me."

"The big deal is I allowed him to live with me, Kelley." Darla shared, looking up into Kelley's eyes, hurting for him over her shame.

"I am not worthy of your love and I am truly sorry." She sobbed.

Kelley was silent, yet his face remained expressionless, his silence making Darla more uncomfortable.

Putting her face in her hands, she cried her hardest. Putting his arms around Darla, he held her close, allowing her to cry in his arms as he comforted her.

"Darla." Kelley started with tenderness in his eyes, as he put his hand on her chin, gently lifting her head, looking into her eyes.

"I assure you, I have never considered giving up on you, not in the past or now. I sincerely love you from the bottom of my heart." He informed, attempting to calm her crying and eliminate her fears.

"I am ashamed of my foolish non-Christian life style. I have hurt you, my family and the Lord so terribly that I am undeserving of forgiveness."

"This is not true, Darla. The Lord forgives each one of us. God commands us, as Christians, to forgive one another. I admire you for telling me what you have. You did not have to, yet you told me because you want to be completely honest with me, even if it meant losing me. This does mean a lot to me." He gently wiped her streaming tears away from her saddened face.

"What you have done, whomever you have dated, or even how you have lived your life, Darla, I will never hold against you or do I have the right. We have not been dating for three years. What happens from this day on most definitely matters, right?" Kelley asked with a gentle smile, looking into her eyes.

"That's right." Darla answered, now looking into Kelley's eyes with his love for her, regardless of her past foolishness.

"There is one thing I would like for you to understand and that is my silence when you first told me. I have known you since we were young children and I do not believe there would have been a roommate if you had not been through the hard times that you have the past couple of years. I was angry that some jerk took advantage of you, of your young age, your upsets and your innocence." Kelley explained, compassionately.

"I did plan a special day for my favorite girl. Do you feel up to enjoying yourself?" Kelley asked, considerately.

"Yes, please." Darla answered, brushing her tears away.

Kelley treated Darla to lunch at a cozy restaurant at the top of a mountain, which deeply impressed Darla. With the completion of their meal, he drove his date to San Diego. They swam and laughed excitedly, as they rode the waves on air mattresses and Kelley was the perfect gentleman, eliminating his girlfriend's fears of her past.

"May I pick you up for Sunday morning services?" Kelley asked, as he walked Darla to her door.

"Sunday night would be great, but in the morning I should attend with my parents."

"Tomorrow night it is then. Good night Miss Roberts, I love you." Kelley said sincerely, and then gave his date a gentle kiss.

"Good night, Kelley." She replied with sparkles in her eyes, from her overwhelming day.

"I had a wonderful time. Thank you." She added.

Darla's summer break seemed to fly past her. She felt steadfast in her commitment to Kelley. Spiritually, she continued to grow daily, witnessing, studying her Bible and time spent in prayer. She had renewed closeness with each family member and with Kelley's family. The urge to be more involved with the park ministry grew stronger and stronger.

Dressing for her last day with Kelley and her family, Darla ran to the bathroom, vomiting. Her stomach ached terribly from her excessive vomiting.

"Darla, are you okay?" Her mother asked worried, entering the bathroom.

"I am sure I will be okay." Darla answered, as she washed her face.

Darla felt awful, as she sat on the patio, waiting Kelley's arrival, taking her to lunch.

"Hi." Darla said pleasantly, as Kelley approached her.

"Hi." He greeted, giving her a kiss and pulling up a chair.

"Your mom seems worried. She said you have been sick to your stomach all morning." Kelley informed, concerned.

"Yes. Perhaps I should cancel our luncheon date, if you do not mind."

"You want to cancel on your last day home? Of course I mind."

"I thought you might disagree." Darla said, with a soft laugh.

"Are you catching the flu?" Kelley asked, placing his hand on her forehead.

"I do not believe so. I do not feel sick enough to be in bed. Actually, I only feel sick when I eat or smell food cooking."

"Darla, you are the most important person in this world to me and I would never purposely offend you." Kelley assured hesitant, as he looked into his young, sensitive, girlfriend's eyes.

"I know this." Darla assured, she searching his eyes with her.

"What is troubling you?"

"I ask this meaning no disrespect to you, I assure you. Could you be pregnant?" Kelley asked bluntly, with flushed cheeks, not intending to insult his girlfriend.

"Oh no, I cannot be pregnant." Darla answered slowly, her young happy face now filled with fright.

"I just can't be, Kelley." She repeated barely above a whisper, her eyes quickly filling with tears.

"You have been going at a strong pace since you have been home, I am sure you have over excerpted yourself." Kelley soothed quickly, taking her hand in his, supportively.

"If you have not improved, see a doctor for a checkup when you return to Missouri." Kelley advised.

"I will." Darla assured barely above a whisper, forcing a weak smile.

It was late morning when the taxi arrived in front of Darla's small Missouri home. Leaving the taxi, she carried her heavy luggage to the porch and then opened the front door.

"Dar, you are back!" Susie exclaimed, hurrying to the front door to assist her friend with her luggage.

"Hi." Darla greeted, pleasantly.

"How was your visit?"

"Fantastic." Darla answered, proudly showing Susie Kelley's college ring on her gold bracelet.

"Who is the lucky guy?" Susie asked excitedly.

"Kelley Peterson. I knew him when I lived in Dunes. He is two years older than I am and he is attending his last year at Southern Cal University to become a minister."

"He is going to be a minister?" Susie asked, surprised.

"Yes, a minister, and no I will not be partying anymore." Darla answered, with a soft laugh over her friend's shocked expression.

"I had a feeling you had changed." Susie confessed.

"I am happy for you, Darla. I have always known your heart belonged to your mystery man. You truly look happy and you have never really enjoyed today's liberal life style. Candy and I always knew this."

"I am happy." Darla replied, with a gentle smile.

"I might have a serious problem that could cause me to lose Kelley forever." She added, nervously.

"I do not understand, why?"

"I may be pregnant with Phil's child." Darla answered slowly, blushing.

"Oh, Darla, you believe you are?"

"Yes and I am scared, Susie." Darla confessed, nervously.

"Come on, I will take you to the free clinic now, so you can find out." Susie suggested, picking up her purse and car keys.

Darla signed her name on a long list, in the clinic waiting room. She silently prayed, asking the Lord not to allow her fears to become reality, as she patiently waited with Susie at her side.

"Miss Roberts." A nurse called with a clipboard in her hand.

Silently, Darla went with the nurse to an examining room. It seemed she waited forever for her results.

"Miss Roberts, you are in excellent health and you should deliver in February." The doctor informed, pleasantly.

"February ... " Darla repeated, as though in shock.

"Thank you, Sir." She spoke, barely above a whisper, quickly leaving the office with tears streaming down her checks.

"Are you okay?" Susie asked, hurrying to her girlfriend.

"Yes." Darla nodded, as she got inside Susie's car quietly, her tears still streaming.

"You are pregnant?" Susie asked, slowly.

"I am due in February." Darla answered, now beginning to sob.

"You are already three months along, but you can still have an abortion." Susie suggested.

"Susie, this would not be right. The Bible clearly teaches one reaps what they sow and me becoming pregnant due to living in sin with Phil, is reaping. I knew better, Susie. I was taught these things since I was a small child." Darla replied, beginning to cry even harder.

231

"I have an entire year of school to complete. I am not prepared to give birth to a baby in only six months. How could I be so irresponsible?"

Arriving at home, Darla entered her bedroom, closing her door behind her. She lay down on her bed, crying her heart out until finally drifting off to sleep.

When awaking from her nap, Darla took a warm shower.

Dressing in a cool summer dress and heels, she left her home to seek employment. After several applications submitted, with the same news of no help needed, Darla felt even more depressed.

Turning down a side street, her gas tank near empty, she turned into a service station. As she watched the attendant fill her tank with gas, she silently prayed.

"My heavenly Father, who art in heaven, You know of my need for work to support my baby. I have only applied at respectable restaurants not serving alcoholic beverages. Please Lord; give me the strength to deal with my responsibilities. Please, Lord, I ask, supply me with work. I thank you Lord, for already meeting my needs. Amen."

Opening her eyes, Darla patiently awaited the attendant to complete servicing her car. Staring out her window, she noticed an exclusive restaurant only a block away. Driving to the restaurant, Darla silently prayed repeatedly that she receive employment. After an intense interview, she was hired as a waitress, setting her mind somewhat at ease.

Darla kept busy with classes, studies, her evening job and church attendance. She spent many hours in prayer, apologizing to the Lord for her foolish actions requesting strength daily to endure.

Pushing her textbook aside, Darla answered the ringing telephone on her desk.

"Hello." Darla greeted, pleasantly.

"Hello, this is Kelley."

"Hi! I miss you." Darla informed, excitedly.

"I miss you too."

"Is someone having a party?" Kelley asked, overhearing the loud stereo music.

"Yes, Susie. She was partying therefore; I am stuck in my bedroom with tons of homework. We have an understanding that the stereo goes off at eleven p.m." Darla answered, with a soft laugh.

"It has been several weeks since you were home. I have not heard from you and I have been concerned. Are you okay?"

"Truly, I am okay. It has been hectic since classes began. My professor's expect nothing less than perfection and you know I am a terrible letter writer.

"Are you working also?"

"Yes, my life consists of studies, work and church attendance. I live a peculiar life." She answered, happily.

"We both live a peculiar life." Kelley replied, with a chuckle.

"You sound good. I am glad everything is going well for you." He added.

"I would be deceiving you, Kelley if I allowed you to believe everything is great. I am pregnant, Kelley." Darla informed with flushed checks.

"I am so sorry, Kelley." She added, as she began to cry.

"I truly did not intend to mess things up for you and I. Surely this is the unpardonable sin I have placed between you and I and my family."

"Do not cry, Dar. We will figure something out." Kelley replied with a sigh.

"What are the father's intentions toward the baby?" He asked.

"I have not talked with him yet. I guess I must make time to do so." Darla answered, blowing her nose from her crying.

"You do not intend to marry him for the baby if he wishes, do you?"

"No, Kelley, I would not do such a thing." Darla answered, her face reddening more, with Kelley's questions.

"That would be even more foolish." She added.

"Have you informed your parents?" Kelley asked.

"No, I do not want my parents to know until I have finished my nurses training. They would want me home if they knew and they worry enough as it is. This is my problem and I will deal with it with the Lord's help." Darla answered, wiping her tears away.

"They will be heartbroken when they do learn of this. I would give anything to erase the last few years." She added.

"I know this, Dar. Please allow your parents to assist you because you will just make this harder on yourself, if you do not."

"I cannot do what you are asking of me, Kelley. My parents would be heartbroken. It is hard enough to keep my chin up and get on with my life. I simply could not bear knowing they were hurting over my mistake, not at this time." Darla protested, gently.

Kelley was silent for several moments.

"Take care, Dar. Write and let me know when you talk to the baby's father." Kelley said.

"Darla, I love you and I want you for my wife." He added, with gentleness in his voice.

"I love you too, Kelley." Darla replied barely above a whisper, her tears coming more quickly with Kelley's touching desires.

Darla kept herself busy, as not to allow depression to consume her over the shame she felt for giving in to Phil. She spent much time in prayer and Bible reading, reassuring her Lord had forgiven her.

It was a chilly Saturday morning as Darla dressed in a pair of jeans and a lightweight, fuzzy sweater.

"Darla." Susie spoke, tapping on her bedroom door.

"Enter." Darla said, pleasantly.

"I really would like to go with you to see Phil. It is not necessary that you endure everything alone." Susie suggested, caringly.

"I am not alone, dearest friend." Darla reminded, with a gentle smile.

"I know, you have the Lord, and the Holy Spirit is your comforter." Susie replied, with a sigh.

"Correct, but I thank you for your offer."

Turning into Phil's driveway, after a three-hour drive, Darla secretly worried what Phil's reaction would be toward the baby. Nervously, she waited at the front door.

"Hi, I received your message." Phil greeted, pleasantly.

"Hi." Darla greeted, politely.

"I will not stay long, Phil. May we talk in private?"

"Sure." He agreed, closing the front door, walking away from the house with Darla.

"I am five months pregnant, Phil." Darla said her face flushed with embarrassment.

"Awe man, you are pregnant? Are you sure?" Phil asked, angrily.

"Of course I am sure." Darla answered, surprised with his response.

"What am I supposed to do? I want no part of a kid and I definitely do not want my family to know." He informed nervously, lighting up a cigarette.

Darla, stunned by his heartless, irresponsible reaction, silently questioned how he could not want his own child, as her eyes filled with tears.

"How could you allow this to happen to me and to yourself?" Phil asked.

Darla stared at Phil, searching his eyes with hers, not understanding him placing blame entirely on her. She desperately fought to hold her tears back.

"I am giving birth to the baby." She spoke finally, as she seemed to acquire an inner strength.

"I will not hold you to any responsibility toward the baby." She added.

"You do realize you are taking on a lot of responsibility, don't you?" Phil asked, as though shocked with Darla's decision.

"Yes, I realize all too well." She answered, disbelieving his lack of responsibility.

"I will have legal papers sent to you, relieving you of all ties." She added.

"Do it fast, I want this done and over." He ordered.

Without another word, Darla walked away from Phil without even a goodbye. As she drove away, she continuously blinked hard to contain the tears that were trying to escape her. She sang praise choruses to the Lord until she was able to let go of the pain Phil had inflicted on her.

In the months to come, Darla never heard from Phil. Kelley wrote, but his letters were brief and far in-between and she wondered if Kelley had felt that her pregnancy was too much to deal with.

Her job at the restaurant had worked out perfectly, with Darla barely gaining weight she was able to continue her job throughout her pregnancy.

Darla was dressed and ready for Sunday morning services when a sharp pain went through her stomach. Sitting down on the edge of her bed, she waited patiently to see if, and when, another pain might follow. With her labor pains now five minutes apart, she went to her girlfriend's room, finding it empty of her.

"Susie, where are you when I am ready to accept your help?" Darla whispered aloud, disliking being alone at this time.

With the labor pains now three minutes apart, she called for a taxi. Placing a note on the table for Susie, she picked up her pre-packed suitcase and waited outside for the taxi.

Arriving at the hospital, a nurse pushed Darla in a wheelchair to the labor room. She seemed to be in labor forever and oh, how she wished her mother were at her side, holding her hand.

With the baby finally arriving, Darla had tears of happiness streaming down her cheeks, as she wearily held her tiny baby daughter.

"You look as though you came from Heaven." Darla whispered, giving her baby a loving kiss.

"I will name you Heaven." She decided proudly, with a weak tender smile. A nurse gently took Heaven from her mother's arms, as another took care of Darla.

"You have a cheering section waiting in the hall for you." The nurse informed, as she pushed Darla on the gurney from the delivery room.

"Hi guys." Darla spoke happily, as Susie and several of her college friends walked next to her side.

"Congratulations!" Darla's friends exclaimed.

"A baby girl Darla, just what you wanted!" Susie said, excitedly.

"Have you seen her?" Darla asked, with tears of happiness over her friend's support.

"Yes and she is beautiful." The young adults answered.

"Have you named her yet?"

"Yes, her name is Heaven and she is a special baby." Darla answered, with an excited laugh.

Spending the first two weeks at home with her baby recuperating, Darla could become acquainted with her precious daughter. It was rough catching up in her classes, with her days of being absent during the baby's birth, but with the Lord's help, Darla survived with flying colors, receiving her diploma along with her fellow class members.

Picking up her telephone, Darla dialed her parent's number, filled with excitement.

"Hello."

"Hi, Mother. I am officially a registered nurse." Darla informed, happily.

"This is great!" Her mother exclaimed, as excited as her daughter.

"I will remain here for the summer, working. I plan to leave for home the first of September." Darla informed, in her soft, gentle voice.

"I believe Dad told you to return home as soon as you completed your schooling."

"He did, but I cannot afford the moving expense at this time."

"Dad will not go for you staying the summer, Darla."

"He will have to, I am one person and I can only do so much." Darla replied, looking at her baby peacefully sleeping in her crib.

"We will see to your expenses, dear." Her mother assured.

"I appreciate your offer, Mother, honestly, but you and Dad have paid my way enough. I must manage by myself."

"Okay, dear, I will tell Dad." Her mother agreed, with a defeated sigh.

"We love you." She added.

"I love you too."

The months of June and July were terribly hectic. Darla's evening waitress job paid so well in tips, she could not afford to give it up, yet with her hospital delivery expense, and her expense to move home, she could not seem to get ahead. Deciding to take a second job during the daytime, she worked at a nursery school, which allowed her to take Heaven with her on her job.

Heaven taking her mid-morning nap, Darla took advantage of her Saturday day off. Lying in the warm sun, sunbathing and reading her Bible, she appreciated the rest from her busy workweek.

"Darla, would you please come inside?" Susie asked, with a mysterious smile.

"I will be right there." She answered, slipping into her thongs and swimsuit cover-up, entering her home through the backdoor.

"Susie?" Darla questioned, puzzled.

"We are in the front room." Susie answered, as she sat in a chair, and their guest sat on the sofa.

Entering the front room, Susie had a radiant smile. Darla seemed to freeze in her tracks, as their tall, handsome visitor politely stood with her arrival.

"Kelley!" She exclaimed, rushing to him, as she hugged his neck tight.

"I cannot believe you are here! I check the mailbox every day for your letters." She informed, thrilled.

"You should have told me you were coming. I look terrible." She added.

"I called and your roommate took my message." Kelley informed.

"By the way, you look great." He complimented, and then gave her lips a light kiss.

"Thank you." Darla replied, looking up into Kelley's eyes.

"Why have your letters come so far in between?" She asked, as she took Kelley's hand into hers, leading him to the sofa.

"I was waiting for you to write, telling me the baby's father's intentions, but you never mentioned him. Then your letters became fewer, so I did not know what to think, until I spoke with Susie a few days ago."

"I am sorry. I forgot you asked me to write on that subject." Darla apologized, feeling badly for creating questions for him.

"Do not worry about it. Susie filled me in."

"Great." Darla replied, with a gentle laugh.

"Susie enjoys telling all my secrets." She explained, lightly teasing her girlfriend.

"I only told what everyone in Springfield already knows." Susie said, defensively.

"Which is?" Darla asked, with a kind smile.

"That Phil is a heartless jerk, whom left you the entire responsibility of Heaven. That you are killing yourself working two jobs because you are too stubborn to accept help and last, but not least, that you are madly in love with some preacher guy from home." Susie answered, bringing smiles to both Darla and Kelley's faces.

"I neglected to add that Susie does tell the truth." Darla shared.

"I am out of here for the weekend." Susie informed.

"Have fun and take Darla home, Kelley, before I am forced to admit her in the hospital."

"I will see what I can do." Kelley replied, his concern for Darla apparent on his face.

"Oh, Dar, you tell the truth also, Kelley is extremely handsome." Susie said, causing both Darla and Kelley to blush with her comment.

"You have actually survived two years rooming with her?" Kelley asked, as Susie left her home.

"Yes." Darla answered, with a pleasant smile.

"She helped me keep a smile on my face when I felt like giving up the past several months. She added.

"How have you been and be honest, Dar?" Kelley asked his concern apparent on his strong, yet gentle face.

"Overall, not too bad, I have been through some real struggles, but the Lord has helped me through." Darla answered, pleasantly.

"How about the baby, how is she?" Kelley asked.

"Heaven is a whole six months now and she is doing terrific. She is presently napping."

"What do your parents think of their granddaughter?" He asked, as he put his arm around her shoulder, gently pulling her closer to his side.

"They do not know of her yet." Darla answered, with reddened cheeks.

"Darla … " Kelley started.

"You had best call them before you leave for home."

"I intend to." Darla said.

"When will you be coming home?" Kelley asked.

"In a few weeks, I need to work a little longer. My living expenses have increased considerably, since the arrival of Heaven." She answered.

"I am sure they have."

"I see you are wearing my ring on your bracelet." Kelley said, with pride in his eyes.

"Of course, like Susie said, I am madly in love with you." She shared, looking up into his eyes.

"I assure you, my feelings for you are mutual." Kelley said, with a gentle smile, and then kissed Darla's lips, long and gently.

"I would like to take you and Heaven out for the evening if you haven't any plans."

"I cannot speak for Heaven, but I would love to go out."

"Then I will get out of here, so you will have plenty of time for both, a nap, and to prepare for our evening." Kelley suggested, getting up from the sofa.

"But you just arrived." Darla objected, lightly, as he took her hand in his, walking to the front door.

"You look terribly tired and you need to rest." Kelley advised, protectively.

"I will pick you up at six." He informed, followed by a light kiss.

"We will be ready." Darla agreed, happily.

Darla tried to follow Kelley's suggestion and rest, yet found her attempts useless because she was too excited to lay or even sit still. Bursting with happiness over her surprise visit from the one she so dearly loved and longed for, she thumbed through her wardrobe searching for the perfect outfit for her evening out, while Kelley was away checking into a motel and planning their evening.

Taking a relaxing bath did seem to make her feel somewhat rested. Working with great lengths on her long, straight hair, Darla made two curls, one on each side of her face, near her ears. Pulling the sides of her hair back, she tied a thin, delicate ribbon around her hair, allowing the long ribbon ends to flow freely down the back of her hair, mingling with the soft curls on the ends of her hair.

With her dark eyebrows arched perfectly, she lightly applied baby-blue eye shadow, mascara, and clear lip-gloss. With the completion of her hair and make-up, she picked Heaven up from her bedroom floor where she played, attempting to crawl.

Bathing her precious daughter with a song in her heart and sparkles in her eyes, Darla thanked the Lord repeatedly for bringing Kelley to visit and making her so happy.

Heaven, dressed in her prettiest Sunday dress and dress shoes with a tiny, delicate matching ribbon on her hair, Darla sat her in her crib with her toys. Darla quickly slipped into her prettiest feminine dress and matching dress shoes and then stopping in front of her full-length mirror, she took one last glance before hurrying to answer the ringing doorbell.

Opening the front door for Kelley, Darla was extremely impressed. Kelley was very becoming in his handsome suit.

"You look very nice." Darla greeted, with a sweet, approving smile.

"Of course I do, the best, for the best." Kelley replied pleased, followed by a light kiss.

"Get your daughter; we have a big night ahead of us." He ordered, impatiently.

Darla went to her bedroom, taking Heaven from her crib, where she sat playing, then returned to her waiting date.

"Hello, Miss Heaven." Kelley spoke, with a look of pride, holding his hands out toward the baby.

Heaven held her arms up toward Kelley, with a big happy smile on her face, as she excitedly kicked her legs. With tenderness in his eyes, Kelley carefully and eagerly took Heaven from her mother, into his arms.

"Heaven is almost as pretty as her mother." Kelley said giving Darla a loving, comforting smile, as he politely opened the front door for their departure.

Kelley took his two choice girls to a very exclusive restaurant for dinner. He played lightly with Heaven, as she sat in a high chair, smiling at Kelley, playfully. Darla's heart swelled with pride, with Kelley's natural ability to amuse her daughter, his caring for Heaven was genuine.

"You are definitely a proud father." Their waitress complimented, her arrival quieting Kelley's play.

"He ... " Darla began, quickly hushing, as Kelley secretly kicked her leg under the table.

"I am." Kelley agreed, addressing the waitress, with a look of pride, before ordering their meals.

"Your mom almost spoiled our evening, Heaven." Kelley said, as the waitress left their table.

"You had best hope I do not get a bruise on my leg."

Kelley ignored Darla's scolding. Taking her hand in his gently, his face grew serious, as he looked deep into her soft, sparkling eyes.

"I told my parents of your pregnancy." Kelley informed, pretending not to notice Darla's face quickly turning its reddest.

"Mom said everyone makes mistakes and Dad said I would make a good father." He shared, with a pleased smile.

Darla was speechless and deeply touched by Kelley's' parent's loyalty toward her, after all she had put their son through.

"I stopped by your home, before I left California to bring you something." He informed, putting his hand in his suit jacket pocket.

"Will you wear this ring, accepting it as becoming my fiancée?" He asked.

"Yes, I accept." Darla answered proudly, with tear-filled eyes.

"I sincerely love you, Kelley." She added.

"I know Dar and I sincerely love you." Kelley replied slipping the dainty diamond, he had gotten her for her sixteenth birthday on her finger.

Following dinner, Kelley took Darla and Heaven to see a play. As Heaven grew tired and restless, Darla gave her, her bottle quickly, quieting her. She was soon sleeping soundly.

"Allow me to hold Heaven." Kelley offered, politely.

"She must be heavy." He added.

With Heaven situated on Kelley's lap, sleeping soundly, Darla slipped her arm through Kelley's, leaning closer to his side.

Returning home late from their busy evening, Darla dressed Heaven for bed then tucked her tiny baby in for the night. Quietly closing the bedroom door behind her, Darla returned to her guest in the front room.

"I prepared a soft drink for us." Kelley said, setting their drinks on the coffee table. He removed his suit coat, laying it over the arm of the sofa, and then loosened his tie.

"Thank you. May I make you a snack, or a sandwich?" Darla asked politely, as she picked up Kelley's suit jacket to hang in the coat closet.

"No, thank you." Kelley answered, taking his coat from Darla's hands, returning it to the sofa arm, as he patiently stood, awaiting her to sit down.

Taking Darla's hands into his, Kelley pulled his fiancée closer to him.

"My jacket is fine where it is and there is no need for you to hang it up. I will not have you waiting on me during my visit. You have enough to tend to already." Kelley informed, considerately.

"You may give me a kiss." He said.

Darla looked up into Kelley's eyes with both pride and compassion, allowing Kelley's lips to meet hers, as he kissed her long, yet with gentleness.

Removing his lips from Darla's, Kelley silently looked at Darla's face for several long moments, with tenderness.

"You have become a beautiful young lady." Kelley complimented, kissing his fiancée once again.

"Kelley." Darla interrupted, in her soft voice, putting her fingers over Kelley's lips, lovingly.

"Is not this the time when Dad makes his appearance informing us we have kissed enough?" She asked with a gentle smile, causing Kelley to blush.

"Yes, I believe so." Kelley remembered, laughing with embarrassment, with his fiancée's wise interruption.

Darla felt as though she could conquer the world, as she walked Kelley to his car, to begin his drive home.

"Call your parents today, telling them of Heaven. I will stop by their home when I return, informing them of my visit." He instructed, thoughtfully.

"Are you still taking your medicine?" He asked, putting his arms around his fiancées waist.

"Yes, faithfully, I am just a little tired."

"Get rid of your waitress job, so you can rest." He gently ordered.

"Do you feel my engagement ring gives you the right to give me orders?" Darla asked, with sparkles in her eyes and a radiant smile, as she looked into Kelley's eyes.

"Yes Ma'am. I will be even tougher when you become my wife and I assure you, I will be most protective of you."

"I can be hard to get along with, also." Darla said.

"I am a bit bigger then you, Dar." Kelley reminded, standing seven inches taller than she does.

"You have a point there." Darla agreed, with a soft laugh.

Tightening his arms around his fiancés' waist, Kelley kissed her long and gentle.

"Take care of yourself and hurry home. I will be waiting impatiently." Kelley said, with a boyish grin.

"I will. Have a safe trip." Darla replied, happily, as she waved goodbye.

Returning inside her home, Darla picked up the telephone, intending to call her parents. Deciding against the call, she wrote her parents a detailed letter of her past instead, informing them of their granddaughter, Kelley's visit, and her engagement.

CHAPTER 8

With only two weeks remaining, Darla would be able to leave Missouri, moving back home to Ragweed, California. Returning home from her nursery job, Darla felt exhausted. Sitting Heaven in her playpen, just inside the front door, she removed her shoes, stretching out on the sofa.

Intending to take a short rest before showering before due at her waitress job in only two hours, she closed her heavy, drowsy eyes. Awakened by the ringing from her telephone, she found it was now past time for her to be at work.

"Oh dear … " She sighed, glancing at her sleeping daughter in her playpen, as she answered the telephone.

"Hello." She answered, with a tired voice.

"Darla, this is Dad."

"Hello Daddy." She greeted pleasantly, taking the telephone to the sofa, lying back down.

"Mother and I received your letter about our granddaughter. How are you, Babe? How is the baby?" He asked concern in his voice.

"Heaven is fine, Dad. She is a good baby and I am fortunate." Darla answered, proudly.

"Good. How is my daughter?" Her father asked.

"You sound tired." He added

"I am tired, but I only have two more weeks of work. If I can manage to hang in, then Heaven and I will be able to come home and I will be so glad to get home." Darla answered, with a tired, weak smile.

"What do you say if I fly up early Friday morning? I will help you pack and drive you and my granddaughter home, where you both belong?"

"Your offer sounds tempting." Darla answered, with a soft laugh, pleased with her father's eagerness.

"I really need to work the remainder of this week and next week. I was not aware how expensive it is being a parent."

"Now perhaps you are able to understand your dear old Dad's reasoning for being conservative." Her father said, with a chuckle, bringing a smile to his daughter's face.

"According to Bill, you handed me my every request." Darla teased.

"You and I both know Bill enjoys stretching the truth."

"This is my darling brother." Darla agreed, with a smile.

"I believe I will come Friday, babe. You can quit your jobs early and I will reimburse you. We will consider it an early wedding gift."

"Oh, Daddy, that would be wonderful." Darla agreed, deeply touched.

"I must have the wrong daughter, I do not hear protesting in regards to independence, and I have to make it on my own." Pastor Roberts laughed.

"I would rather forget about that, Darla, she caused me countless problems." Darla confessed, feeling drowsy.

"I would like to forget that Darla also, Babe." Her father agreed, sympathetic.

"Dad, if it will not be a burden for you or Mother, would it be possible for Mother to fly out until you arrive? I am not feeling well at all. Perhaps, if it is not asking too much, Mother could give me a hand with the baby, so I will be able to rest some, before the drive home." Darla shared, now fighting to keep her eyes open.

"I will put Mom on the phone, Babe." Her father replied, concern in his voice.

"Darla." Her mother spoke, with worry in her voice.

"I will see you in the morning, dear, so you rest now." She ordered, lovingly.

Calling the restaurant, Darla apologized for missing work. Hanging the telephone up, she returned to the sofa, near her daughter's playpen, quickly falling fast asleep.

Awakened early to her daughter's fussing, Darla tiredly got up from the sofa. She slowly, yet lovingly tended to Heaven. With Heaven in her highchair, she fed her, her breakfast.

Picking up the telephone, she called the nursery taking the day off.

Sitting Heaven in her playpen, Darla took a warm relaxing bath. The warm water felt refreshing on her tired, sore muscles.

Hearing the doorbell, she quickly got out of the tub, slipping her robe over her wet body. Hurrying from the bathroom, she could see her mother waiting on the front porch, through the open drapes.

"I am coming." Darla called, excitedly, hurrying to the door.

"Hi Mother!" She exclaimed, giving her a hug and a kiss.

"You are all wet, dear." Her mother said, with a soft laugh, hugging her daughter regardless.

"I am sorry, Mother. I was pampering myself, taking a leisurely bath." She explained.

"I am so glad you could come." She added.

"You should know, Darla, all you have to do is call. Dad and I are always available for you."

"I do know this, Mother." Darla assured, kindly.

"Hello Sweetheart." Mrs. Roberts spoke, happily, taking Heaven from her playpen.

Darla silently admired this precious moment. Her mother was both overwhelmed and thrilled to be a grandmother.

"Heaven is so pretty, Darla."

"Thank you, Mother." Darla replied, with a pleased smile.

"She must have a good appetite. She certainly is the picture of health."

"She is perfectly healthy. Apparently she did not inherit my not so healthy genes." Darla reported, pleased.

"You have a cute home, dear, I like this." She voiced, admiring the girl's decor.

"Thank you."

"I hope you are not going to miss it here and regret coming home."

"Never, I think it is pretty here being able to witness the changing of the seasons, but I want and need to go home. I have had many good times here, mainly play. You may say I have outgrown that stage. I want to be near my family and have each of you become a big part of Heaven's life. I do realize how important it is for one to have a family." Darla assured, touching her tender mother's heart.

"Perhaps you should go change, dear, so you do not see your mother cry." Mrs. Roberts suggested happily, with watery eyes.

"Yes Ma'am." Darla agreed, with an understanding smile, giving her mother a kiss.

Returning to the bathroom, Darla moved at a slow pace, enjoying her day away from the hustle of work. It had been several extremely long months for her going at a fast pace, since her daughter had arrived.

"I made coffee, dear." Sister Roberts informed, placing their cups on the kitchen bar.

"Thank you." Darla said.

"Darla, I am going to give you some orders, and I trust you will obey them. You have disobeyed orders enough." Mrs. Roberts informed, with a gentle smile, bringing a smile to her daughter's face.

"I want you to call both your jobs this morning, informing your employers you will no longer be working. Secondly, I want you to take it easy, and truly be rested this week because I am here to help and this is exactly what I intend to do. Heaven and I will get along fine. Thirdly, I insist you and Heaven live with dad and I until you and Kelley marry. Your room is big enough for both of you."

"Thank you, Mother. I accept, and I will be obedient." Darla agreed, pleasantly.

"Well? Make your telephone calls, and go back to bed. You look worn out."

"Yes Ma'am."

With Darla's mother insisting on taking charge, within a couple of days, Darla felt better. Her mother's presence and fellowship had been most refreshing also. Sleeping until ten Thursday morning, Darla discovered her daughter was not in her crib.

Slipping into a pair of shorts, T-shirt, and sandals, ready for the hot July day, Darla pulled her hair back into a barrette. Ready for her day of packing for her move home with her parents, she left her room to greet her mother and daughter good morning.

"Good morning, sleepy head." Mr. Roberts greeted, getting up from the barstool.

"Hi Daddy, you are here early!" Darla exclaimed, hugging her father tightly, as he hugged her.

"I am an impatient person when I want my family home. I could not wait until tomorrow to see my daughter and granddaughter." He explained, appearing extremely pleased.

"Heaven is a beautiful baby. I am proud to be her grandpa." He added.

"Babe, Mom and I love you more than anything and there is nothing you could do to cause us to love you less. I want you to understand and know this." Mr. Roberts informed, sincerely.

"I understand, Dad." Darla assured, with watery eyes, touched with her parents silently forgiving her for her immature actions, yet offering her their all, regardless.

"Good because I like it best when we understand one another." He said.

"Now, how about some waffles? I am doing the cooking and you are still too skinny in old dad's book." Her father said, with his happy-go-lucky grin.

"Yes, please."

With her parents assisting Darla with her packing, stirred many fond memories. Her parents had always been at her side, encouraging and comforting her, with the exceptions that she had created, when not allowing them to be included.

"They are the greatest." She silently thought as they worked together, enjoying one another's company.

"Babe, I hope you and I survive two days of driving in your compact car, with a dog and a baby." Mr. Roberts voiced, with a chuckle, looking doubtful.

Darla and her mother smiled at one another over her father's doubts as the two women prepared their last dinner in Darla's Missouri home.

"I do too." Darla agreed, with a compassionate smile, feeling for her father having to be involved in the long driving trip.

"Darla, why not allow me to take Heaven home on the plane with me in the morning? I would love to take her and it would be much easier on her, then traveling for two days and nights in this heat." Her mother suggested.

"Mother, Heaven has never been away from me for an entire night. Are you sure she will do alright?" Darla asked, hesitating, concern for her daughter s happiness and security.

"I am sure she will miss you, dear. I do believe she will do well because she seems content and easy to please."

"I am sure Heaven will do much better being with you, then riding in the car." Darla replied, thoughtfully.

"Mother, Dad, I want you both to know how much I appreciate you for being my parents. I could never repay you for all the love, support, guidance, and teachings you have given me. When I was at my worst, you never stopped loving me, or have you ever turned your back on me. I want you to know how grateful I am to both of you, to be your daughter." Darla said, sincerely.

"Thank you, dear, for the kind words." Her mother replied, deeply touched.

"Since I re-dedicated my life to the Lord a year ago, I have sincerely tried to undo all of my mistakes I created while not living a Christian life. I will continue to do my best dad, and not cause you and mother anymore pain."

"We know you will do your best, babe. Mom and I are more than pleased to have our old Darla back."

It had been good for Darla, having first her mother visiting with her, then her drive home with her father. Her parents had said nothing in regards to her behavior while away from them at college. Instead, they opened their hearts and arms to her and their granddaughter, welcoming them both into their hearts and their home.

It was early Sunday afternoon, as Mr. Roberts turned down his street toward his home, with his daughter, her car, and small U-Haul trailer.

"Are you getting excited, babe?" Pastor Roberts asked, with a pleased grin, secretly observing his daughter's silent anxiousness.

"Yes." She answered with a soft laugh.

"I cannot wait to hold Heaven in my arms. This drive has been the longest two days of my life." She added.

"Personally, I enjoyed our time together." Her father said.

"I did too Daddy." Darla assured, giving her father a lovingly smile.

"It appears the entire crew is here, babe. I bet Cindy and Bill already have Heaven spoiled rotten."

"And Mother ... " Darla agreed, pleased.

"I wonder who the blue Vega belongs to?" Her father asked.

"Could it possibly belong to Kelley Peterson?" He added, teasing.

"Do you know anyone besides Kelley that drives a blue Vega?" Darla asked, with a pleased smile.

"It has to be that Kelley's car." Her father answered.

"It looks like the same car I have seen in the drive dozens of times since he visited my daughter in Missouri." He teased, yet held a look of approval on his face and in his eyes.

"Your home and family await your entrance, babe."

"Thank you, Daddy, for everything." Darla said, happily, giving her father's neck a tight excited hug, before entering her home.

"You are welcome, babe. Welcome home." He replied sincerely, pleased for his daughter's happiness, as he opened the backdoor of their home, allowing his daughter to enter first.

Darla soon had tears of joy streaming down her young, tender, pretty face as she received, as well as gave, hugs and kisses to her family and precious daughter. Though her tears continued, her face was aglow with a beautiful smile. She was home where she belonged, as her father had stated.

Kelley waited for his turn, silently and patiently, to greet Darla, as he had a year ago when she had visiting during summer break. Darla secretly longed for his turn to greet her and feel his touch. She had missing him terribly.

The room grew quiet, as Kelley approached his fiancé. Darla's family silently sat down in the family room, watching, observing, as though a spotlight was on the young, deeply in love couple.

Kelley's face bore gentleness, but held a much stronger look from his years of maturing from the teenage boy Darla had fallen in love with, before her stood a handsome young man, ready for marriage and family responsibilities, warming her heart by merely his presence.

"I am glad you are home, Dar." Kelley greeted, taking her hands gently into his, kissing her lightly on her lips.

Darla's face flushed, expressing her happiness, with an excited laugh, as Bill led her family in a round of applause.

"I have something I would like to say." Kelley informed, at the end of their applauding.

Putting his arm around Darla's shoulder, he gently pulled her closer to his side, as he looked at each member at his fiancées family.

Darla silently and politely stood at Kelley's side, as curious as her family, eager to hear what Kelley wished to share.

"To Brother and Sister Roberts, I commend you on a job well done. You have raised a tender, loving, beautiful, dedicated Christian daughter."

Kelley began, in his strong voice, as though he had well prepared his speech.

"Secondly, I thank you both for giving your approval in regards to Darla's and my engagement." Kelley added, in all sincerity.

"With the announcing of our engagement, I give you fair warning Brother Roberts, I intend to kiss Darla very often." He confessed, with a boyish grin, bringing laughter from his fiancés family, at his openness, as his fiancés face reddened with his bluntness, surprising even her.

"Bill, I thank you for not being "rude" and "butting in", as Darla often accused, rather just as bull-headed as your sister, protecting her, caring about her, supporting her when she needed you most. I also thank you for the weekly reports to Darla's feelings toward me."

"You are welcome, Kelley." Bill remarked winking at his sister, as Darla's face reddened again.

"Kelley, I believe you have said enough." Darla informed, blushing with a nervous laugh, not trusting what more he intended to share.

"I am almost through, be patient a little longer, Dar." Kelley replied, ignoring her wishes to hush him.

"God, as well as everyone in this room, knows how long I have had to be patient with you." He added, looking into her eyes, enjoying his play, and holding her firmly at his side to prevent her from escaping.

"Thanks a lot." She said with a tickled, embarrassed laugh, at the honesty in his statement.

"Cindy, I thank you for being there daily and nightly for Darla; nightly, sharing a room with her, enduring her moodiness and daily, keeping track of her activities, informing me of her friends, moods, and whereabouts." Kelley added.

"And Darla ... " Kelley said, looking into her eyes, giving a sigh as though he did not know what to do with her.

"Kelley, I am warning you." Darla said, with a nervous laugh, not at all trusting his next move.

"In all sincerity ... " Kelley began, returning his eyes to the family.

"I am pleased and honored to be marrying into a fine family and I will do my best to take care of Darla and make her happy."

"We are pleased you will be our son-in-law, Kelley." Sister Roberts assured.

"Thank you." Kelley replied, touched by his future mother-in-law's acceptance.

"I would like to marry Darla as soon as the necessary arrangements can be made."

"Are you becoming impatient?" Darla asked, with a happy smile.

"Yes, I am." He answered honestly, his face growing serious once again, as he looked down into Darla's eyes.

"I also would like to adopt Heaven, raising her as our child. I believe this would be best for Heaven, if you agree, Dar. I will treat Heaven as if she was my own child." Kelley said.

Darla had tears of joy in her eyes, as she looked up into Kelley's gentle eyes.

"Are you sure this is what you want, Kelley?" Darla asked slowly, overwhelmed by Kelley's request and endless love.

"I am positive. Have you ever known me to say what I do not mean?" He asked.

"No." Darla answered, with sparkles in her eyes.

"I accept both proposals." She informed, excitedly hugging Kelley's neck, followed by a gentle kiss.

"Brother Roberts, Dar kissed me, I did not kiss her." Kelley remarked quickly, laughing.

Darla quietly moved from Kelley, blushing, as though she had temporarily forgotten her family's presences.

"Excuse me; I believe I will freshen up before dinner." Darla said pleasantly, quickly leaving the family room.

Darla's eyes sparkled and her face glowed with happiness. She assisted the women folk, setting Sunday dinner on the table, with Heaven following behind in her walker.

"I do not know you well, Darla or Kelley." Spoke Paula, Bill's wife.

"What I have seen and heard, I am sure you both will truly be happy together."

"Thank you, Paula." Darla replied, touched by her sister-in-law's kindness.

"Aunt Mary, how soon will you and Darla have the wedding planned?" Cindy asked, excited for her cousin.

"I am not sure, dear." She sighed, as though in deep thought.

"Kelley may have to wait longer than he thinks." She added.

As the Robert's family, Kelley, Cindy and Dan, Bill and Paula, along with Heaven sat eating their dinner, the family experienced the warmth of unity. It was as though the prodigal son had returned, coming back into his family.

"I have a question for you, Bill, and you, Cindy." Darla informed with a smile, yet scolding as she fed her daughter.

"Did you two actually snitch on me to Kelley?" She asked.

"I did not snitch, Darla, but I did answer Kelley's question truthfully." Cindy shared, giving her cousin a loving smile.

"What about you, Bill? I am sure deliberately snitched." Darla accused, in her soft, gentle way.

"Sure I did. It was inevitable that you and Kelley would be together and you should be thanking me, Sis. Look how terrific everything has turned out." Bill said, pleased for his sister.

"Regardless the outcome, Bill, it is pretty bad when your own family sets you up." She scolded, teasingly.

"Wait a minute, Dar; your entire family was not involved." Kelley interrupted.

"I could not get any place with your parents." He informed, with a boyish grin.

"Your dad would say, 'Son, if you have questions concerning my daughter, be man enough to ask her yourself.'" Kelley shared, gruffly, imitating Mr. Roberts, bringing laughter from his audience.

"Your mom would say, 'Kelley, I honestly do not know where Darla's head is these days.'" Kelley added.

"Bill, my thanks go to Mother and Dad then." Darla decided, yet giving her brother a tender smile.

"Bill, we should be going." Paula informed, pushing her empty plate aside.

"Going? Going where?" Bill asked, puzzled.

"My parents are expecting us to visit them today, also."

"Don't you think we should pass today? We see your family every weekend, Paula. I have not seen my sister for a year." He reminded, annoyed with his wife's rudeness and selfishness.

253

"My parents are expecting us." Paula insisted, stubbornly, picking up her purse.

The dinner table grew quiet, as each went about his and her own business, as not to intrude or bring more embarrassment to Bill, then his wife was doing.

"Bill." Darla began, slowly, as she washed Heaven's face and hands.

"I do understand if you have to leave." Darla assured kindly, feeling for her brother's awkward position.

"Thank you, Darla." Paula said, waiting for her husband to join her.

Bill silently got up from the dinner table with a look of fury on his face.

"Sis, I will be back shortly. I would like to go horseback riding with you." Bill said, pushing his chair up to the table.

Darla silently looked at her brother's embarrassed, aggravated face. Secondly, she looked at her sister-in-law's stubborn, insisting face, now filling with anger, with her husband's intentions.

"Okay, Dar?" Bill asked, determined.

"Okay." She agreed, though hesitant, not wanting in the middle of a spat.

Mrs. Roberts' face now appeared drained, as Bill and Paula left the house. Dad had expressions of concern, Cindy and Dan silently began clearing the table, and Kelley insisted on taking Heaven, and putting her down for her nap, leaving Darla alone with her parents at the table.

"Are Bill and Paula having marital problems already?" Darla asked, concerned for her brother's happiness.

"I am afraid so." Mrs. Roberts answered, with a weak smile, not wanting to spoil her daughter's homecoming.

"I am not sure if Bill will hang in his marriage, much longer." Mr. Roberts remarked.

"We will have to pray hard for Bill and Paula." Darla replied, giving her parents a gentle smile.

"You are right, babe." Her father agreed, getting up from the table.

"Mother, you rest. I will assist Cindy and Dan with the dishes." Darla suggested, kindly, changing their thoughts from Bill's upset.

"No, stay put, Cindy is capable of managing the kitchen. You and I have plans to discuss." She explained with a pleased smile.

"Great!" Darla exclaimed, eager to begin her wedding preparations.

Darla and her mother sat at the dining table, busy planning Darla's wedding. Bill had returned alone, assisting his father, Dan, and Kelley unloading Darla's things from the U-Haul and Cindy busily directed the men in arranging Darla's room, unpacking her cousin's things for her.

Completing the wedding plans, Darla and her mother joined their family in the family room. The men sat recuperating from their heavy unloading in the hot desert heat, while Cindy politely served glasses of ice tea.

"How is October first for our wedding date? It is a Friday at seven in the evening, so we may use candles." Darla shared, excitedly, sitting down next to Kelley.

"We have to wait two more months?" Kelley asked.

"October first is pushing it, Kelley." Darla assured gently, understanding his impatience.

"This will be fine then." He agreed, politely.

As evening came, and the air cooling somewhat, the young adults strolled outside to the corral.

"I thank each of you for being here today. You have each made this day most special and you have made me the happiest I could possibly be." Darla shared.

"You deserve to be happy. You have spent your life trying to make each of us happy." Bill replied, compassionately.

Darla felt overwhelmed with compassion and happiness. Her sparkling eyes became moist from her family's love and devotion shown, with their kind words.

"Sis, are you coming riding with me or are you becoming emotional on us?" Bill asked, offering the reins to her.

"I am riding with you and becoming emotional." Darla answered, with a beautiful smile, taking the reins politely from her brother.

Darla felt great, as she galloped her horse next to her brother. Her long hair blowing in the wind, her heart leaped with excitement of the thrill of the horse's speed. Slowing their horses to a trot, then a slow walk, they turned their horses toward home, not wanting to tire them before the others enjoyed their turn for a ride.

"I am happy for you Sis, the way everything has worked out for you." Bill said, breaking their silence.

"Thank you. God has truly had mercy on me, but I wish this day could have been more pleasant for you too."

"Perhaps I am not cut out for married life, as you are." Bill replied.

"Dear brother, you are already married." Darla reminded, carefully, not wanting to add to his upsets by prying or scolding.

"Divorce is becoming acceptable now, dear Sister." Bill said, his face growing tense.

"I will race you home." He challenged, quickly changing their line of talk.

As darkness fell, Darla bathed and dressed Heaven for bed. Picking her daughter up, drinking her bottle, Darla softly sang, "Jesus loves you," to her daughter until she was sleeping, then placing her in her crib, she quietly left her bedroom.

With Cindy, Dan, and Bill, leaving for their separates homes, Kelley and Darla went for a walk alone.

"Are you aware it has been hours since I have had the opportunity to kiss you?" Kelley asked, looking into Darla's sparkling eyes, with a grin.

"I realize all too well." Darla answered, stepping closer to her fiancé, putting her arms around him, looking up into his eyes, allowing his lips to meet hers.

"We truly have to wait two more months?" Kelley asked, with a chuckle and red face, causing his fiancé to blush and laugh with his impatience.

"The time will go more quickly then you presently think." Darla assured, as Kelley put his arm around her shoulders, slowly walking closer to the corral.

"I am sure you are right. Your dad had a rather lengthy talk with me. I got the message, if I let you down after you become my wife, it will probably cost me my life." Kelley shared, followed by laughter.

"I have no doubt Bill will always take your side too." He added, with a pleased grin, bringing a smile to Darla's face.

"We will always be on one another's side, Kelley. We will be a team working for the Lord, and loving one another as God has chosen for us." Darla assured, leaning closer to Kelley, as they leaned against the corral fencing.

"Those were my words, in my defense to your dad." Kelley informed.

"Your dad also explained the importance of you not overdoing it, becoming run down and your daily, prescription of iron medicine. I assured him, I would be cautious of your workload and activities. I will not allow you to become overburdened, Dar. I promise you this." He added.

"I will mention this, only once, unless you wish to discuss this subject at some point and time with me. I also know the full details in regards to your parents adopting you. I assure you; God had a plan for you from the day you were born, just as He has a plan for Heaven." Kelley shared, gently and carefully, as not to offend the one he dearly loved.

"This, I am sure of." Darla agreed, with a loving smile, comforting Kelley, allowing his concern for possibly overstepping his boundaries to fade.

"My parents are hoping to see you and meet Heaven." Kelley said, with a pleased smile.

"In fact, I have been sworn to try to talk you into coming for dinner tomorrow evening." He added.

"I would like this." Darla said.

"I give you fair warning that my mom has already planned a dinner to announce our engagement. She also informed me, that I best remember Heaven will become a Peterson, therefore, she expects equal rights as a grandmother." He shared with a pleased smile, knowing his news would touch his fiancés heart.

Darla's eyes filled with tears, as she looked into Kelley's eyes, deeply moved by his mother's wishes.

"I am not finished, there is more." He informed, bringing an excited laugh from her, as she released her tears.

"Dad wants me to tell you to look up into the Heavens and to never look down again, regardless of trials, and your tears will never last for long." Kelley added.

Darla's tears came quickly now, uncontrollably. Kelley put his arms around his fiancé, pulling her close to him, silently allowing her, her time to shed her tears of joy.

Regaining her composer, wiping her tears from her face with her hands, Kelley handed her his handkerchief.

"I will have to remember to always carry a handkerchief, now that I will be involved with an emotional female, indefinitely." He soothed with a smile, bringing a happy laugh from Darla.

"I trust you have plenty." She said.

"I will make sure I do." Kelley assured her.

"I cannot believe how foolish I was to turn from the Lord, you, and both our families. Between you and our two families alone, there is more love, understanding, and comfort then one could ever endure in a lifetime." Darla said.

"And rules, and responsibilities, and ... " Kelley reminded, with a laugh.

"True." Darla agreed, with a gentle smile, her eyes dancing with happiness.

"I am the Youth Pastor here in Ragweed therefore; I have not been attending the church in Dunes, since I graduated from college."

"Whew, you are already officially a minister. This is great. Congratulations." Voiced Darla, excitedly, giving Kelley a kiss.

"It is good experience. Hopefully this job will prepare me for the day when I accept my first pastoral position for a church."

"I am sure you are aware of my involvement to the street kids, with the park ministry. On Tuesday and Friday nights, I direct this ministry and I go Tuesday and Friday nights. The official services held in the park are still Friday nights. We are desperate for your guitar playing when singing choruses."

"I cannot wait to return full-time in the park ministry." Darla assured.

"But ... " She started, hesitating.

"My parents, I do not want to upset them, Kelley." She added slowly.

"Pray about it and the Lord will lead you in your dealings with your parents. You and I both know the Lord chose us for that ministry as a team." Kelley advised.

"I know." Darla agreed, with a sigh.

"I will simply have to find a way to break this news to them." She added.

"As far as my capabilities to support us, I assure you, I will always be a hard worker. Presently, as you know, I am working as a carpenter for a contractor, but this job will be ending in a few days. Your dad offered me at least six months carpentry work with him. The pay is decent, besides I receive a small salary for my youth pastor position. We will not become rich, but we will do fine."

"Kelley, I intend to seek a nursing position." Darla informed.

"My pay will help and I cannot wait to begin either." She shared, enthusiastic.

"I am glad for you, Dar. I know you have worked hard to achieve your nursing goal. If you want to work, I am behind you one hundred percent, but as far as assisting to support us, I will take care of us on my earnings." Kelley informed, firmly, with pride clearly in his voice.

"Then I will go shopping often." She responded quickly, with a soft laugh, as not to offend her fiancés' pride, bringing an approving smile to his face.

"In all honesty, it is not necessary for you to work. I am sure you will learn, dealing with a daughter, a home, and a demanding, selfish husband, will be a full-time job."

"Perhaps I will work part-time, making each of us happy."

"Perhaps this would be wise. I am sure Heaven would prefer her mother's attention much more than a babysitter's." Kelley replied, thinking of each one's best interest.

"Who will you have sit Heaven?" Kelley asked.

"I have not thought about this, but I will not take her to a nursery, so whoever I choose will be someone I personally know." Darla answered concern on her young face, as Kelley's question tugged at her.

"I am sure you will find someone suitable." Kelley assured.

"We should begin looking for a place to live, within the next couple of weeks. We will need time to furnish a home before our wedding date." Kelley suggested, putting his arms around Darla, pulling her close to him, and looking down into her eyes.

"After I say, 'I do,' I am taking you home with me." He added.

"Until death will we part." Darla agreed, happily, allowing Kelley to pull her closer, kissing her.

"Do you have any objections to living here in Ragweed? Living here would be convenient, with our involvement in the park ministry, and other church activities." He explained, still holding his fiancé in his arms, looking into her eyes as though spellbound.

"I have no objections." Darla replied.

"I have been asked to try out for a pastoral position in Tucson, Arizona. The present Pastor plans to resign in a year and I am considering the position."

"I am happy for you." Darla said, with pride on her face.

"Darla, you know, being the wife of a minister has ups and downs. We may have to move from home to home or state to state, several times in our lifetime, so I want you to be aware of what you may be in for as my wife." He shared, considerately.

"Kelley, I sincerely love you and your interests are my interests. I am sure I will become tired of moving, or aggravated at times with having to share our time with others. You will be at my side helping me through the rough times, as I will be at your side, loving, comforting, and supporting you, through all situations, for as the Bible teaches, we will become as one. I want to be your wife more than anything."

"Aye, your words are music to my ears, Miss Darla."

Walking Darla to her door as the hour grew late; Kelley gently took his fiancée into his arms.

"Could you be ready by six tomorrow evening?"

"I will be ready and waiting." Darla answered.

Kelley kissed Darla long and gentle.

"I had best allow you to go inside. We do not want to upset your parents." Kelley said, considerately.

"Okay, bye."

Entering her home, Darla was startled. "Dad … " Darla said her hand on her chest. "I did not know you were still up."

"I was waiting for you to come inside." Mr. Roberts informed, with concern on his face.

"Daddy, is something bothering you?"

"Perhaps it is nothing." He answered, hesitant.

"You are concerned with me, for being out late with Kelley, am I right?" Darla asked, sensitive to her father's ways.

"Yes, I suppose I am."

"I apologize, Dad. I should not have allowed my excitement over this day to cause you to worry. I promise to remember I am still single, and living under your roof."

"I appreciate this, Babe." Mr. Roberts replied, his face relaxing.

"Goodnight, Daddy."

"Goodnight, Babe."

Monday morning brought busy plans for everyone. Mr. Roberts, his wife, Kelley, and each member of Darla's family had returned to their jobs after their weekend breaks.

Darla made the necessary telephone calls, to get her wedding plans under way. Though it was only mid-morning, she prepared a special dessert for her parents, and planned their dinner preparations. She and Heaven would be away during the dinner hour, so she intended to serve her parents their dinner, making their evening special.

Dinner preparations completed, Darla changed into a pair of cut-offs, tank top, and thongs. Setting Heaven's playpen on the front lawn, she sat Heaven inside. With Heaven playing, enjoying the outdoors under a large shade tree, Darla washed her car.

"Hi, stranger!" Candy yelled, through her open car window, as she turned in the drive.

"Hi." Darla replied, excitedly, hurrying to her neighbor's car.

"When did you come home?" She inquired, getting out of her car.

"Yesterday, you are on my telephone list and I intended to track you down after I washed my car."

"You would have found me. I am on my way to ask my mom if I can move in with her for a while. Mike and I are splitting up."

"I am sorry for you, Candy. I had heard you and Mike married. Do you have a child?"

"Twin boys, they are a year old." She answered proudly.

"My mom is not going to like the boys and me cramping her style." She added with a sigh.

"I do not have a choice because Mike parties all the time and he gets crazy like my dad use to do. I will never have a decent life with him nor will the boys. I am sick of the fighting and worrying how I am going to pay the rent on my pay because Mike drinks his paycheck up."

"Do you still party, Candy?" Darla asked, her heart going out to her friend.

"I party occasionally, but not every day, and never around the boys." Candy answered.

"I heard you turned religious, is this true?" Candy asked.

"I re-conformed a year ago." Darla answered, with a soft laugh, over Candy's disappointed expression.

"What a bummer, I was going to invite you out. We would have a blast, Darla, like the old days." Candy encouraged.

"We would have a blast?" Darla questioned, as though surprised.

"How many parties did I attend where I truly had a blast? I was down more often than not and I was grounded nine-tenths of the time, besides breaking my parent's hearts." Darla reminded.

"I guess that was the reality of our partying teens." Candy agreed, with a smile.

"You were different, Darla. Your heart was never completely in to partying and I secretly thought you would return to your church ways."

"Thank you for the kind words." Her friends' continuing loyalty touched Darla.

"Come meet my daughter, I too am a mother." Darla shared, proudly, leading her friend to Heaven's playpen.

"This is Heaven, Candy. She is six months old."

"She is so sweet." Candy said, taking the baby into her arms.

"She definitely looks like you." Candy added.

"Thank you." Darla replied.

"Are you married?" Candy asked.

"No." Darla answered, her face now flushed.

"I became pregnant while away at college, due to my foolish ways of thinking during my party stage. Heaven has never seen her father and he wanted no ties with a child."

"What a bummer. I bet your parents freaked out when they learned you were pregnant." Candy said.

"No, they shocked me." Darla shared, laughing, embarrassed.

"They have not mentioned my biggest and worst mistake of all. Dad and Mother both have accepted Heaven and me and I am getting married. My wedding is October first, and I want you to be a bridesmaid."

"I accept." Candy agreed, without hesitating. "Who is the lucky guy?"

"Kelley Peterson."

"That preacher guy? I thought you still had a thing for him when you turned down all those cool guys' invitations in high school. You are lucky, Darla."

"The Lord is truly a forgiving God. He is allowing me to marry a wonder person, and giving my daughter the kind of father she deserves, in spite of my mistakes in the past. You do know, Candy, the Lord can mend your marriage and give you real, lasting happiness too." Darla informed, compassionately.

"Perhaps someday, I am not sure I am the church going type, but I promise, you will be the first person I call if I change my mind." Candy said.

"You have a deal. I am glad you stopped by, you look great." Darla said pleasantly.

"Thanks. I will call you, informing you of my whereabouts."

"Okay, bye." Darla agreed, with a sweet smile.

Putting Heaven down for her nap, Darla left her bedroom quietly, hurrying to answer the telephone.

"Hello."

"Hello, Miss Roberts." Kelley greeted, bringing excitement to Darla.

"Hi. How is my hard-working fiancé?"

"I am hot, dirty, and tired." Kelley replied.

"Perhaps we should cancel our dinner plans this evening if you are tired." Darla suggested.

"I am not that tired, Darla." He refused quickly. "In fact, I feel just great, now that I have heard your voice."

"I feel the same way and I was hoping you might get lonesome for me and call." She shared, with sparkles in her eyes.

"I am sacrificing my lunch hour to make this call. This is how good you are for me; you have caused my appetite to curve and you know how I enjoy three square meals daily." Kelley replied, with an excited laugh.

"What have you been doing all morning?" He asked.

"I washed my car, prepared dessert, and started dinner for my parents, so Mother will not have to cook this evening. I set some appointments for our wedding plans, and I visited with my neighbor, Candy." Darla replied.

"Your morning sounds as busy as mine. I thought you would take a few days to rest."

"How am I to rest? I am too excited over becoming Mrs. Kelley Peterson, to sit still for long." Darla confessed, with an excited laugh.

"Then we are equally excited."

"Oh, Kelley, I promised Dad I would not stay out as late as I did last night. You understand, right?"

"I understand and I will respect your dad's wishes." Kelley assured.

"I must get back to work. I will see you and Heaven at six. I love you."

"Love you too." Darla replied, with a pleased smile.

After a leisurely warm bath, Darla did lay down for a short nap, hoping to awake refreshed for her evening dinner date with Kelley and his family.

Dressed in a nice slack outfit and Heaven in a light summer dress for their evening out, Darla put the final touches on her parent's dinner.

"Hello Daddy." Darla greeted, as her father entered the kitchen, returning from work, giving her father a kiss, as she politely relieved him of his lunch box.

"What is all of this, Babe?" Pastor Roberts asked, noting the nicely set table.

"I thought you were going out for dinner with Kelley." He added.

"Your thoughts are correct. This is for you and Mother. You will have the evening all to yourself with Mother."

"Do you think Mom and I need some added romance?" Her father asked, with a chuckle.

"No, I would not say that." Darla answered, smiling at her father's laughter.

"I simply think you and Mother should take advantage of your daughter's thoughtfulness."

"The table looks nice, Babe. I appreciate your efforts and I know Mom will also, especially your added touch of the flowers and candles." Pulling a chair out from the table, he sat down.

"Mom says you plan to take a nursing job." Her father spoke, his face serious.

"Yes." Darla answered, pleasantly, as she completed her dinner.

"I cannot wait, either." Darla added.

"What about Heaven while you work?" He asked.

"I am sure I will find someone suitable to sit Heaven. I intend to take this week to inquire on sitters. Surely there is someone I know that sits."

"Kelley assured me it would not be necessary for you to work, so you could care for Heaven."

Darla's face flushed, as she now realized her father's disapproval of her wishes.

"Dad, I want to work. I have always dreamed of becoming a nurse." She reminded, in her defense.

"I realize this. Your wants do not change the fact that you are a mother now. You will have plenty of opportunity to work in your nursing career when Heaven begins school. Mom and I never left you or Bill with sitters all day, for a week at a time."

"I know, Dad." Darla agreed politely, deciding to end her defense, as not to spoil either one of their evenings.

Hearing a car in the drive, Darla glanced through the window.

"Oh, Kelley is early and Mother is late." Darla voiced, with a sigh.

"Dad, serve Mother dinner, It will make her feel special. Everything is ready."

"I sure will, Babe." Pastor Roberts agreed, as he left his chair to answer the doorbell.

"Hello Brother Roberts." Kelley greeted, politely.

"Hi Kelley, Darla will be in directly. She is getting Heaven." Mr. Roberts informed.

"Are you ready?" Kelley asked, as Darla arrived with Heaven, a diaper bag, and her purse.

"I am ready." She answered, with a smile.

Kelley politely took Heaven's diaper bag from Darla, putting it over his shoulder. He gently took Heaven from her mother's arms, politely opening the door for his date with his free hand.

"Do not have Darla out too late, Kelley." Mr. Roberts advised.

"Yes Sir." Kelley agreed.

Kelley opened his car door, waiting patiently for Darla to get inside. He sat Heaven on her lap, and then placed the diaper bag in the back seat.

"Good evening fiancé." He greeted, as he closed his car door, giving her a light kiss.

"Good evening to you." Darla replied, with a sweet smile.

"You look pretty." He complimented, as he backed out of the drive.

"Thank you. I feel pretty when I am in your company." She replied.

"I will always make you feel most beautiful." Kelley assured, cheerfully.

"I do not doubt you will." Darla said, with a soft laugh, over Kelley's often-complementary ways.

"I have a hard question for you and I trust I will not be over stepping my boundaries." Darla informed, looking at her handsome fiancé.

"There should not be any boundaries between you and me, so ask your question."

"Did my dad suggest to you that you would support us?" Darla asked.

"No." Kelley answered.

"At least I feel somewhat relieved." Darla said, releasing a long sigh, Darla's sigh arousing Kelley's curiosity, though he patiently waited for her explanation.

"I believe I would be considered a terrible Mother if I went off to work." Darla shared, adding a bit of sarcasm to express her irritation, bringing a tickle laugh from Kelley.

"Face it Dar, you and I are stuck with the last of the old-timers for parents."

"I forgot how guilty my parents are capable of making me feel for having a different opinion, until this evening." She shared with a gentle smile.

"I confess, between your dad and my own, I have had to stop and question which was running my life the past few weeks."

"We are doomed, Kel." Darla replied, with a weary laugh.

"No we are not, I have news for both our parents, and I am my own man. I do not intend any disrespect to our elders; on the other hand, I do not intend to be treated without the respect due my wife or myself. We will decide what works best for us as a family, the same as our parents did in their separate homes." Kelley informed, with authority in his voice.

"God will always come first in our lives, in our home, and in our family. We will seek God's will first, one another's second, then our children's thirdly, above anyone and anything. We must be united to produce harmony and our parents will learn to accept this." Kelley informed, sincerely.

"Was it I whom said, only last night, these two months would go quickly?" Darla asked, with a defeated laugh.

"Seven weeks and four days." Kelley corrected.

"Believe me I am counting." He added, with a comforting grin.

"Relax; we will deal with our parents as needed. Kelley assured.

We are capable of having imperfections?" Darla asked.

"Darla." Kelley scolded, teasingly.

"Sarcasm twice from you, where is your passive nature?" He asked.

"I believe I lost it a couple of years ago." Darla replied.

"Great, now you tell me." He teased, bringing a tickled laugh from his fiancée, she feeling at ease once again.

Visiting with Kelley's parents and two younger brothers for the first time in over a year was exciting. They accepted Darla as they had when she and Kelley first began dating as teenagers and they each fell in love with Heaven.

Kelley politely assisted Darla with her chair, as she took her place at the table.

Taking her hand in his under the table, he gave her hand an extra tight grip, as to say, "Everything will be okay."

With the completion of Kelley's father praying over their meal, Kelley let go of Darla's hand.

"Mom, do you know anyone whom babysits that Darla might know?" Kelley asked, as they each passed the bowls of delicious food around the table.

"She would like to take a part-time nursing job." He added.

"You will have your wife work?" Mr. Peterson asked, as though shocked with his eldest son.

"Yes Dad because this is what Darla wants, nursing is important to her and it is her way of helping others." Kelley answered politely, choosing just the right words, and setting his father quickly at ease.

"I would be glad to watch Heaven, Darla." Mrs. Peterson informed, surprising both Kelley and Darla with her offer.

"Aye, this will be good for Mama to have a lassie in the home." Mr. Peterson agreed, pleased for his wife.

"Thank you both. I am appreciative for your kindness and I will feel relieved while I am working, with Heaven here with you, Sister Peterson." Darla said, deeply moved by her generosity.

Darla glanced at Kelley, her heart swelled with happiness, giving him a smile. Kelley winked at his fiancée, returning her a comforting, pleased smile.

"Mom has always wanted a daughter, Darla." Aaron informed, Kelley's younger brother.

"Do not be surprised if mom tries to keep Heaven permanently." He teased with a grin, bringing smiles to everyone.

"Heaven could share my room." Matt offered, Kelley's youngest brother.

"This is kind, son. Miss Darla is a good mama, so she will not allow us to keep Heaven. Maybe she will share with us very often." Mr. Peterson said, with pride in his voice.

"Darla, why did you name my niece Heaven?" Matt asked curiosity on his young face.

"Quit being nosy Matt." Aaron hushed, poking his brother with his elbow.

"I do not mind Matt's question, Aaron." Darla assured, with a gentle smile.

"When Heaven was born, I lived far away from home. I was scared when I was at the hospital to receive Heaven. Besides the doctor and nurses, I was alone. When a nurse handed me my tiny baby, I felt as though she was so precious, she came from Heaven. This thought brought comfort and happiness to me, and this is why I named her Heaven." Darla answered, with a gentle smile, her answer touching everyone's heart.

"That is far-out." Aaron expressed.

"Brother Peterson, I assure you, I will continue to look up into the Heavens. I tripped too often when looking down." Darla said, in all sincerity, with flushed cheeks.

"Aye, me too, Miss Darla, me too." The strong Irish man agreed.

"Dad, may I be excused?" Aaron asked, pushing his plate aside.

"For what reason?" His father asked.

"I am meeting some of the guys at the corner at seven-thirty." Aaron assured, eager to get on with his plans.

"You are not going out tonight, dear." His mother said, secretly attempting to hush her son.

"Mom, the guys are waiting for me." Aaron insisted, not realizing his Mothers warning.

Darla noted Kelley secretly signaling Aaron to be still, yet Aaron had not noticed his brothers warning either.

"Son … " Mr. Peterson started, his voice stern and his face red, quickly quieting Aaron, his face now red also.

"Are your friends more important than your brother and this family?" He asked.

"No, Sir." Aaron answered, his face its reddest, being scolded in front of company.

Kelley quietly took Darla's hand in his, leaning close to her.

"Let's get out of here." Kelley whispered, and then silently, politely led Darla from the table, out of the house, and to the backyard.

"Marriage is a very serious event to my dad. It is a time of family uniting, and party, with music and dancing. Mom will not allow my dad the dancing part. Therefore, my dear brother will probably hear an hour lecture in regards to the marriage event." Kelley explained, with a grin.

The young couple took advantage of their time alone, discussing their future years together, as husband and wife, as a family and as a working team for the Lord, witnessing salvation through Jesus Christ.

"Kelley." Darla spoke slowly, as they walked through the yard, holding one another's hand.

"If I will not be disappointing you terribly, I believe I will wait until we marry to return to the park ministry." She said, looking up into her fiancé's eyes, searching his eyes, desperately not wanting to let him down.

"This is your call to make, not mine." He replied.

"I worry my parents will learn of my returning with living in their home. I honestly am not up to hearing their protesting at this time. These next seven and half weeks should be happy and filled with joy for our friends and families, as well as us. I do not want to spoil my parent's joy by them worrying over me returning to the park."

"You should wait then." Kelley agreed, with understanding.

"For now, we should return inside, as not to delay my family any longer with their plans for us this evening. I certainly do not wish to appear rude by our absence, arousing my father's Irish temper." Kelley informed, with a laugh, as he escorted his fiancée inside his home.

Darla was on cloud nine by the end of her evening spent with her future in-laws and brother-in-laws. They treated both she and Heaven as though each were a princess. Darla knew the wonderful Christian family she was marrying into sincerely blessed her.

CHAPTER 9

It was a hot, humid August morning, yet the day seemed beautiful to Darla. She and Kelley would be marrying in only six short weeks. Her future in-laws were the greatest, and Darla's parents adored Kelley. Even Heaven would soon have her very own daddy. Darla was so pleased and happy. Her face was seldom without a smile, or her eyes without sparkles.

Dressed for her busy day, Darla entered the kitchen, starting the coffee for her parents. Opening the front door, she removed the morning paper from the steps. Sitting down at the breakfast table, she eagerly thumbed through the paper, until finding her picture announcing her engagement. Her heart swelled with pride, seeing her and Kelley's name in print, to become husband and wife.

Turning to the classified section, Darla searched the ads for nursing positions. Though her father was steadfast in his belief that a mother's place was with her child unless circumstances would not allow, he said no more in regards to his daughter's wishes to work.

"Good morning, Babe." Mr. Roberts greeted, pouring himself a cup of coffee.

"Good morning, Dad." Darla greeted, pleasantly.

"Would you like some toast?" She asked.

"I can make it, Babe." Her father replied.

"I know you are able, but I would like to make your toast for you, so enjoy your coffee while you read your Bible." Darla insisted, getting up from the table.

"I will not have many more opportunities to wait on you." She added.

"You are right. I should enjoy you while I can." Her father agreed, opening his Bible.

Darla served her father his toast, and then hurried to her fussing daughter. Heaven bathed, and dressed for the day, Darla returned to the kitchen, sitting Heaven in her high chair.

"Good morning, Dear." Mrs. Roberts greeted, as she had her coffee.

"Hello Sweetheart." She added, giving Heaven a kiss.

"Good morning, Mother."

"I will see you ladies this evening." Mr. Roberts said, followed by a kiss to his wife, granddaughter, and then his daughter.

"Dad, did you see my engagement announcement in the paper?" Darla asked, happily.

"No." He answered.

Setting his lunchbox down, he picked up the newspaper, as Darla prepared Heaven's breakfast.

"This is nice, Babe." He remarked, placing the paper in front of his wife.

"Now the entire town knows we are losing our daughter." Sister Roberts said, with a soft laugh, looking up at her husband.

"All over some guy named Kelley." Mr. Roberts remarked, rolling his eyes up, bringing a smile to his daughter's face.

"You will never lose me." Darla said, politely.

"Yeah, this is what they all say." Mr. Roberts teased, and then gave his wife another kiss.

"I will see you girls at dinner." He added.

"Bye. Have a nice day." Mrs. Roberts replied.

"Bye, Daddy."

"Sweetheart, I must get going also, since I am taking the afternoon off." Mrs. Roberts informed, getting up from the table, placing her coffee cup in the sink.

"Do not forget our plans this afternoon, Dear." She reminded, giving Heaven, then Darla a kiss goodbye.

"How could I possibly forget our one-thirty appointment ordering wedding invitations, three o'clock appointment to decide on my wedding gown, and five o'clock appointment with the florist? I cannot wait!" Darla exclaimed.

"Okay, I confess, this was a silly question." Her mother answered, with a soft laugh over her daughter's excitement, giving her a hug.

With her parents gone to their separate jobs, Darla prepared for her departure. Washing Heaven and her high chair from her breakfast, she sat her daughter in her walker. Putting the scissors back in the drawer from cutting out her engagement announcement, she quickly went to the ringing telephone.

"Good morning."

"Good morning, Baby doll." Kelley greeted, happily.

"I like your choice of greetings." Darla said, with an excited laugh.

"I thought you might. I saw a beautiful picture of my fiancée in this morning's paper."

"The announcement did turn out well. I just cut the announcement out of the paper. When we are old and gray, we will have the newspaper clipping to remember this day, and moment." Darla shared, happily.

"This will be nice."

"Our marriage has definitely put a song in Mom's heart. She is still talking about the dinner she gave yesterday announcing our engagement. To quote her, 'it was superb'." Kelley shared, with a laugh.

"That, it was." Darla agreed, also pleased.

"Fiancé, do you have a job to go to this morning?" Darla asked, glancing at her watch.

"Whoops, I will call you this evening, before I leave for the park ministry. Bye, Baby doll."

"Bye." Darla replied, her heart stirred by hearing his voice.

With Heaven's diaper bag prepared for the day, Darla left her parent's home with her daughter. Driving toward Dunes, twenty miles from her home in Ragweed, her heart was bursting with happiness.

Arriving at Kelley's parent's home, she hurriedly kissed her baby goodbye. Darla drove first, to the hospital in Dunes, applying for a nursing position. With no luck, she returned to Ragweed, applying at the community hospital first, then the clinic. With disappointment on her face and only one hour remaining before due at her first appointment with her mother, she sat in her car in deep thought. Each medical facility she had applied at required full-time, experienced, registered nurses. Starting her car, she had one last thought, her family doctor's office in Dunes.

With much persuading, Darla walked away with a part-time job. Her hours would be perfect for her, Heaven, and Kelley and she could not wait until morning to begin her first day.

Hurrying back toward Ragweed to meet her mother, filled with excitement, she noted she was already fifteen minutes late.

Entering the boutique, Darla found her mother, looking over wedding announcements.

"I was about to give up on you, Darla." Her mother scolded, lightly.

"I am sorry I am late." Darla apologized, taking a seat next to her mother.

"I have a nursing job, Mother." She shared, pleased.

"Part-time?" Her mother asked, giving her daughter her full attention.

"Yes, I will work nine until five, Monday and Wednesday and Friday, I work nine until one."

"I am happy for you, dear. Do keep your work schedule at two-and-a-half days, being a good mother and wife is a full-time job alone."

"I will, Mother."

"Now, may we get on with our plans? Time is passing us by."

"Yes." Darla agreed, excitedly, bringing a smile to her mother's face.

Darla looked at many types and styles of invitations, checking each one carefully, periodically glancing at her watch, so she would not be late for her next appointment.

Finally, choosing the most becoming invitation to her, she shared it with her mother, pleased of her choice.

"Whew, I like this." Her mother approved.

Darla silently, briefly held the elegant invitation in her hand, admiringly. The invitation of white background had a drawing of a young couple. The drawing captured the back of a couple with the young man's arm around his bride with her head looking up into his eyes, as he looked down into hers. The bride had long hair, with the look of the wind blowing her hair and the couple outlined in pronounced blue, expressing both romance and elegance.

"This is lovely." The sales clerk announced, as she prepared the order.

"You know, Miss Roberts, the bride on this invitation resembles yourself." The sales clerk added, her comment bringing a sweet smile to both Darla and her mother's face.

Arriving at their next scheduled appointment on time, Darla carefully looked over the different styles of wedding gowns.

"Darla, you might find what you want, if you would try one of these gowns on. They are all beautiful." Mrs. Roberts encouraged.

"Perhaps you are right." Darla replied, with a smile, taking two gowns to the dressing room with her.

After trying several gowns on, dissatisfied, she politely modeled one more wedding gown for her mother and the sales clerk.

"What do you think, Mother?" Darla asked, as she looked in a full-length mirror at the gown she was wearing.

"You look becoming, dear." Her mother replied.

She silently stood looking at her reflection.

"You are not pleased with this gown, either?" The sales clerk asked.

"No, Ma'am. This is a beautiful gown." Darla assured, politely.

"This is not me though, I feel as though I look artificial." She explained, with a weary smile.

"Perhaps you could explain what it is you do want." The sales clerk suggested, patiently.

"I am looking for something less extravagant because I am a simply person." Darla expressed, with a gentle smile.

"Perhaps a more elegant look, without so much fullness in the skirt, something I could wear a long train with." She added.

"I believe we might have what you have in mind. We had a new style that arrived this morning. Give me a minute to get it from the back." The sales clerk informed.

"Deary, we are about to run out of time."

"I know." Darla confessed, with a sigh.

"Perhaps I should make my own gown, Mother. Darla suggested.

"We do not have the time, Darla." Her mother objected, wisely.

"This is why we are here." She reminded.

"Is this gown more to your liking?" The sales clerk asked, proudly displaying the delicate gown.

"Yes, it is." Darla answered excitedly, as she carefully took the gown and hurried to the dressing room.

As Darla appeared, modeling the gown for her mother, she noted her mother's expression of approval. The gown was simple, yet most becoming.

The gown fit snug, pronouncing Darla's young, beautiful figure. It slightly flowered out at the bottom, allowing Darla to walk freely. Attached, was a long elegant train, setting off the back of the gown.

"I love this gown, Mother." Darla shared, excitedly; thrilled she had found her dream gown.

"Yes." Her mother agreed, happily.

"You look beautiful, Sweetheart." She added.

"Thank you, Mother."

"Ma'am, we will take this gown before my daughter changes her mind." Mrs. Roberts informed, with a soft laugh.

"Oh, Mother, I wish the wedding was tonight." Darla confessed, excitedly, as she left the boutique with her mother.

"I am sure you do." Her mother said, with a tickled laugh over her daughter's excitement and happiness.

"This will definitely be a wedding you will never forget." She added, extremely pleased as she drove toward the florist shop.

"I cannot wait to show everyone my gown." She informed, bubbling with happiness.

"I must be one of the happiest and most fortunate brides to be in the world." She added.

"I will second that. Sweetheart, this is the effect one should experience when preparing for marriage. It should be a beautiful and exciting time. This is the way God intended for us."

"Beautiful and exciting, you have definitely described how I feel. I trust you and Dad will bear with me, until I get through this wedding." Darla said.

"Dad and I may be getting a few gray hairs, but believe me dear, we understand. We have been through this wonderfulness ourselves." Mrs. Roberts assured, with a special glow about her own face, as though recalling her wedding day.

Arriving at the florist shop, Darla assisted her mother with the order for her wedding. It seemed the time whizzed by them.

"Mrs. Roberts, you have a telephone call."

"It is probably Dad, wanting his dinner. See if you can finish up for me, dear."

"How are we doing?" Mrs. Roberts asked, as she returned to her daughter's side.

"We are finished."

"Good. Dad is hungry and cranky, so we had best get out of here." Mrs. Roberts whispered, followed by a soft, beautiful laugh.

"I never thought I would see a day when you would say anything against Dad." Darla said, giving her mother an understanding smile.

"Believe me dear, every marriage has its ups and downs, even Christian couples. The trick is concealing the down times, until you are able to overcome them. Do not tell Dad what I have said; he believes we have a perfect marriage." She threatened, with a soft laugh, her cheeks flushed.

"My lips are sealed." Darla assured, pleased to see her mother in a happy, carefree, youthful mood.

"Would you like to see Kelley this evening?" Mrs. Roberts asked, as she started her car.

"I would love to see Kelley every evening, if this were possible." Darla answered honestly, silently questioning her mother's question with her eyes.

"I thought as much. Kelley brought Heaven home from his mother's for you. Dad, Kelley and Heaven are waiting our company at Pat's restaurant." She explained, happy for her daughter's wish.

"This is great." Darla replied, her eyes sparkling and her face aglow with happiness.

"Mother, I never realized how much you understand being in love and romance until today. I wish your understanding would rub off on Dad. I feel if I even voice I would like five extra minutes with Kelley, Dad would have a two hour lecture for me, followed by some form of punishment."

"I understand, dear. Dad is quite pleased for your marriage, but he is forgetting how he carried on before we got married. Every spare moment Dad had, he was knocking on my door, daily, until we married. Until you are married, I am afraid Dad will continue to be your daddy. I guess this is the way most fathers are with their daughters."

Darla was deeply touched to learn and understand this side of her parents that she had not realized existed. Her mother was not only a mother to her, but she was her best friend. Dad would probably remain her daddy, by wanting to protect her, yet she now understood when he was ready, he too would let go of her as his little girl. She would understand allowing him to change at his own pace.

"I have had a wonderful time with you, today, Mother." Darla informed, as her mother parked her car near Pat's restaurant.

"Thank you, dear. I have had a wonderful day with my daughter, also." She replied, deeply touched by her words.

"Kelley may be getting a wife, but I am not losing my daughter." She informed, with a soft laugh, giving Darla a kiss.

"I am willing to share." She added.

Entering the restaurant, Darla felt both happy and pleased, as she spotted her father, whom she now seemed to see in a different way, her fiancé, young, strong, and handsome, and her precious daughter.

"They each are special, in their own way." Darla thought.

"I agree, dear." Mrs. Roberts replied, with a gentle smile.

"They most definitely are." Darla replied, happily, surprised at her mother reading her thoughts, as she had so often when she was a child.

Pastor Roberts and Kelley politely stood, as Darla and her mother arrived at their table, assisting their dates with their chairs.

Heaven became excited, chattering and hitting her hands on the tray of her highchair, with the arrival of her mother.

"Hello Sweetheart." Darla spoke, giving Heaven a kiss and holding her tiny hands in hers, to quiet her noise.

"Someone missed their mama." Mrs. Roberts said, as Heaven brought smiles to each one's face over her excitement.

"Dad, would you please open a package of soda crackers?" Darla asked, still holding Heaven's hands.

"Heaven, calm down please, Sweetheart." Darla said, giving her another kiss and handing Heaven a cracker, occupying her hands, so she ceased hitting the tray.

"Hello Dad and Kelley." Darla greeted, now that her daughter was busy eating her cracker.

"Hi Babe." Her father greeted.

"Hi, Baby doll." Kelley greeted, covering his mouth with his hand.

"Kelley … " Darla scolded, blushing, with her parent's presence.

"I thought I would see how it sounded." Kelley defended, with a boyish grin, bringing laughter from Darla and her parents.

"Our paths meet this evening after all." Darla said, pleased.

"I called your home and your dad suggested I bring Heaven home for you, and then he invited me to dinner."

Darla secretly winked at her mother.

"Dad, I had not realized you have a romantic side to you." Darla said, with a sweet smile, as Kelley took her hand into his.

Pastor Robert's face reddened, as he laughed.

"Mom, what comment do I make?" He questioned, at a loss for words.

"Darla is talking to you, Mark." His wife answered, her expression serious, causing Darla and Kelley to smile, and her husband to blush even more.

"Babe, I simply thought I would be polite, extending Kelley an invitation. I am sure he would have found some excuse to stop by this evening anyway. In fact, I am sure he will have an excuse to stop by every evening, until he marries my daughter." Mr. Roberts replied, with a tickled laugh, as he passed the blame to Kelley, causing Kelley's face to turn its reddest, though Kelley remained calm.

"Dad ... " Darla scolded lightly, defending her fiancé, after her dad embarrassed him.

"Mark, you do not play fair." His wife scolded.

"If I am going down I am taking Kelley with me." He explained with a chuckle, causing Kelley's uncertain smile to change to a relaxed grin.

"Would you say my actions of wanting to see Darla each evening is normal or abnormal, Sir?' Kelley asked politely, yet with comeback, for his future father-in-law.

"Mom, what do you think?" Mr. Roberts asked, going into another tickled laugh.

"I think Kelley's question just buried you." Mrs. Roberts answered, with a soft laugh.

"My husband is seeing history repeat itself, Kelley. You remind us both of my husband, when he and I were engaged. He was at my door every day until we married." Mrs. Roberts informed, bringing laughter from Kelley.

"You are a worse tease then Bill." Kelley remarked, as both men regained their composer.

"In all honesty, Brother Roberts, I have been concerned you might put a stop to my too often visits." Kelley added.

"I know Son, I have been there." Brother Roberts confessed, with a chuckle.

"My husband even stopped by one evening, Kelley, to see if my mother and I needed help making the wedding gown." Mrs. Roberts shared, embarrassing her husband, sending him into laughter again, along with Kelley and Darla.

"I intended to speed the wedding up." He explained, wiping his eyes from his excessive laughter.

"Mother, tell us more about Dad in his younger years." Darla encouraged, with an eager smile.

"No, Mother, please don't." Mr. Roberts pleaded.

"We will talk later, dear." Mrs. Roberts assured, with a soft laugh, ignoring her husband's warning.

"Remember this Kelley, women always stick together." Mr. Roberts informed.

"I have already found this to be true, Sir."

"Darla, I must leave. I am due for the park ministry in fifteen minutes." Kelley informed.

"May I pick you and Heaven up for Wednesday evening service tomorrow?"

"Can he, Dad?" Darla asked, politely.

"Sure." Her father answered.

"Dinner is at six, Kelley, every evening except Sunday. You have an open invitation, Son. Welcome to the family." Mr. Roberts assured, sincerely, extending his hand to Kelley, touching everyone's heart.

"Thank you, Sir. Thank you for dinner this evening, also."

"You are more than welcome."

"I will call you in the morning, Dar." Kelley informed, giving her a light kiss.

"Okay." Darla agreed, pleased.

"Bye, Princess." Kelley said giving Heaven a kiss, then left the table for his ministry.

"Thanks, Daddy." Darla said, with a gentle smile, and pride in her voice.

"Thanks for what, Babe?" Her father asked.

"Thanks for setting Kelley at ease and for being you." Darla replied.

"You are welcome, Sweetheart." Her father replied, with gentleness on his strong face.

With Darla's added activities, she no longer had time to miss Kelley as terribly and with Kelley now working for her father, she was able to see him briefly each morning over coffee before leaving for his job. Most evenings, when returning with her father to get his car at the end of each workday, they often crossed paths.

Darla spent Tuesday and Thursday evenings at her sewing machine, between caring for Heaven. Her evenings and most Friday afternoons, she found herself involved in some area of her wedding plans. Saturdays, Darla and Kelley spent together on outings or visiting with one another at Darla's home. Kelley and Darla spent their Sunday with their separate families, resting and recuperating from their busy weeks and Sunday services they attended as a couple, worshipping together.

With three weeks remaining until the wedding, Darla had completed making the necessary formals. Darla was as pleased as her bridesmaids and maiden of honor were when each girl visited at her convenience, to try on her gown. With each visit, Darla and her visitors would converse of events they had shared in their years of growing. The Roberts' home was not without excitement, with the wedding drawing near.

Awakened by the ringing of her alarm, Darla quickly turned the ringing off as not to disturb Heaven.

"Oh, it is too early." She sighed, and then lied back down for a few minutes, closing her eyes, quickly returning to sleep.

Awakened again, by Heaven's fussing for her breakfast, Darla glanced at her clock. Slowly getting out of bed, she went to her daughter's crib.

"Good morning, angel, mommy loves you." Darla said, smiling at her daughter, taking Heaven into her arms and hugging her as she entered the bathroom starting Heavens bath water.

"Darla." Spoke her mother, tapping on her bedroom door.

"Come in." Darla replied.

"Good morning, Sleepyhead." Mrs. Roberts greeted, with a smile.

"I heard Heaven, so I thought you could probably use a cup of coffee to help you get moving."

"Thank you. I cheated this morning and turned my alarm off." Darla confessed, taking a sip of the warm coffee.

"I thought as much. You do remember Kelley will be here soon?" Her mother asked.

"Yes, today is house hunting day. Perhaps I will take the day off and allow Kelley to do the house hunting alone." Darla replied.

"Trust me dear, you best go, men are terrible at selecting homes. Allow me to take over my granddaughter. I have plans with Heaven this morning, while you are out and I am concerned with your slow pace."

"Then I will shower, becoming revived, and perhaps almost as fast as my mother." Darla replied, handing Heaven to her mother, giving her mother a kiss on her cheek.

"Do not get cute, Missy." Her mother stated.

"Yes Ma'am." Darla said, with a gentle smile.

The warm shower felt good, doing the trick, making Darla feel in full swing. Dressed for her day with Kelley, Darla quickly made her bed, and tended to Heaven's crib.

"Good morning, Dad." Darla greeted, pouring herself a cup of coffee.

"Good morning, Babe." Her father greeted.

Picking the Saturday morning newspaper up from the counter, taking it to the table with her coffee, checking under "house for rent" twice, Darla circled two choices, then laid the paper aside.

"House hunting?" Mr. Roberts asked, reading over his daughter's choices.

"Yes, Kelley will be here shortly and we need to find a place."

"I am sure you will find something." Her father replied, comfortingly, leaving his daughter's side, to answer the doorbell.

"Good morning." Kelley greeted, giving his fiancée a kiss.

"Are you ready or am I early?" He inquired, taking a chair next to Darla.

"I am ready." Darla answered, showing the two houses she chose.

"This is it?" Kelley asked, though checking the paper for himself.

"These are the only two houses in the country." Darla answered.

"I had not realized you want to live in the country." Mr. Roberts remarked.

"We need a place for Princess." Darla explained.

"Would you like to care for her?" She asked, with a loving smile.

"No, thank you. I have had my fill of your horse while you were away at college." Her father replied.

"You might take Kelley by Uncle Jim's country house. The last I heard it was empty, but it might need a few repairs. I understand the last renters did some damage to the place, but Kelley's young and strong and I am sure he is capable of dealing with any repairs." He added.

"There is plenty of room for Princess and Sam at Uncle Jim's." Darla said, looking at Kelley.

"We will look at the house then." Kelley agreed, getting up from the table.

"Where is Heaven?" Kelley asked, extending his hand to Darla, assisting her to her feet.

"Mother is off and running with her." Darla answered, pleasantly.

"I believe the two grandmothers intend to share Heaven today." Mr. Roberts informed, pleased, bringing smiles to the young couple's faces.

After looking over the two country homes and dissatisfied with both, the young couple drove to Darla's Uncles' rental.

"This is more like what I had in mind." Kelley voiced, as he parked his car in the drive.

Discovering the doors locked, the couple looked through each window.

"Oh, Kelley, this is more than perfect." Darla said, excitedly.

"Then we should speak with your Uncle." Kelley replied, taking his fiancées hand into his.

Sitting close to Kelley, as he drove, giving him directions to her uncle's, home, excitement grew within Darla.

"You have already decided on your uncle's house. Am I correct?" Kelley asked, looking down into Darla's eyes, with tenderness on his face.

"It is not for me to decide, Kelley." Darla answered quickly, concealing her excitement.

"Where we live is a decision for both, you and I to make." She added, not sure of Kelley's wishes.

"I will rephrase my question then." Kelley replied, with a smile, realizing she wanted his wishes met, above her own.

"How well do you like your uncle's house?" He asked.

"From what we were able to see, I like the house very much." She answered.

"Good." Kelley said, now turning down the road Darla had instructed.

"My uncle's house is the last house on the left." She instructed, her excitement quickly growing within her.

"You call this a house? This looks more like a mini-mansion." Kelley remarked, as he parked his car in the drive.

"Uncle Jim does okay." Darla replied, with a gentle smile.

"Come on, they are actually normal, nice people. Besides, I am Uncle Jim's favorite niece." She confessed with a soft laugh, blushing over her bragging.

"Hopefully your uncle will remember this when we talk rent." Kelley said, with a grin.

Putting his arm around Darla's waist, they went to the front door. Darla slipped her arm also around Kelley's waist, noting the tension on his handsome face. Giving Kelley a loving smile, she hoped to comfort his uneasiness.

"Darla!" Her Aunt Nan exclaimed, as she opened the front door, the two women hugging one another, excitedly.

"Aunt Nan, this is Kelley, my fiancé." Darla introduced.

"Kelley and I met at your engagement dinner, hi Kelley." She greeted kindly, leading the young couple inside her home.

"Please, have a seat." She said.

Darla sat next to Kelley on the sofa, slipping her arm through his.

"We saw Bill and his wife at the country club last night." Her Aunt Nan informed.

"I feel for Bill, he is so unhappy in his marriage. One cannot help but notice, his wife is spoiled and arrogant. His happiness is at the top of my prayer list, Sweetheart."

"Thank you, mine also." Darla replied, with a gentle smile.

"Aunt Nan, Kelley and I are house hunting and Dad suggested we look at Uncle Jim's rental. We did this and we liked what we could see by looking through the windows. We would like to speak with Uncle Jim if this is possible." Darla informed, in her slow, gentle way.

"I will locate your uncle, dear." Her Aunt Nan agreed, quickly leaving the room.

"Aunt Nan is like the rest of we average people. Uncle Jim, well, he can be a bit like Bill's wife, Paula." Darla whispered.

"Great. Your uncle is the one I have to deal with." Kelley replied, concern on his face.

"I will talk with him, Kelley." Darla offered, considerately.

"You most certainly will not." Kelley informed, as though scolding, causing Darla's cheeks to flush, and bringing silence to her.

"I apologize, Dar, I did not mean to offend you. True, I am nervous over meeting your uncle, but not a coward, so I do not need you to speak for me, or for us. I will do the speaking in regards to the house, this is my place." He explained, with gentleness in his voice, as he lightly kissed the top of his fiancées head to comfort her, from his tone he had used moments earlier.

"Okay." Darla agreed, giving Kelley an understanding smile.

Darla's eyes quickly left Kelley as her aunt returned followed by her uncle.

"Hi, Uncle Jim." Darla greeted.

"Hi, Princess." Darla's uncle greeted her with a kiss.

"Kelley." Her Uncle Jim greeted, extending his hand, to shake Kelley's hand.

"Here are the keys to the house." He informed, handing them to Kelley.

"I am in a hurry, or I would sit and visit with you kids." He explained, glancing at his watch.

"We understand, Sir." Kelley replied, politely.

"I have not been out to the house for a while and it has been empty for a couple of months. The outside is in good shape, but inside, needs cleaned badly and maybe some paint in a room or two. Look it over, if you kids want it we will say the first couple of months without any rent charge for cleaning it up and we can talk rent after that. Congratulations on your engagement, Darla. You have a nice looking fiancé." Her uncle said.

"Of course, I do." Darla agreed with a soft laugh, bringing a smile to her uncle's hurried business expression.

"See you kids later." He informed, and then started for the front door.

"Darla … " Her Uncle Jim started, from the door.

"Tell your brother to get rid of that wife of his. She is going to make him old before his time." He added, and then hurried from the house.

Darla's face flushed at her uncle's suggestion. She remained silent, as Kelley drove from her uncle's home, in the direction of the country rental.

"Kelley, what does everyone know about Paula that I don't?" Darla asked.

"Whenever her name is mentioned, there seems to be a negative comment." She added.

"You do know who Paula was before she married Bill, right?" Kelley asked, looking into Darla's eyes briefly, as he drove.

"No, I never heard of her until Bill married her."

"You have heard of Marin Yates?" He asked.

"Of course, he is the wealthiest man in this area." Darla answered, looking puzzled.

"Paula is his daughter." Kelley informed.

"I still do not understand my family's dislike for her, nor Bill's upsets."

"I had heard of Paula and what I heard as a kid, was how spoiled she was. According to Dan and Cindy, she still is. She thinks Bill should have a bank account like her dad, one strike against him. Apparently, Paula's father thinks he can run Bill's life and Paula's. You know Bill is his own person, Dar. Cindy says they both drink and party often and they argue most of the time." Kelley explained.

"Poor Bill, I had no idea he was in this much misery." Darla said, heartbroken for her brother.

"Sin always destroys, Babe." Kelley said, putting his arm around her shoulders and pulling her closer to his side.

"We will do as your Aunt Nan; we will put Bill and Paula at the top of our prayer list." He suggested, comforting her.

"We most definitely will." Darla agreed, forcing a weak smile, as not to spoil their day.

"Here we are Baby doll." Kelley said, with a boyish grin, as they entered the drive to the country rental, bringing a happy smile from Darla.

Darla patiently waited for Kelley to open her car door for her. Extending his hand to her, Kelley assisted her from the car.

"Kelley." Darla spoke, with sparkles in her eyes, as she stepped closer to him. Looking up into his eyes, she put her arms around his waist.

"It was been at least two hours since you have kissed me." She reminded, with a soft laugh, blushing over her forwardness.

"Excuse me, Miss Darla, for neglecting you." Kelley replied, as though spellbound, as he looked into her eyes, putting his arms around her.

Kelley kissed Darla, long and gently. Removing his lips from hers, he looked into her eyes briefly in silence as she looked into his and he kissed his fiancée once more.

"We best look at the house." Kelley said, removing his arms from his fiancée.

Taking her hand in his, they both were silent as they walked toward the backdoor.

"Are you ready?" Kelley asked, as he unlocked the door.

"Yes." Darla answered, attempting to conceal her excitement.

"Oh, Kelley, I love this huge kitchen." Darla said, excitedly, as she checked the cabinet space, while Kelley checked the paint and flooring.

"I like this. We could seat half a dozen kids in here." Kelley voiced, in his serious manner.

Darla quickly took her eyes from the room, looking at Kelley. The excitement she had over the room, quickly disappeared.

"What do you mean seat half a dozen kids?" Darla asked, slowly.

"We have never discussed having children, have we?" She asked, hesitating.

"Sure, six kids, the more, the merrier, right?" He questioned, putting his arm around her waist, looking into his fiancées eyes, as though expecting her to agree.

"Tell me you are not serious, Kelley." Darla said, searching his eyes with hers.

"You do not want six kids?" Kelley questioned, as though surprised.

"No, Kelley, I do not want six kids. If you do, I am calling off the wedding." She added, hoping to call his bluff.

"I give, I am teasing." Kelley said, with a chuckle.

"Do not call off the wedding, Dar." He added.

"Kelley, that is not funny." She scolded, forcing a weak smile.

"I suggest we look at the rest of the house, before I get in serious trouble." Kelley said, leading Darla through the other rooms.

Walking through the rooms, twice together, Kelley looked at Darla.

"You like what you see?" Kelley asked.

"Yes, I do." Darla answered, pleased.

"What about you, Kel?" She asked.

"I think we will take it." Kelley answered, observing Darla's expression change from pleased to thrilled, this pleasing him.

"We will have to hustle to have this place ready in three weeks." He informed.

"It will be fun working on our home together." Darla said, excitedly.

With their decision made, the young couple walked through each room, several times, discussing paint colors and decorations. They tried to picture in their mind, how their home would look with their improvements.

The days flew by for Kelley and Darla. Every spare hour they had, the couple worked on the country home, preparing it for their first home. They often had surprise visits from friends or a family member, donating a few hours of their time assisting them in their work.

Entering her parent's home, with Heaven in her arms, Darla wearily sat Heaven on the floor. Removing her nursing shoes, she sat down on the beanbag chair, smiling at her daughter's attempts to stand. With Darla spending most evenings working on her future home, away from Heaven, she appreciated even more her time with her daughter.

"Hello, Sis." Bill greeted, as he entered through the backdoor.

"Hello, dearest Brother." Darla greeted.

"You look tired."

"I am tired." Darla confessed.

"Are you and Kelley still working on your house?" Bill asked, picking his niece up and giving her a kiss.

"Yes, I would like to stay late tonight and finish up, but Dad would have a fit. At the pace Kelley and I are going, we both are going to be too tired to show up for our wedding." She shared with a weary smile.

"What do you say I come help you and Kelley this evening?" Bill offered.

"Sure, we would welcome your assistance and we never turn down free labor."

"I believe I will see who else I can round up. We will work all night, until your house is completed, and I will deal with dad for you." Bill suggested.

"Your idea sounds great, Bill, I appreciate your kindness." Darla replied.

Bill entered the kitchen to make the telephone calls, recruiting additional laborers.

"Hi guys." Darla greeted pleasantly, as Kelley and her father arrived from work.

"Hi Babe." Kelley greeted, giving her a light kiss, sitting down on the carpet near her beanbag chair.

"Is it possible for me to talk you into us taking tonight off?" He asked, as he lovingly picked up Heaven.

"No, we are almost finished, Kelley and you should know by now I am a slave driver." Darla answered, with a gentle smile.

"No, you are not, you would just like the home completed." Kelley replied.

"Bill has the perfect solution for our tiredness; I will allow him to explain when he returns from the telephone." Darla informed, pleased.

"I am all for a solution." Kelley agreed.

"Kelley, would you like a glass of tea?" Mr. Roberts asked, getting up from his chair.

"Yes, please."

"Darla?" Her father asked, kindly.

"No thanks, Dad."

"You look tired, Darla." Kelley said, as Mr. Roberts left the room.

"I assure you, I am no more tired than you are." Darla replied, showing her concern for him.

Darla's father returned, handed Kelley a glass of tea, then hesitated, looking at his daughter. Kelley and Darla both looked at Darla's father, silently questioning his hesitation.

"Did you just arrive from work, Babe?" Mr. Roberts asked concern in his voice.

"I arrived a few minutes ago." Darla answered politely, not understanding her father's question or concern.

"You are supposed to get off at one on Fridays, this makes the second week in a row you have worked a full day on Friday." Mr. Roberts scolded, expressing his disapproval.

"One of the girls went home sick, so I volunteered to cover for her." Darla explained, politely.

"You are going to be sick if you do not slow down." He scolded, causing Darla's face to flush.

"Dad, honestly I am no more tired than you and Kelley. If we can finish the house tonight, I will be able to rest more." She assured, hoping to relieve her father of his worries.

"Hi." Mrs. Roberts greeted pleasantly, as she returned from work. Her smile quickly faded, noting her husband and daughter's expressions.

"Hi." Mr. Roberts greeted, letting out a sigh, as though defeated, walking away from his daughter.

"Mark, did you forget about our dinner plans?" Mrs. Roberts asked, in her soft, gentle way hoping to ease the tension between her loved ones.

"I guess I did, I will get my shower." He replied.

"Darla, did you forget to have Heaven ready when I arrived?"

"Yes, I am sorry Mother." Darla answered, her face flushed again as she got up from the beanbag. Taking Heaven from Kelley, Kelley winked at Darla to comfort her, bringing a smile to her face.

Quickly bathing, and then dressing Heaven in a frilly dress and dress shoes, she sat Heaven in her crib. Changing her nursing uniform for jeans, a sloppy work T-shirt and tennis shoes and brushing her long hair, she made a braid, to allow her to work freely, without her hair in her way. Taking Heaven from her crib and Heaven's pre-packed diaper bag, Darla returned to the family room.

"Goodbye, Dear." Her mother said, she taking Heaven from Darla.

"Excuse me?" Darla asked, surprised with her mother's words.

"I will explain in the car, Sis." Bill said, opening the backdoor for his sister to exit.

Darla silently left her home with her brother, heading for Kelley's car, where Kelley sat waiting. Bill opened the passenger door of Kelley's compact car, getting in the back seat, allowing Darla to sit in the front.

"You should have seen Darla's face, Kelley." Bill stated with a chuckle, as Kelley backed out of the drive, bringing a curious grin to Kelley's face and a now relaxed smile to Darla's face.

"Dar returned to the family room with Heaven, Mom said 'Goodbye' to Darla and I believe Darla thought Mom was throwing her out."

Kelley looked at his fiancée, giving her a comforting smile, taking her hand into his.

"What transpired when I left the room?" Darla asked.

"Dad was in the shower when I finished on the telephone, so I explained my plan to mom to work all night, if need be, to complete your home. Mom suggested I take you and leave before dad returned. She explained she did not want her evening disrupted."

"Mother will tell Dad, then?" Darla asked.

"Yes." Bill answered, relieving his sister of her concerns.

"For future knowledge to understand my parents, Kelley, my mother is the silent head of my parent's home." Darla informed, with a smile.

"Aren't all women?" Bill asked, with a sigh.

"You and I will do things differently, Babe." Kelley said, glancing at his fiancée.

"I will be the head of our home, after we say 'I do', and then I will give you my list of rules." He informed, with a boyish grin.

"I do not think so; I am running low on patience in regards to rules and restrictions." Darla replied, quickly.

"Forget it, Kel; marriage never works like you think it will." Bill suggested.

"If you each do what you want, it works much better." He added.

Darla and Kelley grew silent with Bill's comment; they each were feeling for Bill's unhappiness in his marriage.

"On second thought, I gladly agree to you being the head of our home." Darla started, with a soft laugh.

"You did say you would not allow our parents to continue telling us how to live after we marry, I do not want that job at all." Darla confessed, blushing, with a weary smile, as though even the thought tired her.

"I cannot wait to move out of my dear parent's home." She added, with a laugh, blushing as though sharing a terrible secret, bringing understanding laughter from both Bill and Kelley.

Though tiring, it was fun working on their home for Darla and Kelley, with their volunteer helpers. The light play and teasing while working seemed to make the time go quickly.

Busily scrubbing windows of a completed bedroom, Darla became startled.

"Darla." Spoke Paula sharply, causing Darla to jump.

"Yes?" She questioned, shocked with her sister-in-laws tone and anger on her face.

"Your parents said Bill is here, yet I do not see his car. I want to know where Bill is and I want to know now." Paula shouted, angrily.

"Is there a problem in here?" Kelley asked, as he now stood in the doorway, he clearly expressing his disapproval with Paula's manner.

"No." Darla answered calmly, yet her young pretty face clearly expressed her shock and confusion with her sister-in-law's mood.

"Bill is here, Paula, I assure you, my parents do not lie."

"Then where is he and where is his car?" She questioned, glaring at Darla as though she hated her.

"Bill's car is at my parent's home, he came out with Kelley and me. I will take you to him." Darla said, putting her cleaning cloth aside.

"Are you going to be okay?" Darla asked, with gentleness in her voice and tenderness on her face.

"Take me to my husband." Paula ordered, as though becoming even angrier by Darla's act of kindness.

With her face its reddest from Paula's cold, hateful actions toward her, she silently lead Paula through the house, ignoring the puzzled stares of her helpers.

"He is outside." Darla informed, barely above a whisper, as she opened the backdoor, allowing Paula to exit first, Darla now noting Kelley following behind them, as her protector.

Darla led Paula now through the huge yard and inside the barn.

"Bill, Paula is asking for you." Darla said.

"Hi Hon." Bill greeted, wiping the perspiration from his forehead.

"Did you bring the food for the cookout?" He asked.

"I most certainly did not." Paula answered, glaring at her husband.

"I give up, what did I do wrong this time?" Bill asked, laying his hammer down, leaning against the worktable, as though prepared for a lecture.

"You did not bother to ask me what I might like to do tonight; you left a message with my mother telling me what to do." Paula shouted.

"I cannot ask you when I do not know where you are." Bill defended, rubbing his head wearily.

"In all sincerity, I had hoped you and I could have a normal Friday night for a change." He added.

"We always go to the country club on Friday nights, with my parents and my friends." Paula reminded.

"This is my point, it may come as a surprise to you, Paula, but I have a family also. I have friends that do not attend the country club. I am fed up with our Friday and Saturday nights of you and me over-drinking, and then you stomping off mad dancing with any and every one. I just want us to have a normal life." Bill explained, as though desperately seeking his wife's understanding.

"You call scrubbing, cleaning, and a cookout with a bunch of squares normal?" Paula asked, shouting in Bill's face.

"You need to back off, Paula." Bill warned, his face now tense with his own anger rising.

"What do you intend to do about it if I do not back off?" Paula asked, pushing Bill's shoulders as though wanting to have a fistfight.

"You had best knock it off." Bill ordered, his face bearing his anger.

Darla stepped forward, intending to go to her brother's side, but Kelley quickly grabbed her arm, preventing her.

"Stay out of it." Kelley whispered wisely, leading Darla outside of the barn.

"Kelley, if Paula keeps pushing Bill, I am afraid he will hit her." Darla explained nervously, looking over her shoulder, watching the quarrel continue through the open doorway.

"Dar, Paula and Bill have to settle their differences themselves, brother or not, you must not interfere in a marital quarrel." Kelley replied, in his calm patient way.

"You push me once more and I swear you are going to see stars." Bill warned, his patience gone.

"Kelley, I am telling you, Bill has exceeded his patience tolerance." Darla pleaded, desperately wanting to prevent her brother from becoming violent.

Kelley also feared Bill was near striking his wife with the constant pushing and yelling in his face.

"Do what you have to." Kelley agreed finally, as he let loose of his fiancées arm.

"Stop this." Darla ordered sternly, stepping between her brother and his wife just as Bill started to slap Paula.

"Get out of the way." Paula yelled, deliberately in Darla's face.

"Paula." Darla spoke compassionately, ignoring her sister-in-law's anger.

"Come with me until you calm down. You and Bill are husband and wife, not enemies." Darla said kindly taking hold of Paula's arm.

Paula jerked her arm from Darla. "I said get out of my way, little Miss Perfect." Paula ordered, glaring at Darla.

"I am not perfect, I just care about you and Bill, do not hurt one another." She pleaded, with watery eyes, feeling for their pain.

"I would say you are not perfect, where is your baby's real father, in fact, I doubt you even know who he is." Paula snarled, looking at Darla as though she was the scum of the earth, making Darla feel dirty and cheap.

Darla stood speechless as though in shock by the ugliness that Paula said to her, with tears streaming down her young tender face.

Kelley rushed to Darla's side pulling her from between the fussing couple, holding her in his arms and silently comforting her, his own heart aching for his loved one's pain.

Darla stood silently praying with tears streaming, that Bill would not strike his wife with her hand over her mouth, fearing her prayers were too late.

"This is enough." Bill glared, grabbing Paula's arm forcefully.

Paula swung with her free arm hitting Bill in his face. Bill reared back, with his fist clenched, and then hesitating for a moment. Lowering his fist, he grabbed Paula's free arm instead, holding his wife's arms behind her back, as though she was a criminal.

"Kelley, get Darla out of here and please send Henry out. I will take Paula to her parent's house, and then I will be back." Bill instructed.

"Please take care of Darla." He added, his heart aching for his kid sister due to his wife's foolishness.

"I will be fine, you take care of Paula." Darla advised, kindly.

Returning inside the house, with her tears still streaming, Darla returned to her cleaning as Kelley searched for Henry. She cried for her brother's happiness, she had not realized until now the torment he endured daily in his marriage, or had she known her sister-in-law lived with such grief.

"Oh Lord Jesus, I beg of you, to save their souls and end their strife." Darla prayed repeatedly, as she washed the windows.

"How is my girl?" Kelley asked, slipping up behind Darla, putting his arms around her waist, leaning his face close to her face.

"I am okay, just crying over my brother's misery." Darla answered compassionately, wiping her tears away.

"Kelley?" Darla started, turning around, facing him and looking into his strong, yet gentle face.

"Do you believe Bill and Paula loves one another, I mean, real love?" Darla asked, sadly.

"I do not know, Babe, they most certainly do not have Godly love for one another." He answered, taking his fiancée into his arms holding and soothing her.

"So, this is the way you two work." Cindy remarked, entering the room.

"This is the part I do best." Kelley replied with a grin, bringing laughter from both girls.

"Dar, Kel, what is wrong and where did Bill and Henry rush off to?" Cindy asked.

"They took Paula home." Kelley answered, as he continued to hold Darla, as she allowed him to do so.

"Why? Paula drove herself here." Cindy replied.

"Bill and Paula did not have an argument, did they?" She questioned slowly.

"Yes, they had a good one." Kelley answered.

"Darla, do not worry about Bill and Paula, things will work out one way or another. Cheer up, there is not anything we can do except pray for their salvation and never quit loving Bill, this is for Bill to work out." Cindy added.

"Listen to your cousin, Miss Roberts, wise words from an experienced, happily married woman." Kelley encouraged.

"What would I do without you two always around to boost me back up?" Darla asked, with a gentle smile.

"You would do fine without Cindy, but you could not make it without me." Kelley teased.

"Thanks a lot, Preacher Kel." Cindy remarked, with a laugh.

"Darla, we finished the nursery, come see, it looks beautiful!" Cindy exclaimed, excitedly, taking her cousin's hand, and leading the way to Heaven's new room.

Bill and Henry had returned without a word said about Paula. Henry returned to his assigned project, while Bill filled the grill with hamburgers, as though there had never been an upset.

Though Darla was unable to put her brother's marital upsets aside completely, she was once again filling with happiness, her face aglow and her eyes sparkling with each completed room.

By three in the morning, the house was completed, the yard work completed, and the corral and barn ready for Darla's horse.

"How do you like our home, Darla?" Kelley asked, as the young couple stood back admiring their work.

"I love it, only one more week, Kelley, then you, Heaven and I will live here as a family. Darla said.

We will live happily ever after." She added, with an excited, beautiful laugh.

"Yes and I cannot wait." Kelley agreed, equally excited.

Though exhausted from their hours of labor and dusty shirts and paint-spattered jeans, the seven young adults entered a twenty-four hour restaurant for breakfast. The young people enjoyed one another's company, as they celebrated the completion of Kelley and Darla's home.

"Bill, do not forget to go inside with me when you get your car, I am sure Dad will be up bright and early this morning." Darla reminded, with a gentle smile.

"I told you I will handle dad." Bill assured.

"Just think, Sis, only one more week and you will be with Kelley all you want." He added.

"I intend to be very selfish with your sister from that moment on." Kelley voiced, bringing smiles to everyone's face.

Kelley left Bill and Darla at their parent's home at six in the morning. Darla's father was already awake at the kitchen table, as Darla had predicted, although he was quickly consoled with seeing his son at his daughter's side.

Returning from a leisurely bath, Darla tiredly dressed in her nightclothes, sitting down on the edge of her bed.

"Darla." Her father spoke, standing in her doorway.

"Yes?" Darla asked.

"Mom put Heaven to bed in Bill's room, she said to tell you she and Heaven have plans for the day and you are to rest."

"Thanks, Dad."

"I am relieved your home has been completed, perhaps I will worry less over you now, Babe." Mr. Roberts shared, with gentleness in his voice.

"Thanks, daddy, I hope you will worry less also." Darla replied, giving her father an understanding smile.

Sleeping most of the day, until after afternoon, Darla felt rested. She enjoyed the remainder of her Saturday, being with her daughter and relaxing.

Darla enjoyed Sundays most. She would eagerly await Kelley's arrival, taking her and Heaven to Sunday morning services, Kelley always making her feel special simply by his presence.

Kelley proudly carried Heaven, as he and Darla left their young adult Sunday school class. Lingering briefly in the foyer, visiting with Dan and Cindy, a small group of young teenage girls stood near them. Darla's face flushed and her heart took a saddened leap, as she overheard the girl's whispers.

"That is Darla Roberts." One girl whispered.

"Pastor Kelley is marrying her? She already has a baby." Another whispered.

Dan and Cindy both glared at the teenagers, feeling for Darla. Kelley looked at the girls, extremely annoyed with their actions. The group of girl's faces reddened, as they realized their conversation had been overheard.

"They are just kids, Kelley." Darla reminded, with a gentle smile.

"We best find a seat in the sanctuary." She suggested giving the girls an understanding smile, as she passed them on her way to the sanctuary, surprising the girls with her kind gesture.

"I would have slapped them, Darla." Cindy voiced, as she and Dan chose the pew behind Darla and Kelley, bringing smiles from Dan and Kelley and a soft laugh from Darla.

"If you believe slapping them will change their thoughts and hearts, be my guest." Darla replied, with a gentle smile.

"It is worth a try." Cindy stated, starting to get up, as though she was going after the girls.

"Stay put, silly." Dan ordered, taking hold of his spunky wife's arm.

"Honestly Dan, you are no fun anymore." Cindy teased, bringing laughter from Dan and Kelley.

The young couples quieted their talk now, as Pastor Finks began the morning worship service.

"May I be your guest speaker at youth group this evening?" Darla asked, in a whisper.

"Yes, if you would like." Kelley answered surprised at his fiancées request with overhearing the teenagers talk earlier.

Quickly writing a note, Darla silently waited for the offering plate to come her way, and as the usher approached her pew, she placed the note in the offering plate.

"What is my fiancée up to?" Kelley asked.

"Listen to the announcements." Darla replied.

Kelley waited for the reading of the announcements, silently, but eagerly.

"For our youth service, which begins promptly at six-thirty this evening, our Youth Pastor will be having a special guest speaker. Miss Darla Roberts will be speaking this evening and for those of you who do not know Darla, trust me, you are in for a real treat. She is a remarkable young lady. When Darla had barely turned sixteen, she was the most effective member in our park ministry to the street people." Pastor Finks informed, proudly.

"Come out this evening, young people, bring your friends, I know your hearts will be touched. I realize I am past the age of our youth group standards, but I for one, will attend this evening." He added, encouragingly.

"You are a brave one, Miss Darla." Kelley said, approvingly.

He admired her tender, yet determined will to stand up for Christ and allow her light to shine, regardless of who tried to dampen her spirits.

"No, Kel, the Lord is the brave one; I am but a mere vessel, obeying the leading of the Holy Spirit."

"You are right." Kelley agreed, pleased with her correction.

"This evening's service will begin at the regular time, which is seventhirty." Pastor Finks continued.

"Our Youth Pastor, Kelley Peterson, will be speaking tonight. Should I say speaking or preaching, Brother Kelley?" Brother Finks asked with a grin, as he looked at Kelley.

"This depends upon how the spirit moves me." Kelley answered politely, bringing laughter from the Pastor and the congregation.

"Yes, we must always allow the Holy Spirit to be our guide." Pastor Finks agreed, pleased with Kelley's answer.

"I did not know you would be in charge of tonight's service." Darla whispered, pleased.

"Apparently tonight is both our big night." Kelley replied.

With Heaven napping after Sunday dinner, Darla sat at her desk, preparing her talk for the youth service. She spent time in deep prayer and Bible studying, she wanted to say just the right words to reach the teenager's hearts.

"Babe ... " Pastor Roberts started, tiptoeing to his daughter's desk, as not to wake Heaven.

Come join me in a short walk, I will not keep you long." He said.

"Sure." Darla agreed, pleasantly, quietly getting up from her desk, and going outside with her father.

"I am a curious person, Babe, I am sure you are aware of this by now." Mr. Roberts said, as they slowly walked toward the corral, bringing a smile to his daughter's face.

"Darla, do you intend to return to the park ministry?" Her father asked.

"I do not feel this is the right time to discuss this, I do not intend any disrespect, Dad." Darla answered, becoming nervous with her father's question.

Mr. Roberts silently leaned against the corral fencing. He seemed to remain silent forever. Darla patiently remained at her father's side, wishing she knew where he stood, what his feelings were of her hidden desire.

"You know, Babe, it takes both a mother and a father to completely understand their child. Sometimes a mother understands when the father does not and sometimes a father understands when a mother lacks the understanding. I will share with you what has been on my heart for three years, when I finish; perhaps you then will feel free to answer my question openly." His eyes grew moist, touching his daughter's compassionate heart.

"I knew I let you and the Lord down, Babe. I had all of the right reasons to justify my decision, none-the-less; I blew it as you kids say." Mr. Roberts looked at his daughter with tears in his eyes.

"I should have allowed you to return to the park ministry, but I interfered with the Lord's plan in your life. I know you belong there with Kelley, working as a team for the Lord." He shared, with tears running down his cheeks, as well as his daughter.

"Oh, Daddy, you do not know how good it makes me feel to have you understand. It is like a drive inside me to return to the park." Darla shared, with happy tears, hugging her father's neck.

"I understand the drive and the desire, Babe. Learn from my mistake, do not ever interfere in the Lord's work, and obey the leading of the Holy Spirit. God has great plans in store for you and Kelley."

"Does Mother now feel as you do?" Darla asked.

"No, I am afraid Mom may never be able to put aside what happened to you, Babe."

"To make my returning to the park ministry easier on the family and myself, I thought I would wait until after the wedding, I do not want mother unhappy, especially now." Darla shared.

"I agree with your timing, Babe." Mr. Roberts replied, walking his daughter back to the house, with his arm across her shoulders.

Darla felt a revival beginning within her, her father's talk stirred many old feelings. She longed to be involved in a work for the Lord.

Completing her outline for youth group, Darla left her room. Entering the family room, she picked up the telephone, dialing her brother's number.

"Roberts." Bill answered.

"Hi." Darla greeted, happily.

"How has your day been?" She asked.

"Okay." Bill replied.

"Good, I would like you to do something that would mean the world to me, are you game?" Darla asked, pleasantly.

"Of course, I am game." Bill answered, considerately.

"I want you to attend the youth service tonight, yours truly is the guest speaker."

"I have been invited by Kelley, Cindy, Dad, and now you. You forgot to invite me to the evangelist service to hear Kelley also." Bill replied, with a chuckle.

"I intended to, Dear Brother." Darla confessed, with a soft laugh.

"Will you come?" She asked, hopeful.

"I will not promise, but I am considering attending. I would like to hear you and Kelley."

"Do inform Paula that I invited her also." Darla added.

"This is not possible; I have not seen Paula since Friday night, Sis." Bill informed.

"Oh, Bill, call her and invite her to come with you, tell her your family wants her to come." Darla insisted.

"I will think about your suggestion. Thank you for the invitation."

"You are welcome; I expect to see you at least tonight, bye." Darla concluded.

Darla silently prayed repeatedly for Bill and Paula's marital upsets and for their salvation while she prepared Heaven and herself for the evening services.

"What are you going to speak on?" Kelley asked, as he prepared the youth chapel for the coming teenagers.

"I am going to speak on trials of a Christian teenager." Darla answered, pleasantly.

"Sounds interesting, I am sure your talk will bring results." Kelley said.

The youth chapel was full, and to Darla's surprise, several of the young married couples had come.

Darla sat reverently, with Heaven on her lap, as Kelley approached the pulpit. She held admiration for his talent as a Youth Pastor.

"Had I known having Darla as a guest speaker would fill these pews, I would have had her speak much sooner." Kelley informed, with a pleased grin.

"For you who do not know Darla, I assure you, you are in for a treat. She is a special person, a dedicated Christian and my lovely fiancée. I have witnessed Darla experience both mental and physical torture over the years and still offer love and strength to others, burying her pain as not to burden another. Before I call Darla up, I say to each one present, listen to her, and allow your hearts to be dealt with as the Holy Spirit speaks to you." Kelley instructed, in all sincerity.

"Darla." Kelley spoke, turning the services over to her.

"Sis, I will take Heaven." Bill informed, sitting behind Darla, surprising her with his arrival.

Handing Heaven to her brother, Darla left her seat, approaching the front of the chapel. Laying her Bible on the pulpit, she glanced at Kelley as he sat down next to Bill.

"I appreciate your attendance this evening." Darla informed, with a happy smile and sparkles in her eyes.

"I would like to correct a statement both Kelley and Pastor Finks have made today. I am not special. I am no different from any of you in this chapel tonight, or the wino on the street. I am not without flaws, I am capable of making mistakes, and I am an imperfect sinner, a sinner saved by grace." Darla clarified.

"The title of my talk is trials of a Christian teenager, because I can relate so well to this topic. It seemed my trials as a Christian teenager became too great for me to endure. I do not wish this for any of you, so if only one statement I make this evening helps prevent one person out of this crowd to remain steadfast in the Lord and not stray because you feel your trials are too great, how marvelous this will be for you." Spoke Darla, with sparkles in her eyes and a glow about her face.

As Darla spoke, choosing her words carefully and wisely, her excitement grew stronger within her. Her zealousness to share the love of God, salvation through Jesus Christ and the comfort of the Holy Spirit, and her excitement to witness for Jesus was quickly rubbing off on the teenagers. The inner peace she had within her, her strength from the joy of the Lord that she possessed, the excitement she expressed with simply speaking the name of Jesus, stirred the teenagers.

"Regardless of your young age, the Lord has a work for each and every one of you. Seek out the Lord's will, if you presently know your work. You must stay busy in the Lord's work because idol time is dangerous; it creates boredom and restlessness between you and the Lord. You know as well as I, it is a hard job to be a Christian. It takes a very strong person to say yes to the Lord, and no to the ways of the world. We are the Lord's army, and we must be strong to be overcomers, and examples, that our ways will be a daily reflection of the Lord to others, that a sinner will yearn for what you have and seek salvation. This is every Christian's duty in life, to be soul winners."

"I found as a Christian teenager, as well as now, as a young adult, there are two most important necessities in Christian living. The first necessity is involvement, as I stressed, and the second is rules and believe me, no matter how old we become, we have rules. The Bible is full of rules for us from parents, teachers, employers, and traffic laws. Rules can seem endless, petty, and unimportant, but do not take a short cut to avoid a rule. We must be obedient because when one breaks a rule, one always suffers the consequences."

"Being a preacher's kid, I have sat through many church services. I have probably heard the scripture, "you reap what you sow" thousands of times. For every action, you sow either good or bad. There is no in-between. If you sow good deeds, you will reap well and if you sow badly you reap badly. Ensure your reaping to be good by sowing all good deeds. Please do not forget this extremely important piece of scripture. We will reap what we sow and there is no escaping this."

"To the young girls I overheard whispering about me this morning, I owe you an apology." Darla said, her face now flushed and her eyes watery.

"For all present who did not hear the whisper, I will share with you." She added, slowly hesitating.

"I must clarify a misunderstanding otherwise, I am allowing my Christianity to be questioned. If there are doubts my reflection is not pleasing unto the Lord, I do not want my reflection blemished." Darla assured, sincerely.

"The girls were whispering about my having a child before marriage. No, I was not serving the Lord when I conceived my child. Had I remained steadfast in the Lord, I would not be a mother at this time, nor would I have this blemish in my Christian walk today. I was a one-hundred percent, sold-out Christian teenager. I was involved in my work for the Lord. My time was never idol and as Pastor Finks shared; my work was in the park ministry. I was as happy as I could possibly be in my youth, with everything going my way. I still for one split second was very foolish." Darla shared, blinking hard to contain her tears, hesitating, as she cleared her throat.

"Pastor Finks had set rules to ensure our witness in the city park would be successful, and rules insuring our safety. One rule I will remember until I am old and gray."

Darla said, with a nervous laugh.

"The rule was to never enter the park alone at nighttime. I had been at the park earlier with the witnessing group and I was thrilled with the outcome of our visit. I was flying high on Jesus and in my excitement; I had forgotten my Bible in the park. Knowing I would be breaking a rule, I returned to the park regardless, alone for my Bible."

Darla was silent now, closing her Bible on the pulpit, blinking her eyes hard, and regaining her composer. Under control, she walked from behind the pulpit, standing closer to the group.

"I was severely beaten; my family was crushed, and forbid my returning to the work the Lord had chosen for me. I broke one rule, which seemed so petty, but that mistake led to many mistakes. I let our pastor down by disobeying; I let my family down, the Lord and myself down. I became restless without my involvement for the Lord. I eventually became frustrated with myself for failing. Little by little, I strayed for the Lord. For three years, I was empty, lonely, searching elsewhere for inner peace. I found, firsthand, there is no peace without the Lord, teenagers, none."

"I was involved for and with the Lord, but I broke a rule. With the breaking of the rule, I began sowing bad seeds and I had to reap what I had sowed when I became a mother.

Do you think, for one second the Lord is going to jump in and pull you out from reaping what you have already sowed? Everyone pays for his or her mistakes, sooner or later; this is just the way it is." Darla informed, sincerely.

"Teenagers, I beg of you to be a much stronger Christian than I was. If you have had bad times in your life, eliminate it now. If you are restless, or are uninvolved with the Lord, seek His will, and live by His rules. Plant seeds of good, so your reaping will be exciting, fun, joyous, challenging, and most rewarding." Darla encouraged, excitedly.

"As I turn the service back to Kelley, I leave each of you with this. I Darla Roberts, challenge you to be a much better Christian teenager, than I was. Never become weak, taking your eyes from the one who truly loves you, our Savior, Jesus Christ. Be strong always, in the Lord." Darla challenged excitedly, with her eyes sparkling and her face aglow.

"Kelley." Darla spoke, removing her Bible from the pulpit. Leaving the pulpit, to return to her seat, Kelley winked at Darla, as they passed one another. He held a look of approval, pleasing and reassuring her.

Taking a seat next to her brother, Darla kindly relieved him of her daughter.

"You are good; you even touched my hardened heart." Bill shared, with a pleased smile.

"Good. It is past time you get your life in order also, Dear Brother." Darla replied, giving her brother a gentle smile, quickly bringing silence to him.

"I would like for everyone to stand please." Kelley informed his voice strong, his face sincere, yet his eyes gentle.

"I believe the Lord is ordering each of us to search down deep in our hearts and eliminate any sin and all sin. I believe the Holy Spirit is dealing with some of you to have a closer walk with the Lord. For some, the Holy Spirit is pleading, take my hand and follow me you have wasted enough time. It is time to get serious, for the Holy Spirit is saying, hold steadfast to the Lord's ways." Kelley said.

"Darla, will you join me please?" Kelley asked, he patiently waiting for her, as he looked out over the crowd, seeing eagerness on the teenager's faces.

Bill quickly took Heaven from his sister. As Darla joined Kelley, he put his arm briefly across her shoulder.

"Cindy, Dan, please join us."

"Gail." Kelley called, instructing the pianist.

"As Gail plays, 'Just as I am, I come', I want you to search your hearts. Can you truly look into the Lords' face and say, 'yes Lord, I know my heart is where you want it', or are you yearning to open your heart unto the Lord? Are you seeking more from the Lord than ever before?" Kelley questioned, as the music softly played.

"Teenagers, it is time to quit playing church. Your entire futures are ahead of you, so make the difference in your future now. There is no time for delays and as Darla has shared, delays are much too painful and costly."

"As I close in prayer, Cindy, Darla, Dan, and myself are here to pray with you and for you, that your walk with the Lord will be steadfast and victorious. Those of you who are seeking salvation, seeking answers, seeking a deeper walk, come, and let us pray together." Kelley encouraged.

The front of the chapel quickly filled with many stepping forward. Shedding both, tears of joy and sorrow, the young people broke down their barriers to self, and opened their hearts willingly and eagerly unto the Lord.

After several moments of prayer, Kelley approached Darla, where she stood praying with some teenage girls.

"Babe, I must go to the sanctuary. I am already late." Kelley whispered.

Darla, along with Cindy and Dan remained until the last teenager ceased their praying. It was a joyous event, being filled and/or refilled with the presence of the Holy Spirit, with a feeling of victory accomplished.

Arriving at the back of the sanctuary, Darla discovered the evening service had already begun, as she, Cindy, and Dan silently searched for a place to sit.

"Do you see Bill and Heaven?" Darla asked, in a whisper.

"Bill and Heaven are in the front, with your parents, and Kelley's parents." Cindy answered.

"Oh, Kelley must be pleased having his parents visit this evening instead of attending their home church." Darla said, excitedly.

As the congregation sang from the hymnals, the three young adults tiptoed to the front of the sanctuary, sitting down on the pew in front of Darla's family. Briefly greeting her future in-laws, and retrieving her daughter, Darla glanced at her handsome fiancé sitting on the platform with the pastor, as she joined in the song service.

As the song service was nearing a close, Darla put her hymnal aside. Glancing up at her fiancé, again, she noted him and Pastor Finks laughing, both men putting their hand over their mouths, as though attempting to conceal their laughter, with being up front for the entire congregation to see, their actions.

"Thank you, Brother Smith." Pastor Finks spoke into the microphone, as the song leader left the pulpit.

"I feel excited tonight." He informed, with a radiant grin.

"Knowing that I am a child of the King excites me." Pastor Finks said.

"Amen." The congregation agreed.

"I am excited knowing that I am involved in the greatest occupation on earth teaching, and preaching salvation through Christ Jesus." Spoke the Pastor, excitedly as though he was about to shout.

"Amen." The congregation agreed.

"How many of you remember what if feels like to pray though?" Pastor Finks asked, holding his hand up, looking over the congregation, many raising their hands.

"I just left a group of our teens that could teach a few of you old timers who have forgotten. Thank God for our youth, they are the future. Back our teens, encourage them, and pray for them. I assure you, they will not hesitate to pray for you." He added.

"Our church has been blessed by many of you, through your talents, your hours of labor, and your hours of prayer. Our church has been blessed with a fine, dedicated youth pastor who will be speaking shortly."

"Kelley came to me in private, with a burdened heart a few months ago. He shared some personal concerns with me. He was seeking direction due to the importance of him being the best Christian example he could be. We talked, and we prayed, on several occasions, until Kelley received his answers. He requested this evening, and this time to justify his ministerial calling to you. I told Kelley, this was not necessary. His reply was, 'It is necessary Pastor, and I must stand up for the Lord and put an end to the hindrance to the Lord's work.' This is a dedicated Christian's response. This is the response of one called by the Lord to minister under the Lord's anointing." Pastor Finks informed, in all his sincerity.

"Amen?" Pastor Finks asked, looking into the faces of his congregation.

"Amen." The congregation answered.

"Brother Kelley." The pastor instructed, for Kelley to join him at the pulpit. The pastor put his hand on Kelley's shoulder, as he looked into Kelley's face.

"I asked you this morning if you would be speaking or preaching tonight. Which is it?" The pastor asked.

"After attending youth service earlier, and this superb introduction I have been given, I will probably speak, preach, and shout." Kelley answered with a grin, bringing laughter from the pastor and the congregation.

"We do serve an exciting and an amazing God, a loving God, a merciful God." Kelley spoke, looking into the faces of his congregation, as Pastor Finks left the pulpit.

"Amen."

"I was not aware that my fiancée would be speaking in the youth service until this morning, nor was she aware I would be speaking this evening, until this morning, when learning of this when the announcements were given. One would think she and I prearranged this coincidence. I assure you I did not know the title of her talk until attending the youth service this evening. She has yet to learn the title of mine." Kelley informed sincerity on his young face.

"When Darla hears what I feel I must say I may not have a fiancée." He added with a chuckle, his face reddening, as he glanced at Darla.

Darla returned Kelley a loving smile, looking into his eyes, as to say, "It is okay, Kelley, obey the leading of the Holy Spirit."

"Darla spoke on 'the trials of a Christian teenager.' I will speak on, 'trials of a Christian couple.' Neither Darla, nor her family is aware of comments made to me or about me, questioning my judgment in regards to marriage." Kelley spoke, his face growing tense, as he now bore his hidden pain on his face.

"Oh, Kelley, I am sorry." Darla said, silently, repeatedly, her eyes quickly filling with tears. She knowing his pain was due to her past haunting him.

"Misconceptions of facts can create turmoil and confusion. I stand before you tonight to release those of you who have misconceptions about myself and/or my fiancée as both individual servants of the Lord, and as a Christian couple working as a team for the Lord. I hold a position in this church, which I intend to keep." He informed, with authority in his voice.

"Amen." Pastor Finks said, as he sat on the platform.

"The comments are creating confusion in our youth's minds. This is a tremendous hindrance to my position as the youth pastor. This certainly is not pleasing unto the Lord. I will try to undo the false accusations and confusion by properly introducing Darla and myself to you. From what I am hearing, some of you do not truly know either of us." Kelley explained, pausing, looking out over the congregation.

"I met Darla when she was five and I was seven. We watched one another grow up and we kids admired Darla. She was sensitive to others feelings, she was overly happy and she was a warm, caring, and loving person. Her love for the Lord started sometime before I met her." Kelley shared, with a smile, and admiration on his face.

"Amen." Brother Peterson voiced.

"As a teenager, Darla's love for the Lord only grew deeper and stronger. I saw Darla give up fame in high school because she felt it would hinder her duties as a child of God. Her life during these years consisted of pleasing the Lord first, her family second, always being available for her friends, and dating me."

"I fell in love with Darla when I was seven. We both shared this bond as teenagers. We set plans to marry after we both completed college and our goal was to be partners for the Lord."

"When Pastor Finks began the park ministry a few years ago, Darla was one of the first Christian teenagers involved. She lived for that ministry and she knew the Lord put her in that work. Later, I joined the witnessing group. She and I worked as a successful team. The success was only possible because both Darla and I obeyed the leading of the Holy Spirit. We knew then, as well as now, the Lord intended we be a team." Kelley shared.

"Amen."

"Honey, hold your head high, look up not down." Kelley's father whispered, from the pew behind Darla, as he supportively patted her on her back. Cindy silently took hold of Darla's hand, giving her a smile.

"Brother and Sister Roberts, I trust you will bear with me." Kelley said, hesitant, as he looked into the faces of his future in-laws, as though feeling their pain.

"Do what you have to do, for your future, Son." Darla's father said, understanding all too well how rumors could destroy a minister.

"Yes. Amen." Pastor Finks voiced.

"Thank you, Sir." Kelley replied, respectfully.

"The last visit Darla made to the park, as a member of the witnessing team, was the beginning of three years of mental pain for her, her family, and me." Kelley informed his eyes watery and his voice now shaky.

Kelley remained silent for several moments. Each member of Darla's family as well as Kelley and Pastor Fink's eyes also grew moist.

"This happy-go-lucky dedicated child of God, with the innocence of an infant, this sixteen-year-old teenager had more compassion and understanding of anyone I have yet to meet. The girl the street people gave the name Angel, was so severely beaten and mistreated, for no reason, other than Satan trying to destroy a child of God. Satan trying to destroy a successful soul-winning ministry, Satan trying to destroy the future the Lord had planned for Darla and me as a team, and as becoming husband and wife." Kelley stressed, hitting his fist on the pulpit, expressing this disapproval.

"Yes. Amen." Pastor Finks said.

"Amen." Several from the congregation voiced.

"My fiancée has been through so much physical and mental pain, more times in the past three years then I have personally known of anyone, yet she sits inside the Lord's house, humbling herself before God. If she did not have a child to remind one of her past, most of you would not have questioned my choice for marriage, regardless of the past. Sin is sin, and my Bible tells me when the Jews nailed my Jesus, my Savior, on the cross of Calvary, He bore all my sins. Did you hear what I said?" Kelley asked, raising his voice.

"I repeat He bore all my sins." Kelley stressed.

"Amen." The congregation agreed.

"My father taught me as a small boy, if I did not understand something to ask, so I might learn the correct answer. He also taught me to ask my question in a respectful manner. Allow this to be a lesson for us all, so we are not guilty of falsely accusing our brother or sister. For if we do, we have sinned by passing false judgment and in doing so, we may cause one to lose their salvation." Kelley warned, with authority in his voice.

"When I stand before God on judgment day, I do not want a lost soul on my hands."

"Amen." The congregation agreed.

"I recall telling my lovely fiancée a few weeks ago, that I am my own man. I relay this fact to you folks. I am my own man, God is my boss, I will be a man, and be obedient unto my master regardless the price I must pay, for He is the one I choose to please. In fact, I refuse to be a pleaser and doer of men, I refuse." Kelley declared loudly, striking the pulpit again.

"Amen."

"Preach it Brother."

"The Lord brought Darla and I together. In my eyes and in my heart, the Lord will be presenting me with a priceless gift, when Darla and I are married. I would never dream of refusing a gift the Lord has given. If anyone sitting in the sanctuary could, I would be forced to question that person's walk with the Lord."

"When I sometimes get beside myself over silly, ridiculous, petty complaints, or hear one pointing a finger condemning, my mind goes back. I see my fiancée at sixteen years of age lying in bed." Kelley started, briefly hesitating removing his handkerchief from his pocket as tears began down his cheeks.

"I see a broken arm, a broken leg, a battered face that looked as though it belonged to another. I see a young girl almost destroyed. She looked at her brother and me and said, 'please understand this was my fault. I was foolish. I broke an important rule, I entered the park alone, and I know better.'" Kelley shared, his tears coming more quickly.

"She told her brother who was in a rage over her being hurt, 'Bill, she said, the street people would never hurt me, please understand an escaped convict did this to me.'" Kelley shared, and then briefly walked away from the pulpit wiping his face with his handkerchief.

Returning to the pulpit, he looked into the faces of the people before him.

"When Bill left his sisters, side, leaving Darla and I alone, she looked into my eyes with deep compassion and said, 'Kelley, my family does not understand the street people, but you and I are fortunate we understand. They are special people, let's never become too busy for them.'

"Broken-hearted, broken spirit, physically, and mentally in severe pain, she put others first. This is the deep, sincere, kind of Christian love my fiancée possesses. She possesses a Godly love, and she is a strong-willed overcomer." Kelley spoke, with pride on his face and in his voice.

"I trust I have eliminated all confusion from your hearts and minds. This is so important, so that we each can keep our minds on our individual callings and not fail the Lord. God is not the author of confusion. Let's kick Satan in the teeth, assuring him, we each are overcomers, servants unto our Savior Jesus Christ." Kelley spoke, in all sincerity.

"Pastor ... " Kelley removed his Bible from the pulpit, leaving the platform. Arriving at Darla's pew, he sat down beside her.

"Kelley." Darla stated, her tears still streaming down her young face. Kelley turned his eyes from the pastor up front, to his fiancée. He comfortingly put his arm around his fiancées shoulders.

"I am ..."

"Don't you dare apologize." Kelley interrupted, with sternness on his face, yet gentleness in his eyes.

"Will you be okay?" He questioned his voice more gentle, as he brushed his beautiful fiancées tears away.

"I am always okay when I am with you." She answered, with a loving smile, her words relaxing his tense face.

"This is the way I feel about you, Babe." He replied, with a comforting smile.

"I believe the Holy Spirit would have me invite each one to the altar for some serious soul searching. Come, let us pray, so our walk with the Lord will be more humble, more obedient." Pastor Finks advised.

Darla, nor Kelley's family made mention of Kelley's heartache of others questioning his judgment in the choosing of his bride, nor did either family mention Darla's past. Each family member looked ahead, in hopes with each new day; they each would be a much wiser servant unto the Lord.

Awakened early by the ringing telephone, Darla quickly answered it as not to disturb her family.

"Good morning." Darla answered, in a half-whisper, taking the extension to her bed, slipping back under her covers.

"Good morning, Sweetheart." Kelley greeted.

"Kelley Peterson, you could have woke my parents, you crazy guy." Darla scolded, lightly.

"Just so I did not wake my daughter." Kelley replied, with pride in his voice.

"I like this also. I like the sound of 'our' daughter, better though."

"In a few hours, Dar, we will never again say 'mine or yours.' Anything and everything will become 'ours.'"

"Kel, will you please tell me why you called me at five o'clock?"

"I wanted to hear your voice, assuring myself we really and truly are marrying this evening." He answered with a chuckle.

"Yes, dear, you have the correct day." Darla answered, with a soft laugh.

"How long have you been awake, anyway?" She asked.

"All night, Dar, I am going crazy. No one told me I would be a nervous wreck, on the most important day of my life." He answered, with a nervous laugh.

"Awe you poor guy." Darla sympathized.

"I have to see you this morning, Dar." Kelley said.

"Then we will bend the rules, come have coffee with me at seven." Darla replied.

"Two more hours, do I have a choice on the time?" Kelley asked.

"Of course not, if you will allow me, I will make myself presentable for your arrival and we may have our coffee on the patio."

"I will meet you on the patio at seven, Miss Roberts." Kelley agreed.

Completing her shower, Darla slipped into a pair of slacks and lightweight sweater, for the cool October morning.

With the coffee made, she looked through the window, finding Kelley had already arrived. Picking up the thermos of coffee and coffee cups, she left her home to join her fiancé on the patio.

"Good morning." Darla greeted, happily, with sparkles in her eyes.

"Good morning." Kelley greeted, appearing his happiest. He politely stood as his fiancée approached, greeting her with a kiss.

"Yum, doughnuts … " Darla said, helping herself to one.

"Will you have a doughnut with me?" She asked, politely.

"No, thank you, I cannot sleep or eat." Kelley answered, with a boyish grin, blushing over his nervousness.

"Kel, all you have to do is walk down the aisle this evening and say 'I do.' What is so difficult about that?" Darla questioned, giggling over his nervousness.

"I do not know, honestly." Kelley answered, smiling over his fiancées laughter.

"I do know, I will be there, ready and waiting." He assured proudly.

The young couple visited until Heaven awoke from her sleep. Kelley left his fiancée to tend to her preparations for their wedding. If Darla had ever felt like an angel, it was now. To her, becoming Kelley's wife would be as though she had her own piece of heaven.

Dressed in her elegant wedding gown, with her mother at her side, while she waited for her father to join her, Darla was now as nervous as Kelley had been earlier.

"Dear, you be a wonderful wife to Kelley. Do your best to make him happy and proud, stand by him, encourage him, and comfort him. You do these things for him and you both will profit, throughout your lives." Mrs. Roberts advised, with happy, watery eyes, as she gave her daughter a tight hug followed by a kiss.

"I will Mother." Darla assured, deeply touched by her mother's words of wisdom.

With Mrs. Roberts escorted down the aisle to her seat, Mr. Roberts proudly took his place at his daughter's side.

As the wedding ceremony began, Darla slipped her arm through her father's arm as she waited for her walk down the long aisle, becoming even more excited.

"I have not got a speech prepared for you, Babe, but I am very proud of your outcome. I am afraid you will remain my little girl in my heart for some time." Mr. Roberts said.

"You will always be my daddy, no matter how old I become." Darla replied, lovingly, giving her father a kiss.

As the door opened into the sanctuary, Darla's heart leaped with excitement. The church decorations looked even more beautiful than she had imagined they would. Her eyes slowly swept across the sanctuary, observing the flowers and candlelight.

"Dad … " Darla whispered, excitedly.

"The sanctuary is so beautiful it reminds me of the event to come, when Jesus returns for His bride. That will be a marvelous event." She said, her eyes sparkling, and her face aglow with happiness, as she looked up into her father's face.

"It most certainly will be marvelous, Babe." Her father agreed.

Darla quickly returned her eyes to the sanctuary, as her four bridesmaids began their walk in their knee length, powder-blue formals, with their handsome escorts, and then the maiden-of- honor, in her long floor length formal.

"They each look beautiful Daddy." Darla remarked, excitedly. She was too thrilled to be silent.

"They do look beautiful, Darla." Her father agreed, pleased with the outcome of the wedding.

With the beautiful flower girl and handsome ring bearer, making their walk, Darla's heart beat faster.

"It is our turn, Babe." Mr. Roberts said, looking down into his daughter's eyes with pride.

"Are you ready?" He asked, with a pleased grin, knowing she was overly anxious.

"I am most definitely ready." Darla answered, with a radiant smile.

Her dad walking her down the aisle, Darla felt so happy; she wanted to laugh aloud.

"I am so happy." She whispered, looking up into her father's eyes.

"I am glad, do be quiet now, Babe." Mr. Roberts reminded, with a pleased smile, as their guest's eyes were upon them.

"Yes Dad." Darla replied, with a beautiful smile, as they neared the front of the sanctuary.

Approaching her destination, her eyes fell on Kelley, as he stood, waiting her walk to join him. Darla felt even more joy and excitement as Kelley's pleased, loving, gentle face, was watching her every step. He appeared as though he was about to be presented a princess.

Standing at Kelley's side, Darla looked into his eyes, giving him a loving smile.

Though the minister began their vows, Darla's eyes remained on Kelley, gently, tenderly, proudly, silently sharing her love and happiness for their marriage with Kelley.

Kelley in return, looked into her eyes, proudly, as her abundance of love and happiness touched his heart.

"I now pronounce you man and wife." Pastor Finks announced.

"I love you, Mrs. Kelley Peterson." Kelley spoke, gently taking Darla into his strong arms, kissing his bride long and passionately.

Though blushing with Kelley's forwardness in front of their guests, Darla released an excited laugh and Kelley smiled a pleased smile, as well as their observing guests.

Kelley proudly escorted his bride from the front of the sanctuary, down the long aisle.

"What do you say you and I pass on the reception, and have a solitude party?" Kelley asked in a whisper.

"Yes." Darla answered, excitedly, bringing a pleased smile to Kelley's face.

Leaving the church, rice was thrown on the bride and groom.

"Are you ready to make a run to the car?" Kelley asked, as the rice fell on them.

"You expect me to run in heels, husband?" Darla asked, looking up into her groom's face with sparkles in her eyes.

"I suppose not, hang on." Kelley answered, sweeping his bride off her feet, into his arms.

Kelley made a dash to his now fully decorated car. With assisting Darla inside his car, Kelley hurried to drive away as several of their friends hurried to their cars, to follow the bride and groom.

"Kel, who is going to cut the wedding cake?" Darla asked, as Kelley drove through their small desert town, followed by friends, blowing their car horns.

"Whoever would like to." Kelley answered, putting his arm around his bride's shoulders, pulling her closer to his side.

"I say, allow our families and friends to enjoy the reception, while you and I enjoy our honeymoon. Do you agree?" He asked, looking into her eyes.

"All the way, until death do we part." Darla answered, happily, leaning her head against her grooms, strong shoulder.

ABOUT THE AUTHOR

Sherry is the proud mother of four, grandmother of nine, and great-grandmother of one. She spent her early years working with other's children while raising her children. Her latest years have been spent working with the elderly. Though residing in Indiana, the desert climate and scenery of her childhood remain close to her heart. Promoting family with godly principles is top priority. She believes all ages will enjoy this inspired, easy read.

Printed in the United States
By Bookmasters